The Secrets of Everlight

JULIE HALL

ACE
New York

ACE
Published by Berkley
An imprint of Penguin Random House LLC
1745 Broadway, New York, NY 10019
penguinrandomhouse.com

Book design by Ashley Tucker
Illustrations on pages vi–vii and 480–481
by Sasha Lee Coleman, sashalee-art.com
Illustrations on pages viii, 57, 76, 112, 137, 230, 275, 297, 413, and 440
by Irene Barboni

ISBN: 9798217191390

Library of Congress Cataloging-in-Publication Data

Names: Hall, Julie, 1981- author
Title: The secrets of Everlight / Julie Hall
Description: First edition | New York: Ace, 2026 | Series: Shattered kingdoms; book 1
Identifiers: LCCN 2026000178 (print) | LCCN 2026000179 (ebook) | ISBN 9798217191390 trade paperback | ISBN 9798217191406 ebook
Subjects: LCGFT: Fantasy fiction | Romance fiction | Novels
Classification: LCC PS3608.A547266 S43 2026 (print) | LCC PS3608.A547266 (ebook)
LC record available at https://lccn.loc.gov/2026000178
LC ebook record available at https://lccn.loc.gov/2026000179

First Edition: October 2026

Printed in the United States of America
1st Printing

The authorized representative in the EU for product safety and compliance is Penguin Random House Ireland, Morrison Chambers, 32 Nassau Street, Dublin D02 YH68, Ireland, https://eu-contact.penguin.ie.

The Secrets of Everlight

To those who once dreamed of being princesses
but found their strength in becoming warriors

Chapter 1

HIDDEN IN THE SHADOWS, I PEER THROUGH THE wavy glass window of Sinclair's office down at the pub floor below. It's late enough in the evening for the patrons to be well into their cups, but I'm far enough removed that the shouts and boisterous laughs of their revelry are muted. As I scan the crowd, I spot the usual drunkards who frequent the Lame Horse.

My upper lip curls into a sneer as Barnaby Elmwish takes a long swallow of his mead. His arm is wrapped around Greta, the young serving wench perched on his lap. She's probably half the age of his wife, who's no doubt at home tending to his litter of children, the youngest of which can't be more than a year old. At the table next to him, a group of males plays a rowdy game of cards. One loses, and he throws his drink in the face of the player next to him. The fae at the tables around them hardly give the brawling duo a glance as their companions jump in to break them apart. The fight ends quickly; new mugs of mead are passed to the pair, and after they each take a hearty swig, everyone sits back down and they continue their game.

The male patrons in the pub outnumber the females at least eight to one. Typical for most of the taverns in Everlight. Females are encouraged to stay at home and tend the house and children while the males have the freedom to explore whatever debaucheries their hearts desire.

I'll never willingly put myself in a position below a male again. Once I'm no longer indentured to Sinclair, I'll be free, and I'll never get married. Why would I trade one type of servitude for another?

My stomach growls as I watch fae share a hot meal and drink deeply from their cups. When was the last time I ate? Yesterday afternoon, I think. At least the water from the stream is free or I'd be dehydrated as well.

I rub my thumb over the ruby brooch in my pocket that I nicked from a highborn lady this morning. This bauble alone would feed me for months, but instead I have to turn it over to Sinclair and hope it earns me a half-decent meal tonight. After all, Sinclair knows I need some energy to keep me sharp enough to steal him a new treasure tomorrow. Losing his best thief would hurt his pocketbook.

As I scan the evening crowd below, passing the time while waiting for Sinclair to show up, my gaze catches on two males seated at a table by the wall. There's nothing particularly interesting about the pair, who appear to be enjoying a cup of mead and a bowl of stew, but one of the males is clearly older than the other. Perhaps it's a father and son? That's not very uncommon or unusual to see, but there's something about their body language that makes me think otherwise. Like the power dynamic between them is swapped.

They are dressed similarly, in simple tunics with black cloaks and breeches. Both quite fit, and the younger fae looks like he's not too many years older than me. Early twenties, perhaps?

He's too far away for me to determine eye color, but he has sandy-blond hair that's on the longer side, not quite reaching his shoulders. A strong jaw, straight nose, square face. Along with his broad shoulders and a seemingly muscular build, he's ruggedly handsome. Even from a distance. But that's not what causes me to linger. Something tickles the back of my mind. Even when I try to look away, he draws my eye. It's not that I think I've seen him before, but there's something about him that's maybe not familiar, but distracting.

He wears an easy smile; his body is nonchalantly sprawled in his chair. To a casual onlooker, he'd appear to just be enjoying a night at the Lame Horse like everyone else, but something about the way his gaze moves over the crowd gives me pause. I get the impression he wants to give the air of someone carefree, but he's really attentive to everything going on in the pub.

His companion isn't even trying to fit in. His brown hair is speckled with gray and his body is rigid. He sits with his back to the wall, and his hand rests lightly on his weapon. Both the drink and stew in front of him look to be untouched.

As I'm watching, Sinclair appears before the pair, and I lift my eyebrows. Even though Sinclair owns the Lame Horse, he doesn't typically interact with the patrons. He prefers to keep a low profile and is usually content to sit in his office, watching all the money pour into his business from above.

Placing his hands on the table, Sinclair leans forward, his potbelly pressing into the wooden tabletop and a clump of greasy black hair falling over one eye. When the older of the two fae grips the hilt of his sword and slides it out a few inches, the younger fae puts his hand on his shoulder to stop him.

I was right. They're not a father and son duo. The younger male is clearly the one calling the shots. Perhaps it's an employer-employee relationship.

The males listen, leaning in as Sinclair talks. I wish I knew what he was saying, if for only curiosity's sake. For a few minutes,

Sinclair does most of the talking and the younger male nods a few times. The older fae stays as rigid as a board.

Eventually, Sinclair gestures toward his office, up where I'm standing, spying on the crowd. The blond-haired male lifts his gaze and I step more fully into the shadows so I won't be seen. Yet I swear his eyes connect with mine and a self-satisfied smirk lifts the corners of his mouth. The look on his face seems to say, "Gotcha," and that unnerves me.

Sinclair's mouth is moving again, and the younger male's face lightens, his body language going languid and unthreatening once again. He throws back his head and laughs at something Sinclair says in what can only be false merriment. Sinclair isn't funny at all. A fae would be more apt to laugh *at* him than *with* him.

The blond drains his drink and shoves backward from the table. His companion stands, still without having touched his drink or food, and they both follow Sinclair toward the stairs that lead to his office.

Shit.

Sinclair should know that I'm here waiting for him like I do every night, so why is he bringing them up here?

I have the urge to hide somewhere in his office. I don't like to be seen. Good thieves are masters at blending in, and anonymity is a must. Even now my hair is braided up and hidden under my hood so that I'm not identified by its color; my face is smudged with soot to hide my freckles.

I eye the curtains to my left. I'm small enough that I could slide behind them and not leave a bulge, or perhaps even to lie flat under the couch, but if I were to get caught, the consequences would be severe. If Sinclair could prove misconduct, he would have grounds to extend the contract I have with him. It's best to stay put and just wait to be dismissed when he enters with the two fae.

So long as I keep my head down, the hood of my cloak will hide most of my face. My clothes are oversized to hide my petite and slightly curvy frame. Under the right circumstances, I can easily pass as a young boy rather than a female. Not many females would be proud of that, but I am. With some luck, I'll be unrecognizable and unmemorable to them to the extent that they could pass me on the street later and not even know it was me.

Boots stomp along the wooden floor outside Sinclair's office, and I tense. I'm standing in the corner, and I don't look up as the door swings open. Sinclair talks loudly about the bosom of one of the barmaids as they enter, and even though the other males don't seem to be joining the conversation, my face still heats. I have to clear my throat before I'm noticed.

"Rowan?" Sinclair says, and I lift my head only high enough to see him from under my hood. "You shouldn't be here."

I grind my teeth, forcing myself to bite back a comment. I come here every night, not because I want to see his ugly face or rotund figure, but because if I skip a day, he tacks it on to my contract. He's probably several drinks in and just forgot about me and is making this look like my fault so he doesn't look bad in front of these fae.

"I'll wait and come back when you're finished with whatever business you have here," I say as I head for the door, but a body steps in front of me before I can escape.

"Wait," says one of the males. His voice is deep and smooth.

Without glancing up and revealing my face, I can tell from his polished black boots and his matching cotton breeches that it's the younger of the two. The other fae wore brown boots and pants.

From a distance, I had assumed the blond fae was unarmed, but I spy a dagger concealed in one of his boots. I'd bet coin there's a weapon in the other one as well.

And although his clothing appeared nondescript from my

vantage point before, now I can tell they are well-made with expensive materials. Definitely not the typical commoner garb. Yet this male is trying very hard to portray that they are.

Interesting.

"Excuse me," I say, and try to sidestep him, but he just moves with me.

"We're happy to wait until *your* business is concluded," he says, his tone mocking.

My insides bunch. Just another entitled male trying to throw his weight around.

"Rowan can wait outside," Sinclair says, and out of the corner of my eye I can see him shooing me away.

I start forward a third time only to get blocked again.

Insufferable brute.

"Hey now, no need to run the boy off," the blond says. "We can wait until your business with the lad is finished. He's clearly been waiting for you."

I bristle at being called a boy, even though I'm dressed specifically to look like one.

Without thinking better of it, I jerk my head up to glare at the stranger, only to find him staring down at me with a knowing look in his bright blue eyes and a smug smirk.

He said that on purpose. He knew I wasn't a male and wanted a reaction from me, which is exactly what I gave him.

I'm annoyed that he's just as handsome up close as he was from a distance. The pull to him is still there. It irritates me like the last little piece of a splinter that's buried too deep to remove.

"Violet eyes," he says thoughtfully, then glances at his companion. "Very rare."

I lower my gaze immediately, cursing my own stupidity.

Violet eyes are indeed rare. My most distinguishing feature

that I can't change. I do my best to hide my face under my hood or keep my eyes downcast so I'm not identified by them. I'm uncomfortable with these strangers knowing my most recognizable feature, but there's nothing to be done about it now.

"Fine, Neo, if you insist. This should only take a minute," Sinclair says, sighing as he takes a seat.

Neo, what an unusual name.

"Get over here, Rowan, and show me your tribute for the day." I look sharply at Sinclair as he beckons to me from behind his desk.

I can't show him the brooch in front of these strangers. If it gets reported as stolen, they'll point the authorities right at me.

"I don't think now is—"

"You aren't supposed to think," Sinclair barks. "That's my job."

Could have fooled me.

"Now get over here and show me what you have so that I can get you out of our hair."

My nostrils flare, but I keep my mouth sealed shut as I walk woodenly over to him, feeling the strangers' stares on my back with every step. Casting a glance over my shoulder, I make sure Neo and the other fae aren't close enough to see the brooch when I pull it out. They're in a quiet conversation between themselves, not giving me the least bit of attention.

Good.

I pull the piece of jewelry out of my pocket and slide it over to Sinclair for inspection. Rather than being discreet in his examination of the item, he lifts it high, bringing it close to his face, twisting and turning it.

The piece is beautiful. Made of gold with inlaid jewels, it's shaped like a peacock, which is part of the Blackwell family crest. There's one large ruby set as the peacock's eye, and smaller gems, colored bright red to vibrant pink, make up the tail feathers.

I have no doubt the piece is an heirloom and easily recognizable, which will make it difficult for Sinclair to sell. But that's his problem, not mine.

"Hmm. It looks like a fake to me," he says, and then places the brooch on the desk in front of him. "This will only count as a half day's work."

"What? No. There's no way it is a fake. I got it off—"

Cutting myself off, I seal my lips shut, horrified that I almost admitted to lifting it off Lady Blackwell herself.

There's a cunning glimmer in Sinclair's eye that says he knows I can't say anything more in front of the strangers, and my shoulders sag in defeat.

"Because it's only a half day's work, that means you'll only get a half day's portion of food. Get out of here. I'll be checking in with Zia to make sure you aren't cheating me."

Me, cheat him? That's rich. I've been indentured to Sinclair for six and a half years now, yet have barely worked off four years of my ten-year contract. It's clear who's cheating whom in this scenario.

If only I could end him.

I'm not particularly bloodthirsty, but Sinclair is not a good man. If I had known that, I never would have indentured myself to him in the first place. But I was young and starving and would have sold my soul for a loaf of bread back then.

The Ember Kingdom might be the mightiest fae nation in Vaeloria, but the streets of Everlight aren't kind to orphans, or any fae who fall on hard times, for that matter.

I can't so much as lay a finger on Sinclair since the contract binds my life to his. If he dies, every fae who's contracted to him, including me, dies with him. Thankfully, or unfortunately, depending on how you look at it, it doesn't work the other way around. If one of his indentured dies, he's unaffected. And injuries don't transfer through the bond between indentured and contract holder either. But he's already ordered me never to lay a hand on him, so if I did, I'd be in breach of contract, and he'd be able to add more time to my servitude.

But even so, it doesn't stop me from imagining burying a blade in Sinclair's gut. I've killed him more than once in my mind, but the only thing I want more than to see Sinclair bleed is my freedom. There are very few ways to get out of an indenture contract, so to gain my freedom, I have to bide my time. One torturous day at a time.

Clenching my fists, I manage a half nod and then start to turn away, but Neo, who is somehow now directly behind me, reaches around me and touches the brooch. I freeze, a zing of warning shooting up my spine at his closeness.

I'm more than a little unnerved that I didn't realize he was there. I shift so he's no longer standing at my back, looking over my shoulder.

"Hmm. This seems rather familiar," he says conversationally. "It's the Blackwells who have a fondness for peacocks, right, Bram?"

"You're right about that," Bram, the other fae, answers from somewhere behind us.

Sinclair shifts in his chair, finally appearing to have enough sense to be a little apprehensive about being so open in front of these males.

"Never mind that." Sinclair swiftly grabs the brooch and deposits it in his desk drawer. "You said you were looking to procure my services."

Sinclair flicks his hand at me in a silent command to leave, and I'm only too happy to oblige. If these males, Neo and Bram, are interested in hiring Sinclair, then they are into some shadowy deals I want no part of.

Thievery is one thing, but I'm not naïve enough to believe that Sinclair's misdeeds stop there. He has his hands in a plethora of different illegal activities, ones that don't involve just losing a minor appendage or imprisonment if caught, but rather death.

When I go to flee, Bram is standing directly in front of the door, a stern look on his face as he stares at me with his hand back on the hilt of his sword.

The fine hairs on the nape of my neck prickle in warning.

"You know, that brooch reminds me of one of the Blackwell heirlooms. They are partial to rubies," Neo says.

On the outside, I appear unchanged by his comment—not so much as a single twitch of muscle, the cadence of my breath the same—but on the inside, warning bells are ringing and my heart rate has doubled.

I scan the room from under my hood, looking for a second exit despite knowing there's only one way in or out of Sinclair's office: the door that Bram is blocking. Even so, I eye the windows that overlook the dining area below. In a pinch, I could break the glass and jump. I don't think the fall is so far that it would kill me. If I aim for a well-fed patron, they could cushion my landing.

"Nonsense." Sinclair waves Neo's words away, but I can see the gleam of sweat forming on his forehead. "I send Rowan to the old quarter to barter and trade. Her job is to bring me back something that's more valuable than what I sent her with." He snaps his fingers at me. "What was it I sent you with this morning?"

"A gold chain necklace," I answer without missing a beat. Lying comes a little too easily for me, but I'm not complaining. The talent is certainly handy when I'm in a tough spot.

"See," Sinclair says, as if that explains everything. "And the twit-brain traded it for a worthless piece of fake jewelry."

"Still . . ." Neo rubs his chin as if considering. "I'd feel better if we brought the authorities in, just to make sure."

What is he playing at? Whatever business he's here to conduct with Sinclair certainly can't be aboveboard. The only legitimate business Sinclair conducts is for the pub downstairs, and even that is a front for a bevy of illegal activities. I know for a fact he stores smuggled goods in the cellar and has fae cooking illegal substances in a back room behind the kitchen, and I have heard rumblings that some of the long-term residents in the rooms upstairs are assassins for hire.

Everything Sinclair has his hands in is dirty, including the number of indenture contracts he holds. Only nobility can hold more than three indenture contracts, but Sinclair has dozens of us working for him.

Sinclair's face reddens. "I'll not have you getting one of my best workers arrested."

That was as close to a compliment as Sinclair has ever paid me. I'd be half flattered if I wasn't so terrified I was going to get thrown in prison or worse.

Neo shrugs, as if me rotting in a cell or hanging from the Silverleaf Bridge by my neck makes no difference to him. "I know how attached the Blackwells are to their heirlooms. I'm sure if you were to catch the thief who stole it, you'd be rewarded for your efforts."

My stomach drops even lower. Sinclair would turn over his own child if it meant a payday for him. It's good he doesn't have any . . . that he knows of. There's no way he'd spare me if it meant protecting himself *and* earning coin.

"Just be glad you don't hold her indenture contract, because if you did, that would mean you'd be held responsible for the theft as well," Neo adds.

So, that's what this has all been about. They want something from Sinclair they think he might refuse and have backed him into a corner to make sure they get it. I'm as impressed as I am horrified.

Sinclair gets to his feet and sputters in fury as Neo walks over and flops down onto the couch, throwing his long legs up on the cushions and folding his arms behind his head as if he's about to take a nap.

"Bram, please fetch the constable. I'll wait here to make sure the brooch is secure and we can get all this settled with the law."

"Wait," Sinclair shouts, although he needn't have. Bram hasn't so much as budged from his position in front of the door. These fae both know they have Sinclair where they want him. The question is . . .

"What do you want?" Sinclair's gruffly spoken question mimics my thoughts exactly.

"Want?" Neo asks with a frown, cocking his head as if confused.

"Yes, what is it you want in exchange for your . . . discretion?"

Neo takes his time answering, rubbing at his mouth as if considering the options, which is silly, because it's obvious he knows exactly what he wants from Sinclair. Sinclair is truly an idiot if he's buying this fae's act.

I inch toward the window as he continues his performance. I want to be close just in case I still need to make a run for it. I hate being in the middle of this manipulation.

"Hmm. Since you mentioned it, it so happens I'm in need of a female with certain . . . talents."

Neo's gaze tracks over to me, and nothing about the calculated look on his face puts me at ease.

"You want me to make arrangements for you at the brothel?"

Sinclair chuckles. “Why didn’t you just say so? That’s done easily enough.”

Disgust flicks over Neo’s features. “No, that won’t be necessary. I believe this female here will do.”

Oh, so now he admits I’m a girl?

I’d be more alarmed if I were under the impression Neo was looking for a female to bed. His gaze as he stares at me isn’t lustful, it’s calculating. Besides, no one would go to this much trouble to bed someone, especially not a skinny, soot-covered female like me.

No, this fae knows exactly what he’s doing. He’s searching for a thief.

And he knows that he’s just found one.

Sinclair laughs. “You want *her*? But there’s hardly any meat on her at all. Nothing to grab on to. Surely you can’t be serious.”

I bite my cheek to stop my words. It’s not that Sinclair is morally against pimping me out, but rather he thinks the idea of someone wanting me for that purpose is preposterous. He’s not wrong, but the slight on my physical appearance still stings a little.

Neo looks over at me, his gaze bloated with interest as he assesses me. “Oh, I believe she’s exactly what I need.”

Chapter 2

A SLOW SMILE SPREADS OVER NEO'S MOUTH, and a sliver of trepidation slides down my spine. He may not be interested in bedding me, but that doesn't mean his intentions aren't nefarious.

Discreetly sliding my hand under my cloak, I brush my fingertips over the handle of my dagger to soothe myself. My talents aren't limited to thievery. I know a dozen ways to bring a grown male down with the small blade, from a distance or close range. I can also hold my own with only my fists and feet.

Mastering defensive and offensive fighting skills and weaponry was a must. I never would have lasted this long on my own had I not.

"Well . . ." Sinclair clears his throat. "I suppose if you're set on this one, I could loan her to you for a period of time."

"No." Neo shakes his head. "I want her contract."

Sinclair's face reddens with anger. "Hey now, I already told you she is one of my best workers. And she still has six years left on her contract. Parting with her will put me out. Let me find you a different girl."

"We could always still call the constable," Neo says, glancing over at Bram, who remains silent, guarding the door.

"That's blackmail," Sinclair roars.

I wrap my hand around the dagger, and Bram takes a step toward me, his eyes moving from my face to where I'm gripping the concealed weapon. He shakes his head to tell me not to try it, and I stare back blankly, like I don't understand what he's saying. He assesses me as Sinclair and Neo argue over my contract.

Playing stupid is a tactic that works more often than not, especially against fae males.

Idiots.

I have to work to keep a straight face when Bram crosses his arms over his chest and steps back to his sentry position in front of the door. Slowly, I move another step closer to the window overlooking the pub floor. Despite my skills with a blade, intuition tells me I'll have a better chance of surviving a fall than up against the stoic Bram.

Neo rises to his feet. "It's settled, then."

My attention snaps back to him and Sinclair, who are shaking hands, having just come to some sort of agreement.

My heart rate spikes and a feeling of panic bubbles in my gut. These two males just negotiated my life, my future, and I didn't even get a say in the matter.

I clench my fists and bite down hard enough on my tongue that I taste blood, promising myself that someday I'll break free of this yoke that's been imposed on me.

"Oh, one more thing," Sinclair says. "I want your word that you'll order the little urchin not to lay a hand on me."

Neo's eyebrows lift. "Worried about retribution from a waif?"

Sinclair snorts. "She's as wicked with a knife as any seasoned warrior, and her aim with a throwing blade is deadly. Appearances can be deceiving."

Neo's eyes light with unabashed delight. "They certainly can be. Interesting development."

One he's obviously excited about, but his interest just makes me more nervous.

"I want assurance she won't come back and slit my throat in my sleep once I relinquish her contract."

The fae tips his head in acquiescence. "You have my oath." Grabbing Sinclair's letter opener, Neo jabs the sharp end into a fingertip and a bead of blood wells up, sealing the oath.

I grind my teeth. A fae blood oath is unbreakable. If they don't fulfill it, they slowly go mad until they die. Which means the second I'm contracted to the fae, he's going to order me not to kill Sinclair.

That's a real shame, but also an unnecessary precaution. Too many lives are connected to Sinclair through the indenture contracts he owns. If I kill him, I doom every fae indentured to him as well. That doesn't mean maiming or dismemberment is off the table, though. Chopping off one of Sinclair's hands won't kill him, but it would give me a great deal of satisfaction.

Neo pulls out a pouch of coins, and Sinclair's eyes light with glee. I inch toward the pair, knowing that when my contract is transferred and the ancient magic binding me to Sinclair drops, there will be a single moment before the contract ties me to this new fae. That will be my opportunity to strike.

When the pouch drops into Sinclair's open hand, he wastes no time overturning it and counting the money. I blink at the number of coins he sifts through. There have to be at least twenty pieces of gold. A small fortune to someone like me.

The fae has definitely overpaid for me, especially considering he had leverage over Sinclair. It makes me even more suspicious of him, and for a moment I consider striking at Neo's heart during my brief seconds of freedom instead of at Sinclair's hand. But I know I can't. I might be skilled at killing, but that doesn't make me a killer.

I get distracted by a shine from Neo's belt—a dagger he has partially concealed. The handle is etched silver, and the blade is some sort of black metal. It's clear the intricate weapon is valuable and was meant to be hidden, but with the way his body is bent over Sinclair's desk, I can see it peeking through.

Part of the reason I make such a good thief is my ability to spot rare treasures, but sometimes the items are so alluring that the compulsion to snatch them is too strong, overpowering my common sense.

As I stare at the small weapon, the familiar impulse washes over me. My fingers itch to have that dagger and my mind goes a little foggy.

I must have it.

Before I even realize what I'm doing, my deft fingers have plucked the dagger from Neo's belt, and I've slipped it under the folds of my cloak and into an empty sheath.

I hold my breath, waiting for Neo or Bram to call out what I've done, but neither of them does.

That was lucky.

Going to the back of the office, Sinclair opens his wall safe. I get a brief look at its contents from around his large form. He has stacks of rolled contracts neatly layered in the safe. Every one of those contracts is a life he holds, and it makes me sick.

Maybe I should take an arm instead of a hand.

It takes him a moment to locate my contract, and when he turns with the piece of parchment in his hands, it's hard to hold myself back from vaulting over the desk, snatching it from him, and tearing it up.

Not that I'd be able to destroy the contract. There's very little magic still left in our world, but when it started to disappear centuries ago, the magic imbued in certain objects and rituals held strong. It's said that each fae used to have magic of their own in varying degrees, but those stories feel more myth than truth, as there's not a single fae today who can produce even a spark of magic.

The parchment of indenture contracts is made from the skin of ancient unicorns and is one of the few remaining objects that has held its own magic. Nobody knows why these skins, and a handful of other objects, are the last existing magic in our culture, but it means that even if I ripped the parchment to shreds, it would just re-form.

Grabbing a quill, Sinclair writes a quick note on the parchment saying that the contract is being transferred to Neo, then signs it. Neo signs as well, then Sinclair grabs the same letter opener Neo used and pricks his thumb. A bead of blood wells up on it. The only way to release me from the contract, or transfer it to a new owner, is through blood. He looks at me before letting any blood drop onto the parchment.

"If I ever see you near me or this establishment, I won't hesitate to run a blade through you," he warns, and I only arch a brow at him.

Besides the fact that I'd be happy to never see his face or the Lame Horse again, we both know I'd never give him the opportunity to stab me.

"I can assure you she won't be coming here anymore," Neo answers for me when it's clear Sinclair isn't going to proceed without some sort of verbal agreement from me. "Can we be on with this already? I have other things to do tonight." His tone is bored, but I pick up a hint of anxiousness.

Sinclair scowls but finally presses his thumb to the parchment.

The thin sheet of skin absorbs the bead of blood immediately, greedily slurping it up as if it's a meal. As soon as the red bloom disappears, the magic of the contract lifts from my skin like a cloak that's been removed.

It's not exactly an external feeling, but an internal sense. Or perhaps it's all in my head. Either way, I don't get to revel in the moment of freedom. Neo has already pricked his finger and is about to add his own blood to the scroll, sealing my fate with his. I have to act fast if I want to take my pound of flesh.

Ripping my dagger from its sheath, I launch at Sinclair, catching him completely by surprise. In theory, he knows I'm dangerous, but I've never been more than quiet and respectful toward him in the years he's owned me—a meek mouse he's ordered around and mistreated.

It's time he felt my bite.

The desk is between us, but I'm over it and in front of him in less than a blink. He only has time to bring up his arm to defend himself, which is exactly what I wanted.

I angle the blade toward his wrist and slash with enough force to sever the hand clean off. My dagger is a hairsbreadth from cutting into his flesh, the smile already on my face, when I'm yanked backward. The dagger is twisted out of my hand and then clanks to the floor. I find myself trapped in a vise grip with my arms pinned to my sides.

Sinclair roars in anger and pain, and I look down at my contract to see a chubby severed finger sitting on top of it. The unicorn skin soaks up the blood until there isn't so much as a stain.

"Bloodthirsty little thing, aren't you?" Neo says into my ear. "But he's not worth it. And just so we're clear, you're not allowed to hurt me or Bram, and I forbid you from killing the piece of cow dung that was your last contract owner."

I try to jerk out of Neo's hold, but it's too tight. I growl at him like a beast, furious that he stopped me from taking Sinclair's hand like I'd intended.

"Sorry about that," Neo says, sounding a touch sincere. "But I need to fulfill my blood oath. Madness would be highly disruptive to my plans."

Neo lets his blood drip on the parchment and then the magic of the contract squeezes me once again, and I know that this fae is my new owner. I let out a growl of disgust, bitterly aware that I won't be able to disobey that command.

"You cut off my finger!" Sinclair howls as he holds his injured hand. "I'll take your head for that!"

He tries to grab the sword at his side, but I'd cut off a finger from his dominant hand and now he's clumsy. By the time he gets it in his grip, Bram stands between us and Sinclair, his sword brandished in a clear warning.

"Grab the contract," Neo tells Bram. "Time to go."

Bram swipes the contract and we are out the door and down the hallway. I'm no longer trapped in Neo's arms, but he has an iron grip on my hand that I can't break.

Sinclair's furious bellows follow in our wake, and a satisfied smile blooms over my face.

Chapter 3

I'M THANKFUL FOR THE PADDED SEAT AS WE roll down one of Everlight's cobblestone streets. I've never been in a carriage with padded seats before, or one lined with silk tapestries. Yet here I am. If someone had told me this morning this was how this day would end, I would have laughed in their face.

There's no denying I'm glad to be free of Sinclair, and cutting off his finger gave me no small measure of satisfaction, but I'm far from relieved to be in my current situation. And now that I'm seated across from the mysterious and handsome stranger whose presence fills every unoccupied nook and cranny of the small space we share, I can't shake the feeling that I've jumped out of the boiling cauldron only to land myself in the fire.

We left the Lame Horse by the back entrance with Sinclair's roars echoing in the building behind us. Neo and Bram's carriage had been waiting unattended around the corner. Risky for this part of the city. Things go missing here all the time. If the Briarwood gang had stumbled across it, Neo and Bram would never have seen their carriage again.

Neither Bram nor Neo bothered to ask if I needed to take anything with me as they rushed me into the carriage. Thankfully, I've always carried anything of value on myself, so I didn't *have* any valuables to collect, although I am a little peeved I didn't have a chance to grab the dagger that Neo twisted out of my hand.

After I got into the carriage, Neo climbed in behind me, while Bram jumped up onto the box seat up front, and we were off.

Once we were seated across from each other, I blinked back at Neo, surprised Bram was riding up top. I wasn't so sheltered as to think I needed a chaperone, but it was strange there wasn't a coachman already, since these fae clearly had enough coin to hire one.

For the first ten minutes of the ride, Neo and I remain silent as we size each other up. My mind whirls, coming up with reasons why he may need a thief, each possibility worse than the last. I feel like I may go mad if I don't discover what it is soon, but I refuse to be the first to speak.

"Are you mute?" he finally asks.

I glare at him. He already knows I'm not.

"If you are, I definitely overpaid for you."

"Are you going to tell me what the job is?" Or rather the first job. Since he owns my contract, he now has power over me for the remaining six years. For the foreseeable future, I'm at his disposal.

"Not yet," he answers.

I discreetly run my thumb over the outline of the remaining dagger I have hidden within the folds of my cloak. All the uncertainties are starting to make me feel stabby.

Neo doesn't miss a beat. He taps his fingers against the rolled parchment sitting on the bench seat next to him, not so subtly reminding me that I can't actually hurt or kill him since he now owns my contract.

Neo holds his hand out. "I'll take my dagger back now."

"What dagger?"

His gaze is cutting as he gestures for me to hand it over.

With an eye roll, I pull the black metal blade out and slap the handle into his palm. It takes a second to force myself to release the prize. I want that dagger—it feels like it should be mine.

Neo lifts a questioning eyebrow and I finally let go, sitting back against the seat with a huff. I don't bother apologizing. I'm a thief; it's what I do. I may not be able to steal from him anymore, but if he expects me to stop doing what's natural to me, he's in for a world of disappointment.

I try to distract myself by gazing out the window, but he pulls the curtains closed after I've opened them. I look at him for an explanation, but we sit in silence for what is probably another twenty minutes. I take the time to study Neo, wondering if we've ever met before because of my initial reaction to him—that touch of familiarity that's already starting to fade. I certainly don't know every elite in the city, but I've stolen from my fair share of them. It wouldn't be surprising if our paths crossed at some other point.

"Have we met before?" I ask, mostly to try to draw out some sort of information about him rather than because I think that we have.

His gaze drifts back to me and his eyebrows arch high. "Most assuredly not."

"Are you sure?" I prod. "Have you been to the Lame Horse before?"

He shakes his head. "Tonight was my first and last time setting foot in that place."

"Are you an elite?"

Everlight is considered one of the most modern cities in Vaeloria, complete with several printing presses. It seems like all they ever want to circulate are the latest scandals of the elite class: those fae with more power, wealth, and prestige than the rest of us. Perhaps I've seen his likeness in one of the papers? He may be trying to downplay his wealth, but with the amount of coin he paid for me and the expensive fabrics of his clothes, he's clearly not a regular Everlight citizen.

He frowns. "I just have one of those faces."

Something tells me that's not it. I open my mouth to ask him another question, but we take a turn and the carriage slows.

"Where are we?" I ask as we come to a gentle stop.

"An ally's home," is all he says, right before the carriage door swings open.

A lady smiles up at us from the ground outside. Older than both of us but by no means past her prime, she's beautiful, with raven hair piled high on her head, bright green eyes, and a pair of pearl baubles dangling from the lobes of her elegantly pointed ears that would fetch enough to feed me for a month, at least.

Definitely an elite. The cut of her dress and the material it's made of suggest she's probably even a member of the nobility.

"Good, you've found her," she says, casting her gaze between Neo and me.

Found me? Like they were searching for *me* specifically?

There's clearly more going on here than I realize, but I keep my mouth shut even as my anxiety spikes. If I stay quiet, I'm much more likely to learn about them and their plans than to accidentally reveal something about myself.

"Not as easily as I'd expected," Neo says.

The lady's smile widens. "That means she's proficient at her craft." Stepping aside, she leaves room for us to get out of the carriage.

Neo gestures for me to go before him, and I find it curious his manners extend to a lowly, dirty fae such as myself.

Pulling my hood back over my head, I climb out of the carriage. My breath catches the moment my foot touches the graveled path, and I take in the giant manor house in front of me. It shoots six stories into the air and is the width of at least five normal townhomes, with manicured gardens. It has marble statues and an entrance one story off the ground almost as grand as the palace at the center of Everlight. And that's all I can see in the dim light of the moon and the torchlit path. I can only imagine what it looks like during the day in its full glory.

I had no way of knowing where we were going as we traveled through Everlight. Neo didn't let me peek through the curtains. But we have to be in Hyde Hill. It's the only place that has homes this large.

The lady tilts her head back, glancing up at Bram. "Pull the carriage along the south side of the manor and then join us in the study. The servants are all abed or have left for the night, but even so, try to keep quiet."

He shoots her a look that says he doesn't need to be reminded to stay quiet, and she chuckles. With a gentle flick of his wrists, Bram rides off in the direction she indicated.

"Come, come. Let's get inside in case any of the servants wake and decide to glance out their windows." Picking up her skirts, she walks briskly up the stairs toward the manor house.

Neo once again gestures for me to go ahead of him, and this time I wonder if rather than it being about manners, he just doesn't want me at his back.

I wouldn't blame him if that was it. I don't particularly feel comfortable with him behind me as I scale the steps and follow the lady through the front door, but my mind skids to a halt the moment I walk over the threshold.

My mouth drops open as I take in the cavernous three-story foyer.

In front of me, a pair of curved staircases lead to the second and third floors. The floor is polished white marble with veins of gold running through it like mini streams. Hand-painted murals of fae folk cover the walls, and a giant crystal chandelier hangs above our heads, the light dim because half of the candles have burned down to their wicks.

Neo has to nudge me along, as the dark-haired lady is already on the other side of the room, inserting a key into a carved wooden door. By the time we join her, she has the door unlocked and ushers us inside, closing it behind us.

The room we enter is large, but nowhere near as grand as the foyer. It's obviously a study with filled bookshelves and a desk against one wall, but as opposed to the opulence of the foyer, this room feels lived in. There's a small seating area composed of a love seat and two wingback chairs in front of a fireplace where only a pile of embers still burns red.

A jeweled letter opener on the desk catches my eye, and my hand twitches to snatch it, but I shove it into the pocket of my cloak to keep myself in check. I can't help that my eyes continue to roam the space, cataloging each of the expensive items that are small enough to conceal within my clothing. It's just how my mind works, but I have enough self-control to keep my hands to myself . . . for now.

The female moves around the room, lighting a couple of lamps, and Neo starts rebuilding the fire. I move toward one of the corners, feeling most comfortable with walls at my back, and do what's natural to me: blend in and hope people forget I'm there.

It's only a few short minutes before Bram enters, locking the door behind him just as the lady and Neo finish their tasks.

"Do you think you were seen?" she asks Bram, wringing her hands.

He shakes his head. "The house was quiet as I entered. We're in the clear."

"Good," she says, visibly relaxing. "I'd hate to have to battle rumors of your arrival. I'd much prefer to set the narrative for my staff in the morning. Now that we're settled, let me meet this girl." She scans the room, a furrow appearing between her eyebrows when she doesn't immediately spot me.

Neo knows exactly where I am and shoots me an annoyed look. "Rowan, stop hiding in the corner. Come over here and let me introduce you to your new patron."

I narrow my eyes at him, not liking the way he's already ordering me around. I may have willingly gotten myself into this life of servitude, but I've always known it wasn't meant for me. I'm meant to be free, and once I am, I'd rather die than allow myself to be indebted to another again.

When I shuffle over to them, Neo says, "Olette, this is Rowan. Rowan, this is Lady Greyblossom."

My stomach drops. Lady Greyblossom. I know that name, and I was right about her being nobility. She's a duchess, and the queen's sister, at that. I'm relieved I've never stolen from her before, but had I spotted her in the market, I'm sure I would have tried.

Lady Greyblossom smiles warmly at me. "Rowan, welcome to Autumnburn Manor. I'm very glad to meet you."

I bow my head in respect to her title and keep my eyes downcast. The hood of my cloak conceals the upper part of my face.

"Nice to meet you," I mumble and try to retreat, but Neo puts a hand on my back to keep me from going too far.

Lady Greyblossom steps forward. I can tell she's trying to catch my gaze, but I keep my eyes fastened on the skirts of her dress instead of her face. A single bolt of the fabric would also probably feed me for a month.

"May I see your face, dear?"

I shift my weight, not comfortable revealing myself to yet another stranger this evening.

"Rowan, please remove your hood," Neo says, and although his words are spoken gently and politely, I know what they truly are. An order.

Clenching my jaw, I reach up and pull back my hood.

Lady Greyblossom clicks her tongue thoughtfully as she walks around me, her gaze moving from head to foot several times. "It's a bit hard to tell under those baggy clothes, but I think her build is good. Her hair is the right shade, or at least close enough." She puts two fingers under my chin, and the contact makes me jolt and look up and into her eyes, which go a little wide when she sees mine. "Does she have violet eyes?"

"Yes. But they appear blue in some lights."

I snap my gaze to Neo. How does he know what color my eyes look like in different lights?

If he registers my alarm, he ignores it. "Do you think that will be an issue?" he asks, and I'm utterly confused about why the shade of my hair, my eye color, or my build would matter in the least to them. But like always, I keep my mouth shut and my ears sharp.

"Let's hope not." She taps a finger against her lips as she assesses me. "Perhaps we can plan her wardrobe to downplay the unusual color. And her freckles shouldn't be a problem either. They can be easily covered with makeup."

Shoot. I must have accidentally wiped some of the soot off my face if they can see my freckles.

"Freckles?" Bram says, narrowing his eyes as he takes a better look at my face from his spot behind Lady Greyblossom. I don't know how well he can see in the low lighting. "Huh." He rubs his chin. "I just thought they were flecks of dirt."

I purse my lips and shift from one foot to the other. This is the most attention anyone has ever given my features, and their scrutiny makes me incredibly uncomfortable. My hands itch to yank my hood back up and slink into the shadows, away from their view.

Lady Greyblossom retreats a step, her gaze softening as she tries again to catch my eye. "Thank you so much for being willing to help us out. Your participation is vital to the success of our endeavor."

"Willing to help?" I snort. "It's not as if I have a say in the matter, do I?" The words are uttered under my breath, but everyone hears them, and the room goes uncomfortably silent.

I sense Neo go rigid next to me, and I tip my gaze up to see Bram's mouth pressing into a straight line as he shakes his head at me behind Lady Greyblossom.

I've clearly said something I shouldn't have.

A frown forms on Lady Greyblossom's face. She glances between Neo and Bram. "She isn't here of her own free will?"

"Not exactly." Neo clears his throat and avoids eye contact with her, appearing uncomfortable for the first time since we've met. "I own her contract now."

Lady Greyblossom's eyes widen and she gapes at him. "She's indentured to you?"

She looks horrified by the thought of Neo holding my contract, but since when do the fae nobility balk at fellow-species ownership?

Neo runs a hand through his hair, messing the soft strands so that a blond lock falls onto his forehead.

I've seen several sides of him this evening. Calculated, cunning, flippant, and even jovial, but this is the first time I've detected nervous energy from him.

"It's not as if I *want* to be linked to her. There was nothing to be done about it. She was already indentured, and her contract holder was a vile fae who would do anything to gain coin. We couldn't proceed with our plan with her still attached to him."

It's not as if I want *to be linked to her.*

I cross my arms over my chest and lift my chin. I shouldn't be offended by his words, but I am.

"But . . . you *own* her now," Lady Greyblossom says with a frown.

Neo sighs, suddenly looking very weary, and plops into the wingback chair to the side of the mantel. "Once this mess is taken care of and we have the answers we need, I'll deal with the contract. But first things first."

It's beyond late, and I've had enough this evening. There's only so long I can suppress my temper, and I've finally hit my limit. "What mess? And what do you mean, 'deal with the contract'?"

Three sets of cunning eyes swivel toward me.

"Neo," Lady Greyblossom chides. "She knows nothing of why she's here?"

Neo pinches the bridge of his nose. "There was hardly time. I figured it would be best to explain the details here."

Lady Greyblossom shakes her head at Neo and Bram and then comes over and urges me to sit on the small sofa in front of the fire with her. "What do you know of politics of the kingdom?" she asks, her voice gentle and eyes soft.

I shrug. "As much as the next citizen of the Ember Kingdom, I suppose."

Vaeloria is divided into sixteen separate kingdoms, which, in theory, all hold equal power. But everyone knows that's not true. The Ember Kingdom is considered one of the most powerful and influential kingdoms in Vaeloria, if not *the* most powerful. And while our kingdom is lauded for being the largest and for its abundant resources and wealth, what really sets the Ember Kingdom apart is the crystal housed in the highest tower of the palace—a crystal that burns like an ember, and for which the entire kingdom is named. It's the one resource all of Vaeloria depends on, and it's the key to our kingdom's unrivaled influence.

Lady Greyblossom's voice draws me back. "Have you had much interaction with the royal family or any members of the nobility?"

"What do you think?" I ask, gesturing to my clothes. "I don't exactly fit in with the highborn." I leave out the part where I've stolen from a number of nobles. The fae in this room might know I'm a thief, but I'm not about to further incriminate myself.

Lady Greyblossom smiles warmly. "That works in our favor. Rowan, you need to know that we've been searching for someone exactly like you. You're our very own needle in a haystack. The things you don't know, we can teach you, but the skills you already have are invaluable to us."

I don't know where she's going with this, but I wish she'd get to the point already.

"Where to start?" she says, almost to herself. Neo and Bram remain silent, letting Lady Greyblossom take the lead. "As I'm sure you realize, the Ember Kingdom is one of the most prosperous kingdoms in Vaeloria, but we do still have our enemies. Other kingdoms might not try to directly conquer us, as we're too strong for them to come up against, but they would certainly like to see our demise and jump on any opportunity to take control of our land, resources, and citizens, or use subterfuge to try to indirectly steer the kingdom in one direction or the other."

I nod. That is the way of things, after all. But we haven't been at war in my lifetime, and even then, usually squabbles between fae kingdoms are short-lived and settled without much loss of life.

"And then, of course, there are the other threats that lie beyond our lands."

I know what she's hinting at. Our biggest enemies are actually the otherworlders, the vampire and werewolf kingdoms outside of

Vaeloria and beyond the sea. We all know that otherworlders exist and the threat they pose if they were ever to get a foothold in Vaeloria, but you'd be hard-pressed to find a fae alive today who has ever come face-to-face with either of those species. Vaeloria is isolated on its own island, far away from the vampire and werewolf kingdoms on the mainland, with the ember crystal upholding a magical barrier that otherworlders can't get through. It's been the responsibility of the Ember Kingdom's royal family for generations to ensure it stays active.

Even so, the vampires' and werewolves' biggest enemies are each other, and their bloody battles far away on the mainland have kept them preoccupied for centuries.

"Are you trying to tell me there are reasons to be worried about otherworlders?" I ask, holding back an eye roll.

Vaeloria has been isolated for so long, anything beyond our fae land borders feels more myth than reality. Scary tales of werewolves and vampires aren't good for much more than keeping children obedient—the proverbial monsters that will snatch you if you step out of line, as the headmistress at the orphanage used to say to keep us compliant.

Before going on, Lady Greyblossom glances at Neo, who nods as if giving her permission. "There have been some concerning reports over the last year."

"About otherworlders?" I ask in disbelief.

She nods. "King Darius is looking to make an alliance with another fae kingdom to strengthen us against potential future threats, including possible ones from otherworlders. Alliances are made in many different ways, but one of the most unbreakable is through marriage. Several months ago, he sent invitations to the rulers of the kingdoms of Vaeloria, welcoming them to send an eligible royal female of marriageable age to our kingdom as a tribute."

"So the king is planning to marry?"

King Darius has only been the ruler of our kingdom for a little over a year. He was crowned after his father died unexpectedly, leaving the throne to him, the eldest son. The marriage between his parents was said to be a love match, and his mother, Queen Teresa, Lady Greyblossom's sister, has rarely been seen since her husband died. At least that was what I've picked up from eavesdropping on conversations between elites and from the gossip sheets.

King Darius is in his early thirties, still relatively young for a king, but certainly old enough to take a bride. And political marriages among royalty are commonplace, so the news isn't too shocking.

What *is* surprising is his sudden belief that the otherworlders pose an imminent threat to Vaeloria. Supposedly, the fae kingdom rulers manage to keep loose tabs on the ongoing conflict between Lunaris and Drakhar—the werewolf and vampire kingdoms across the sea—but it's not the kind of information that's ever disclosed to the public.

Lady Greyblossom shakes her head. "No. The alliance between kingdoms will be made when his brother, the prince, marries. King Darius has called an official courting season. In a way, this is a competition, with the prize being the prince's hand in marriage and an alliance between our two kingdoms."

I snort. I've heard the stories of Prince Dryden, the twenty-two-year-old younger brother of the king. We all have. He's handsome, to be sure, but he's said to be lazy and frivolous, concerned more with chasing skirts than protecting the kingdom, and spending many nights at the card tables, deep in his cups.

"What?" Neo asks, finally speaking up.

When I glance over, he's leaning forward with his arms draped over his knees and his gaze sharp.

I shrug. "I just don't see the prince's hand being all that much of a prize," I say honestly, and Neo scowls.

Perhaps I shouldn't be this open about my irreverence for the royal family. Lady Greyblossom is, after all, the prince's aunt.

"My apologies. I spoke too freely," I say to her, but she simply laughs.

"I think you picked the perfect female for the job," she says to Neo, then turns back to me. "The tributes from the different kingdoms will all be housed in the same part of the palace and spend much of their time together. We need someone on the inside who can have access to these females. Learn who they are and their true motives."

I snort again. "There's no mystery there. These princesses will be hoping to secure a title for themselves and an alliance for their home kingdom. If the prince is expecting a love match from this charade, he's going to be sorely disappointed."

The room falls silent. I may have been a tad blunt, but I didn't say anything that wasn't obvious. Since we are the strongest kingdom in Vaeloria, an alliance with us, trade or otherwise, is highly coveted among the other fae kingdoms, which means every single one of these princesses is going to arrive in Everlight with her eye on the prize. And regardless of how handsome Prince Dryden may be, he's not truly the prize. It is the Ember Kingdom itself.

"The prince is acutely aware he doesn't have the luxury of marrying for love," Neo says, breaking the tension.

"We have intel that suggests one of the tributes may be sent with a different agenda than marriage and securing an alliance with the Ember Kingdom," Lady Greyblossom tells me.

"An agenda that could be deadly to the prince or harmful to the kingdom," Bram cuts in from several feet away. I twist in my seat and watch Bram as he pours caramel-colored liquid into a set of crystal cups and then walks and hands one to Neo, who downs it immediately.

"Which brings us to the part where we need you," Neo says. "We want to place you as one of the tributes for the prince's hand."

My heart stalls for a moment. I couldn't have heard that correctly.

"You want me to seduce the prince?" I scrunch my nose at the thought.

Bram, who had just taken a sip of his drink, starts to choke. Lady Greyblossom covers her quiet laugh with her hand.

"No," Neo says blandly. "That won't be necessary."

"Your interactions with the prince will be brief and never alone," Lady Greyblossom supplies. "You're not there to actually compete for his hand in marriage. No one else will have as much access to the other princesses as you will. Your directive will be to learn as much as you can about them and relay any information you have back to us."

I look each of them in the eye, convinced they must be joking. But I don't read a single line of levity on any of their faces. "I'm not a spy."

"No," Neo says. "But you are a thief. And I've seen you in action, more than once now, in fact, and the skills you have will serve you well for this task."

"More than once?" I didn't take anything else from him or Bram besides the dagger.

A smile lifts the corner of Neo's mouth. "I saw you snatch that brooch from Lady Blackwell. Then we tracked you down at the Lame Horse. We were only at that vile tavern for you."

He saw me? What? How?

I'm an amazing thief; the fact that he caught what I did makes me grumpy. "Today must have been an off day for me," I grumble, and Neo's half smile turns into a full one. "And there's one big problem in your plan."

Neo arches an eyebrow, tilting his head for me to go on.

"I'm not nobility. Not even close. The palace won't accept me as a tribute."

A sly smile lifts the corners of Neo's mouth. "We don't plan to present you as yourself. You'll be pretending to be a very real royal."

My stomach drops. The penalty for impersonating nobility is lifelong imprisonment, if not death. "I don't know anything about fae royalty or how to impersonate one. There has to be someone better suited for this mission. Perhaps a palace spy?"

Neo shakes his head. "This has to be done without the king's knowledge. He doesn't believe any of the princesses pose a threat to his brother's life or the kingdom. Any of the regular spies might be recognized in the palace. Princess Greer of the Glacier Kingdom has never set foot in the Ember Kingdom. Their lands are so remote that very few fae would have had the opportunity to meet her in person."

Lady Greyblossom gestures to me. "Your physical appearance is close enough to hers in terms of stature and eye and hair color that we feel confident you will be able to pass as her. We don't want anyone outside this room knowing who you truly are."

"But what about the real Princess Greer?" I ask. Surely that could be a complication. "What if she shows up, hoping to win the prince's hand?"

"She's not coming," Neo says. "My spies intercepted a missive from the Glacier Kingdom claiming Princess Greer is too ill to travel. But since the note was never delivered, as far as the palace knows, she's still coming, giving us the opportunity to use her identity without raising suspicion."

Lady Greyblossom surprises me by taking my hand. I want to

rip it from her grasp because her hand is clean and free of blemishes or calluses, where mine is rough and dirtied, but if she notices, she doesn't let it show on her face. "Rowan, when I said before that you were our own needle in a haystack, I meant it. As a thief, you've proved that you know how to blend into your surroundings and be discreet. But we were also looking for someone who matched Princess Greer's physical description and who could mimic the elites' speech and mannerisms as well."

I press my lips together, frustrated with myself. I long ago learned to adjust my accent and speech patterns to the various classes in Everlight. It made it easier to steal from the different members of society without drawing attention to myself. Since entering Autumnburn Manor, I've slipped into speaking like an elite almost without thought, unintentionally revealing that ability.

"We've truly been looking for someone *just like you*, so when we heard whispers of a blond female thief who was somewhat of a chameleon, Bram and Neo went looking for you."

I frown, more concerned than flattered by my apparent notoriety. If I'm as good of a thief as I think I am, there shouldn't be whispers about me at all.

Realization dawns and I cast a startled glance over at Bram and then at Neo. "You didn't just accidentally catch me stealing that brooch. You knew I'd be working that market and were watching me the whole time."

Neo nods. "We wanted to see you in action before approaching you."

"Who told you where I would be?" I demand, unsettled that someone knows my patterns well enough to betray me.

Neo crosses his arms over his chest, a self-satisfied look on his face. "No one. I followed you most of the day."

A knot forms in my gut. I don't know if I should be relieved I wasn't betrayed or disturbed that I was followed without realizing it.

Lady Greyblossom squeezes my hand, drawing my attention back to her. "The courting season doesn't start for another month. You'll spend the next four weeks here, with me, as Princess Greer. The elusive fourth daughter of King Silas, ruler of the Glacier Kingdom. I will teach you everything you need to know about interacting with the elite in fae high society. How to dress, eat, blend in. All of the highborn customs and who you need to know." A smile spreads on Lady Greyblossom's face. "When I'm done with you, your own mother won't recognize you."

I almost snort again. My mother died the night I was born, so that's not saying much. "If no one outside this room is to know who I really am, that means the prince will think I'm this princess as well. But what if Prince Dryden discovers our deception? He's not going to take lightly to being deceived in such a way. I'll be imprisoned . . . or worse."

"That won't be an issue," Neo says.

What they are asking me to do is beyond dangerous, but Neo's face is hard and closed off, telling me I'm not going to get a further explanation than that, at least not now, so I tuck the question away for later.

"And if I don't agree, then what?"

The three of them exchange a look, but it's Neo who answers.

"You can refuse. I won't force you to do this, but since we've already divulged sensitive information, you'll have to be kept somewhere until this mess is over."

"Somewhere safe, like a dungeon?" I ask, my voice cold now that I see what they intend to do with me.

"No, not a dungeon," Neo says with an eye roll. "Somewhere like a country home away from court. But yes, you'd be highly monitored and ordered not to reveal any of these plans to anyone else. Then after the courting season is over, I'll release you from your contract and you can do whatever you'd like with your life."

I catch my breath. *Release me from my contract? I'll be free?*

Hope blooms in my chest, but almost as soon as it starts to grow, I pull it out by the root. I want it to be true, but how could it be? There has to be a catch.

"And just like that? You'll let me go?" I find it easier to believe that if I don't agree, they'll just kill me. Keeping me monitored or even locked up is a lot more trouble than just making sure I'm not around to spill their secrets.

Neo crosses his arms over his chest, his face hard. "Yes, I'd let you go. I don't agree with forced servitude. It's something I want to change one day."

I let out a humorless laugh. "Well, unless you are the king himself, I don't see much chance of that happening. This has always been the way of things. It will never change."

Neo frowns. "I hope, for your sake and the kingdom's, that's not true."

I shrug. He can believe and hope for whatever he wants—who am I to burst his bubble? Although rather than his outlook endearing him to me, it just makes me think he's a fool.

"But if you decide to help us with this mission, I'll make it worth your while," he goes on.

I cock my head and narrow my gaze, waiting for him to explain.

"If you help us, when it's over, I'll destroy your contract and arrange for transportation to any of the other kingdoms. Not only that, I'll send you with enough funds to buy a home, perhaps even open a shop if you so desire. You'll be free to start a new life, however you choose."

I'm stunned silent. Freedom and a fresh start?

But just like before, doubts creep in. "What if nothing comes of it? What if, at the end of it all, I don't discover anything useful? Will I be punished?"

Neo shakes his head. "No, that's not a stipulation of this offer."

"Neo," Bram starts, but the younger fae holds up his hand, cutting him off.

"The only condition of this offer is that you allow Lady Greyblossom to train you for the next four weeks and then participate in the courting season as Princess Greer Stormfeather of the Glacier Kingdom. With or without uncovering the truths we are seeking, when the courtship period is over, you'll be released from your contract and sent with a small fortune to live in another kingdom. But if you do find some evidence that leads to uncovering a potential assassin, your reward will be greater."

My mind spins. It's too good of an opportunity to pass up, even if it might all be a lie. For years, all I've hoped is to be free of my contract, but to be given money to start a new life, that's beyond my wildest dreams.

"How long is the courting season?" I ask.

"Six weeks," Neo says.

That means that in ten weeks, just a little over two months, I could earn my freedom. And a new life as well. This mission has dangers that I'm not even aware of yet, but I already know they are worth it.

"And I have your word on this?" I ask, looking deeply into Neo's eyes, searching for a hint of deception and finding none. That tells me he's either being truthful or that he's a very skilled liar.

Neo stands and walks the short distance to me. I have to crane my neck to keep our gazes locked. "You have my word."

I suck in a sharp breath of air through my nose and hold it in my lungs before slowly releasing it again. "Then I agree."

Neo's face doesn't show much emotion as he acknowledges me with a curt nod. "Good." Turning to Lady Greyblossom, he says, "Bram and I have to leave. It's getting close to dawn, and we need to return before anyone realizes I'm gone."

Lady Greyblossom's gaze tracks to a large grandfather clock against the wall, her eyes widening when she sees the time. "Yes, of course. You need to be off."

"I'll be back next week to check on her progress."

"Neo, do you think that's wise?" she asks.

"You know I have a vested interest in this endeavor." His gaze drifts over to me, his eyes calculating. "I want to see her progress."

Lady Greyblossom's eyes narrow. "You doubt me?"

Neo leans over and kisses Lady Greyblossom on the cheek. The gesture speaks to their familiarity, and I start to wonder about their relationship and why these three people are working so hard to protect Prince Dryden. Lady Greyblossom is his aunt, so her interest makes sense. But who are Neo and Bram?

"Never," Neo says. "But there will be details that need discussing regardless, and I'd like to be able to gauge her progress. You don't need to worry. We'll arrange a discreet location. Your reputation will be intact."

Lady Greyblossom sighs. "You know it's not me I'm worried about."

Neo only smiles fondly at her and then waves to Bram before they both head toward the door.

"Wait," I call after them.

Neo pauses with his hand on the doorknob and glances over his shoulder at me.

"Will you be . . . requiring anything else of me until the courting season begins?"

"What do you mean?" he asks with a head tilt.

I press my lips together, frustrated and slightly embarrassed that I have to point out the obvious.

"You're my contract holder. If I'm expected to do more over the next month than learn to be a pampered princess, I'd like to know."

Neo still looks confused.

"As you've said numerous times, I have a particular set of skills. Will you be requiring I use them?"

Neo lifts his eyebrows, finally catching on. "No. You won't need to use those skills until you are embedded in the palace, and even then, they are only to be used to further your mission. And if I hear of items missing around Lady Greyblossom's estate, our deal is off."

I gasp. "You wouldn't. You gave me your word."

But maybe he would. What do I really know about this fae? I feel stupid for not insisting we do a fae blood oath when the opportunity was there.

The smile he shoots me is wicked and does uncomfortable things to my stomach.

"I don't advise trying me," he says, and then without another word, he and Bram are out the door.

Chapter 4

AFTER NEO AND BRAM LEAVE, LADY GREYBLOSSOM shows me to a guest room, which consists of an antechamber and a small seating area that leads into the bedroom. Inside the room is a large bed draped in red fabrics, several chests for clothes, a vanity, and a small, unlit fireplace.

The room is chilly, but not uncomfortably so. I've certainly slept in colder circumstances. There's a bowl of water with a cloth on the vanity. She tells me I need to strip out of my clothes and wash as best I can. She quickly lights the fire before leaving to get me a nightgown.

Anticipating she would be training a girl to act as Lady Stormfeather, Lady Greyblossom has already prepped her staff that Princess Greer would be arriving sometime this week. Our cover story is that I lost my luggage during a storm at sea, which explains why I don't have any clothes or baggage. She said that until items can be purchased, I'll be wearing some of her clothes. Lady Greyblossom is a petite female as well. I'd guess our measurements aren't too far apart from each other.

While Lady Greyblossom is gone to find something for me to sleep in, I undress, slipping the jeweled letter opener I grabbed from the study beneath one of the pillows. Despite Neo's parting threat, I'm not about to sleep in an unfamiliar place without a weapon within reach. With my dagger still in Sinclair's office and Neo having reclaimed his own, I didn't have many options. His warning echoes in my mind, but I tell myself I'm only borrowing the opener, not stealing it.

When Lady Greyblossom returns, I've stripped down to my underclothes and scrubbed my face, hands, and arms as clean as I'm able. She immediately takes my discarded clothes off the floor and tosses them into the fire. Handing me a white nightgown, she tells me all my undergarments will have to be burned, so the staff doesn't see what clothes I arrived in and get suspicious. I slide the nightgown over my head and shimmy out of my underthings as well, only to watch them go up in flames next.

"How are you doing?" she asks me as I stand in the middle of an unfamiliar room in someone else's clothing, most likely looking more lost than I ever have in my entire life.

"I'm fine."

Her mouth turns down.

"Are you sure? Everything about your life has changed in the last few hours. It would be okay to feel a little apprehensive or unsteady right now." When I remain silent, she adds, "We're going to be spending a great deal of time with each other over the next several weeks. My desire is for you to feel comfortable sharing your truths with me."

"Thank you, Lady Greyblossom. That's very kind of you."

"Please, call me Olette."

"Oh no, I couldn't. That wouldn't be proper."

Stepping forward, she grasps my calloused hands in her soft ones. "You must remember that in everyone's eyes we are equals. In fact, a princess outranks a duchess."

She's not wrong. Switching that mentality is going to be difficult for me.

"But beyond that," she continues, "I would truly like to be friends, and my friends all call me Olette."

She squeezes my hands once.

The enormity and seriousness of what I'm about to do finally sets in. I can no longer think like Rowan, the street thief. I have to start thinking like Princess Greer.

I take a deep breath and nod. "Thank you, Olette. I'd very much like to be friends as well."

It's the truth. She has been nothing but kind and warm to me since the moment I stepped into her home, which is more than I can say about most fae in Everlight. At least the ones I've encountered. I'm sure after this whole ordeal is over, I'll never see her again, but something tells me being friends with Olette, even if just for pretend, will make the next weeks more bearable.

A smile blooms on her face. "I'll leave you to get some rest. The sun will be up shortly, but I'll let my staff know not to rouse you. You're going to need all the rest you can get."

When Olette leaves, I climb into bed and sink into the plush mattress and pillows. It feels like heaven. I almost don't want to sleep so that I can enjoy the luxury of it all instead, but I can't fight my heavy lids, and within minutes I'm out.

✦

I DIDN'T GET to bed until the sky was already turning pink, and I wake slowly hours later. I've never slept in a bed this comfortable. It's like sleeping on a cloud. It's not until I hear soft humming that I realize there's someone else in the room.

My eyes pop open and I sit up with a gasp. I haven't forgotten where I am, but waking in such a different place is disorienting, and I forget that Olette said a maid would be in midday to attend to me.

A young fae, a year or two older than me with hair the fiery red of a burned sunset and bright blue eyes, stands next to the bed with a silver tray in her hands. "Oh. I'm so sorry, Lady Stormfeather. I didn't mean to startle you. Her Ladyship mentioned you arrived early this morning and asked me to bring you some tea and wyldberry muffins. They just came out of the oven and are still warm. I can just set them here if you'd like"—she indicates the nightstand with a nod of her head—"and let you continue to rest."

"Oh, um . . ."

The young maid stands patiently in front of me with the tray still in her hands, waiting for me to give her directions.

"Yes, that would be lovely."

The maid smiles warmly and sets the tray down.

"I'm Eilowyn. I'll be acting as your lady's maid while you are staying at Autumnburn Manor. I'm very sorry to hear your lady's maid perished during the storm at sea, and also that you lost all your possessions. It sounds like a terrible ordeal you've just been through."

I blink back at Eilowyn, racking my brain for an appropriate response. I know nothing about the Glacier Kingdom except that it's a kingdom of several small islands off the northernmost coast of Vaeloria in the Obsidian Sea. I know even less about ships and sailing. Olette said she would be telling her staff that I lost all my belongings on the trip, but we never talked about the particulars of the story. It makes sense to say I lost a lady's maid as well. Why else would I be without one now?

"Yes, ah, thank you for your concern?" That wasn't supposed to be a question, but it came out like one.

A small furrow appears on Eilowyn's brow, letting me know that I'm really making a mess of things.

Fantastic. My first morning as a fake princess and I'm already blowing it. How did I think I could pull this off? What seemed like an achievable task last night now feels impossible. I blame exhaustion and food deprivation for my bad decisions.

"I'll just let you continue to rest, Your Highness. I'll be back in a few hours to help you dress." Eilowyn gives me a wobbly smile and then bows her head and turns to leave.

"Wait," I say too loudly, and wince.

Eilowyn turns back with a muted smile on her face. "Is there something I can do or get for you?"

"On second thought, I think I'd just like to get up and start the day. I've slept enough."

"Of course. If you wait here, I'll bring in the clothes that Lady Greyblossom set aside for you. I think she's planning on bringing you to the seamstress today to start purchasing a new wardrobe." She curtsies and then departs.

That's going to take some getting used to.

I snatch a wyldberry muffin from the tray and shove it in my mouth, trying to chew and swallow before Eilowyn returns. It's delicious, and it's been over a day since I've eaten, so one muffin isn't enough. I'm halfway through my second when she returns with a gown draped over her arms. I do my best to wipe the crumbs from my face, but my cheeks are crammed with the delicious breakfast treat.

"I see you have quite an appetite this morning," she trills. "I'd be happy to have the cook whip up something a little more substantial for you if you'd like."

I take a sip of the tea to try to wash the rest of the muffin down, careful not to reply until my mouth is empty. I may not know much about highborn fae, but I'm sure they take care not to spit food at people when they talk.

"How embarrassing," I say with a forced laugh. "I just didn't have food this appetizing during the voyage here and skipped the evening meal yesterday."

Eilowyn smiles warmly. "Don't fret about that, Lady Stormfeather. It's just you and me here."

"Please, call me Ro— Greer," I say, forgetting that I'm playing princess and that Eilowyn wouldn't consider it proper to call me by my given name. The moment the words leave my mouth, I want to suck them back in. I force myself to pretend like what I've asked of Eilowyn is perfectly acceptable and not a slap in the face of decorum.

The young maid looks reluctant, and I know she probably feels exactly as I did last night when Lady Greyblossom asked the same of me.

Grasping for a plausible excuse to cover my blunder, I say, "Lady Stormfeather is just so formal. My last lady's maid and I were actually very close, so I asked out of habit. I apologize if I made you uncomfortable."

Yes, that sounded feasible. Who's to say the real Princess Greer isn't close with her lady's maid?

"Oh, milady, I'm so sorry. How insensitive of me. You were close and you lost her on your voyage. Of course I'll call you Greer if it gives you comfort."

I smile politely at her and dip my head. "It would. Thank you ever so much."

Eilowyn smiles back at me so warmly that I can almost believe I did make a new friend. She holds up the dress she brought me, a dark blue cotton day dress, similar to what I've seen other elites wear when they take outings to the market or for picnics around one of the city ponds. It's a simple design but still far nicer than anything I've ever worn before.

Eilowyn helps me out of my nightgown and into a loose chemise, then slides a corset over my head, which is an entirely new and awkward experience for me, but I do my best not to let that show. She goes behind me to lace it up. When she's done, I'm not sure I can take in a full breath, but Eilowyn appears pleased by her handiwork, so I don't say anything. After helping me into a petticoat and putting on stockings and flat slippers, the blue dress comes next.

"That color is lovely on you." Eilowyn beams at me, but then her gaze travels to my head and her smile wobbles. "Why don't you sit at the vanity, and I'll brush out your hair and pin it up."

I reach up to my hair, only now considering how it must look. It's been in the same braid for several days, which isn't unusual for a fae of my class, but surely isn't a style a highborn would be caught dead in.

Hopefully, the cover story of me having been on a ship for days without my maid is a plausible enough excuse for its state that Eilowyn doesn't question it.

I nod and let Eilowyn direct me to the small wood vanity in the corner. I concentrate on sitting up straight and not wincing as she undoes my braid and works a brush through the tangled mess. It feels like she's tugging on my hair for ages before she's finally done, but even I can admit the torture was worth it. She's managed to tame my long locks. Now my hair hangs down to my lower back in soft honey waves. The sides have been pulled back and twisted into small braids. Eilowyn has even woven fresh flowers into the plaited hair.

When I stare at the fae in the mirror, I don't see Rowan, the penniless shadow waif anymore. Instead, Lady Stormfeather, princess of the Glacier Kingdom, looks back at me.

"Eilowyn," I say, turning my head left and right to inspect her handiwork. "You are a sorceress. What you've done with my hair is true magic."

Eilowyn blushes at my praise. "You have beautiful hair, milady."

"Greer," I correct her, happy I remembered my fake name this time.

"Right, Greer," she says with a nod. "I do enjoy styling hair, but your locks simply needed a little bit of love after your journey to truly shine."

A bit of love is an understatement. It wasn't any journey that caused my hair to be in its sorry state; it's the nineteen years of neglect. I never cared much about my hair before. It was only so long because I never bothered cutting it.

I smile warmly back at Eilowyn. "Oh, you're too kind."

Look at me, sounding all highborn and fancy. I'm already starting to get the hang of this.

Just then the door to the bedchamber opens and Lady Greyblossom walks in. I turn and stand to greet her as she drifts gracefully toward me. Leaning forward, she plants a kiss on each of my cheeks, an elite formal greeting. I fumble through the motions, hoping it doesn't come off too awkward.

"I'm so glad to see you are awake and dressed. You look divine in that dress. It really makes your blue eyes sparkle," she says with a wink when Eilowyn turns to put away the hairbrush and leftover bobby pins. "I was hoping we'd have time to go to the seamstress today. If we're going to replenish your wardrobe before the courting season begins, we have to start ordering dresses and fabrics right away. How advantageous it was that you arrived a month early."

I dip my head politely. "How advantageous indeed."

Chapter 5

OLETTE'S CARRIAGE IS EVEN MORE OPULENT than Neo's. The exterior is painted gold, with decorative carvings of intricate vines and flowers running over the sides and the Greyblossom crest on each door. I have to swallow a gasp when the footman helps me enter the carriage.

Every inch of the interior is swathed in damask silks except the floor. The benches are tufted, and there are small pillows placed on the seat to put behind your back or rest your arm upon during the ride.

When Olette settles on the bench across from me, she murmurs her thanks to the coachman and informs him to go to the back entrance of the shop. She pulls the heavy curtains closed, blocking his view, but also preventing anyone from seeing us inside as we travel.

The carriage starts moving and Olette says, "I'm sorry we can't have the curtains open. It's a lovely ride, actually, but we need privacy." She frowns. "The staff has been ordered not to mention that you have arrived. However, I don't think the news will stay under wraps for very long. But I need to keep you to myself for as long as possible."

"What do you mean?" I ask.

"I mean that once the public, and specifically the elite, learn you're staying with me, they're going to want to meet you. The invitations will start rolling in. And I need to warn you now, there may be some I won't be able to refuse. The longer we can keep the arrival of Lady Stormfeather a secret, the more time we'll have to prepare you."

"I wasn't aware I'd have to take on the mantle of Lady Stormfeather in society so soon."

"From now on, that is who you are." Olette covers one of my gloved hands with her own and squeezes. The gloves are a necessity until we can get my nails cleaned and polished and the skin softer. "Remember, you are not alone. I'll be with you every step of the way, and as your official chaperone, you won't have a single social engagement without me. We will start your etiquette studies immediately. You'll also be learning extensive details about the Glacier Kingdom, and any other details you'd be expected to know as one of its princesses. It will be all right. I promise."

As I stare at Olette and the earnestness shining on her face, I believe her. A warm feeling fills my chest. For as long as I can remember, I've been on my own without a single soul to care or watch out for me. Knowing that there's someone in my corner is completely new to me. Part of me fears I'll get used to it.

"Thank you." I give her a small smile. "I can do this."

Olette's face brightens. She squeezes my hand another time before sitting back. "I know you can. Now, let's go have some fun."

I learn quickly that Olette's idea of fun and my idea of fun are not the same. When we arrive at the door of Madame Larkfire, the seamstress, we are immediately escorted into a private room. We don't see anyone except the seamstress's assistant, who brings us tea and finger cookies that Olette informs me I'm not to eat when we aren't alone. Apparently, there's a specific way to eat I haven't been taught yet.

When Madame Larkfire finally joins us, she spends the first five minutes apologizing profusely for making us wait. After stripping down to my underclothes—with the help of the assistant, because there's no way I could get out of this corset on my own—I stand on a pedestal in the middle of the room with my arms raised while the seamstress takes my measurements and talks about fabrics with Olette.

The assistant reenters the room with several bolts in her arms. The seamstress takes them from her and drapes the fabrics over me while Olette gives her opinion about each. Olette picks many shades of blue, and then warm tones, and when the seamstress and her assistant step out of the room to bring us a design book to pick dresses from, she tells me she's picked the colors that will bring out the blue in my eyes and hopefully downplay the purple hue.

When the pair returns, the assistant finally helps me back into my dress. I sit down on the small settee next to Olette as she flips through a thick book of hand-drawn designs of dress after dress.

Madame Larkfire spends the next hour fawning over Olette. If she thinks it's odd that I'm not speaking up about any of my preferences, she doesn't show it. I don't think she cares, though, because Olette is purchasing so many items she'll probably be able to retire with the funds being spent on my wardrobe.

"I brought some of my dresses that I'd like you to alter for Lady Stormfeather as quickly as possible while we wait for you to make the rest of her wardrobe," Olette says.

Madame Larkfire nods enthusiastically. "Yes, of course, Your Grace. I can work on some tonight and have them sent back to you right away." She clucks her tongue, turning her attention to me. "Poor thing. We'll get you looking like a *proper* princess again in no time."

I smile politely and thank her for everything, when what I

really want to do is stick out my tongue. I know an insult when I hear one.

When we finally get back into the carriage, I'm exhausted. Olette takes one look at my face and offers me a sympathetic smile.

"I know this is a lot, and I'd like to tell you it will get easier, but it won't."

I appreciate Olette's directness more than she probably realizes. "No, no, I'm okay."

"You handled yourself well."

"Because I only said two words the whole time." I snort, and Olette's eyebrows arch.

Whoops. Noted. Snorting is not ladylike behavior.

"Lady Stormfeather isn't known to be chatty, so we aren't looking for you to be the center of attention. Just the opposite, in fact. Blending into the background is probably the best strategy. We think that if the other girls see you as too much of a threat, they may not confide in you."

Thank goodness for that. Blending in is one of my specialties. I can spend the next several weeks learning everything I need to know about being a fake royal, but if they expect me to overhaul my entire personality and turn into the social butterfly of the season, that would be asking too much.

Olette spends the rest of the carriage ride giving me random facts about different members of the Ember Kingdom's nobility: who's related to whom, their vices, the recent gossip I would be expected to know even as a visiting princess. I struggle to stay focused on the conversation. And it's not only because I find the information completely boring and generally useless, but because I'm distracted by her necklace: a string of pearls with a large emerald pendant. I didn't notice it before, as the pendant was tucked into the bodice of her dress, but now it hangs loose, dangling enticingly at the end of the string of pearls.

My fingers start to twitch in the familiar way they do when I see an object that I can't resist snatching, but I ball up my fist and press it into my skirts. Neo's warning that the deal will be off if I steal anything from Lady Greyblossom rings in my ears. He might be able to overlook the letter opener I stashed under my pillow as a makeshift weapon, but I doubt he'd be as forgiving about stolen jewelry. I tell myself I'm stronger than the compulsion to steal, but even so, I can't seem to keep my eyes from the necklace. The longer I stare at it, the less I catch of what Olette's saying.

"Do you like it?" Olette says, picking up the emerald between her fingers, and I snap free of my trance.

"Oh, yes." I squirm in my seat, embarrassed to have been caught eyeing it so intently.

"It's an heirloom. It's been in our family for seven generations. I would have passed it on to my daughter or daughter-in-law if . . ." She lets her sentence drop off, and I know why.

Olette doesn't have any children to pass the heirloom on to. If I remember correctly, her husband died early and she never remarried. I don't blame her for that. Why remarry when she's so free on her own? But perhaps her lack of a family is something that hurts her heart.

For a moment, her eyes get a little misty before clearing again. "I suppose it will go to Prince Dryden's bride, my soon-to-be niece, whoever she may turn out to be," she says with a false smile.

We both fall silent after that, Olette lost in her thoughts and me forcing myself to focus on anything but the necklace.

When we arrive back at Autumnburn Manor, Olette leads me to the study from last night. She informs her staff we'll be eating together, and when they bring the food, she dismisses them, requesting that they don't disturb us for the rest of the day.

Olette is relieved to find out that I can read. Not every fae in the kingdom knows how, but I taught myself to read, as well as to modulate my speech, in order to better blend in when I'm working—particularly when I steal from the elite. Sinclair always scoffed when he caught me practicing, grumbling that a gutter fae didn't need to know how to read, but it's a good thing I never listened. Every princess will be expected to be literate, and it would be near impossible for me to learn in the time we have.

We stay up well past midnight as Olette teaches me all the basic information about the royal family, politics, and history of the Glacier Kingdom I'm to pretend I call home. I learn all of Princess Greer's relatives, and I am given a small stack of books to start reading to familiarize myself with the culture and customs of not just the Glacier Kingdom, but the Ember Kingdom as well.

By the time I trudge up the stairs to my room, I'm as tired as I've ever been. My head throbs with the amount of details and facts I force-fed it today, but I have a full belly and a soft place to sleep. That's more than I've ever had before, so I go to bed feeling lucky.

Chapter 6

OVER THE NEXT WEEK, OLETTE HAS ME TAKE all my meals in my room, where I am if I'm not in the study cramming as much political, social, and economic information into myself as I can hold. Besides looking the part of a pampered princess, I'm expected to be well-versed in all things related to the various kingdoms of Vaeloria. That includes knowing each one's resources and strategic value to the Ember Kingdom, even going as far back as studying the magical resources they once possessed before magic began to fade.

The lessons are both tedious and fascinating. I've uncovered pieces of history I never would have guessed, like with the River Kingdom. Everyone knows its main exports are fine textiles woven from river flax, and that it's famed for hand-carved driftwood furniture and bows and arrows. But when magic was still strong, the kingdom was said to possess far stranger wonders. Its intricate canal systems could carry whispers, messages that only the intended recipient would hear, even in other kingdoms. And those who sang to the river claimed it would carry their boats faster.

I'm not sure how useful much of this will be during the courting season, particularly in my mission to sniff out a potential assassin, but Olette was adamant that these are facts all princesses would know, so I do my best to absorb everything regardless.

Olette joins me for most meals in my room, and after sending Eilowyn away, she schools me on dining etiquette as we eat. I had no idea before her tutelage started that dining was so technical. So. Many. Rules.

Don't overload your fork. You're to take only small bites.

Sip, don't slurp.

Never rest your arm or hand on the table.

Make good eye contact with your dining companions.

Cut only one piece of meat and eat it before cutting another.

Never, *ever* speak with food in your mouth or take food out of your mouth once you've started eating.

The list goes on and on.

And then there's the silverware. It feels like there's a different utensil for every food. My eyes almost crossed the first time the table was set for dinner and there were four forks, three spoons, and three knives.

Olette makes me eat my meals with a book perched on my head to learn to keep my back straight. The first three meals, I splatter myself with food when the book drops onto my plate. Olette takes every setback with grace and a seemingly endless wellspring of patience, but mine is definitely running thin.

The luster of staying in Olette's grand manor starts to wear off as the days tick by and all I see are the inside of my room and the study. I've never been cooped up like this before. It doesn't suit me. By day seven, the study starts to feel like a gilded cage, one I'm desperate to escape, so when Olette comes in and announces we're headed back to the seamstress for another fitting, I'm more enthused about the outing than I should be.

In my haste to enjoy some time out of Autumnburn, I stumble

a little on the steps leading toward where the carriage waits for us. Olette gives me a stern look. Even with the alterations the seamstress made to some of Olette's dresses, I've been struggling to walk gracefully in such voluminous skirts. The layers of petticoats get wrapped around my legs, causing me to trip or stumble often. I also frequently miscalculate the clearance I need to get past people or objects, and more than once have knocked something from its place.

Yesterday, I sent a vase crashing to the floor when my skirts bumped into its pedestal. Olette assured me it was okay that I broke what was probably a priceless heirloom, but I can tell my clumsiness is starting to grate on her.

The coachman is on the ground holding the door open for us when we reach the carriage. Olette nods her thanks without glancing in his direction and then steps up. I go to follow her, but before I get my foot on the first step, my gaze travels over to the coachman. I stop, recognizing him.

"Bram?"

Wearing tight royal blue breeches and a matching coat, Bram is dressed like one of Lady Greyblossom's staff. I haven't seen him or Neo since the night they dropped me off at Autumnburn Manor, and I can't say that I've given them too much thought. I've been too busy with my lessons, so I'm taken aback to see him now.

Does he work for Olette? Has he been around the manor somewhere all week and I just never saw him?

Bram tips his head to me. "Your Highness," he says, then waves me into the carriage after Olette.

Not knowing what else to do, I climb in and take a seat across from Olette. Bram closes the door, then the carriage shakes a little as he climbs up into the coachman's seat.

"Bram works for you?" I ask when we jolt into motion.

"Not exactly. He's here to take us to a spot to meet Neo. I don't trust any of my other staff enough with our meeting location, or to keep their lips sealed about it afterward."

At the mention of Neo, an unexpected zing of awareness shoots through me that I diligently ignore.

Instead, I glance toward the front of the carriage. "He doesn't say much, does he?"

"Bram?" Olette smiles faintly. "He never has. But don't let that fool you."

"You put a lot of trust in him," I say, not quite a question as I fish for information, still curious how Bram and Neo fit into all this.

She nods. "I do. Bram and I have known each other for years. Since we were young. It probably shows," she adds with a small smile, the easy familiarity between them making more sense now. "And I'm not the only one who trusts him. He's been watching over the prince in one capacity or another since Dryden was a boy. Saved his life once, actually."

That catches my attention. "Really?"

Olette shrugs like it's nothing, though there's a flicker of something deeper in her expression. "It was a long time ago. Not many people know the details. But let's just say Bram's loyalty to the royal family is hard-won—and absolute."

I settle back into my seat, my thoughts drifting unbidden from Bram to Neo before I yank them back again.

I give my head a light shake. "So this means we're not going to the seamstress?" I ask, not at all disappointed about the change of events. I didn't particularly enjoy the last trip we made to Madame Larkfire's.

Olette sees the hopeful look on my face and chuckles. "I'm afraid we are still going there as well. Your wardrobe is a very important part of this deception. But we'll make a stop to see Neo after."

I scrunch my nose but then smooth out my features like Olette taught me, and she gives me a nod of approval. We travel with the curtains drawn again, but we're out of the house, so I tell myself I don't really care that I don't get to enjoy the sights as we bump along the cobblestone streets in Olette's lavish carriage.

When we arrive at Madame Larkfire's, Bram opens the door and steps back with a bow, allowing Olette and me to climb out of the carriage. Once again, Olette doesn't acknowledge him any more than she would any of her other servants, so I follow her lead and keep my gaze fixed forward.

The seamstress's assistant once again brings us to a private room, and when Madame Larkfire meets us less than a minute after we arrive, she wastes no time showing Olette and me the sketches of the dresses she is making. Fashion is not my area of expertise, but even I must admit that the designs are stunning.

After we view the designs, the seamstress's assistant helps me into the first dress and then puts me up on the pedestal right away. I stand with my arms lifted, trying not to wince when Madame Larkfire repeatedly pokes me with pins as she adds another layer of fabric to my already oversized skirt.

There's no denying that the dresses they're making for me are true showpieces, but they are so cumbersome that I don't understand how noble ladies wear them day in and day out. I'm already struggling in Olette's hand-me-down day dresses, and some of these skirts are twice as large. There's a real fear that I won't be able to handle the more formal attire—not to mention there's no way to sneak around the palace in these gargantuan things.

The seamstress starts chatting with her assistant about adding another petticoat to give the dress more volume, and the thought of being even more constricted becomes too much.

"I have a request," I say, cutting off their conversation. Madame Larkfire and her apprentice, surprised by my interruption, stop talking and glance at Olette.

"What is it, dear?" Olette asks.

"I was thinking that perhaps instead of wearing only the styles popular in the Ember Kingdom, we could incorporate some of the styles from the north into my wardrobe . . ."

Setting down her teacup, Olette gets to her feet and walks over to me. "What did you have in mind?"

I've done enough research about the Glacier Kingdom to know that pants with a detachable overskirt is a popular style there, even among the nobility. The terrain in the north is more rugged, and they've adapted their fashions to allow females more range of motion, something I highly support. Their styles might be a bit progressive for the highborn females here in the Ember Kingdom, but I might go mad if I can't wear pants at least some of the time.

I explain what I have in mind, and Madame Larkfire regards me like I've lost my mind.

"You want to wear . . . pants, Your Highness?"

I nod. "It would make me feel more at home here in the Ember Kingdom. I would also like to showcase some of my own culture."

Olette smiles and gives me a small nod of encouragement, and I'm instantly relieved. This isn't something I thought to discuss with her beforehand, but I'm glad she approves.

Olette turns to the sour seamstress with a bright smile. "Madame Larkfire, I'm sure if there is anyone in the kingdom who could combine the far northern styles with our fashion, it would be you. Just imagine what everyone will say when they see Princess

Greer in your one-of-a-kind designs. I'm sure they'll all want to know who created the masterpieces."

Stroking the seamstress's ego works like a charm. Color blooms high on Madame Larkfire's cheeks as she most likely imagines the piles of coins that will come her way. "Well, yes. I'm sure I can make her an exquisite collection. And now that I think about it, I have a new fabric in the store that would look amazing with your golden hair."

She jets off with her assistant following in her wake, and I let out a sigh of relief.

"That was very cunning," Olette says, and I beam under her praise.

I've never had anyone treat me with the respect that Olette does, so even in this short time, her opinion has started to matter to me.

"You've seen me struggle in these skirts."

"I certainly have. I was trying to figure out what to do about that myself, but you've already taken care of the problem. Well done."

The seamstress and her assistant return with a length of rose gold silk in their hands. The fabric is stunning. It looks like liquid metal under the warm lantern lights.

"I've only enough of this silk to make one dress this season. As you can imagine, it's very expensive, but I thought a fae of your taste would appreciate the quality," Madame Larkfire says, once again addressing Olette rather than me, and I don't care one bit. As long as she makes me some pants and cuts down on the overskirt volume, she can pretend I don't exist for all I care.

Olette reaches out and brushes her fingers over the decadent fabric. "Oh my, it is truly heavenly. Look, Greer, it will bring out the blush on your cheeks and be lovely with your honey-gold hair."

I smile demurely and nod. I've never given even a fleeting thought to what colors would look good on me.

Can we just get out of here already so we can meet up with Neo?

Where did that thought come from?

I shake it off. Spending a full week cooped up, on top of the torture of having to pretend to be interested in highborn fashion, must be messing with my brain. And sadly, verbally sparring with Neo probably *will* be the highlight of my week. So it's not too bizarre that I'm looking forward to it.

The next hour ticks by slowly. I have to force myself to take measured steps out the back of Madame Larkfire's shop rather than make a run for it. Bram is there waiting for us. He jumps down from the coachman's seat to open the door for us when we exit the shop.

"Everything is on the passenger's seat," Bram says in a low voice as Olette passes him.

"Thank you," she replies quietly.

Bram's gaze stays on me as I climb into the cab, and I know he's assessing me.

"Where are we going?" I ask Olette when I sit down across from her.

Olette explains that Bram's taking us to meet Neo at a small pub in the Emberhollow district. My eyebrows shoot up at that, knowing that our carriage is going to stick out like a sore thumb in that neighborhood. The Emberhollow district isn't an area of the city highborn frequent often, but I suppose that also means there's less chance that Olette will be recognized.

She hands me a long black cloak and tells me to keep the hood up and my head down when we get there. We slow to a stop in a narrow alleyway between two buildings—a clever way for Bram to keep the carriage partially hidden. There's hardly room for the door to open, but Olette and I manage to squeeze out.

"I have to stay with the carriage, so try to make it quick," Bram says, his wary gaze on the open road beyond the alley. He doesn't seem happy at all to be stuck with the horses.

Keeping our hoods low and the dark cloaks wrapped tightly around us, we walk the short distance to the end of the alley. I sneak a peek at our surroundings from under my hood—I recognize where we are. This part of the city doesn't truly come alive until after dark, so the streets are sparsely populated, only a few fae in threadbare clothes scurrying by with their heads stooped low.

My heart twists when I spot a young boy sitting on the ground in front of the pub we're about to enter. His legs are bent, knees pressed against his chest, head dipped. He's probably no older than ten, and it's obvious by the state of his worn and faded clothes and almost skeletal frame that there's no one taking care of him. He doesn't even glance up when we pass, probably too tired to bother.

I was that little boy.

Abandoned as a baby and kicked out of the orphanage by nine because of overcrowding, I lived on the streets for years, barely scraping by and coming close to death more times than I care to remember.

As much as I hate to admit it, my contract with Sinclair saved my life. I traded freedom for a chance to keep breathing. There have been many days when I wondered if the trade-off was worth it, but what's done is done and has led me to where I am. If I can make it through the next couple of months without losing my head or ending up in a dungeon, I'll have the life I always dreamed of somewhere far away from this wretched kingdom.

A small bell chimes when we enter the pub, but the only two

people I spot, a weathered bartender and a drunk patron, don't bother to look up.

Olette moves swiftly toward the back corner of the establishment and pushes through a wooden door that leads to a small room no larger than the one I used to rent from Sinclair. Bookshelves line two of the walls, and there's a single small table with two seats next to a dingy window that barely lets in any light. Neo is seated in one of the chairs and stands when we enter.

He looks just as I remember, similar to before in a simple but well-made shirt-and-breeches combo with high boots. Our eyes connect, and a small shiver of awareness runs through me that I instantly brush off as nothing. Just a chill from some errant breeze.

Shifting his gaze from me, Neo steps forward to greet Olette. He brushes a kiss against her cheek and then asks, "Were you spotted?"

Olette shakes her head. "I don't think so, but we shouldn't tempt fate by leaving my carriage out in the open for too long."

Neo tilts his head in agreement. "And Bram?"

"Waiting with the carriage."

Neo smiles. "Good. I didn't think he'd listen to me and stay with it."

"Well, you know he has a mind of his own."

"One of the reasons why I like him," Neo quips, then adds with a twinkle in his eye, "A trait I know you admire as well."

Olette shoots him a look that makes me wonder if the nature of her relationship with Bram is even closer than I assumed, but before I can dwell on it, Neo turns to me. He makes a motion with his hand that I take to mean he wants me to take off my cloak, so I untie the fastening close to my neck and slip it off.

His eyes flare slightly when I'm free of the dark material, but he recovers, making sure his face is blank as he looks me over. Making a motion with his finger, he indicates that I should spin, but instead of heeding him, I press my lips together and cross my arms over my chest.

Undeterred, he walks over, taking his time as he circles me in the tight space. My face heats under his perusal, but I refuse to squirm. I keep my head held high while I wait for him to finish.

Finally, Olette speaks up: "Neo, cut that out. She's not an auction horse."

He strides back to the table, shrugging as he slouches into a chair.

What, he can shrug and I can't? Not fair.

"She looks . . ."

I hold my breath, waiting for what he's going to say about my transformation.

". . . presentable."

Seriously? "You flatter me," I say flatly.

"My pleasure," Neo says with the shadow of a smirk and a faint note of amusement.

I roll my eyes, chastising myself for caring even for a moment about Neo's opinion. What does it really matter if he likes my hairstyle or thinks I look shapely in my new clothes? A week ago, I took pride in fae assuming I was a boy. My new clothes and style of hair are not really me anyway, just another disguise.

Olette gives Neo a stern stare. "Stop goading her."

Neo stares back at her innocently, his eyes wide as if he doesn't have the slightest clue what she's talking about, though we all know he does.

After shaking her head, Olette casts her eyes heavenward, sighing. "Your note said you have news," she says, changing the topic.

In a single heartbeat, Neo's whole persona goes from relaxed and playful to no-nonsense. "Right," he says, after clearing his throat and sitting forward. His shoulders square as he rests his hands on the table, his face set in stone. "There have been reports from the south that otherworlders have been spotted. News straight from the Coral Kingdom. And a few attacks that have been . . . suspicious."

Olette's eyes widen, and I have to smother a gasp. The night we made our bargain, Olette mentioned that King Darius was seeking to strengthen his alliances with the other fae kingdoms to guard against potential threats from otherworlders, but I hadn't taken it all that seriously at the time. Otherworlders haven't set foot in fae lands since the ember crystal was used to erect the barrier around Vaeloria over two hundred years ago. Yes, there was a time when our lands were open to vampires and werewolf visitors from the continent, but they began to covet our lands, our magic, and even our citizens, and so we closed ourselves off to outsiders to protect ourselves.

If it's true there are otherworlders in Vaeloria, why now? How were they even able to enter our lands in the first place?

"Is it true?" Olette asks. She sits in the chair across from Neo. With no other seat in the room, that leaves me standing awkwardly to the side.

Neo sighs, dragging a hand through his sandy hair. "It should be impossible, but there are victims with markings consistent with what we know of their attacks. And . . . their bodies were found nearly bloodless."

Olette lets out a quiet gasp, and I don't blame her.

Nearly bloodless? What kind of attack could do that to a fae?

I rack my brain for what I know about werewolves and vampires, but it's not much.

"The barrier is still intact," Neo continues, "which means the crystal is doing its job, but considering what happened last year, this isn't something we can afford to ignore."

What happened last year? I wonder.

"Is your—?" Olette cuts herself off, casting her eyes over toward me. I realize this isn't a conversation for my ears, but there's nowhere to go in this small space to give them privacy. Even so, I back up until I feel shelves behind me. At the very least, I don't need to be hovering.

Neo waves his hand in the air, not seeming to care one way or another if I'm here. "The king refuses to send out anyone to investigate since it happened in another kingdom, so I've commissioned a few trusted fae to go and make discreet inquiries. Perhaps it's nothing, but . . ."

"It seems too much of a coincidence considering all we know and with the warning you already received," Olette finishes, and Neo nods.

I'm trying to follow their conversation, but it's obvious I'm missing pieces. They go on to talk about which princesses have already arrived in the kingdom and who is hosting them, but my gaze drifts to the rows of books beside me and catches on a small black leather-bound book with no marking on the spine. There's nothing overtly special about the book, but still, an uncomfortable compulsion swells inside me; my hands start to tingle and itch, begging me to snatch it.

I should be paying attention to Olette and Neo's conversation. Knowing which princesses have arrived this early might become useful to me later. But I can't drag my eyes from the spine of the tome resting on the dusty bookshelf.

I drift over toward the book, Neo and Olette becoming a quiet buzzing in the back of my mind as I reach out and pull the volume off the shelf. The moment my fingers connect with the cover, a warm rush shoots up my arm, but it passes so quickly I almost wonder if it happened at all.

The spine cracks when I open the book to one of its faded pages.

The words are so faint they're hard to read. It takes me a moment to realize the text is written in Faelith, an old fae language we haven't used for hundreds of years.

I trace a finger over the page and note it's not made of wood pulp, but rather parchment, and a chill runs down my spine.

The book is obviously old, so it makes sense it's made of animal skin since the fae have only been using wood pulp paper for the last hundred years or so, but something about this book and its ancient pages makes my stomach hollow.

I can't understand any of the text, but there are washed-out pictures splashed over many of the pages, everything from silver and gold star maps curling across the margins to lunar phases sketched beside crimson sigils and anatomical drawings that trace glowing lines through fae forms. There are also scenes of war: ghostly depictions of creatures locked in battle, some with sharp fangs, others with snarling muzzles, and fae with their pointed ears fighting on both sides. It's probably my imagination, but as I turn pages, they seem to warm beneath my fingertips, as if the ancient parchment is coming alive under my touch.

"Does she know how to dance?" Neo asks, his voice finally breaking through to me. I look up at the pair huddled together at the small table on the other side of the tiny room.

Olette's face falls and she shakes her head. "I'm afraid that's been a bit tricky. I can teach Rowan a great many things on my own—etiquette, political intricacies between the kingdoms, style and fashion—but to learn how to dance she needs a partner, and it would bring too much suspicion if I tried to hire a teacher. Do you think we can get away with her not knowing how to dance?"

Neo considers the issue for a moment and then shakes his head. "No. There's no way a princess of any kingdom wouldn't have been taught how to dance. I'll teach her."

My heart jumps into my throat and I shut the book, tucking it under my arm. I shrug my cloak back on, hiding the book from view.

"Neo," Olette says. "I don't think—"

"It's fine," he says with a wave of his hand. "We can arrange twice-weekly meetups. That should be enough time for her to learn the basics."

"Do you really think you can get away that often?" Olette asks, concern etched on her face.

"It will be tight, but with Bram's help, I can make it happen. The hours might be a little . . . odd."

Olette doesn't seem happy about it, but she nods. They both turn toward me. I try not to look guilty, though I feel like they can see through my cloak to the book I have wedged under my arm. The amount of dust on the books on the shelves makes me doubt this one will be missed, but I'd rather not chance asking for permission to take it. I want the book, and I don't want them to tell me I can't have it.

"How are you doing? Have you been settling in well enough?" Neo asks, the questions surprisingly thoughtful and caring.

"I'm well," I answer truthfully. "Lady Greyblossom is a gracious host and wonderful teacher. It's a lot of information, but I feel like I'm picking it up well enough."

"She's being modest," Olette says with a grin. "She's a sponge. There are a few areas that will need extra work and practice, but she picks up and remembers information faster than I expected. I think she'll be ready to go out on a few outings in the next week."

Neo's brows lift. "Do you think that's wise?"

Olette nods. "You know she's going to be exposed to society sooner or later. We can't have her initial introduction be the first day of the courting season. That could be a disaster. And of course, the news that she's staying with me is already circulating. I've received several invitations for her to attend social engagements."

Neo's brows notch even higher. "So soon?"

Olette laughs lightly. "She's a young, pretty, and perhaps most importantly, *eligible* princess. In a normal setting, there would be suitors lined up for her."

That's a bit alarming. I hadn't considered I'd have to discourage male attention while I was here, other than from the prince, of course.

"But Princess Greer is one of the prince's tributes. She wouldn't be free to encourage a suitor," I say, confused.

"Yes," Olette affirms. "But Prince Dryden will only be picking *one* bride, which will leave all the other princesses unattached at the end of the courting season. Opportunistic males from the kingdom will want to get a head start with some of the eligible—"

"—and don't forget wealthy and connected," Neo cuts in to add.

Olette tips her head in acknowledgment. "Like I was saying, there are a great many of our kingdom's elite who would benefit from a marriage to any of the eligible *wealthy and connected* princesses who will be present in Everlight for the courting season. As a matter of fact, I'm sure that's something King Darius planned as well. The more solid connections our kingdom can make with the other fae kingdoms, the better. There are several balls and events where you'll be mingling with not just the prince but also with the city's elite."

That makes sense, especially with all I've learned about the kingdom's politics over the last week, but I'm not exactly thrilled with the idea of mingling with wealthy or highborn fae outside of the courting season. It's not that they intimidate me, per se. I've spent years around the elite—stealing from them. But I have little to no experience navigating courtships, let alone deflecting romantic interest, so the thought of being the center of attention rather than another face in a crowd twists my stomach in knots.

Getting to their feet, Neo and Olette start strategizing about our next meetup, but my mind wanders to the book hidden under my cloak.

"I need to go check with the proprietor and pay him for the use of the room, as well as his discretion," Olette says. "Rowan, would you mind waiting here with Neo for a few minutes?"

I shake my head, but my stomach does a small flip, and I'm instantly annoyed at myself. I have much bigger issues than being alone with a handsome fae, so why the nerves?

When Olette leaves, the air in the room thickens with the silence.

"Are you truly all right?" he asks, surprising me again with his concern. His gaze searches my face, making my cheeks warm. "I know what we're asking you to do is no small task."

I cock my head at him, searching his face for a hint of insincerity, but find none. Is it possible I misjudged Neo, that he's not the unfeeling cad I originally pegged him to be?

"Truly, I'm doing well," I assure him, touched by his regard, despite myself.

Neo takes a measured step closer to me, and I shift back to keep him out of my space, but he matches my movement.

I arch a brow at him, not knowing what he's trying to do.

He takes another step forward, and I back up until I bump gently against the wall behind me. He's so close now that I have to tip my head back to keep my eyes locked on his face.

My heartbeat picks up, but not in fear.

I know that even in all these skirts I could take Neo down. I lived on the street; I'm scrappy. It's obvious Neo's lived the life of a pampered elite. Who knows if he's ever even raised a weapon against a foe? I'm sure Bram does all the heavy lifting.

No, my heartbeat is racing for an entirely different reason. One that I don't have much experience with at all. And when his gaze drops to my mouth and he runs the tip of his tongue over his lower lip, my stomach bottoms out. I'm not so naïve to not know what that means, but I am too inexperienced to know what to do about it.

Maybe I was right to have nerves about being alone with him after all.

Chapter 7

"THERE'S SOMETHING I DO WANT TO KNOW," NEO murmurs, dipping his head.

"Yes?" *Why am I so breathless?*

"What I want to know . . ." he starts, his gaze heavy-lidded as he stares down at me.

"Yes?" I say again, almost in a whisper as I fixate on his mouth, my half-muddled brain starting to wonder about things it never has before. Like how it would feel to have his lips pressed up against mine. Or what they would taste like. Or how soft they would feel.

He lazily lifts a hand, and I'm conflicted about whether I should duck out from under his arm, knee him in the crotch, or stay put.

Indecision makes my choice for me, keeping me rooted in place.

His hand hovers in the air next to me, his fingers so close to my neck I expect to feel their graze at any moment.

". . . is what are you doing with this?" As quick as a striking snake, he drops his arm and shoves his hand through the folds of my cloak, grabbing the small book I have wedged under my arm and yanking it away from me.

It all happens in a blink, and by the time I gather my wits, he's already opening the spine and flipping through the pages.

"Give that back," I demand, and lunge for my stolen treasure, but Neo easily spins out of the way, holding it in the air too high for me to reach. Short of causing him physical harm, which he's already banned me from doing, or jumping up and down to try to grab it, there's nothing I can do.

Anger boils my blood. I step back, crossing my arms over my chest and glaring at him.

When Neo sees that I've settled, he lowers the book, flipping it over to look for a title, but I already know he won't find one. "What do we have here?"

"That was a dirty trick," I say, my hands itching to snatch the leather-bound book back.

Neo glances up at me with a smirk on his face. "What trick?"

My nostrils flare, and I take back every nice thing I ever thought about him. He knows exactly what I mean, and that I won't embarrass myself further by pointing it out.

I hold out my hand. "Give it back," I demand again, then make a dive for it when he just shakes his head.

He twists out of the way and snags me around my waist, pinning my arms as he yanks me back against his chest. All with one hand still holding the book.

"Did you expect I wouldn't notice you pocketing this?" He shakes the book in front of me. His breath fans my neck as he speaks quietly into my ear: "I told you not to steal." There's a faint hint of growl in his voice, letting me know that he's as upset with me as I am with him.

"No. You told me not to steal from Lady Greyblossom," I correct him. "And don't even think about commanding me not to steal at all. That would just handicap my mission. You know as well as I do my skills as a thief are the primary reason you sought me out."

With a frustrated sigh, he releases me and prowls to the other side of the small space. "What is this anyway?" he asks, flipping the book open again and thumbing through its pages.

"I don't know," I admit, and his brows arch when he lifts his face to look at me.

"Then why take it?" he asks.

"Why do you care?" I ask, deflecting his question because I don't have a good answer. I'm not about to explain how I feel compelled to steal objects from time to time. He already owns enough of me. I'm not going to give him that piece as well.

He narrows his gaze and snaps the book shut. "I care because if you get caught stealing, your cover will be blown, and I want to know what you are willing to jeopardize that for."

"There's no one here to catch me," I argue.

"I caught you," he says. "And if I notice you stealing, then someone else will too."

"I'll be more careful around other people. Besides, you only noticed I took the book because you're highly attuned to me. You're watching and waiting for me to take something. Other people won't be as observant."

"That's a bad assumption," he says. "When you're in the palace, you'll have eyes on you almost every minute of every day. All it will take is a single slipup to land yourself in King Darius's dungeon, or worse."

I try not to let it show, but Neo's words frighten me.

"You should be scared," he says, reading me easily. *Too* easily.

"Let me worry about myself," I snap, my emotions a weird, knotted jumble. I'm not used to feeling this much in such a short period of time, and it's throwing me off my game.

"I can't," he says, and I see a bit of something that might be concern cloud his eyes. "When the courting season starts, there's only so much I'll be able to do to protect you."

"Protect me?" I say with a laugh. The idea of someone else watching out for me is so foreign to me it's laughable. "I didn't ask or expect you to take on that role. I can take care of myself."

The door opens, interrupting our argument. We both clamp our mouths shut when Olette reenters. She glances back and forth between the two of us, picking up on the tension immediately.

"What happened?" she asks.

Neo's gaze hasn't left me since Olette entered the room. I can feel the weight of it even though I'm trying to look anywhere but at him.

"Nothing," Neo finally says, then holds the book out to me. I grab it with mumbled thanks, tucking it back under my arm.

"What's that?" Olette asks.

"Just a book Rowan found that she'd like to borrow. There's enough dust on these bookshelves to prove Bernard won't even notice it's gone."

I shoot him a look. Why did he give me such a hard time if he was going to hand over the book in the end anyway?

"I'll see you later this week," Neo says to me with a stern expression. He kisses Olette on the cheek and then sweeps out of the room.

Olette seems like she wants to ask me something, but she just says, "Let's get going. Bram is probably itching to leave."

I keep my head down as I follow Olette through the pub, and when we push out the front door, the little boy is in the same spot as before. Olette passes right by him with hardly a downward glance, but I find myself crouching in front of the tiny child and reaching into the folds of my cloak to grab a small chocolate biscuit and a silver teaspoon I nicked from Madame Larkfire.

I'm extra thankful in this moment that Neo only forbade me from stealing from Olette, not stealing in general. There's no doubt my fingers are still sticky. Years of habits I developed as a thief can't be unlearned in only a week, and I had snagged the biscuit and small serving spoon on the way out. But I'm glad I have them. At least it's something to give the starving boy.

The boy lifts his head when I pull the biscuit and spoon out. His round eyes are filled with apprehension and a drop of fear as he watches me. I offer both prizes to him and his hand moves quickly to snatch them from me, like if he doesn't hustle, the small bounty will disappear. Without a word of thanks, he shoves the chocolate treat into his mouth and pushes to his feet before taking off. I watch him sprint away with a frown pulling down my mouth.

Up until Neo and Bram plucked me from Sinclair, survival was a daily concern, and so my ability to see and feel the suffering of others was limited. There simply wasn't room inside my head or heart to concern myself with others' misfortunes when I was buried under the weight of my own. But my mind is starting to clear, causing my perspective to change, illuminating the disparity in our kingdom in a new and heartbreaking way.

I'm only one girl. One girl with no power, no wealth, no standing in society. There's nothing I can do to change the way of things, at least not on a grand scale. But today I could make a difference for one soul. Because to others, a sweet and a silver teaspoon might seem trivial, but in a world that's doing its best to erase you, even the smallest kindness can remind you that you still matter.

Olette calls my name softly from down the street, where she and Bram are waiting for me. Nodding to let her know I heard her, I get to my feet and come face-to-face with Neo through the pub's dirty window.

I don't know how long he's been standing there, but I get the feeling he witnessed the whole exchange. His brow is pinched and he tilts his head, his eyes searching mine as if looking for something. For what, I don't know.

I hope he didn't notice the stolen spoon.

With effort, I tear my gaze from the blue-eyed fae and hurry to catch up with Olette. She and Bram wear similar expressions to Neo that I'm not sure how to interpret.

I duck my head, suddenly embarrassed. I don't know what the big deal is. Have they never seen someone show a touch of kindness to the less fortunate?

✦

I CHECK THE clock on the study wall for the third time in the last ten minutes. It's past midnight. Neo is late for our first dance lesson.

Olette informed me earlier in the day that they couldn't secure a discreet off-site location, so we'd be conducting our lessons here at Autumnburn Manor. But to keep them secret and work around whatever strange schedule Neo seems to keep, the classes are going to be held in the middle of the night, after the staff have retired.

Early that evening, I went through the nightly motions with Eilowyn, letting her help me out of my day dress and into my nightclothes, taking down my hair and brushing it out, and then I bid her a good night's sleep. After she left, I waited a few hours, keeping myself awake by reading by the dim firelight, before I slipped into a robe and padded my way downstairs to the first-floor study.

I practice the appearance of calmness as I wait for Neo, but in truth I'm a ball of nerves. The anger and embarrassment of our last encounter swirl with the same strange sense of anticipation to see him again. I don't know how I'm going to react when he arrives. Will I feel awkward for mistaking his actions as flirtatious? Will anger rise to the surface for the trick he played on me? Or will I see that I built the whole interaction up too big in my mind and be able to move forward with ease?

I truly hope it's the last option.

But even as I order myself to calm, my mind and heart are at war. I tell myself to push it all out of my mind. Neo is coming to train me, and that is all. Our lessons will be professional. I need to learn a skill if I'm to perform this deception, and he's the only one who has the ability to teach me.

The door creaks as it opens behind me, and I tense. I keep my gaze fastened on the small fire still burning in the hearth. Neo's unhurried footsteps sound on the hardwood, and then on the padded rug as he moves toward me, yet I still refuse to peek over my shoulder at him.

It's not until he's standing almost directly in front of me that I slowly lift my gaze to his. With the fire behind him, Neo's backlit, his face shaded in the dark room. My heartbeat picks up a notch when we remain locked in a stare-down, neither one of us seemingly in a hurry to speak first and break the thick tension in the air.

It's not helping me to know Neo can see every inch of my face, every twitch and blink, where I'm struggling to read his expression in the shadows.

"I need to apologize," Neo says, taking me off guard.

"Apologize?" I parrot, blinking up at him.

Neo steps to the side, letting the firelight illuminate his face as he takes a seat on the small couch next to me. I resist the urge to lean away, reminding myself that we'll be standing quite close once the lesson starts, so I need to get used to his proximity.

There's a small furrow between his eyebrows as he picks his

next words carefully. "I've thought a great deal these last couple days about what this experience must be like for you," he starts. "The truth is . . . you're not accustomed to this world, but from what I can see and how highly Olette speaks of you, it's clear you've been working hard to adjust. It wasn't fair of me to go on the attack about the book the last time we met."

A blush rises to my cheeks at the mention of that incident. The book is currently tucked into a corner cabinet in my room here at Autumnburn, along with a little stash of items I've stolen from the seamstress. Through sheer willpower, I've been able to restrain myself from taking anything of Lady Greyblossom's, including the necklace that I can't seem to get out of my mind. I'm embarrassed that I wasn't able to stop myself from snagging the book, but I don't let myself look away in shame. Instead, I lift my chin, daring him to call me out on it.

"I acted inappropriately toward you that day," he goes on. "I should not have been as hard on you for taking the book. You're right. Your mission will no doubt require you to steal. Please believe me that my initial reaction was born out of concern for your ultimate well-being."

I'm stunned into silence as I stare at Neo's face, which reflects nothing but sincerity. I feel a part of my heart that I'd purposefully turned cold toward him start to thaw.

I realize I've been staring for longer than appropriate and clear my throat, glancing away from the intensity in his gaze. "Thank you. Let's put it behind us."

There. That was certainly magnanimous of me.

Reaching forward, Neo places his hand gently over mine where it rests in my lap, making me jolt. Physical connection is jarring for me, even more so from Neo.

"Can we start over?" he asks, and I find myself looking up into his blue eyes and nodding.

A smile spreads across his face, and rather than letting my hand go, he adjusts his grip and pulls me to my feet, tugging me to the open space in the middle of the room. Leaving me there, he goes over to a music box at the side of the room and fiddles with it until a slow melody starts to play.

Returning to me, he slides one arm behind my back. Pressing his hand against my spine, he drags me toward him as he takes one of my hands and places it on his shoulder, then grabs the other. His rough palm rubs against my skin, making my stomach flip as we stand with only a spread hand's worth of space between us.

His hand tightens around mine, making me take note of the calluses on his palms and fingers, similar to my own despite the nightly paraffin wax soaks. Perhaps my assumption that he's a pampered elite who doesn't know how to work hard or wield a weapon was hasty.

"Now," he says, "we dance."

Chapter 8

FOR OVER THREE WEEKS I'VE BEEN MOSTLY COOPED up in Autumnburn Manor, in either my bedroom or the first-floor study, absorbing everything I can in order to play the part of a princess. My only reprieves have been dress fittings and dance lessons with Neo.

I'm starting to go stir-crazy, so I'm near euphoric when Olette announces we're going to make my first official outing: strolling through Greenbriar Park, which is what she tells me the elite do in order to be seen.

Olette says I'm ready, but I'm not as sure as she is.

But I also don't care.

I'd risk a great many things to finally have a change of scenery.

I'm not meant to be a pampered bird in a gilded cage. I'm a wild thing that thrives on the freedom to come and go as I please. When this is all over and I leave the Ember Kingdom for good, I'd like to live in a cottage near the ocean. Somewhere remote where I can swim when I want and don't have to answer to anyone but myself.

Life will be perfect. I just need to learn how to swim first.

It isn't until we're in the carriage, ambling through Everlight's most prestigious neighborhoods, this time with the curtains open so I can drink in the sights as we rumble past, that the nerves finally take hold. My palms grow damp, and the breeze drifting through the window does nothing to cool my overheated cheeks.

"Now, remember what I told you. Think of this like a mini trial run," Olette reminds me when the carriage comes to a gentle stop. "If anyone tries to talk to you, keep the conversation light. Don't forget that you are Princess Greer of the Glacier Kingdom. Look the elite in their eyes. They are your peers now. Your peers *and* your inferiors."

I nod, taking a deep, calming breath.

Leaning forward, Olette squeezes my hand in a now-familiar gesture of comfort and encouragement.

"You'll do fine. I'll be with you the whole time."

I give her a smile, letting her know I'm ready, and she knocks on the door, signaling to the coachman. The door swings open, and I'm hit with the scents of jasmine and honeysuckle. A stark contrast to the stench of urine, sweat, and stale mead that permeates the alley behind the Lame Horse.

Olette climbs out of the carriage, and, straightening my posture, I follow after, keeping a neutral look on my face like I've been instructed.

Greenbriar Park is enchanting. The meandering trails are sparsely forested with willows, their branches hanging heavily toward the ground, creating hidden spaces beneath their cover. There's a large pond in the distance and neatly trimmed green grass as far as the eye can see. Finely dressed fae stroll in groups of two or three throughout the park.

I never spent much time in Everlight's elite neighborhoods, given how I would have stuck out like a sore thumb when my modus operandi has always been to blend in. So because of that, I only ever preyed on the elite who ventured out of their comfortable bubble of luxury and into the real part of the city, the gritty neighborhoods where the majority of the fae in Everlight live and die.

Glancing from one well-dressed elite to another, it's hard for me not to see them through the eyes of a thief. This would have been a veritable buffet for me a month ago, but a lot has changed since then.

Olette wouldn't let me wear one of my new pant-and-overskirt dresses today, saying that she didn't want me to garner too much attention, so I take care with each step, praying that I've learned well enough how to move in these dresses over the last few weeks as to not make it obvious how unused to them I am.

Olette keeps a slow pace as we stroll on one of the park's gravel paths. Along the way, several fae tip their heads or give Olette small waves of greeting, which she returns. In low tones, she tells me who each of the fae are and any information she thinks I may need to know about them during the courting season.

I keep a pleasant smile on my face as we meander, looking to the world like I'm enjoying a leisurely day outdoors, when in reality I'm concentrating on every tidbit of information Olette feeds me while simultaneously making sure each step is measured and stable.

"Oh no," Olette says, and I glance over at her. Her lips are pursed, and a small furrow has formed between her brows. She smooths it over by plastering what I know is a fake smile on her face.

"What?"

"Lady Sylvan and her son, Lord Sylvan, are headed this way. I'd turn us around if it wouldn't be so obvious I did it just to avoid them."

I rack my brain, but I can't recall hearing that surname before. The pair heading straight for us look much like any of the other fae enjoying the park. The son, dressed in dark green slacks and an overcoat with a green damask vest underneath, is pleasant-looking enough. He has rust-colored hair with a natural wave and brown eyes. His chin is square and his nose is straight. His mother is wearing a dark blue dress made of thick velvet that swoops just a little too low in the front for someone her age.

I don't have time to ask Olette why she's opposed to speaking with Lord and Lady Sylvan before they come to a stop in front of us.

"Lady Sylvan, Lord Sylvan, how nice to see you," Olette says politely.

"As well as you, Your Grace," Lady Sylvan says to Olette. Then her gaze darts over to me in a clear message that she wants to be introduced.

"I don't think you've met my ward, Lady Stormfeather, princess of the Glacier Kingdom," Olette says, then introduces them to me as decorum dictates.

Lady Sylvan drops into a small curtsy and her son bows before they both straighten.

"We haven't," she says. "Although we've heard all about her." She turns to me and says, "So awful that your voyage was so rough. To lose all your belongings!"

She holds a hand to her chest as if losing a wardrobe is the worst thing to ever happen to anyone. She says nothing of the fictional maid who was supposed to have died as well, as if material possessions are more important than the loss of life.

I instantly don't like her, but I'm careful not to let that show on my face.

"Thank you for your concern," I say politely. "But Lady Greyblossom has been the most wonderful patron, and helped me replace all that was lost."

"Oh yes," she goes on, "we've heard about that as well. Your new fashions are the talk of the town." She looks me up and down quickly, and she isn't nearly as good at hiding her feelings as Olette. I can tell right away that she finds the dress I'm wearing lacking. "You must be waiting to reveal Madame Larkfire's creations for when the courting season starts."

I find myself at a loss for words, but Olette steps in smoothly. "It was nice to see you and your son, Lady Sylvan, but Lady Stormfeather and I must be off."

Olette tries to turn away from the pair, but Lady Sylvan speaks up before she can do so.

"Oh, but Lady Greyblossom, before you go, I was hoping we could speak of the opening ball. I so wanted to know what you are wearing, because of course you're going to be the envy of every fae in attendance." She glances at me with a sugary-sweet smile. "Besides the tributes, of course."

Olette starts to decline, but Lady Sylvan cuts her off. "It won't take more than a few moments, and in the meantime, perhaps my son could keep Lady Stormfeather company."

Up until this point, her son hasn't uttered a word, but now he steps forward and offers me his arm. If I don't take it, it will be an affront, so I slide my hand into the crook of his arm.

"We'll just take a walk around this small pond while you ladies work out your business," Lord Sylvan says in a smooth timbre that has absolutely no effect on me.

Olette shoots me a quick apologetic glance, but I give her a small nod to let her know it's okay. I'm nervous to be alone with Lord Sylvan, but only because I'm worried I'll say or do something un-princess-like. But the reality of the matter is that I need to learn to be comfortable in these very types of situations, so I take this as a learning experience as Lord Sylvan leads us away from his mother and Olette.

"How are you finding the Ember Kingdom?" Lord Sylvan asks when we are out of earshot of Olette and Lady Sylvan.

"Everlight doesn't have the same rugged beauty as the isles, but it's still a lovely city," I say with a touch of practiced haughtiness. "I'll admit that I am looking forward to seeing more of it, and perhaps some of the country as well."

Lord Sylvan's eyes light up, and I realize my mistake right away. "I'd be honored to show you some of the highlights of Everlight while you are here."

My mind spins, but I can't think of a way to turn him down outright, so rather than agreeing, I simply plaster a pleasant noncommittal smile on my face.

"I would love to show you the theater district," he says, taking my silence as agreement. "I do enjoy a good show. When the house lights dim, there's something about sitting in the dark that just feels so . . . intimate."

Reaching up, he lays a hand over mine where it is resting on his arm, and I immediately want to jerk away from his grasp, but I know well enough not to. Tilting my head away from him, I bite the inside of my cheek to keep myself from doing something rash, like pulling free and slapping him.

"Don't you agree?" he asks in what I think is supposed to be a seductive way, but it just comes off as predatory.

"I don't like the theater," I say bluntly, not overly concerned with offending him anymore. I've already decided that in the future I will avoid this particular lord's company at all costs.

Lord Sylvan's hand slides off mine, and a rush of relief runs through me.

There seems to be some sort of commotion going on over by the pond, and I tilt my head to get a peek. A group of fae have congregated, and others are drifting in that direction, especially the females. Lord Sylvan, noticing my gaze has traveled past him, glances off to the side and then turns back with a frown.

"Do you know what's going on?" I ask, curious, but also wanting to steer our conversation toward something neutral.

I don't like how Lord Sylvan looks at me. Like I'm something he wants to acquire. Any conversation that leads us away from the one he seems to be trying to start is good for me.

"My guess is Prince Dryden has arrived," he says in a bored tone.

"The prince?"

I feel the blood drain from my face, and I start searching for a place to hide. I know I'll be meeting Prince Dryden in a few days, but I'm not exactly looking forward to it. I may be curious about the rakish prince, but that doesn't mean I want to make his acquaintance any earlier than I must.

"He does so like to take any opportunity he can get to have his ego stroked," Lord Sylvan says, and I lift my eyebrows, surprised he'd speak that way about the prince when he knows I'm here to compete for his hand. It's clear he doesn't hold the prince in high regard, but I wonder if he realizes how bitter he sounds.

"Well, no need to add to his fan group," I say, and start to walk in the opposite direction, trying to catch Olette's eye but failing to do so because Lord Sylvan's mother won't stop jabbering.

Lord Sylvan grins. "I knew I liked you right away."

He matches my steps with an appreciative gleam in his eye as we walk farther away from the group growing around Prince Dryden. If it's possible, Lord Sylvan appears even more interested in me than he was before, and that's not good.

"I'm not supposed to be introduced to the prince until the

opening night of the courting season. It wouldn't be proper for me to meet him in this informal setting. But I must confess that I'm looking forward to that evening." I lie easily, and I'm happy to see some of the glee disappear from Lord Sylvan's gaze. "Immensely," I add, pouring it on thick.

"Yes, well, I suppose Dryden is still the most eligible bachelor in our kingdom, after King Darius, of course. It's to be expected that his title alone would sway any young female's head."

I'd be offended if I were actually one of the tributes and thought for a minute I had a chance of wedding Prince Dryden someday.

He scoffs, and I lift my head to see that he's watching two finely dressed females cross the path in front of us, beelining toward Prince Dryden. The older of the two is practically dragging the other. A mother and daughter, perhaps? The daughter doesn't appear happy to be headed toward the prince. If anything, it seems like she's dreading it, but there's a determined look on the mother's face that can't be misinterpreted.

"As if the daughter of a merchant has a chance with a prince," Lord Sylvan sneers, disgust clearly imprinted on his features. "Mrs. Holloway has been parading her daughter around Greenbriar Park for the better part of the year, hoping to snag the interest of some poor titled lord. It doesn't matter how comely she is or the size of her dowry, no respectable lord is going to wed the girl. They need to trade stalking the park for stalking the card tables, because the only way that will ever happen is if they find a lord desperate enough to lower himself and his family name to get out of debt."

This fae is really something else.

It takes effort to hide my disgust of Lord Sylvan, but I manage. Mostly by making a point not to focus on his face. But even though I think he's vile, he's given me good insight into the mind of a highborn.

So far, my access has been limited to Olette, Neo, and Bram. Olette has only ever treated me with respect and dignity, despite my station. Neo and Bram, as well . . . for the most part. But there's no question that if Lord Sylvan knew who I really am, he'd be appalled and probably the first person to advocate for my neck to be stretched for impersonating a royal.

When we finally make it back to Olette and Lady Sylvan, it feels like we've trekked around a massive lake rather than a small pond. I quickly slip my hand from the crook of Lord Sylvan's arm and step away from him.

Lady Sylvan glances between her son and me with an unconcealed gleam of interest in her eye. I can practically see the gears turning in her head. During our walk, I learned that Lord Sylvan is only a viscount. Technically nobility, but not very high up on the royalty food chain. Marrying a princess, even from a smaller Vaelorian nation, would definitely be a step up for him and his family.

Lady Sylvan's body language says she's going to try to keep us longer, but Olette manages to tactfully extract us from the social minefield that is the Sylvans.

I let out a sigh when we finally walk away from them.

"You did well," Olette says, and a bubble of pride starts to grow in my chest.

I smile back at her. "Thank you. That was exhausting. He's awful."

Olette presses her lips into a firm line and nods in agreement. "They're not my favorite of the highborns, but I'm afraid you're likely to meet many more just like them before the courting season ends."

I nod, understanding that what she says is true. In some ways, fae are fae, no matter their station. Lord and Lady Sylvan remind me of Sinclair, just with more polish—fae who look to elevate themselves at the expense of others.

Olette steers us back toward the carriage, and I'm glad for it.

"Oh, look," she says, gesturing toward the crowd Lord Sylvan and I already spotted around Prince Dryden. "Someone truly interesting must be here if it's causing that much of a fuss."

When I tell her Lord Sylvan thought it was Prince Dryden, Olette's eyebrows rise.

"You don't think it's him?" I ask.

"Perhaps. He just hasn't been seen out in society much these days." The corners of her mouth are turned up in a tiny, sly smile that I get the impression she's trying to suppress.

We reach the carriage, and the coachman opens the door for us. Olette climbs in first and I turn my head back toward the small crowd in the distance. For a moment, the fae part, and even from a distance I pick up on the back of the prince's dark head of hair and his broad shoulders. He stands out as the tallest fae in the group, wearing a dark blue coat with gold embellishments.

I've seen pictures of Prince Dryden in the papers—who hasn't?—but I've never laid eyes on him in real life. I wish he'd turn so I can see his face.

"Greer?" Olette calls from within the carriage, snapping me out of it.

I give my head a small shake and place my foot on the step to climb in. Just before I enter the carriage, something compels me to take one final glance, and my stomach bottoms out. The prince has twisted in my direction, his gaze fixed over the heads of the fae gathered around him.

He's far enough away that I can't make out his expression, but it feels like he's staring right at me. I duck my head and settle in the seat across from Olette, hiding myself from view.

"Are you all right, my dear?" Olette asks, her brow knitting as she stares at me.

I stop myself from raising a hand to press against my suddenly flushed cheeks. Using every bit of training from the last few weeks, I compose myself, putting on a pleasant smile like I've been taught. I assure her I'm fine and then change the subject.

For the rest of the ride back to Autumnburn, we discuss strategies for getting close to the other tributes, but my mind keeps creeping back to the dark-haired prince and the sense of foreboding that I can't seem to shake.

Chapter 9

NEO WINCES WHEN MY HEEL COMES DOWN ON his foot for the third time this lesson.

"I'm actually getting worse at this," I grumble, breaking away from him to rub my eyes. It's three hours until dawn and I've not slept yet, but it isn't exhaustion causing me to have two left feet. I'm simply awful at dancing, and there's nothing to be done about it. It's embarrassing being so bad at something.

"You're not," he says, but I don't believe him.

"It's hopeless. Maybe I can get away without dancing. I'll just stick to the wall and try to blend in."

He shakes his head. "That won't be possible. There's a ball almost every week during the courting season. At some point you're going to have to dance, if not with the prince, then with one of the highborn fae at court. It will be suspicious if you have no idea what you are doing."

"Maybe we should break one of my ankles so I have an excuse not to dance."

Rather than dignify that with a response, Neo rolls his eyes and holds out his hand, beckoning me back to him. I release a frustrated sigh but accept his hand, placing my other hand on his shoulder.

He wraps his arm around my back and pulls me close until we're almost touching.

A soft flutter, like butterfly wings, tickles my gut, and I blurt the first thing that comes to mind to distract myself. "Did you know that when the fae still had magic of their own, it often reflected the region they were born in? The Ember Kingdom fae, for example, were renowned for their illusions. Like the crystals mined in our lands, they could bend light and perception, weaving illusions so convincing that even other fae could be fooled."

"I see Olette is being very thorough in her teachings," he says, a touch of amusement in his voice.

I nod. "And our kingdom's name was changed from the Crystal Kingdom to the Ember Kingdom when the barrier over Vaeloria was put up. I'm not entirely sure how any of this is going to help with my mission, but I do find it fascinating." I chew on my lip as Neo leads me in lazy circles around the study.

Neo's gaze drops to my mouth, and I quickly release my lip, assuming the gesture displeases him. Princesses are only supposed to chew their food.

There's a brief pause, one filled with something I can't quite name, before Neo assesses me with a look that's close to appreciative. "A sharp mind along with your other . . . unique skills. We truly did luck out when I found you, Rowan."

I find I can't hold his gaze after that compliment and shift my focus to adjusting the placement of my hand against his shoulder, using the motion as an excuse to look away. I'm not used to compliments, and the warm feeling it stirs in my chest is oddly disarming. "Yes, well, perhaps in another life I would have been a scholar."

He tilts his head slightly. "Is that true?" he asks, taking my comment far more seriously than I intended.

I offer a faint, dismissive smile. "I was only joking."

But he doesn't let it go. "But if given the choice, would you have liked to become a scholar?"

The question catches me off guard, because in truth, I've never spent much time thinking about what I would or wouldn't like to be—except free.

"I'm not sure," I confess. "No one's ever asked me that before, and I've never given much thought to what I could be. I was too busy becoming what I had to be in order to survive."

Neo stares back at me, and a touch of sadness colors his gaze, but not pity. For that, I'm grateful. He's silent for a while as we continue to sway to the music before he finally says, "At the risk of sounding insincere, I can relate."

I may not know much about Neo—his past or his present—but the look on his face tells me that he means what he's saying, and that gives me a measure of comfort I don't quite understand.

"I truly hope that when all of this is over," he says, "you have the chance to discover what makes you happy, and the freedom to chase it. Because if anyone deserves a happily ever after, it's you."

I try to ignore how the air between us feels charged. Dancing is more intimate than I imagined it would be, and I think spending these lessons with Neo, mostly alone and unchaperoned, has started to mess with my head. More than once, I've found myself staring into his eyes, trying to determine the exact shade of blue or wondering about the scar he has high on his forehead. I even recognize his scent now—sandalwood with a hint of vanilla. It's far too appealing, and more than once I've held my breath to try to keep from inhaling it.

"You're really not, you know," he says, moving me gently through the basic three steps of the dance.

"Not what?" I ask, realizing my mind drifted again to places it shouldn't. I sternly remind myself that Neo is my contract holder.

I'm nothing but a means to an end for him, and after the courting season is done, I'll be off to another kingdom, never to see him again.

"Getting worse," he says, skipping right over the last few minutes of conversation to circle back to my earlier comment about my dancing. "When you aren't thinking about it, your steps are actually quite graceful. It's when you try too hard that your feet get tangled."

So of course, as soon as he says that, I start thinking about where my feet are supposed to go and stumble. Neo's arm around my back tightens and he pulls me to his chest to keep me from falling.

I glance up at him, which is a mistake, because his face hovers right above mine. If I lift up on my toes and tilt my head back a fraction, our mouths will meet.

Shocked by the thoughts running through my mind, I jerk back, forcing more distance than necessary between us.

"Sorry," I mumble.

Neo doesn't comment on my strange behavior. He simply starts dancing again, letting me keep the extra space I put between us.

We dance in silence for a few minutes, allowing the soft melody from the music box to lead us.

"You know, there's an element of trust in dancing," Neo says quietly.

"How so?"

"The male has to trust the female to follow his lead, and the female has to trust the male to lead her. If that's missing, the dance won't flow. But if there is trust between partners . . ." Lifting his arms, he spins me out and then pulls me back. I execute the move without incident and find my way into Neo's arms with ease. "They can create something beautiful."

As Neo looks down at me, I hold my breath.

"If you follow my lead, you'll be fine," he murmurs, then gives my hand a reassuring squeeze. Something about that small gesture warms my heart.

I was wrong about Neo. He's not cold and unfeeling. He's actually incredibly sweet and caring. I see it in how he treats Olette and Bram. I see it in how much he cares that this mission not only goes well, but that I'm protected throughout. And I see it in how he's holding me now, and it makes a vulnerable place inside of me melt.

The music ends and we stop swaying but don't immediately break apart.

"You're ready," he says quietly.

"I don't feel like I am."

"You are. I promise." His stare is so intense, I can't find the strength to break it. I don't know what's going on right now, but it's something. "Prince Dryden won't be able to take his eyes off you."

Licking my lips, I break eye contact with Neo and slip from his grasp. "That's not part of the plan, so that would be very inconvenient," I say, letting my gaze drift back to him now that we have some distance.

Neo's gaze lifts, and I flush when I realize he was staring at my mouth.

"'Inconvenient' is an understatement," he says, then clears his throat, his demeanor stiffening. "'Disastrous' is more accurate."

Neo probably didn't mean it as an insult, but it still feels like one. It reminds me who I really am. I'm not Princess Greer of the Glacier Kingdom. I'm Rowan, gutter fae and thief. The idea that the prince would notice anyone like me, let alone develop feelings for them, would horrify the entire kingdom. And as much as Neo—and Olette and Bram, for that matter—treat me like I'm more than my station, they'd all be horrified as well.

"Right, disastrous," I echo, and Neo frowns.

"Rowan, I don't mean—"

"No, no, I understand perfectly what you mean. I have a few days left. I'll be ready."

He silently stares at me, his gaze penetrating. A wrinkle appears between his eyebrows, and I can't help but feel he's trying to figure me out. It's unnerving to be stared at like that by anyone, but especially Neo.

He's opening his mouth to say something when the study door creaks behind him. He twists around quickly, instinctually pushing me behind himself. His body relaxes when he sees that it's only Olette, and he lets me step around him again.

Dressed in a heavy night robe with her long hair plaited into a dark braid that runs down her back, she carefully closes the door behind her. "How is she coming along?" she asks.

"Horrible," I say at the same time Neo says, "Well."

Olette's gaze travels back and forth between the two of us as a smile curves her mouth. "Is that so?"

"She'll be fine," Neo says with conviction I don't feel. "And if not, we can break her ankle so she has an excuse not to dance." He grins down at me and I roll my eyes.

"Well," Olette says with a smile. "Let's hope it doesn't come to that."

Neo chuckles. "I'm sure it won't."

But really, it might.

Neo casts his gaze at the grandfather clock and then runs a weary hand over his face when he sees the hour. "Another sleepless night for me, I'm afraid," he says, then grabs his overcoat, which he'd discarded on the couch when he arrived.

I hold back a groan, knowing it will be sleepless for me as well.

Olette frowns. "Yes, that's why I'm up, actually. The palace staff will be waking soon, and I wanted to make sure you'd ended your session. You don't have much time to make it back unnoticed."

"Palace? You live in Whitespire?" I ask.

I didn't know that. Neo has always been very careful not to talk much about himself. I don't really know a ton about him except for little bits and pieces I've picked up here and there. But even though I suspected he was an elite, I hadn't considered that he lived at the palace. The only fae who live in the palace are the royal family and their staff. But it is clear Neo has some connection to the crown, or else he wouldn't be so concerned with ferreting out the true motivations behind the tributes.

Rubbing the back of his neck, he shoots Olette a look that I can't see, but she winces a little, telling me I wasn't supposed to know that.

"I don't think 'live' is exactly the right word for what I do there, but yes, I spend a great deal of time at the palace," he confesses.

"If you spend a lot of time there, that means I'll probably see you when I'm living there during the courting season."

The thought of that causes a trace of excitement to run through me. I tell myself that's only because seeing a familiar face when I'm pulling off my deception will be comforting, but perhaps it's more than that.

"It's doubtful you'll see my face very often," he says, and I deflate a little. "But I do know the palace very well. I'll be able to find you when I need to. Either myself or Bram will be checking in with you regularly to learn what information you've gathered."

"Oh. That's good."

We've already been over this. There's a false bottom on one of my trunks should I need to conceal anything. The plan is to check in with one of them once a week, at least. And I've been told I'll be given instructions on where and when to meet after I'm settled in at the palace. If there's an emergency, I'm to write a coded message and have my lady's maid deliver it to Olette.

After giving Olette his customary kiss on the cheek, Neo nods goodbye to me and sweeps silently out of the room.

"Are you all right, Rowan?" Olette asks, and the use of my real name sounds strange on her lips. Since the first night I arrived at Autumnburn Manor, she's rarely used it.

I nod. "My dancing isn't my finest skill, but I do think it will be passable," I say with a shrug. She gives a chastising look at the motion.

"I'm sure you're being too hard on yourself. I'm confident you'll do splendidly."

I hold back a grimace, because she wouldn't be saying that if she'd walked in on us ten minutes earlier.

"Come." She gestures for me to follow her out of the study. "Let's get you back to bed. I'll tell Eilowyn you aren't feeling well this morning and that she's not to rouse you. You've been working so hard. You need some rest to save up your energy for next week."

Sleeping in sounds like heaven right now, and I thank Olette, but as we climb the stairs, I can't stop the pressure that builds with every step. It will take more than Olette's confidence to help me pull off this deception, but I do hope she's right.

Chapter 10

THE LAST FEW DAYS OF MY TRAINING WITH Olette pass quickly. We fit in another stroll around Greenbriar Park and attend a whist party with a baroness and other highborn guests. It's a struggle not to cheat, especially when I can see my partner's every card in the window reflection behind her, but I don't want to draw too much attention to myself by winning every hand. Neo isn't able to get away for another dance lesson, so I just need to hope I don't have to demonstrate that particular skill, or lack thereof, very often.

I try not to let it bother me that I don't see Neo again before Olette and I get in the carriage to go to the palace, but it does. And the fact that it does bothers me even more.

When we arrive at the palace midday of the courting season's opening ball, I expect there to be more fanfare than there is. Rather than pulling up to the front entrance and the expansive staircase that leads to the interior of the royal dwelling, our coachman pulls up on the side of the property, not far from the stables. A footman opens the carriage door for us, and I follow Olette out into the sun, where a short male with a small potbelly and a large mustache waits for us.

"Welcome, Your Highness and Your Grace." He greets us and then offers a small bow. "I'm Thaddeus Tumblebee. I'm to show Her Royal Highness to her rooms for the duration of her stay at Whitespire Palace."

The palace was aptly named after the pearlescent tower in the middle of the palace that shoots high into the sky. Over the years, the palace has been added to, but the spire was the first part of it to be erected hundreds of years ago. It's said fae magic was used to stack the marble slabs that make up the structure. The tower's topmost room houses the ember crystal that casts the barrier around Vaeloria, and as such, the spire is heavily guarded. To this day, it's by far the highest fae-made structure in the Ember Kingdom.

Olette and I both dip our heads in acknowledgment and follow the gentleman into the palace.

"All the tributes will be staying in the palace's west wing," he announces.

Even though we don't enter through the main entrance, the moment we step inside the palace, I'm still overcome by its opulence and beauty. So much so that Olette has to give me a small nudge to remind me to hold my façade. A bolt of fear runs through me that I broke character so easily, and I vow to myself not to let it happen again.

I sneak a covert glance around me to make sure no one was looking. Luckily, it's just the three of us, and Mister Tumblebee is in front as he leads us to our rooms. I shoot Olette a small apologetic smile and she nods to let me know it's okay.

As Mister Tumblebee leads us through the open corridors lined with damask wallpaper and paintings of former monarchs, he prattles on about some of the history of Whitespire Palace. All things I already know from the extensive studying Olette put me through. What all the studying didn't prepare me for was the grandeur, and despite my vow, I struggle not to gawk.

"Here we are," Mister Tumblebee says as he takes hold of a gilded handle and pulls the door open.

The antechamber we enter, and the bedroom beyond, are just as grand as what I've seen of the palace so far. From the curtains to the bedding to the area rug that covers the stone floors, the room is draped in ice blue and deep purple, the colors of the Glacier Kingdom.

"Your things have already been brought in and put away," Mister Tumblebee says.

"Lady Greyblossom, your room for the evening is just across the hall. Shall I show it to you?" he asks, gesturing back out the door.

As my patron these past weeks, Olette is staying this first night of the courting season. After tonight, she'll return to Autumnburn Manor. Each of the tributes is allowed their own lady's maid for the duration, so Eilowyn will be staying in the palace as well, just in the servants' quarters, which are in an auxiliary building somewhere on the north side of the grounds.

Olette shakes her head. "No thank you, Mister Tumblebee. I'd like to spend some time with my charge, and I'll make my way over there to get ready later."

The footman nods. "As a reminder, the opening ball starts at six this evening. I'll be back to escort you both to the ballroom before then." With a bow, Mister Tumblebee leaves, shutting the door quietly behind him.

When we're alone, I go straight to the chest beneath the window, lifting the lid and checking to make sure the false bottom hasn't been disturbed. A quiet sigh of relief escapes me when I see it's still intact.

Right now, the hidden compartment is nearly empty. Just the black leather-bound book from the pub tucked safely inside. The last few weeks have been so chaotic, I haven't had a chance to properly go through it, but it hasn't been far from my mind. Somehow, just knowing it's nearby is oddly comforting.

"Everything as it should be?" Olette asks, and I nod. "Good."

We take afternoon tea in my room and spend the next few hours testing my knowledge of Princess Greer and the other tributes. Two hours before six, Eilowyn arrives to help me get ready, and Olette retreats to her own room to get dressed as well.

I barely say anything as Eilowyn helps me into my gown and styles my hair. I'm a ball of nerves, going over the names of Princess Greer's siblings, parents, aunts, and uncles in my head, as well as her likes—disgusting rose-flavored jellies, cross-stitch, and archery—and dislikes—animals, the opera, and swimming.

"You look lovely," Eilowyn says, her beaming face clear in the mirror behind me.

As I twist my head from side to side to take in her handiwork, it's hard to disagree with her. I truly look transformed, but it's due to her skill with my hair and makeup. She swept the front part of my hair back in elaborate twists and braids and threaded rose gold ribbons throughout that match my gown. She applied oils to my hair to make it shimmer in the light, and the part that is loose hangs in gleaming gold waves down my back. She kept my makeup subtle, a good choice considering the drama my gown already brings. Rather than clashing with the yards of buttery smooth rose gold fabric draped around me, my makeup enhances the effect, making the apples of my cheeks look sun-kissed and my lips dewy; the bronze and gold shadow on my eyelids, accompanied by only a touch of kohl, is light and fresh. My only complaint, and slight worry, is that my eyes look more purple than blue with this color combination.

Concern flashes across my face that Eilowyn is quick to pick up on. "Do you not like the hairstyle, Your Highness?" she frets, mistaking my frown for dissatisfaction with her work. "There's still a little time for me to adjust something if you'd like. I don't—"

I hold up a hand to stop her. "No, no, I love what you've done. Truly," I say. Twisting, I take her hands in my own so she knows I'm sincere. "It's just that I'm nervous."

At least that's a half-truth rather than a flat-out lie. I truly can't recall a time I've ever been this nervous. I'd rather work a crowded marketplace any day of the week than walk into that ballroom. I just have to trust that my eye color won't become an issue.

Relieved that I'm happy with her work, Eilowyn smiles. "There's nothing to be worried about. There's no way any of the other tributes will surpass your beauty tonight. Prince Dryden will be smitten."

I laugh lightly, but it's wobbly, because that's actually the last thing I want to happen this evening. Perhaps Olette should have picked a more subdued gown for the opening ball? Something a little dowdier? But instead she insisted I wear the gown made from the exquisite silk Madame Larkfire showed us.

There's a soft knock on the door, and Eilowyn rushes to see who it is. A moment later, Olette sweeps into the room.

Olette is nothing short of stunning in her deep purple gown, the dusky color complementing her cool-toned complexion and dark features. The top isn't low-cut, but the dress's off-the-shoulder style shows off her graceful neck and delicate bone structure. Her hair is swept up into a sophisticated updo full of raven-colored curls and braids.

Even though she's almost old enough to be my mother, she's beautiful and youthful enough to be mistaken for a tribute this evening. I'm more convinced than ever that it's been Olette's decision to remain unmarried all these years. I'm sure there is a line of noble fae who would take her hand in an instant were she to make herself available.

Olette's gaze travels from my head to my toes and back up again, lightly assessing me. The gown is one of the designs we worked on closely with the seamstress, blending the Glacier and Ember Kingdoms' styles.

The top is a corset style, with overlapping strips of fabric cinching me in at the waist. Yards and yards of thick rose gold fabric crisscross over my hips and upper thighs and then cascade to the floor, making up the voluminous overskirt with a cutout subtle enough to mostly camouflage that I'm wearing pants that allow me to move more freely. It's a stunning creation that quite literally took my breath away when I first laid eyes on it.

A small smile lifts the corners of her mouth when Olette's gaze reaches my face. "Greer, you look lovely."

"Thank you," I say, tipping my head in acknowledgment.

"Eilowyn, dear, you did a wonderful job," Olette praises, and Eilowyn blushes.

"Thank you for saying so," she says with a small curtsy.

"Would you mind if I have a few minutes alone with the princess before we go to the ball?" Olette asks kindly, and Eilowyn nods. After wishing me luck and telling me she'll be back in the evening to help me into my nightclothes, she slips from the room.

I turn to Olette the instant Eilowyn leaves, on the edge of panic. "Are my eyes too purple?"

Olette's eyebrows bunch together for a moment before she smooths them back over. "It will be fine. If anyone brings it up, we'll just blame it on the lighting in the room. It will be quite dim this evening. Everyone looks better in dim light, and they like to start courting season on a good foot."

I run nervous hands over my skirts. "Yes. All right. If you say so."

Reaching forward, Olette clasps my hands to stop me from fidgeting. When I look down, mine match hers. After a month of no manual labor, I finally have the hands of a lady. The nails are filed to rounded points and painted gold. The calluses I spent years building up have smoothed over. There isn't dirt under my nails or coating my knuckles. On the outside, I look exactly how I need to, but on the inside, I am still me.

"You're going to be wonderful. No one will suspect you aren't Princess Greer. And I know we've told you there is inherent risk in this mission, which there is, but no matter what, you will still have me, Bram, and Neo looking out for you. If you ever get the feeling that someone is on to you, you are to send a message directly to me like we talked about. Do you remember how to do that?"

I swallow, wetting my suddenly dry throat. "Yes. I'm to send Eilowyn back to Autumnburn asking for the violet dress that somehow got left there."

Olette nods. "Right. And then one of us will get you out of the palace. Everything will be fine."

Before I have a chance to reply, there is another knock on the door, followed by Mister Tumblebee announcing he's here to escort us to the ballroom when we're ready.

I take one last fortifying breath and then square my shoulders, ready as I'll ever be to head into the trenches.

Chapter 11

RATHER THAN HEADING STRAIGHT TO THE BALLroom, all the tributes and any of their advisers or patrons are led to an adjoining room. Olette is permitted to stay with me until it's time for the tributes to be announced. Then we'll be called out one at a time and paraded before King Darius, Prince Dryden, and the rest of the court.

The holding room is large, with twenty-foot ceilings, hand-carved scenes on the walls, and plenty of room for the tributes to walk around without bumping into each other.

When Olette and I enter the room, we appear to be one of the last to arrive, and more than one gaze turns toward us. I do well in keeping my expression neutral and aloof, as if their regard means little to me. In truth, it feels like every set of eyes pointed at me brands my skin.

Olette and I have hardly arrived before the patrons are asked to take their places in the ballroom. Olette gives my hands a squeeze. "You've got this. I'll see you in there."

I give her a tight smile that I hope doesn't reveal my nerves. Olette has spent the last four weeks patiently teaching and nurturing me, and by now, I want our ruse to succeed almost as much for her sake as my own. That is, until I remember that if I'm caught impersonating Princess Greer, I'll most likely be executed.

The thought sends a chill down my spine, like a bony finger trailing along my back. I've always known the stakes, but they've never felt quite as real as they do now.

I glance around. The princess closest to me is dressed in a gold gown that makes her dark skin look radiant. She looks to be a few years older than me, and her hair is intricately braided into hundreds of small plaits, expertly woven together to form a crown atop her head.

From her features, I believe it's Princess Lakelyn of the Honey Kingdom.

Catching her mahogany eyes, I offer a small smile, hoping to make my first introduction to another tribute, but the princess doesn't return it. Instead, she gives me a stoic nod of acknowledgment and then turns away.

Beyond Princess Lakelyn is a tribute in a blush-pink ball gown with matching hair. In her getup, she reminds me of some sort of sweet confection, but the sharp look in her eye tells me her appearance is deceiving.

That has to be Princess Primrose of the Bloom Kingdom. If the dyed hair hadn't given her away, her game face would have tipped me off. I read a whole report on how cunning the beauty is, and of her alleged exploits in her own court. She has a nasty habit of getting into trouble and then framing other fae for her misdeeds. She's high on my list of suspects.

One by one, I take note of the different princesses with their glamorous gowns and elaborate hairstyles and try to place them with the vast amount of knowledge I have on each.

Princess Octavia of the Desert Kingdom, with butter-yellow hair and warm brown eyes. Her gown flows in yards of cream-hued desertlace—fabric spun through a closely guarded technique that transforms coarse desert plant fibers into something soft, breathable, and impossibly elegant. It's a textile highly coveted by the Ember Kingdom's elite for both its beauty and its rarity.

Princess Soraya of the Spice Kingdom stands out in a burnt orange ball gown, her strawberry-blond hair shimmering under the light. There's some kind of glitter or makeup dusted over her skin and hair that catches the light with every movement, and I can't help but wonder if it's meant to tie in with her kingdom's primary resource.

With fourteen tributes besides myself, the list goes on and on, and I believe I've correctly identified over half of the princesses when one of them surprises me by coming up and introducing herself.

Princess Willow of the River Kingdom.

Petite in stature and wearing a ruffled blue and white gown, she looks like a porcelain doll, with flawless cream skin, delicate features, and large, unblinking blue eyes. Her brown ringlets hang free just past her shoulders and brush against her cheeks as she twists her head.

It doesn't take me long to figure out that Princess Willow is an open book. Within minutes I've learned about her younger siblings, her favorite activities, and even every high and low of her journey to the Ember Kingdom. At first, the ease of drawing information from her boosts my confidence, but as time ticks by, the real challenge becomes finding a way to slip out of the conversation and meet some of the other princesses while I have the chance. But every time I try to extract myself, she pulls me back in, until eventually we're told to gather our belongings because the ball is about to begin.

Aside from Princess Willow, who seems utterly unfazed and eventually flounces off with a carefree wave, the atmosphere shifts.

The room grows heavier, filled with nerves and anticipation, as the rest of us gather into a line to await our introductions. I catch more than one curious look and even a few narrow-eyed glances cast in my direction. Even though I know I'm not here to compete for the prince's hand in marriage like these females are, it's hard not to feel the pressure in the air.

It doesn't help that some of the tributes are carrying weapons. The blue-eyed female in front of me, who I'm pretty sure is Princess Pluma of the Forest Kingdom, has small throwing blades strapped to both arms. Her short auburn hair is styled in loose waves that stop just below her chin.

Princess Meer of the Gold Kingdom, her hair pulled back into a sleek brown ponytail that reaches her waist, wears an armored gold breastplate and sleek shoulder pauldrons over her jet-black gown. A sword belt cinches her waist, and as she turns, I catch the glint of a gold-hilted sword in its ornate scabbard.

Jealousy sparks instantly.

I would feel so much more comfortable if Olette had let me strap a dagger to my thigh. Just in case. We may all be here under the guise of a courting season, but it's clear from the look on some of their faces that these princesses consider this war, and I'm a potential enemy.

Horns blare from somewhere beyond the curtains separating us from the grand staircase that leads to the ballroom floor below. Any chatter quiets immediately, and a room attendant announces it's time.

I do my best not to fidget as I wait for the first princess to be announced. As my gaze drifts over the other tributes standing in a loose line before and behind me, a prickle of unease runs over my skin.

Most of the princesses are holding something, whether it be a weapon, an instrument, or some other token, while I stand empty-handed.

Ahead of me, Princess Pluma toys with her blade, flipping it through her fingers as if she were born with steel in her grasp. I know enough about daggers to recognize that the gilded-hilted blade is dulled, meant for practice or demonstration rather than true combat. Farther up the line, another princess moves through fluid motions, as though rehearsing a performance, and a little farther still, Princess Juniper of the Tide Kingdom holds a cello in one hand and sheet music in the other.

Behind me, the brunette Princess Tessira of the Salt Kingdom carries nothing in her hands, but that doesn't soothe me. She is quietly humming scales, warming her voice as we wait.

My heart starts to quicken, and the back of my neck starts to heat.

What's going on?

As soon as I have the thought, a deep voice that I assume belongs to King Darius sounds from the other side of the curtain. He thanks his guests for attending the opening ball of the courting season, and then all too soon, the first princess, Princess Tien of the Grassland Kingdom, is announced.

I happen to catch Princess Tien's profile before she walks forward when the curtain is opened. Her face is tinged a shade of green that makes me think she's going to lose whatever bit of food she managed to get down this morning. After taking a deep breath, she pulls it together enough to straighten her spine and glide forward. Her giant green dress—which isn't helping downplay the sickly pallor of her skin—and its ten-foot train disappear when the curtains are closed after her.

It's silent at first, and I hold my breath. Then comes a faint rumble that I think might be King Darius or Prince Dryden speaking with the princess, but they are much too far away to hear unless they deliberately project their voices. The room beyond the curtain falls quiet again, and I start to relax. That is, until a single wobbly note pierces the silence, and Princess Tien begins singing an unfamiliar song.

The sound of blood rushing in my ears drowns out the rest of her performance as the horrifying reality settles over me.

These princesses are all prepared to perform for the king and prince, and I am not.

Did Olette know?

For a moment, a sharp sting of betrayal sweeps through me, but I shove it away. Olette spent weeks preparing me for this day. She wouldn't have worked so hard just to set me up to fail. And something like this wouldn't have simply slipped her mind. Surely she must not have known either.

Nothing about this makes sense.

The next princess is called: Princess Juniper, her seafoam dress flowing around her and her red curls loose. She hefts her cello and disappears behind the curtain. Princess Laurel of the Coral Kingdom, dressed in a bright fuchsia organza gown with tiny bells at the hem that chime with every step, moves into the place Juniper left, waiting for her turn to be announced. Within minutes, the deep notes of Juniper's instrument reach us.

This isn't happening. It can't be happening.

But it is.

My hands are slick with sweat, and I don't need a mirror to know my face is flushed.

What am I supposed to do? Go out there and admit to the king that I have nothing prepared, when it is obvious every other princess does?

I am somewhere in the middle of the line of tributes, so I still have time.

Time to run, or time to come up with a last-minute solution. I am not sure which.

Two more princesses are announced, and I feel like I might be sick. I still have no plan.

I've always prided myself on thinking quickly on my feet, but I'm completely out of my depth. What do I know about the skills a princess is supposed to possess? I can't sing or dance. If I had blades like the princess in front of me, I could probably hit a target, but I'm weaponless.

My mind is frozen, caught on a single question that loops again and again: *What am I going to do?*

Another princess is called, and then only Princess Pluma stands between me and my turn. My gaze sweeps the room, desperate for some miracle, when it catches on the door.

With that cursed question still spinning through my head and the rush of blood pounding in my ears, I step away from the line, escape the only option I can see.

A trickle of relief seeps through me as I near the door, but just before I reach it, a round body steps in front of me, blocking my escape.

It takes my muddled mind a moment to recognize Mister Tumblebee. His thick mustache bobs as he asks if I'm all right, his voice breaking through the fog that has held my thoughts captive.

"Um, yes. I'm just feeling rather warm all of a sudden. I thought I'd get some fresh air."

A frown tugs at his features. "But Your Highness," he says, clearly frazzled, "you're about to be announced. You can't leave now."

"Well, about that—" I begin, but a round of applause from the crowd beyond the curtain cuts me off. The princess must have finished her performance or demonstration, because Princess Pluma is promptly announced, and all the blood drains from my head.

I've run out of time.

Mister Tumblebee gently takes my arm and tries to guide me back toward the curtain, but I plant my feet and refuse to move.

"Your Highness, I understand you might be feeling some nerves about your performance and introduction to the king and prince, but we really must get you back in place."

I shake my head, unable to force a single word past my lips.

Frustration flickers in Mister Tumblebee's eyes. "Princess Greer, I must insist—" he begins, but my gaze snags on something red sticking out from his pocket, and a sudden idea sparks.

"Give me your handkerchief," I order, surprising the portly fae.

"Pardon me?" he asks, his brow knit with confusion.

"Your handkerchief," I say, reaching into his pocket and pulling it out myself. It's a garish red color, which is perfect, because it will draw the eye like I want it to. I quickly shove it into my pocket and then point to the table in the corner, the one with empty water goblets on it. "Bring that out after I'm announced and place it in front of the king and prince."

His eyes go wide with shock, maybe even a flicker of fear, and he begins to sputter a protest, but I don't have time to explain. I just pray he listens as I turn and hurry back to my place.

I slide in front of Princess Tessira just as I'm announced.

"Her Royal Highness, Princess Greer of the Glacier Kingdom."

My stomach drops. There's a real chance I'm now as green as Princess Tien.

Gathering as much false confidence as I can muster, I give a small nod to the fae stationed at the curtain to signal that I'm ready.

I don't know if my plan will work, but I pray it does.

Chapter 12

THE MOMENT THE CURTAINS PART, A WAVE OF brightness from the ballroom hits me, and I flinch instinctively. My feet root to the spot as I freeze, caught in the sudden hush that falls over the room.

All eyes are on me. The royals and courtiers wait in heavy silence, expecting me to step forward.

Why didn't I flee when I had the chance?

I can't do this, I think, but then I hear Neo's voice in my head—telling me that I won't fail, telling me that he'll protect me—and a strange sort of peace settles over me.

Taking a deep breath, I sweep ahead and into the ballroom. A quiet murmur starts the moment I enter into view. I keep my head high and my expression neutral like I was coached as I descend the staircase, my eyes fixed forward on nothing in particular. Until I catch Olette's startled gaze in the crowd below. She's wringing her hands, looking exactly how I feel—terrified—and in that instant, any lingering doubts that she knew about the performance requirement are snuffed out.

In a way, it gives me comfort to know I'm not the only one

caught unaware. Our eyes lock, and I give the smallest nod, hoping she'll understand that I have a plan.

When my foot touches the bottom step, I allow my gaze to drift to the dais at the end of the room where King Darius and Prince Dryden preside.

King Darius, dressed in the deep blue of the Ember Kingdom, sits on a high-backed throne with a gold crown perched on his head. His brother, Prince Dryden, stands to his right, his arms clasped behind him and his back ramrod straight. The monarch and heir are nine years apart in age. Quite a large age gap, but after her first son was born, the queen had a heartbreaking four miscarriages before giving birth to Prince Dryden. Despite the age difference, the king's and prince's builds are similar, and they have matching heads of dark hair, though King Darius's looks more closely clipped than his younger brother's.

I'm still too far away to make out the details of their faces, but their body language radiates a mix of arrogance and boredom. I'm not even sure that either of them is looking at me, and I don't exactly know how to take that.

From the bottom of the stairs, we've been instructed to walk straight across the ballroom and stop in front of the dais. The journey across the ballroom takes forever, with each step feeling like I'm marching to my doom. When I finally reach the foot of the dais, I lower my eyes, skipping over Prince Dryden and letting them settle on his brother instead. I still remember the feeling of my stomach bottoming out when I thought the prince was looking at me in the park. I remind myself that the less interaction and interest from the prince, the better. Let him think I'm rude and aloof. That would serve me well.

King Darius tips his dark head to me in acknowledgment, then extends his hand. With a slight tremor in mine, I step forward, grasp his fingers like Olette instructed me, and dip into a deep curtsy. Just before rising, I press my forehead lightly to his knuckles in respect for the Ember Kingdom's ruling monarch, then release his hand.

Stepping back, a trickle of relief runs through me, knowing I executed the maneuver exactly how I intended.

"Princess Greer," King Darius says, immediately silencing the murmuring crowd. "I welcome you to the Ember Kingdom. You honor me and our kingdom with your presence and participation in this courtship season."

"Thank you, Your Majesty. I'm very pleased to be able to stand as tribute on behalf of the Glacier Kingdom."

"I understand you've been in Everlight for several weeks now," he says, while Prince Dryden does nothing but watch our exchange. "How do you find our capital city?"

Having expected to perform immediately after the official welcome to the kingdom, I'm not mentally prepared to converse with the king. But I put a pleasant smile on my face and try to stay calm as I say, "Everlight is beautiful, Your Majesty. So much life and vitality. I've found the citizens of your kingdom to be particularly warm and welcoming."

Out of the corner of my eye, I think I see Prince Dryden cock his head in interest, but with my focus on his older brother, I can't be sure.

"I'm so glad to hear it." King Darius's dark gaze sweeps me from head to toe and back up again. It's not a lecherous look, but I can't say the perusal is comfortable. "I must say, you are as beautiful as the rumors suggested."

The soft hum of whispered conversations starts up again behind me at his compliment. I feel my face flush. "You flatter me, Your Majesty."

King Darius glances over at his brother. "Don't you agree, Dryden? This potential bride is particularly appealing."

I smile as I should at the supposed compliment, but my insides are crawling. This parade of "potential brides" is starting to feel like a buffet where the tributes are part of the meal.

When he doesn't automatically respond to his brother's comment, my curiosity gets the best of me and I finally shift my focus to Prince Dryden, only to find him staring back at me with a slight look of disdain.

"She is comely enough," the prince says, then averts his attention to something behind me.

The slight isn't missed by the highborns in attendance, and the hum of conversation increases to a low murmur.

I shouldn't care if I am spurned by the prince. I *don't* care. It works to my favor if he finds me disagreeable. But the slight was made so publicly that I can't help the flush of embarrassment that rushes through me.

King Darius frowns at his brother but then glances back at me. "I'm sure my brother looks forward to getting to know you more in the upcoming days."

Prince Dryden presses his mouth into a hard line, as if to stop himself from refuting the king, only making the moment that much more uncomfortable.

"I'm anxious to see what performance or demonstration you have planned for us this evening," King Darius says smoothly, a hint of interested amusement in his gaze.

I swallow hard. Every nerve I've been trying so desperately to lock away rushes to the surface.

Can I do this? Can I actually pull this off without the entire room seeing right through me?

I don't know. But I don't have much of a choice.

A hush settles over the ballroom as everyone waits for me to do something. I catch Prince Dryden's gaze as it sweeps over me, perhaps searching for an instrument, weapon, or some kind of prop I intend to use for my performance. A small furrow forms between his brows when he realizes I'm empty-handed.

I have to fight the urge to glance over my shoulder, searching for any sign of Mister Tumblebee and the items I asked him to deliver. Instead, I draw a steadying breath, do my best to calm my frayed nerves, and offer the king a graceful smile.

"As everyone knows, in my kingdom, everything reflects, refracts, hides. Because of that, the fae of the Glacier Kingdom were once steeped in illusion magic, not unlike some of the ancient magics found here in the Ember Kingdom, though perhaps not as powerful," I say, nodding toward the king and his heir. "Tonight, I plan to bring back a touch of that magic."

The king leans forward in his chair, genuine interest lighting his eyes. "How intriguing."

"Your Majesty," I say with a polite curtsy, "may I borrow your ring for the purpose of this demonstration?"

King Darius raises a brow, hesitating before he reaches to slide his signet ring—a wide gold band with a flat engraved family crest on the face—from his finger, only to freeze as I hold up my hand, revealing the very same ring already gleaming between my fingers.

A murmur of surprise sweeps through the crowd. Even the prince looks startled, his dark brows leaping up his forehead.

I offer the king an innocent smile. "Apologies. I may have gotten ahead of myself."

Laughter ripples around the room, and I turn to the center of the floor, letting the ring's gold sheen catch the light. Pulling the red handkerchief from my pocket, I drape it over the ring, twist it once, and with a flick of my wrist, the piece of silk snaps open, the ring seemingly having disappeared into thin air.

Gasps echo from the crowd as I flip the cloth inside out, show both sides, and then, just as quickly, make the ring reappear.

I repeat the move twice more, letting the rhythm lull them, pulling their attention where I want it. Disappear. Reappear. Disappear again.

Where is that table? I wonder, knowing I can only keep this sleight of hand going for so long.

A stir at the back of the ballroom draws my eye, and I sigh inwardly with relief as two footmen enter, carrying the small table I requested, its cluster of opaque goblets, originally meant as refreshments for the tributes, still arranged at the center.

I wave the pair over, directing them to place the table in front of the king and prince. Once it's set down, I quickly select three ornate glasses and ask the footmen to remove the rest. They obey without question and swiftly exit.

I arrange the goblets upside down in a neat row, then glance up at King Darius.

"Let's make it a game," I say, placing his ring beneath the center cup. "Watch closely."

It's a trick I learned as a child on the streets, used to cheat the elite out of a few coins to keep food in my belly. Over the years, I became so skilled at it that it almost looks like magic. My hands blur as I shuffle the goblets. Once, twice, three times. When I stop, the entire room leans forward.

"Which one?" I ask, turning to the king and prince.

King Darius gestures to the left, and the prince, to the right.

I lift both. Empty.

The audience murmurs in confusion. With a slight smirk, I tap the center cup and lift it slowly, revealing the king's signet ring beneath.

I repeat the trick a few more times, inviting members of the crowd to guess its location. Each time, they choose incorrectly.

For the final round, I turn to the king and prince, asking them to make their selections once more. As before, both of their chosen cups are empty. Without a word, I reach for the third and lift it.

Empty.

More gasps. A few startled laughs. Then I raise my free hand and reveal the ring balanced on the tip of my finger.

Applause breaks out, louder this time, accompanied by delighted laughter and scattered cheers.

Moving around the table, I return the ring to the king, setting it gently in his open palm. "Thank you for lending it to me," I say sweetly.

He stares at the ring in his hand, then at me, half amused and half baffled. "How did you get it in the first place?"

I offer a demure smile. "Every kingdom has its secrets," I say, not about to admit that I slipped the ring off his finger when I pressed my forehead to his knuckles in greeting.

A flicker of calculation enters his gaze, but it disappears so quickly I wonder if I imagined it.

"Rightly so," he says, a smile curving his lips. "Thank you for the entertaining and intriguing demonstration, Lady Stormfeather. It was truly enlightening to meet you."

I know a dismissal when I hear one, so I drop into another curtsy. As I start to retreat to the side of the ballroom, I can't stop myself from letting my gaze pass over Prince Dryden one last time. The disdain that had hardened the prince's expression earlier is gone. In its place is a conflicted look that is no less bewildering, and when his gaze locks with mine, the intensity sends a streak of heat through me, making my steps falter and leaving me off-kilter.

I hurry away as fast as I dare. By the time I fall in line beside the other tributes who have already been announced and are now waiting for the rest of the introductions, I feel instantly lighter. Whatever else the night might bring, it can't be as harrowing as the last half hour.

Princess Tessira of the Salt Kingdom is announced next. I watch as the brunette princess descends the staircase in a lavender gown with a skirt large enough to hide at least four children underneath. Her dress is ridiculous. I have no idea how she plans to dance in that thing, but I'm still impressed with her grace as she glides down the steps. No matter how much practice, I could never look that smooth or elegant.

"Psst." Someone makes a sound next to me and I glance over at the beautiful black-haired girl with a flawless olive complexion to my right.

Princess Shayla of the Iron Kingdom, I believe. A wealthy nation nestled in the northern mountains, rich in iron deposits that it exports to other kingdoms for forging weapons and armor. It's not large in size, but its military strength is widely respected.

The princess leans in close and says quietly, "Want to take bets about what she's hiding under those skirts?"

I blink back at her. She can't be serious.

"I think she's got a footman she's having an affair with under there. Either that or maybe she has a tail or a pair of hooves she doesn't want the prince to find out about until the wedding night."

I can't help the giggle that escapes, and Princess Pluma on my other side turns to glare at me. I quietly clear my throat to cover the faux pas and am relieved when it seems like no one else caught my slipup.

When Princess Tessira reaches the dais and starts talking with the king and prince, I put my hand in front of my mouth and whisper back to Princess Shayla. "I was trying to figure out if she was smuggling small children, but I think your guesses are more amusing."

We grin at each other conspiratorially. After Tessira flawlessly performs her opera piece and takes her place beside us, the next princess is called, then the next, then the next. One of the tributes comes out juggling knives, another with a train of silk flowers off the tail of her gown at least fifteen feet long.

The last tribute to enter, Princess Tori of the Fire Kingdom, wears a high-necked black gown embroidered with intricate gold filigree that glints like flame across the front and back panels. Twin slits run up each side to her waist, revealing rich red side panels that billow with her movements like rising embers. Half of her glossy black hair is swept into an elegant twist, secured with oversized red blooms that echo the fiery palette of her kingdom, while the rest cascades down her back in a waterfall of silk. In each hand, she carries a torch lit with emerald-green flames that match the color of her eyes. The fire flickers dangerously close to her hair, and I hold my breath as she glides through the ballroom toward the dais, certain she's going to catch fire.

She reaches her destination unscathed, but then spits some liquid she was holding in her mouth at the flames, which makes the entire assembly gasp, myself included. The torches blaze brightly, shooting out red sparks that match her dress's side panels, before extinguishing.

Princess Shayla and I make quiet comments back and forth throughout the spectacle. At one point, I think Prince Dryden notices. I glance up to see him scowling at us, or rather at me, so I make sure to keep my mouth closed and feign interest until the last princess joins the large group of tributes on the side.

When all is said and done, fifteen of us line the left side of the ballroom.

Part of me is relieved. With so many other females around, blending in won't be a problem. But the other part is overwhelmed. How am I supposed to get close enough to all these females to ferret out which one has nefarious plans for the prince?

King Darius finally stands from his throne and walks to the middle of the room. "Friends, courtiers, and visiting tributes—thank you again for being here to celebrate the start of Prince Dryden's courting season, a long-standing tradition in our kingdom. I'm confident that one of these ladies will make a wonderful bride for my brother and a new daughter of the Ember Kingdom."

Applause echoes throughout the cavernous room, and when it dies down, King Darius launches into a short speech about the importance of alliances and standing as united fae against our enemies outside Vaeloria. He goes on to tie in how Prince Dryden's marriage to one of the tributes will only strengthen the name of Vaeloria.

He ends with, "Please enjoy the rest of the evening." As King Darius returns to his throne, the orchestra starts playing a soft melody that alerts the guests that we can now mingle. A few fae nobility approach him and strike up a conversation. Prince Dryden, who I noticed looked bored and uninterested while his brother was talking, snags a champagne flute off the first serving tray that passes him.

"He looks about as excited to begin this process as I feel," Princess Shayla says.

"You're not looking forward to competing to win the prince's hand?" I say, trying to keep my voice neutral.

"Heavens no," she says with a laugh. "I'm not planning on competing at all. If you want him, he's all yours."

"You don't really mean that," I say.

I may not be here to win Prince Dryden's hand, but from the hungry look on the other tributes' faces, I can tell they all want to become the next princess of the Ember Kingdom.

The dark-haired princess beside me takes a healthy sip from her champagne flute, something Olette told me never to do, and then shrugs, something else I was told never to do. "Regardless of who I marry, my life will be relatively the same. I'll live in a palace and my every need will be met. Why should I care who fills the role of husband?"

Is she just saying that because she thinks it's something I want to hear? It could be her strategy if she's hoping to catch some of the girls unaware.

Regardless, I don't really care if she is or isn't interested in marrying Prince Dryden. What I *am* interested in is knowing whether or not she's the one I'm looking for.

"Well, I don't know how much of a chance I have against a princess who can yodel in Ancient Faelith. There's really no competing with that."

She throws back her head and laughs, startling a few of the courtiers closest to us and earning her several glares. She doesn't care in the least.

"I knew we would get along. I'm Shayla, by the way," she says, then shifts, revealing a red bow and empty quiver leaning up against the wall behind her. The sight tickles free more information about the Iron Kingdom. Centuries ago, when magic still thrived, the weapons and armor crafted there were often imbued with enchantments. Daggers that never missed, armor that couldn't be pierced, shields that could deflect magical attacks. It makes me vaguely wonder if her weapon might still hold a touch of that magic.

"Greer," I offer with a light smile.

"Oh, I know who you are. I was here for that spectacular entrance."

I give her a funny look. I don't know what she's talking about. Perhaps my sleight of hand was amusing, but my entrance had to be one of the most forgettable, just as I planned it.

"You should have heard the whispers when you first appeared in that phenomenal rose gold dress. And the look on Prince Dryden's face." She fans herself dramatically. "For a moment there I thought he was going to propose to you on the spot. But of course, he composed himself before you reached the dais and managed to slap that uptight aristocrat mask back on." She rolls her eyes. "But just so you know, I'm going to have my seamstress make me a gown like yours right away. It's gorgeous and looks refreshingly comfortable. It's past time fashions were updated. I'm over these ridiculous skirts and corsets."

Shayla's gown is beautiful in its simplicity. She doesn't have embellishments like bows or long trains like so many of the other tributes have, but the red color paired with her black hair adds drama, and the cut is very flattering to her slender frame. To her point, though, the skirt is still very full.

I run a hand along the silky fabric of my overskirt. "It is a more functional outfit," I agree, not touching her comments about Prince Dryden. I don't believe for a second that he had that strong of a reaction. Shayla must be trying to flatter me. Either to be genuinely nice or to lull me into a false sense of complacency as a strategy to get me to lower my guard. I know because that's going to be part of my strategy with the other tributes.

I glance at her bow resting on the wall again. So far, I like Princess Shayla, but any tribute who is skilled in weaponry is higher on my list of threats to Prince Dryden, so I'll have to keep an eye on her.

"I lost my belongings on the trip over and asked the seamstress here to make me a dress similar to what we wear at home," I tell her with an easy smile. "I think she did a lovely job combining the flavor of my kingdom with the drama of Ember fashions."

"Agreed," Shayla says, tipping her champagne flute at me in a salute.

The song ends and the orchestra starts a new one that signifies that dancing should commence. I look up, scanning the room to see who the prince will decide to choose for his first dance, and see him cutting through the crowd, headed straight for me.

My stomach flips; he can't possibly mean to ask me to dance.

According to Olette, whomever Prince Dryden asks to dance first will not only be the subject of the most gossip, but also signal whom he intends to start courting.

Shayla follows the direction of my gaze. "What did I tell you?" she says quietly in my ear.

No, this won't do. I sweep the room for a quick exit, but I'm not fast enough and Prince Dryden stops directly in front of me.

The noise in the room dims as everyone watches what will happen next. I can only hear the orchestra and my ragged breathing.

"Lady Stormfeather," the prince greets me with a small bow, and I return the gesture with a graceful curtsy. "I found your demonstration this evening to be . . . unexpected."

My pulse skips. There's nothing in his tone to suggest suspicion, but my thoughts instantly spiral. Did I reveal too much? Does he suspect I'm not who I claim to be? Is he about to call me out for the fraud I am?

I force a polite smile, shoving my fear into a small box and locking it. "Ah. Yes," I say, fumbling for the right words. "I hoped it would be memorable."

He nods, though the glint in his eye suggests he's still turning it over in his mind. Then, more gently, he adds, "I've been told you had a bit of trouble sailing down from your kingdom. I'm sorry for your loss."

I latch on to the change in subject, happy to be able to move past my performance. "Thank you for your sympathies, Your Highness. I was fortunate to have enough time for the seamstress to make me a new wardrobe."

"I was referring to your lady's maid," he says, surprising me. He's the first highborn to acknowledge her life as a loss, and it takes me aback.

"Oh, yes, her," I say, stumbling over my words once again before regaining my composure.

Despite the slight earlier and the sore look on his face when we were formally introduced, I find myself warming a bit to the arrogant prince for caring enough about my fictitious maid.

"It was a great personal loss to me indeed. I miss Daisy immensely. She was a wonderful fae and friend. But I am indebted to your aunt, Lady Greyblossom, for being such a generous hostess the last month. She has graciously provided me with a new lady's maid who is more than satisfactory."

A twinkle of warmth enters Prince Dryden's eyes at the mention of his aunt. It reminds me of the fond way Olette always spoke of him, regardless of his reputation.

"I can think of no better hostess in our kingdom than my aunt. I don't doubt you've been in good hands."

"She's become a very good friend and confidant," I say with a small smile, feeling like I'm actually experiencing a moment of connectivity with the prince. It's all quite unexpected, and my guard starts to slip as I look into his bright green eyes that are so much like his aunt's and so different from his older brother's near-black gaze.

Up close, I realize that the images I've seen of Prince Dryden haven't done him justice. He's classically handsome in an undeniable way. He's tall and broad, but not overly so. He has a strong jawline, and his thick head of wavy black hair, which is shorter on the sides than it is on top, is just shy of being a touch too long. Tonight, his hair is tamed back and off his face, but I imagine it makes him look quite the rake under the right circumstances. His cheekbones are sharp and high, and his nose is straight except for a slight bump on the ridge that only adds to the interest rather than taking away. I wonder if the bump is natural or if he broke his nose at some point. It's rumored that the prince likes boxing, but that's not something Olette ever confirmed to me.

Prince Dryden clears his throat and frowns, making me realize he asked me something that I completely missed while I was cataloging his features.

I rack my brain, but for the life of me, I don't know what he said.

"I'm sure Princess Greer finds Whitespire Palace just as impressive as the rest of us," Princess Shayla says smoothly, coming to my rescue. Glancing at me out of the corner of her eye, she gives me a small nod, encouraging me to keep speaking. Not exactly the move of a tribute trying to show up the competition.

"Yes. Very much so," I say with a forced smile. "I love our palace; it's home, and our ice sculpture courtyard is second to none, but Whitespire is truly spectacular."

Prince Dryden scowls down at me. The warmth he showed while we spoke about his aunt is gone, replaced by something that looks like disappointment.

His gaze travels past me to Shayla. "Lady Ravenforge," he says, ignoring me now, "will you honor me with this first dance?"

Shayla looks between the both of us as whispers start from

around the room, a small crease between her eyebrows. She seems just as confused with this turn of events as I am, but despite her irreverence for the courting season, she has enough decorum to know that you don't deny a prince a dance, especially in his own kingdom.

Setting her half-finished champagne flute down on a table, she dips into a curtsy. "Of course, Your Highness," she says, then places her hand in his outstretched palm, leaving her bow and quiver where they rest.

She flashes me a look as she passes, and I get the impression she's saying "I'm sorry." But she needn't worry. Dancing with a handsome prince is the last thing I should be doing tonight. And now that all eyes are on them and off me, I can finally get to work.

Chapter 13

PRINCESS SHAYLA AND PRINCE DRYDEN MAKE A striking pair as they head toward the dance floor, but I don't bother watching once the music begins. What they do together is inconsequential. In a month and a half, I'll be living in another kingdom, finally free. Regardless of how handsome Prince Dryden might be, as long as Princess Shayla isn't the potential assassin we're looking for, I couldn't care less if he chooses her for his wife.

I spot Olette across the ballroom and weave my way toward her, keeping my light smile perfectly in place. She's talking to an elderly woman—Princess Willow's patron, I think—but when she notices me, she excuses herself quickly.

"Rowan," she says, her voice low but her expression bright for anyone watching. "I—I'm so sorry."

"What happened?" I ask, still smiling.

Her own smile wavers for only a second. "From speaking with a few of the other patrons, it sounds like a message went out from the palace last week to every princess, explaining the mandatory performance. Except ours never arrived," she murmurs through her teeth.

My stomach tightens. "Why?"

She nods, her expression steady even as her tone hardens. "I'm not sure. And I don't like it." Determination sharpens her words. "I'll look into it."

Her gaze lingers on me for a moment, pride flickering through the worry. When she speaks again, her voice gentles, the edge fading. "You handled yourself beautifully tonight."

The praise warms me in a way I don't expect, a small spark of pride lighting in my chest. I nod, unable to do more with so many eyes nearby.

Before I can say anything else, another mentor approaches, and Olette tells me not to let it ruin my focus before she turns with effortless grace, slipping back into the crowd as if we'd been discussing the weather.

I keep my smile in place as I drift away, but inside, my thoughts are spinning. A missing message. A performance no one warned us about.

Someone wanted us unprepared.

Since the prince is dancing, a lot of the guests stand ringed around the dance floor, waiting for the signal from the king that they can join in as well. Pushing thoughts of the performance out of my mind, I refocus my attention back where it should be—the princesses. Scanning the crowd, I find a group of three tributes talking among themselves not far from me and make my way over. As I near, I overhear part of their conversation.

"That dress is divine, but it doesn't make up for that embarrassment. I thought for sure he was going to ask her to dance, but then to turn to Princess Shayla instead . . ." Princess Laurel of the Coral Kingdom, with her dark auburn hair piled high atop her head, makes a *tsk*ing noise. "If it were me, I would have wanted to melt into the floor."

Oh goodie, they're talking about me.

When I join the group—Princesses Juniper, Sonjai, and Laurel—all three of them clam up, pressing their lips together and staring at me wide-eyed.

"Hello, I'm Princess Greer," I say, the name rolling off my tongue easily by this point. "It was embarrassing," I say with a small self-deprecating smile. "But my kingdom is so small I hardly consider myself in the running for Prince Dryden's heart. I'm just happy to be here and get the opportunity to experience all Everlight has to offer. Is this your first trip to the Ember Kingdom, or have you spent time here before?"

Matching looks of relief wash over their faces. My guess is they are just as relieved to hear that I'm not a serious contender for the prince's attention as they are that I don't care they were talking about me.

They take turns introducing themselves, and, pretending like I didn't already know who they were, I ask them questions about their homes and families. After several minutes of light chatter, I determine that I've done well at infiltrating the first group of tributes, giving myself a mental pat on the back for handling the situation so well.

If only Neo could see me now.

The sudden thought of Neo makes something in my chest squeeze.

"Are you all right?" Sonjai asks me with a small frown, her ice-blue eyes standing out against her dark complexion.

I give a light laugh, concerned that I let my emotions break through. "Oh yes, I'm sorry. Perhaps just too much wyldberry wine." I touch my forehead as if I have a small headache. "I think I'll switch over to flavored water for the rest of the night."

"That's a good idea," Juniper says with a nod. "The wyldberry wine is very strong, especially if you aren't used to it."

“Excuse me, ladies,” I say, explaining that I’m going to get a refreshment. Really, I’m going to look for some of the other tributes. It’s not that any of the princesses I just met are off my suspect list, but with their softer demeanors, I have a hard time seeing any of them as an assassin. “I’m looking forward to getting to know you better over the coming weeks.”

After giving Sonjai and her impressive train of silk flowers a wide berth, I head toward a refreshments table along the edge of the room, my gaze sweeping the crowd for other tributes, but most of them are on the dance floor. I catch a splash of red out of the corner of my eye and turn to see Princess Tori of the Fire Kingdom standing off to the side, her dark head ducked as she speaks with a male fae I don’t recognize. They are partially hidden by the sweeping staircase we all descended to enter the ballroom, but something about their body language gives me pause.

Stepping closer to the wall, I have a better view of them, and it’s clear they’re arguing. Princess Tori keeps checking over her shoulder to see if anyone is watching them, but since I’m peeking at them from behind a potted plant, she misses me. At one point, the unfamiliar fae tries to reach out to Princess Tori and she jerks away from him quickly, clearly upset that he tried to touch her.

“Princess Greer, you look ravishing this evening.”

I squeeze my eyes shut. I don’t need to turn to know it’s Lord Sylvan. His voice slides over me like eels through water, leaving a slimy feeling in my gut. I reopen my eyes just in time to see Princess Tori walking back toward the dance floor, plastering on a wobbly smile.

Making sure to wipe the disgusted look off my face, I school my features into a neutral expression before turning.

“Lord Sylvan, how nice to see you this evening,” I lie smoothly.

“I would never miss the opportunity to appraise so many lovely flowers at the same time.”

Gross.

The smile he gives me is polite enough, but the way his eyes roam down my body and back makes me want to grab a cloak and cover myself. I have the urge to jab him right in the nose for ogling me so openly, but I can't afford to create a scene tonight, so instead I squeeze my fist, pressing it into my skirts to hide the action.

Lord Sylvan leans forward into my space, and it's physically hard not to rear back. His voice dips low, which I only find creepier. "Never fear, my sweet. Your beauty eclipses them all."

My stomach roils, and I have to give myself credit for not throwing up all over him. As a titled noble, Lord Sylvan may be considered a highly sought-after bachelor, but there's an oiliness about him that I don't trust. He makes my skin crawl, and the fact that he has his sights set on me just makes this whole experience more complicated.

I know what I'm supposed to do in this situation: laugh lightly and play off his comments as harmless flirtation like Olette taught me, but I can't bring myself to do it. There's a good chance I'm about to make an enemy, but I need to shut this down right now.

"How kind of you to say," I start, and Lord Sylvan's smile widens. "But I feel the need to remind you that I'm here for a reason, and that's to get to know Prince Dryden and see if we would make a suitable match for each other as well as our kingdoms." As I talk, his smile fades and his gaze turns hard. "Your attention toward me, although flattering, is not appropriate in this setting, and I have to insist that we keep our distance for the duration of the courting season."

When I finish, Lord Sylvan's face reminds me of a spoiled child who's had his favorite toy taken away. As his anger boils, a muscle twitches in his jaw, and he balls his fists. He opens his mouth to speak, but then his gaze shoots to my left. Snapping his mouth shut, he dips into a shallow bow.

"I believe it's time for our dance," Prince Dryden says from right beside me.

I smother a gasp, and my heart beats double time. How much of what I said did he hear?

When I turn, Prince Dryden has his hand extended to me but is glaring at Lord Sylvan. Lord Sylvan, although having shown Prince Dryden the respect he deserved through his bow, stares back at the prince with a similar look of disdain.

I dip into a quick curtsy and place my hand in Prince Dryden's, knowing this is a request I can't refuse. He tucks my hand into the crook of his arm and starts to lead me to the dance floor.

"Make sure to leave a dance open for me, Princess Greer," Lord Sylvan calls.

Prince Dryden pauses to glare over his shoulder at the vile fae. "Are you having so much trouble finding a willing dance partner that you need to harass one of my potential brides?" he asks, his voice cool and calm, at direct odds with how he's staring at Lord Sylvan.

"Don't worry about me," Lord Sylvan answers with a smirk. "If I were having trouble finding a willing female, I'm sure I could ask the king to make some arrangements for me like he has for you."

Prince Dryden tenses under my hand, and for a moment I'm worried he's going to go after Lord Sylvan for insinuating that he can't find a bride on his own, but after a couple heartbeats, his muscles relax again and a smile that doesn't reach his eyes stretches his mouth.

"I'll let him know you'd be open to marrying for the sake of the kingdom. I'm sure there's a list of eligible maidens he'd be happy to arrange for you. I hear Lord Stoneridge has been looking for a match for his daughter."

I'm unfamiliar with Lord Stoneridge or his daughter, but Lord Sylvan must know who they are, because the smile slips off his mouth and his face pales.

Check. Mate.

I have to press my lips together to keep from smiling.

Well done, Dryden.

As the prince leads me through the crowd toward the dance floor, eyes follow our progress. I catch tidbits of whispered conversations.

". . . from the Glacier Kingdom . . ."

". . . has been staying with Lady Greyblossom . . ."

". . . no one has ever met her before . . ."

". . . the gall she has, wearing pants beneath that gown . . ."

The last comment makes me smile, and I catch Prince Dryden giving me a curious look. I'm sure he heard as well—the partygoer wasn't trying to be quiet. The prince probably expects me to be appalled that someone was criticizing my gown. The other princesses surely would have been, particularly on a night as important as this one. But the female just reminded me of the frivolity of the elite class. They must lead truly shallow lives if the design or color of my outfit matters to them.

Their opinion of me is of no consequence. I'm not here to win their approval, or even to win the prince's hand. I'm here to do a job so I can earn my freedom. They can say or think whatever they want of me as long as they never learn the truth.

Prince Dryden leads me to the middle of the dance floor. We get into position with one of his hands anchored at my lower back and the other grasping mine, just as I practiced with Neo. I thought

I'd escaped having to show my dancing skills—or more accurately, my lack thereof—earlier this evening.

I'm thankful to the prince for interceding for me with Lord Sylvan, but I wish I could have done something to avoid this fate. Now that I'm standing face-to-face with Prince Dryden, waiting for the orchestra to start the next song, my nerves kick up.

The music starts and the prince leads me into the dance. The melody is a slow one, which I'm thankful for. I always had an easier time with slow tempos when practicing with Neo, but even so, I'm nervous. I stumble a little over my feet on the fourth step. Prince Dryden's frame remains strong as he easily covers my misstep.

I mumble a quiet apology.

"Interesting company you choose to keep," the prince says, rather than acknowledging my blunder.

"He's not anyone I choose to do anything with, let alone keep," I say in response, my nose scrunching in disgust.

He tilts his head slightly, his gaze assessing. "Yet you spent time with him before the courting season began."

It's not a question, it's a statement, and that takes me aback. He must have seen me and Lord Sylvan in the park that day.

I blink up at him, not sure what to say to that.

He arches one dark brow. "Surprised I would have taken note? Rest assured, I know many things about each and every tribute," he says cryptically, making warning bells go off in my head.

Is he suspicious of me already? Did my last-minute sleight of hand performance doom me?

I mentally kick myself now for not demanding more training on how to interact with the prince. I spent so much time learning the tributes and hardly any time working with Olette on how to convincingly converse with Prince Dryden. Whenever I did bring him up, Olette would steer the conversation elsewhere, claiming that we needed to focus on the other princesses because my interactions with Prince Dryden would be few and far between and I shouldn't worry about it.

Well, I'm worrying about it now.

"There's not much to know about me. I'm very boring, I assure you," I say, trying not to sound evasive, but missing another step right as I say it.

Prince Dryden covers for me again, and I think I see the corner of his mouth twitch. "I wouldn't say that. You're staying with my favorite aunt, after all. That, in and of itself, inherently gives you interest."

"Isn't she your only aunt?" I ask, avoiding the topic of how interesting I may or may not be altogether.

He dips his head, lowering his voice when he says, "I see you've done your homework on me as well."

A bit of warmth enters my chest at his nearness, and I'm struck again at how attractive he is. I can practically hear female fae swooning whenever we dance past, and I have to give myself a mental shake to snap myself out of it as well.

Frustration at myself rises in my chest. I've seen lots of handsome fae over the years. A pretty face has never swayed me before, so why should it now?

The fact that he is the prince should only make him less desirable to me, not more. But at least now I understand where the rumors of his charm come from. It's like all he has to do is bat his dark eyelashes and flash a smile and females line up for him. Apparently, myself included.

How embarrassing.

If I didn't know better, I'd say he was using some sort of unknown magic on me. But magic in fae faded centuries ago.

"I'm sure having you know bits and pieces about us isn't half as unnerving as knowing there are fifteen tributes here who have probably done very little the last several months other than study you."

He chuckles lightly, and for the first time I see a little life in his eyes. "I was born a prince, so it's something I'm very used to."

The real Princess Greer would be able to relate, but I certainly can't, so I just offer him a demure smile.

"Have you enjoyed your stay in our kingdom?"

"Immensely," I answer honestly. Or at least mostly.

There were certainly grueling and unpleasant parts of the last four weeks, but I enjoyed getting to know and spend time with Olette and Eilowyn, and even Bram and Neo. I'm not new to the kingdom, but I may as well be. Living as an elite is as different to my prior life as you can get.

I'm still getting used to the opulence and luxury. Where I once slept on the hard ground with only a threadbare blanket to chase away the chill, I now lie to rest on a feather bed with soft sheets, a thick comforter, and a fire in the hearth to warm me. Many of my meals used to consist of rotten food and scraps I'd scrounged for in the alleyway behind the Lame Horse or stolen from marketplace vendors, but now my meals are brought to me, prepared by some of the best cooks in the kingdom and often looking like works of art as much as food.

But I can't let Prince Dryden know any of these luxuries are new to me. I'm playing the part of a princess who most likely has no idea how the other half lives, so I offer a pleasant smile and recite the well-rehearsed reply we devised for when I'm asked how I find it here.

"The climate in the Ember Kingdom is so very pleasant. I shall miss it when I return north."

Something about that response seems to amuse Prince Dryden, and this time when the corner of his mouth twitches up, it doesn't immediately flatten. "I'm glad to hear that some parts of our kingdom are to your liking. I'm sure it's very different from your home. I hope it hasn't been too disorienting being in this foreign land."

"I've been managing well," I say with a practiced smile.

He nods. "Yes, you seem to be fitting in just fine."

Is there a double meaning in his words, or am I just paranoid?

"You must miss many things from your home, though," he says, and I'm surprised by the sincerity in his voice. Perhaps my impression of Prince Dryden being a spoiled and arrogant royal who only cares about himself was a touch off the mark.

I dig in my brain for a bit of information about the Glacier Kingdom to make up a convincing lie.

"I do miss the hakarl. My mother used to make it, and it was delicious."

The prince gives me an odd look. "Truly?"

"Oh yes. It's my favorite local dish."

"How interesting that you should have such a fondness for fermented shark."

Wait . . . what?

I bite back the cuss that suddenly rises in my throat. I confused hakarl with kleinur. I meant to say I liked kleinur, which is a twisted doughnutlike pastry that the north is famous for. But instead, I mixed it up with hakarl, which I now remember is, in fact, fermented shark pieces.

Whoops. Now I'm committed.

"It's an acquired taste," I admit.

"I'd say so," Prince Dryden says. "One of my bodyguards visited the Glacier Kingdom several years back and described it as the worst thing he ever put in his mouth."

I give a wobbly smile. "It's not for everyone's palate."

Prince Dryden's eyebrows rise. "It's supposed to taste like piss and rotten eggs."

Lovely. The smile I keep frozen on my face feels more like a grimace, but Prince Dryden doesn't give any indication of noticing. Or perhaps it's just that he doesn't care.

We've been dancing over the course of our short conversation, and although I know I'm nowhere near graceful, I haven't made any more mistakes in the last minute. Maybe Neo was right and when I don't think too hard about it, this is something I can do.

But as soon as I think that, we fall into a prolonged period of silence and I start to get into my head again. My feet feel like bricks, and I step on the prince's toes not once, but twice. The second time he winces slightly, but still doesn't bring it up. He does put a couple more inches between us as we move together and takes extra care with each step.

The dance finally ends, and Prince Dryden releases me, stepping back and giving me a small bow as is the custom. I dip into a curtsy in reply.

When I lift my gaze and our eyes connect, he says, "It seems like you need a little more practice with your dancing, Your Highness. I may have to ice my toes tonight."

A couple of light giggles reach my ears, and I glance over to see that several couples overheard the prince. Two of the female fae are fellow tributes: Princess Primrose with the pink hair and Princess Tien, whose complexion no longer matches her green dress. They cover their grins behind their hands, their eyes twinkling.

I flush from the top of my head down to my toes. True, I wasn't the best dancer, but he didn't need to call me out on it so publicly.

Taking a slow breath through my nose, I remind myself it's better that these other tributes don't see me as real competition. So really, Prince Dryden just did me a favor.

But then I catch Prince Dryden's smile. It's a wicked one, letting me know that he's completely aware of what he just did, and in that instant I'm sure every awful thing I've heard about him is true.

I always thought the worst part of this mission was going to be trying to get information out of the other tributes, but I know now I was wrong. The worst part is going to be putting up with this spoiled prince for the next six weeks. The only way I'm going to make it through this courting season alive is to stay as far away from Prince Dryden as possible.

Chapter 14

THE MORNING SUN SNEAKS THROUGH A SLIT IN the curtains like a thief, silently and unwanted, hitting me square in the face. With a groan, I roll over, shoving a down-feather pillow on top of my head.

The opening ball went well into the night. I didn't find my way back to bed until almost daybreak. I've had plenty of sleepless or almost sleepless nights over the last month, but never coupled with faewine. My head pounds and my mouth tastes fuzzy. I curse every drop of wyldberry wine I consumed the night before. It wasn't worth it.

The soft clink of metal reaches my ears, and with a groan, I throw off the pillow and sit up, catching Eilowyn trying to carefully place a silver tea set on the nightstand next to me.

She jumps a little at my sudden movement, and cream splashes over the rim of the creamer. "Oh no," she says, setting the tray down quickly and using her apron to wipe up the mess. "I'm terribly sorry, Your Highness."

"Greer," I remind her, sounding froggy.

"Yes, yes. Of course. I didn't mean to wake you," she says as she finishes cleaning up the small mess.

I wave her off. "Please don't worry about that," I say. "It's just a bit of cream."

But despite my protests, she finishes her task. "Shall I let the light in?" she asks once she pours me a delicious-smelling cup of wyldberry tea.

I nod. It's probably well past the time I should be awake.

Holding the petite cup between my hands, I take a big whiff, letting the sweet berry flavors wake my taste buds—and hopefully the rest of me as well.

Eilowyn goes over to the main windows and yanks apart the heavy drapes, letting in a waterfall of sunlight that blinds me. It feels like the rays are piercing straight into my skull, and I have to bite back a groan. Eventually, I force my eyes open.

With a gasp, I set down my tea and slide from the bed. From the position of the sun, it has to be almost midday. I immediately start searching my wardrobe, looking for a presentable day dress. All the tributes were supposed to meet in the gardens before lunch for orientation. I must be late.

I yank out the first thing I find, an embroidered light blue day dress that isn't one of my overskirt-and-pants combos, but it will have to do. It's not so large that I think I'll trip on it. I don't have the time to leisurely search for the perfect thing to wear.

"Hurry, help me into this?" I call to Eilowyn.

"Yes, of course," she says, rushing to my side. "But you should know that the orientation this morning has been postponed."

I freeze with my arms trapped above my head as I'm shedding my nightgown. I wiggle back into it and look Eilowyn in the eye. "It has?"

Her head bobs up and down. "So many of the tributes were under the weather this morning that they pushed it back until right before afternoon tea."

Under the weather. A polite way of saying *hungover* because they got completely pissed the night before. At least I wasn't the only one who lost track of their glasses of wine last night.

Eilowyn leans in to whisper, even though it's just the two of us in the room: "And the gossip this morning is that Prince Dryden didn't make it to bed until after the sun rose, so they didn't think he would be in any shape to entertain the tributes after the orientation."

I snort a laugh and then wince at my lapse in decorum, but Eilowyn just giggles as well.

"Well, in that case, I think I'll take a moment to wake up before rushing to get ready."

Eilowyn nods and carefully lays the day dress over the end of the settee at the foot of the bed so that it won't wrinkle. Grabbing my robe from where I flung it over a wingback chair the night before, I slip my arms into it, tie the sash, pick up my tea, and take a sip. It tastes divine and does wonders settling my stomach.

Going into the other room, Eilowyn returns with another tray full of food and sets it on a small bistro table by the window. Bringing my tea with me, I take a seat at the table. Some of the items in front of me, like an egg dish smothered in some sort of yellow sauce and greasy sausage links, make my stomach churn, but I eye a buttery croissant, debating whether it's worth the risk or not.

"Is Lady Greyblossom still here?" I ask Eilowyn as I pick up the pastry and give it a sniff. It doesn't seem to make my stomach clench, so I take a small bite, happy when it doesn't immediately come back up.

I'm never touching faewine again.

"Her Grace and the rest of the patrons and advisers left this morning," Eilowyn says as she hovers above me with her hands clasped in front of her.

"Oh, right," I answer. I knew that Olette would only be staying in the palace one night, but I'm still sad she's gone. I pat the seat next to me. "Please, sit."

Eilowyn's eyes round. "Oh, Lady Stormfeather, I couldn't."

"Please," I say again. "I grow tired of my own company."

Looking very uncomfortable, Eilowyn sinks into the seat across from me. I nod toward the food, encouraging her to take whatever she'd like. When she argues again, I let her know I won't be eating more than half of this croissant and don't want the rest of the food to go to waste. After that, Eilowyn finally makes herself a small plate of food and digs in, and I smile.

A twinge of guilt runs through me. It's not that I wouldn't be kind to Eilowyn regardless, but I also know she could be a great source of information for me. The palace staff is bound to gossip while we are here. I need Eilowyn's lips loose.

"Are any of the other tributes up and about?" I ask.

"Some are," she admits. "I believe they are congregating in the solarium. It's been partitioned off from other palace guests. A place just for the tributes during the courting season."

I nod. That's where I need to go, then.

"What have you heard of the opening ball?" I ask her with interest, hoping she has some tidbit of information that I will find useful.

Eilowyn grins. "I heard you made quite an impression," she says. "Everyone was impressed with your performance with the king's ring and goblets, but the whole kitchen staff couldn't stop talking about your gown and how Prince Dryden could hardly look away from you."

I have to stop myself from rolling my eyes. That's an exaggeration. Prince Dryden spent plenty of time eyeing every other tribute besides me the evening before. In fact, after our dance, he barely glanced my way the rest of the night.

But Eilowyn thinks I want to know what fae are saying about me, when in fact I want to hear about the other tributes. I push her for information, to know what the palace staff thinks of them, but she doesn't have much gossip. The biggest news was that a few of the tributes drank a bit too much and were found passed out in the palace gardens this morning.

After finishing my tea and half of my croissant and waiting for Eilowyn to have her fill, Eilowyn fixes my hair and brushes on a little blush before I'm on my way to the solarium.

It is only a short walk from the wing of tribute rooms. Although two guards stand on either side of the solarium doors, they don't try to stop me when I enter.

Stepping into the solarium is like stepping into another world, and for a moment my breath is taken away. A small stream meanders through a space that's dripping with lush flora and bathed in soft sunlight. Walking bridges are placed throughout the room to navigate from one side to the other over the stream. Plush couches and quaint seating areas are cleverly tucked in between budding fruit trees and moss-covered stones.

The majority of the solarium is made of glass and iron, but the architect was very nature-focused when they pieced together this stunning room, making the ironwork holding together the glass panels look like trailing vines. It doesn't even feel like I'm inside, but rather tucked into a whole separate microcosm.

The pearlescent tower that inspired the palace's name, Whitespire, has always been regarded as the most impressive part of the opulent royal residence, but standing in the solarium, I have to disagree. The solarium is the real hidden gem.

"It's something, isn't it?" I look over to see Princess Shayla standing next to me.

"I've never seen anything like it," I confess with a smile. I'm glad to see her. Out of all the tributes I interacted with the night before, I liked her the best. I truly hope she isn't the assassin we're looking for, but I remind myself to still be on guard. Without anything else to go off, the tributes who demonstrated their skills with weapons are highest on my list of suspects. She showed off her skill with a bow, so it could very well be her.

"We have a small solarium in the Iron Kingdom," she says. "It's full of night-blooming flowers. The only way to truly appreciate it is to go after dark. It's my favorite place in the palace, but I'll admit this rivals its beauty."

"We don't have much flowering vegetation in the Glacier Kingdom. So this," I say, gesturing toward the room, "is a real treat."

"Come," Shayla says, linking her arm through mine and pulling me farther into the solarium. "Did you meet all the other tributes last night?"

I nod. I made it my mission to meet each and every one of them. It was one of the main reasons I was at the ball so late. Otherwise, I would have left immediately after my dance with Prince Dryden.

"And?" she asks with a grin.

"It's a lovely group," I say neutrally, and she laughs.

"That can't be what you really think," she says, then nods over toward the side, where I notice a blush-pink head of hair. Princess Primrose. "Let's both at least admit she's horrible."

I don't disagree. My first interaction with Princess Primrose last night was when she sneered at me after my embarrassing dance with Prince Dryden. When I tried to talk to her later, she gave me a look, arched an eyebrow, and walked away. Beyond her beauty, I have a feeling Primrose is an acquired taste. But part of my strategy for sussing out the traitor is to stay neutral. It doesn't matter who I like or don't like. I need to try to get close to them all.

"I'm sure she's lovely once you get to know her," I say, and Shayla shoots me a look that I take to mean she thinks I'm mad.

Shayla and I walk across one of the small bridges toward a seating area, where a few of the princesses are sitting together on padded chairs and settees.

Princess Soraya, her strawberry-blond hair still shimmering like the night before, sees us first, and with a smile waves Shayla and me over. Princess Willow and Princess Octavia are seated with her. Princess Octavia glances at me with a hint of apprehension in her gaze but still shifts down on the settee, moving her butter-yellow dress that matches her hair almost perfectly out of the way so I can sit on the other side.

Princess Willow gives both Shayla and me a shy smile as she brushes a curly lock of her brown hair behind her pointed ear. I make sure Shayla takes a seat between us. I got caught in another conversation with Princess Willow the night before, this time learning not only her favorite dish but also that of every member of her family. There is such a thing as knowing too much about a person. For now, her oversharing has pushed her to the bottom of my list, considering how much I know about her compared to how little I know about the other tributes.

As I settle, my gaze catches on the bracelet around Princess Octavia's delicate wrist. It's a simple silver chain bracelet. There aren't any jewels on it, and it probably wouldn't even fetch a high price, but from the moment it catches a ray of sunlight, I can't take my eyes off it.

"Greer . . ." Shayla says my name and I glance up, blinking. She's looking at me expectantly, and I realize I've missed something, again.

"Oh, I'm sorry." I touch a hand to my forehead and give a self-deprecating chuckle. "I'm still a little fuzzy. I had a bit too much fun last night," I say.

Princess Soraya nods enthusiastically. "I suggest staying away from the punch at the next event. It will sneak up on you. My poor maid had to shake me to wake me up this morning." She laughs, and the rest of the princesses in our group smile along with her.

Princess Octavia's bracelet catches the light again out of the corner of my eye, luring me to distraction, but I straighten my spine and stiffen my neck to keep from glancing over at it again.

After that, we all fall into easy conversation. The goal of these first meetings for me is not so much to dig for information, but to make the other tributes comfortable in my presence. I don't expect loose lips to come until they've gotten to know me and don't see me as a threat anymore. With the exception of Princess Willow, who is clearly a chatterbox. I think Princess Shayla only took to me so quickly because she doesn't care or want to be chosen by Prince Dryden, so her guard isn't up. Or maybe it's just a front? That is, after all, what I'm doing.

We continue to chat about nothing until Octavia makes a noise of disgust. "Those two are already thick as thieves," she says, pointing over to where Princess Juniper and Princess Laurel of the Tide and Coral Kingdoms are huddled together in conversation.

"Their kingdoms are very close, so they already knew each other before the courting season began," Princess Willow chimes in. "I think they're even related somehow. Cousins, perhaps."

Not cousins. Juniper is technically Laurel's aunt, even though there's only a two-year age gap between them. In fact, they're the only two princesses here who aren't daughters of the reigning monarchs but rather nieces to their kingdom's ruling king and queen. That alone could put them at a disadvantage when it comes to vying for Prince Dryden's hand. Still, I keep my mouth shut. The last thing I want is for all the tributes to realize how much I already know about them.

Octavia is about to reply when a bell chimes, drawing our attention to the back of the solarium, where a footman stands with a small bell. "If Your Highnesses would please make your way to the garden gazebo, the orientation is about to begin."

We all rise and walk toward the back door leading directly to the palace gardens. I find myself once again transfixed by Octavia's silver bracelet. Coming up beside her, I wait until one of the other princesses says something to her, then with featherlight fingers I detach the bracelet.

I realize fully what I've done the moment the silver pools in my palm. Neo and Olette might have wanted a thief for this mission, but they weren't looking for one who takes unnecessary risks simply because a shiny piece of jewelry catches their eye.

I still slip the bracelet into a hidden pocket in the folds of my skirt. We had all my dresses designed with something like that, anticipating I might need to steal evidence from time to time. It's also a good place to store a small weapon. We had to tell the seamstress it was so I could hide a bottle of smelling salts on me at all times so she didn't raise an eyebrow at the odd request.

My guilt makes the bracelet feel like it is heating in my pocket as we travel as a group through the queen's roses. Down boxwood- and daylily-lined paths, I shift away from Princess Octavia, holding my breath that she doesn't notice her bracelet is missing until later.

When we reach the gazebo, the remaining tributes are already there, waiting, most of them chatting in small groups. Princesses Tien and Tessira are standing off by themselves, looking sickly and miserable. They were likely the tributes found passed out in the gardens this morning.

When we're all standing in the gazebo, there's a fair bit of side-eyeing going on. The tributes checking out one another's dresses and hairstyles, whispering behind their hands to one another. The atmosphere is decidedly tense, and if I were really here to win the prince's hand, I'd no doubt be feeling the nerves right now.

The whispers immediately cut off, and I glance over to see King Darius ascend the gazebo steps. I cock my head as I watch the king take his place in front of our group. I wasn't expecting the king himself to take part in this orientation.

Prince Dryden isn't far behind him, and as soon as the tributes catch sight of the prince, their whole demeanor changes. Princesses who were looking at one another with sharp eyes and pinched lips moments before suddenly soften, forcing pleasant and flirty facial expressions.

I laugh and have to turn it into a soft cough to cover the sound. When I look up, my gaze connects with the prince's hard green eyes, a stern expression on his face.

Swallowing, I arrange my features into something milder and glance at the king rather than the prince, who I've somehow already seemed to offend today without even uttering a word or dancing a single step on his foot.

"Princesses," King Darius starts, pulling the princesses' gazes from his brother. "Thank you again for honoring us by traveling to our kingdom."

He launches into a speech about how delighted he is that Prince Dryden's bride is in our group, and what a lovely life the tribute who weds the prince will have here in the Ember Kingdom. It's a little over the top, but when I scan the faces of the princesses around me, I can tell they are eating it up.

Prince Dryden remains stone-faced, but his eyes slowly move over the tributes, one at a time.

I wonder what he's thinking.

King Darius goes on to remind everyone that the duration of the courting season is six weeks, in which time there will be scheduled activities. Activities that will, of course, include the prince, but also opportunities for us to learn more about the Ember Kingdom that may one day become our home. Upon the request of the prince, some tributes will also have one-on-one time with him throughout the process.

"There's been one slight change to the courting season that we want to make you aware of." King Darius shoots a side look to his brother, and it seems to me that he's a little annoyed, but he goes on to say, "If it becomes obvious that you aren't a match for Prince Dryden, he will have the option of letting you return home before the end of the season."

A murmur goes through the tributes, and the breath stills in my lungs.

This is new. I was told that every princess would remain in the palace for all six weeks.

This could create a problem. A big one.

I didn't anticipate having to hold the prince's attention to remain at the palace. Every interaction we've had so far indicates I haven't started out on the right foot with him.

What if he sends me home early, or even today? Will Neo still let me out of my contract if I can't complete my mission? He said so, but what if he changes his mind?

"Ladies," King Darius says to stop the rising concerns. "This decision was made with you in mind and for your benefit. The prince and I felt it was cruel to keep you from your kingdoms and families for so long if it becomes clear you aren't a good match. I want to assure you that Prince Dryden is committed to this process."

Prince Dryden makes a noise that sounds suspiciously like a scoff, and King Darius shoots his brother another look, one full of warning, but now the prince's face is so blank it makes me wonder if I heard him make a sound at all.

"Over the next month and a half," King Darius goes on, "my brother's sole purpose will be to get to know each and every one of you. No one will be sent home without having their time to get to know Prince Dryden. I vow it."

If I wasn't pretending to be a princess, I would let out a groan. Time with Prince Dryden? That's the last thing I want.

King Darius goes over some more details of the courting season: The princesses will all have free time to do as we please, as well as planned functions; a rundown of the other balls coming up over the next several weeks; we're not to leave the palace without supervision . . .

But I'm only half listening now.

I need a new game plan. And a good one, or else I'm going to get sent away before my job here is done.

I hope Neo's prepared, because the next time I see him, we're going to have to strategize not only how to uncover a potential assassin, but what it takes to attract and keep a spoiled prince interested.

Chapter 15

WHEN I GET BACK TO MY ROOM LATER THAT AFternoon, I notice a sealed letter placed beneath a small box that someone must have delivered while I was gone. Many of the elite have very specific signets, but I don't recognize the design of a phoenix with feathers morphing into smoke pressed into the wax.

Slipping my finger under the sheet of paper, I break the seal and open the note. Written on the paper is a time—one o'clock—and a hand-drawn map.

Neo, I think. And my heart rate picks up a beat.

Since it's past one o'clock now, I assume he means in the middle of the night. I study the map. The lines don't seem to exactly mirror the palace corridors, so I can't quite work out where the map is leading me. From my memory, it appears that some lines go straight through walls, which makes no sense.

Placing the note aside, I pick up the box, a bit larger than a traditional jewelry box. My breath catches as I crack it open. Inside rests a milky white gem I recognize instantly: a lumestra stone. One of the magical crystals once mined in the Ember Kingdom, it releases a soft glow when held in a fae's hand. Long ago, fae used them to light their way at night instead of lanterns or candles. But over the centuries, most lumestra stones have gone dark, their light dimming with the slow unraveling of Vaeloria's magic. It's incredibly rare to find one that still works, and those that do are worth a small fortune.

Holding my breath, I gingerly pick up the stone. It rests perfectly in the center of my palm. At first, nothing happens, and my heart begins to sink. But then a gentle warmth starts to radiate from the milky gem. Like something slowly waking, a faint pulse of light flickers to life—soft at first, then gradually growing into a steady, brilliant glow. It's beautiful.

Even though I'm certain the lumestra stone is only on loan—a practical gift to help me slip through the palace unseen in the dead of night—I'm still captivated and overwhelmed by Neo's gesture. It's as thoughtful as it is unexpected, and it stirs something in me I'm not ready to name.

The antechamber door behind me opens and Eilowyn enters, coming to help me get ready for dinner. Before she enters the main bedroom, I quickly put the lumestra stone back in the box and shove the note in my pocket, right next to Octavia's bracelet. A flash of guilt goes through me that I try not to let show on my face.

When Eilowyn goes to pick out a gown for the formal dinner tonight, I manage to get the bracelet along with the lumestra stone and note safely tucked into the false bottom of the trunk. All too soon, I'm re-dressed in a royal blue gown, another overskirt-and-pants combo that makes me feel considerably better than the day dress I wore earlier.

Dinner this evening is to be held in the palace's formal dining room, and when I enter and see the setup, I have to press my lips together to keep from giggling. It's clear all the tributes are to be sat at a long table with the prince at the head. It's going to look ridiculous with all of us sitting at a table with him, but if this is how they want to move forward with this whole song and dance, who am I to stop them?

I pick a seat as far away from the prince as possible, motivated to find this would-be assassin as quickly as I can. The faster I find this assassin, the less I have to worry about Dryden sending me home early—and the sooner I can collect my money and freedom and leave the Ember Kingdom to start my new life.

Being strategic about where I sit, I spend the dinner talking with Princesses Pluma and Meer, two of the tributes I wanted to get to know because of their show of physical might during the opening ball. Meer's dress that evening had been half gown, half armor, and Pluma had entered armed with throwing blades strapped to her arms. Both princesses are polite, and I feel like I'm making some headway with them as we eat, but at the same time, not enough of anything useful.

Curiosity gets the best of me, and I sneak a glance or two down the table at Prince Dryden throughout the meal. It's clear he's trying to hide it, but he looks miserable. His eyes are glazed over as Princess Tessira talks animatedly next to him. It makes me wonder what she can possibly be saying that would bore him so much. The Salt Kingdom princess is wearing another ridiculously large gown this evening. The chairs next to her had to be shifted to accommodate her skirt.

Dinner lasts almost three hours, and when we're done, I'm more than ready to go back to my room and wait until it's time to meet with Neo. After we're formally dismissed, many of the tributes hang back, hoping to get a word or two in with the prince, but I head straight for the exit.

I glance over my shoulder right before slipping out the doors, and my eyes lock with Prince Dryden's. As if his gaze is a physical touch, an unwanted shiver runs over my skin. He's wearing a hunter green vest and matching overcoat that makes his bright green eyes pop, even from a distance. I know I should keep going, but something in the intense way he's staring at me, like he's trying to peel back the layers and see what I'm hiding underneath, freezes me in place.

Princess Primrose is trying to talk to him but notices his attention isn't on her. She turns and scowls in my direction when she sees he's staring at me.

That's not good. The conniving tribute is high on my suspect list. She may not have displayed skill with any weapons during the opening ball, but her cunning and ruthlessness are as sharp as any blade. I don't need to be making an enemy of her so soon, but I also need to keep the prince somewhat interested—or at least intrigued—in order to remain in the palace until I can uncover the assassin.

Ducking my head, I rush out of the dining room, my heartbeat racing. I try to keep my steps measured, but I am practically running by the time I make it to the safety of my chamber door.

I barge into the room abruptly, startling Eilowyn, who's there to assist me before bed. She's already laid my nightgown out and stoked the fire, which has chased away the evening chill.

Eilowyn holds a hand to her chest and lets out a wobbly laugh. "Your Highness, you scared me."

"Greer," I remind her, and she nods.

Eilowyn helps me out of my gown and into my nightclothes, asking me questions about the dinner. I tell her about the decadent chocolate berry cake we had for dessert, that I stayed far away from the wyldberry wine, and which princesses I sat next to during the meal.

"Did you not have any time with the prince?" she asks with a frown after I've donned my nightgown and sat down in front of the vanity for her to brush out my hair—a nightly routine I'm still not used to but have learned to live with. It's a wonder these highborns can function at all, considering they don't seem to do much for themselves.

I shake my head. "The seating arrangements didn't allow for you to talk to someone on the other end of the table."

"I'm so sorry to hear that. But I'm sure there will be opportunity enough to mingle with him tomorrow. You're all going to visit Eldergrove together, aren't you?"

"Yes, we are."

"Well, there, you see. You'll get your chance then."

I smile politely back at her when inside all I feel is apprehension. I really hope Neo has some good ideas to hold the prince's eye while still keeping him at arm's length.

Before Eilowyn leaves, I ask her if she can have the kitchen deliver some sablethorn tea to the room.

"Yes, of course. But are you sure you wouldn't prefer some nice herbal tea instead?" she asks, a line appearing between her furrowed brows. "Sablethorn tea will keep you up half the night."

That is exactly the plan.

If I'm going to remain awake and alert until my late-night meeting, I'm going to need some help.

I wave off her concern. "Oh, sablethorn tea never affects me that way," I lie. "I've been drinking it for years. I'm immune to its effects. But I just adore the flavor. It sounds very comforting right now."

With a reluctant nod, Eilowyn leaves, bidding me good night. Less than half an hour later, a kitchen maid knocks on the door and delivers my tea. I sit in an overstuffed chair by the fire, sipping the dark tea and watching the grandfather clock in the corner count down the time.

My mind swirls as I wait, mulling over each of my interactions with the fellow tributes, trying to come up with strategies for pulling out their secrets. It's clear that for many of them, I'm going to have to do more digging than simple conversations in the solarium. Getting into their rooms to check their belongings will be a must. Perhaps one of them is harboring weapons. Maybe I can find secret correspondence.

The remaining tea in the pot has long gone cold when the clock chimes, letting me know it's a quarter till one. Standing, I quickly throw a thick robe over my nightgown and fish the map and lumestra stone out of the trunk where I left them. When I go to grab the note, my gaze catches on Octavia's bracelet resting next to it. Reaching out, I stroke my fingers over it. I swear I can feel warmth on the metal.

Shaking my head, I straighten and replace the false bottom on the trunk. I listen at the door to make sure I don't hear any sounds before stepping out into the corridor. Oil sconces, turned low, line the halls in each direction, but they don't provide enough light for me to make out the details on the map in my hands, and so I reach into my pocket and pull out the lumestra stone. As before, it takes a few seconds to warm before the faint glow begins to build.

One of the stone's rare magical traits is that the fae holding it can control its brightness through sheer intention, a feature I'm especially grateful for now. I don't want to flood the corridor with light and risk alerting any patrolling guards. Instead, I keep the glow low, just bright enough to read Neo's map.

With light steps, I follow the lines on the map the best I can until it takes me to a dead end. In front of me is a life-size portrait of King Drake, the last king of the Ember Kingdom, and Queen Teresa, his wife. In the portrait, they look young. She sits in a chair, the red and gold silk of her skirts fanning out around her. King Drake stands next to her, his hand lovingly on her shoulder. Their bodies are tilted toward each other.

I think about the dowager queen. I haven't met her yet, and her absence from the opening ball was obvious. It's been said that she's still in mourning for her husband, who died suddenly less than a year ago. His cause of death was never officially released, which caused a stir at the time, but the royal family said it was a private matter, and so that was that. Who was really going to argue with them?

King Drake and Queen Teresa were said to be very much in love, though, which is unusual for nobility of their rank. According to Olette, who visited her sister twice while I stayed with her, the queen hardly leaves her apartment at all these days. I'm curious what type of fae she is, but it's possible I'll go the whole courting season without meeting her, so I'll probably never find out.

Dragging my gaze from the portrait, and my mind from my thoughts of the absent dowager queen, I glance back at the map, mentally retracing my steps. I must have made a mistake somewhere. I can't just walk through the wall.

I start to turn back when I hear voices and freeze. Shoving the map and lumestra stone back in my pocket to extinguish its light, I spin in a circle, looking for a place to hide, but there's nothing around me but carpet and walls.

The voices grow louder, and I think they are just around the corner. They're talking about one of the maids, arguing between them about whom she likes more.

My mind scrambles for a believable excuse to be out of my rooms this time of night. I left my room because I couldn't sleep. I was looking for the kitchen to get a glass of warm milk, but I must have taken a wrong turn and gotten lost.

Is that believable? Will they question why I didn't simply ring for my lady's maid? Will this be what leads to my discovery?

I'm sure they are going to appear any second when a hand clamps over my mouth and an arm wraps around my middle. I try to scream, but it's muffled. Suddenly, I'm yanked back into the dark.

Chapter 16

"SHHHH, ROWAN. IT'S JUST ME," SOMEONE SAYS quietly into my ear.

Neo.

My body goes limp, and I lean back into Neo's embrace rather than fight against it. Somehow, we're within the wall, behind the portrait of King Drake and Queen Teresa. My heart's beating against my ribs hard enough to bruise, and I hold my breath as the muffled voices on the other side of the portrait grow fainter.

When their footsteps finally fade, I let out a harsh breath but then become acutely aware of Neo's arm wrapped around my waist, holding me close.

I clear my throat and tap Neo's arm.

He releases a curse under his breath and then his arm disappears. When I turn, he's several feet away.

Neo winces. "Sorry. When I opened the portrait to get you, I heard voices and knew I needed to get you out of there quick. There wasn't time to explain."

"Yes, well . . ." I clear my throat and brush at invisible wrinkles on the skirt of my robe. "You're lucky I'm unarmed. If you'd pulled something like that on the streets of Everlight, I'd have gutted you without a second thought."

Neo barks a half laugh. "I suppose I am very fortunate, then. I'll have to keep that in mind."

"Yes, you will," I say, then take a moment to get my bearing. It appears we're in a narrow tunnel behind the walls. There's a dimmed lantern hung near Neo's head, letting off just a touch of light, but I can't see very far down the passageway behind him. "Where are we?"

Neo grabs the lantern off the hook. "Corridors like these run throughout the palace," he says. "You'd be surprised at how many places you can get to using these hidden passageways."

That explains why the lines on his map didn't make sense to me. "And you just expected I'd realize I needed to look for hidden entrances when you left me that map?"

He shakes his head. "No, but that's why I came to get you. Next time you'll be able to get there on your own. Come on," he says, waving me forward. "Bram's waiting."

I follow Neo throughout the narrow and cobweb-filled corridors for several minutes, trying to remember which turns we made, but knowing I never will. But I suppose that's why I have the map. We hear voices on the other side of the wall a couple times as we navigate through the narrow passageways. Whenever that happens, Neo slows our pace so that our steps can't be heard.

Eventually, we come to a half set of stairs down that lead to a plain wood door. There's a sliver of light showing from the crack underneath. Neo grabs the handle and swings the door open, beckoning for me to come in after him.

Bram, who's seated at a small two-chair table when we enter, immediately gets to his feet.

"What took you so long?" he barks at Neo, then slides accusatory eyes my way for good measure.

"Calm down," Neo says, setting the lantern on the table. "We were only a few minutes late."

Bram grumbles and then flops back into his chair, but Neo and I remain standing.

I take a moment to scan the room. Besides the table where Bram's seated, there is only a tiny single bed shoved in the corner and a few shelves on the wall holding a smattering of random objects: a couple of books, a thick candle that's been burned halfway down, and the black-bladed dagger that I tried to steal when we first met.

I whip my gaze back to Bram right away, doing my best to ignore the dagger so I'm not tempted to grab it. "Do you . . . live here?" I ask, unable to keep the note of horror out of my voice. This windowless room is more like a jail cell than a bedroom.

Bram shakes his head. "No. No one lives here. It gets used when we need someplace private. Only a few fae even know about it."

"But there's a bed and books."

Bram looks at Neo, and I turn to glance at him as well.

Neo rubs the back of his neck. "Sometimes I stay the night here," he admits, and I can't help the small shudder that runs through me. Sleeping here would be like sleeping in a crypt. "How did you find your first day in the palace and the opening ball?" he asks, changing the subject. "Anything noteworthy?"

Before I get a chance to respond, he crosses his arms and adds, "Besides that surprise performance."

I clear my throat. "Oh, you heard about that?"

He narrows his eyes. "I think the whole kingdom heard about

that. The princess who can make objects disappear. Half the fae in Everlight now think you have magic."

"And the other half?" I ask, somewhat alarmed.

"Seem to have written it off as a clever trick."

I sigh in relief. Performing sleight of hand had been a risk. Anyone truly clever, or even just street-smart, might have seen right through it. But I didn't exactly have a choice. I had to perform something.

Neo's gaze softens, his voice dropping as he shifts closer. "I heard you weren't aware of the last-minute performance requirement, though. I'm sorry about that," he says sincerely.

"Do you have any more insight into why the message from the palace never arrived?" I ask, curious if he can make sense of it.

He shakes his head. "I didn't realize the update hadn't been delivered. I would have made sure you were prepared myself, but I didn't have a chance to see you in those last days before the season started. I've made some light inquiries, but the best Olette or I can tell, it just slipped through the cracks."

I huff. "That slipup probably took ten years off my life."

Bram leans forward. "I'm impressed you were able to come up with something so quickly on the fly."

A nervous half laugh bubbles up my throat. "You wouldn't be impressed if you'd seen me panicking behind that curtain. I won't tell you how close I was to bolting."

"Which makes your innovation in the moment all the more impressive," Neo says. The admiration in his gaze unsettles me, making my cheeks heat and a shy warmth curl low in my chest.

I clear my throat. "Well, I was able to meet all the tributes," I say, steering the conversation to more comfortable topics. "But there's not much to report so soon. With a couple exceptions, most of the princesses are pretty tight-lipped. And the information I have gathered so far probably isn't of much use."

That is, unless it's somehow important to know the River Kingdom monarch's favorite dessert.

"I'm sure it's going to take a little time," Bram says with an unconcerned shrug.

I nod, agreeing with him. But when I glance over at Neo, there's a frown on his face, and I can't help but feel like I let him down.

"I'm sure I'll find out more tomorrow," I quickly add. "And if not, I plan on trying to sneak into their rooms at some point. My guess is I'll be able to learn a lot from the princesses by what they keep in their private quarters."

Neo gives his head a small shake. "I'm sorry, it's not that. I have every faith you'll find something. I'm just distracted."

"What's wrong?" I ask.

He waves a hand in the air. "Just more reports of some suspicious attacks throughout the kingdom."

"Vampire attacks?"

"We don't know. There are some factors that are rather specific to otherworlders, but the barrier is still holding, so it doesn't add up."

"Did you ever find out anything about the incident in the Coral Kingdom?" I ask.

He shakes his head.

"What's the king doing about it?" I ask.

Bram scoffs and I glance over at him. "The king doesn't want to check them out."

"Whyever not? I'd think reports of a potential otherworlder attack would be worth verifying."

"Because he doesn't believe it could possibly be otherworlders," Neo answers, then sighs. "But that's not what we're here to talk about."

"That's right," Bram says with a hint of a grin. "So, Rowan, what do you think of the prince?"

I roll my eyes. "You don't want to know."

Bram leans forward, a spark of interest lighting his eyes. "Oh, now I definitely do."

"Well, if you must know, I think he's as spoiled and arrogant as everyone says he is. And to be honest, I feel a touch of pity for whatever princess ends up with him."

Bram thinks that is hilarious and starts hooting with laughter, slapping his knee and everything.

"Did you hear her, Neo?" he says. "Spoiled and arrogant. She has the prince pegged, that's for sure."

I frown at Neo, hoping he'll explain what's so amusing, but he just shakes his head at Bram and says, "Yes, I heard her. Can we move on, please?"

"Actually, we can't," I say, then explain the unexpected twist from earlier this afternoon, when King Darius announced the new rule for the courting season.

When I finish, Neo and Bram don't appear nearly as concerned as I expected.

"That won't be a problem," Neo says confidently.

"Not a problem?" I ask, eyeing him with doubt. "It's a *huge* problem. The prince already half hates me."

"I can't imagine that's the case," Bram says.

"Trust me, it's true. We didn't exactly get off on the best foot." As in, I smashed his foot more than once during our first dance and things went downhill from there. "He looks at me like he can't stand my presence."

Bram's eyebrows go up. "Well, that is . . . unexpected."

"How so?" I ask. "It's not like I spent even a single lesson learning about the prince. I have no idea how to appear alluring and know next to nothing about him except he's Olette's nephew and fond of animals."

"Fond of animals. Who told you that?" Neo asks.

"Olette." Not that it should matter.

"Seems like an odd thing for her to tell you," he muses.

I shrug, not caring that I'm not supposed to. "Who cares if the prince likes animals or not?" I say, my voice coming very close to a screech. "The point is that if I'm not careful, I'm going to get thrown out of the palace before I get a chance to figure out which princess is here to hurt him."

Or worse, I'll be discovered as a fraud and imprisoned or killed.

"Rowan, you needn't worry," Neo says. "The new rule won't be a problem."

"Why do you keep saying that?"

Neo and Bram exchange a glance. It feels like they are talking over my head. I don't like it. Finally, Neo looks back at me as Bram reclines, crossing his arms over his chest as if he's getting comfortable to watch the show.

"It's just that you are a very lovely girl, and we know that the prince will find you appealing."

I scrunch my nose. "Are you trying to say that I'm his type?"

Bram chuckles, and Neo shoots him a death glare.

"Something like that."

I give him a skeptical look. The prince may be into honey blonds with unique eye colors, but that doesn't mean I can't still frustrate him enough to get myself sent home.

"Regardless, I'm going to insist on some training. If for nothing else than to put my mind at ease."

"What sort of training?" Neo asks, looking confused.

I can't believe he's going to make me spell it out. "I need to know more about the prince. His likes, his dislikes. And . . ." I clear my throat for nothing else than to give myself another moment.

It's not that I don't have any experience with males, because I do have some, but it's not what I would call extensive. My priority has always been to keep myself alive, and that didn't leave much time for other activities.

"And . . . ?" Neo prompts with raised brows.

"I'll need to know what entices a male."

Bram doesn't say anything, but out of the corner of my eye, I see him lift a hand to cover his mouth.

"Are you asking me to teach you how to seduce the prince?" Neo asks carefully, his face giving nothing away.

My cheeks heat. "Entice, not *seduce*," I say through clenched teeth. "It's not as if I'm willing to take the prince to bed to complete this mission."

Bram starts choking on nothing.

Aren't you, though? my mind whispers, an image of Prince Dryden rising unbidden in my mind. His green eyes flash in intensity as he looks at me. More heat rises to my cheeks, and I'm just thankful Neo and Bram can't read my mind.

Without sparing Bram so much as a cursory glance, Neo's gaze remains locked on me, his blue eyes just as intense as the unwanted image of the prince that came to mind. His features turn thoughtful; he rubs the pad of his thumb over his bottom lip. "All right, then," he finally says.

"All right?"

He nods. "Yes, I can give you some lessons." He takes a step closer. "If that's what you truly desire."

A flash of heat runs through me when he utters the word *desire*, but I shove it away. "It is," I answer, my tone flat as to not give away my inner turmoil.

"Perfect," he says.

Neo shifts even closer, close enough that I have to tilt my head to hold his gaze. As I stare up at him, I unconsciously wet my lower lip with the tip of my tongue. His gaze drops to my mouth, and the blood starts to cycle through my veins faster, warming me everywhere.

"Neo," Bram says, coming to his feet behind the younger fae and breaking the spell between us. "You can't be serious."

Neo slowly drags his eyes from me to glance over his shoulder at his friend. It's only when he's facing away that I feel like I can breathe normally again.

"You heard her. She wants to feel more comfortable around the prince. It will help her complete her mission. Besides," he says, turning back to me with a wicked smile. "We've already had our first lesson."

My eyes flare and a small gasp escapes me. *That's* what that was? A lesson.

Pressing my lips together in a hard line, I glare at Neo if for no other reason than to cover my own embarrassment. "Yes, well, duly noted," I clip. "Males fall under thrall easily with a longing stare. Good to see your gender is as simpleminded as I always suspected."

Bram chuckles again. "Never mind," he says. "I see Rowan has everything under control."

"Now," I say, needing a change of subject. "About the tributes."

We jump into talking about the different tributes, coming up with strategies for digging deeper into all of them. I don't know the hour, but at some point, the sablethorn tea starts to wear off and my eyes get heavy. When my head bobs as Bram is trying to show me the map of the palace's hidden passageways, Neo announces it's time for me to go back and try to get a couple hours of sleep before morning. I don't fight him. At this point, I'm not retaining much anyway.

Bram surprises me by giving me a big hug before I leave the room, telling me to be careful and good luck, and then I follow Neo back through the labyrinth to the same portrait of the former king and queen. We pause behind the painting before entering the main corridor.

"Can you make your way back to your room from here?" Neo asks, only the left side of his face visible in the dim lantern glow.

I nod and then say yes, realizing he may not be able to see me well either.

Reaching into my pocket, I pull out the lumestra stone, letting it brighten to a soft glow.

"Thank you for this," I say quietly. "It was incredibly thoughtful of you. I promise to keep it safe until I can return it."

Reaching out, he closes my fingers over the stone, dimming the light once again. "It's a gift, Rowan. It's yours to keep."

My breath catches. It's not only the first true gift I've ever received, but it's arguably the most valuable object I've ever held. Worth more than the baubles I was forced to steal for Sinclair.

I shake my head. "It's too expensive. I couldn't—" I begin, but Neo stops me with a light touch against my lips.

"If it helps, you can think of it as a down payment on what I've already promised you for your help."

I'm overwhelmed, not just by the gift, but also the feel of Neo's hand still wrapped around mine and the lingering brush of his fingers on my lips.

Neo blinks lazily down at me, and the space between us hums, thick with tension. But then he suddenly clears his throat and takes a step back, his hands falling away from me.

The loss of contact feels sharper than it should, and I glance down to re-center myself.

"The security through the hallways is sparse this time of night," he says, his voice a little gruff. "You should be able to make it back to your room without anyone catching you. But if you do get caught, tell them you rang for your maid because you woke up feeling ill and she didn't come, and so you were out looking for her and got lost."

I don't like the idea of possibly getting Eilowyn in trouble, but it is a plausible excuse, so I tell him I understand.

When I turn to push open the portrait, Neo catches my hand, staying me. Although we're only connected through our fingers, the entirety of my arm buzzes with awareness.

"I won't let anything happen to you. You know that, right?"

I didn't, but looking into his eyes makes me want to believe it.

"Yes, you wouldn't want to lose your investment," I say with a forced chuckle, trying to make light of the situation, but Neo's face darkens.

"Your worth is far greater than what's written on a piece of parchment."

Emotion clogs my throat. I have to push back against it to speak. "I have to go. If I wait any longer, Eilowyn might beat me to my bedchamber and find it empty."

Neo nods and steps back, releasing my hand and my gaze.

"Honeysuckle," Neo says, right before I'm about to slip back out into the corridor.

"Excuse me?" I whisper to him.

"The prince's favorite scent. Honeysuckle. You want to keep his attention? Have some added to your perfume."

I blink back at Neo. It's on the tip of my tongue to ask him how he knows that, but it doesn't really matter. I nod and then carefully open the hidden door and reenter the palace corridor. Within minutes, I am safely back in my chamber, but when I finally lie down to sleep, it eludes me.

Chapter 17

I MAY NOT KNOW MUCH ABOUT COURTING, BUT a picnic with fifteen females fighting for the attention of one male certainly doesn't sound romantic to me. A point that's confirmed within the first half hour of our outing as I watch the tributes vie for Prince Dryden's attention. Who will ride in the carriage with him? Who will walk next to him to the picnic spot? Who will get to sit next to him for lunch?

I'm convinced that despite the pedigree of the tributes, a catfight could break out at any moment. Just now, behind Prince Dryden's back, I watched Princess Primrose yank on Princess Juniper's dress to keep her from stepping up next to him.

It's hard not to find it humorous, watching these refined highborns bicker and shoot death glares at one another when Prince Dryden isn't watching. The moment he looks in their direction, they turn into perfectly polished and demure princesses.

"Are you finding this as amusing as I am?" Princess Shayla asks as she settles onto the pink twill blanket I'm sitting on.

"It is quite a sight," I agree as I watch four different tributes squeeze onto Prince Dryden's blanket. Princess Soraya is practically in his lap, and the prince doesn't look happy about that at all. In fact, it's becoming increasingly clear he'd rather be *anywhere* but on this grassy knoll overlooking Everlight with us right now.

"Well, I suppose I can't blame them. If they don't make an impression now, they may never get a chance to," Shayla says as she takes her time arranging her emerald-green dress around her legs.

"What do you mean?"

She glances up at me. "You mean you haven't heard?"

I shake my head. "Heard what?"

"Princess Tessira was sent home early this morning because Prince Dryden already ruled her out as a potential bride. It's probably what's caused the stench of desperation in the air today."

Sent home? So soon, and after just one dinner?

I turn wide eyes to the group, scanning the tributes, and realize that Princess Tessira is indeed missing.

"Oh no. Please don't tell me you're worried too?" Shayla says, her face falling.

I force out a light laugh and drag my gaze off the prince and other tributes. "Of course not. If I'm sent away today or in a month, it doesn't make a difference to me."

Shayla regards me with a touch of skepticism. "If you say so," she finally says, picking up a raspberry and popping it into her mouth.

Shayla and I make light conversation, and I find myself laughing easily with her. She's more down-to-earth than the other tributes. I can't help but think that if she wasn't a princess, or if I were one, we might actually be friends.

As the midday wanes into afternoon, I track the prince and his harem of revolving princesses. I'm torn between making the rounds with the other tributes and trying to find time to talk to the prince. I can't decide if trying to talk with him will make things better or worse for myself. One thing I know for sure is the stress of potentially getting kicked out is taking valuable mental energy away from my real task. If Neo and Bram could just explain to the prince what I'm doing here and come to an arrangement, then it would make my job so much easier.

Out of the corner of my eye, I catch Princesses Primrose and Tori walking off by themselves, and my interest is piqued. Their heads are bent toward each other as they round a corner and disappear from view.

Primrose and Tori are two of the tributes I want to look into next. Primrose because of her reputation for being ruthless, and Tori for the interaction I saw between her and a guard at the opening ball that seemed to upset her so much.

I tell Shayla and the other tributes who'd joined us that I'm going for a walk. When Shayla asks if I want company, I wave her off, letting her know I just want some light exercise to clear my head.

Following the path Princesses Primrose and Tori took, I walk around a large boulder and out of view of the prince and tributes. There are palace guards stationed around for our safety, but since we are guests in the Ember Kingdom, we are free to roam the area.

At first, I don't spot Primrose or Tori anywhere, but I hear voices in the direction of the forest up ahead, so I pick up the pace. Only a handful of steps into the shady forest, I'm thankful for my pants and overskirts. I can step over roots and underbrush with ease.

The voices are growing louder. Another minute and I can see a flash of pink hair: Princess Primrose. I veer off the trodden path to try to get closer to the pair without alerting them I'm there, thankful for the muted gray and olive colors of my dress today. It's difficult to be stealthy among all this foliage, but the colors do blend into the forest relatively well. Certainly better than the butter-yellow dress I almost picked. I manage to get within ten feet of the pair without them noticing by quietly creeping forward and hiding behind a dense spicebush.

"If your parents ordered you to, what other choice do you have?" Princess Primrose says to Tori. "Even if it's something you don't want to do, they're the leaders of your kingdom. You can't defy them."

My heart starts to pick up. Could Tori's parents have ordered her to harm Prince Dryden?

Princess Tori chews on her bottom lip as she wrings her hands, and even from my hiding place, I catch the conflict in her green eyes.

"I don't know that I can go through with it," she says.

"Well, you're going to have to," Primrose snaps at her. "I don't need to tell you what's at stake."

I strain my hearing, knowing how important this conversation is.

"I'm fully aware of the stakes," Tori snaps back. "But if you were in my position, you can't tell me you wouldn't be hesitant, too. If I'm caught, I'll be branded a traitor. In the Ember Kingdom as well as my own."

"All the more reason to see it through," Primrose says, and I unconsciously lean forward, sure that at any moment Princess Tori is going to confess, and my mission will be complete.

What luck to have stumbled across the would-be assassin so soon in the courting season. Admittedly, Tori doesn't seem like the type, but appearances can be deceiving. Just look at me.

Eager to hear what the pair will confess, I inch forward and a small branch in front of me cracks beneath my foot. Both princesses jolt and then freeze.

I drop into a crouch, using the thick underbrush as another layer of camouflage, cursing myself for being so careless.

"What was that?" Princess Tori asks.

Princess Primrose's gaze turns shrewd as she scans the area. I'm convinced she'll spot me the moment she looks in my direction.

Should I get up and flee or stay put?

Princess Primrose's eyes are almost on me when Princess Tori exclaims, "Your Highness!"

A moment later, Prince Dryden appears next to the pair. "There you are," he says with a suave smile that has both princesses practically swooning. "I've been looking for you both."

"You have?" Primrose asks, batting her lashes at him.

I grimace. Do males really fall for that?

But it seems to be working on Prince Dryden, who smiles down pleasantly at her.

"I was," he says. "We're packing up to leave, so I'm looking to round up a few of the princesses who seem to have wandered off."

"Oh, I see," Primrose says, her smile dimming a little. "Well, in that case, should we be off?" she asks, smoothly sliding her hand into the crook of his arm for him to escort her, but Prince Dryden manages to extricate himself from her grasp.

"Go on without me. I'll just be a little behind you," he says. "There's another princess I'm still looking for."

Princess Primrose can do nothing but nod, and she and Tori—who was suspiciously quiet and looking a bit ill as she stared at Prince Dryden—turn to leave. Before departing, Primrose sweeps the bushes with a keen gaze, her eyes sliding right past me. I release a relieved sigh when the pair finally disappears from view.

Prince Dryden's back is to me as he watches them as well, but rather than continuing on the path once they're gone, he turns and looks right at me.

"You can come out now."

I freeze.

What do I do?

Prince Dryden crosses his arms over his chest, his gaze trained in my direction. "I'd prefer not to have to go in there and pull you out myself."

I squeeze my eyes shut, letting the shame roll through me for exactly five seconds before opening them again and standing. Picking my way between bushes, I stumble over a root right before reaching him.

He catches me, his grip firm as he braces my arms to keep me upright. The roughness of his palms against my bare skin instantly makes me think of Neo, but I shove that thought from my mind. Interesting that his hands are calloused, though. Who would have thought it from a pampered prince?

When I'm steady, he lets go, but the warmth from his hands lingers on my arms. I want to brush the sensation away, but can't with him staring at me.

He leans toward me and sniffs. "Is that honeysuckle perfume you're wearing?"

My cheeks heat. I had Eilowyn find me some this morning based on Neo's suggestion last night. I'm not sure whether to be pleased or not that Dryden noticed.

I nod and force a small smile that I hope comes off as coy and flirty, but I'm so bad at this it might just look deranged. "It's always been a favorite scent of mine."

"Oh, is it now?" Even though he doesn't smile, I get the feeling that he's mocking me.

"Yes. I simply adore how sweet and . . . honey-like it is."

What am I even saying right now?

His eyebrows rise slightly. "Hmm, I see. And what, may I ask, were you doing back there?" He nods toward the bush I was hiding behind.

"Well, I was . . . relieving myself," I answer, not knowing what else to say. I certainly can't tell him the truth.

The corner of Prince Dryden's mouth twitches, but besides that, he remains a veritable statue. "Is that so?"

Heat rises to my cheeks, but I refuse to look away from the prince. I lock my violet gaze on his green eyes and raise my chin.

"It is," I say, daring him to question me further. Prince Dryden is, after all, a gentleman. This type of conversation isn't considered proper between highborns. I'm confident he'll drop the subject, which is why I'm so surprised when he doesn't.

"And you thought less than a stone's throw from two other tributes was a good place to pick to do that?" He arches one brow, challenging me to lie again.

Which I do. Easily.

"I was here first. I was just finishing when they arrived. It would have been embarrassing for all of us for me to announce my presence."

"Hmm," is all Prince Dryden says.

This is not going well. I'm so annoyed, but I can't let that show. If I irritate Prince Dryden, I could find myself packing my belongings, just like Princess Tessira.

"Well, Your Highness. I won't keep you any longer. You can go look for your missing princess, and I'll see you back at the picnic site."

"*You* are the missing princess," he says with the hint of a smirk.

"Oh. Right. Well, I guess we should return, then."

I turn to leave, but he stops me by grabbing my hand. When I glance up at him, he steps closer and reaches forward. I catch my breath as his fingers dip into my hair, my heart suddenly drumming.

As I stare into his bright green eyes, I hold my breath, waiting to see what he's going to do, but he just pulls his hand back. A sprig from the spicebush I was hiding behind is pinched between his fingers. Letting go of my hand, he drops the twig, and I reach up to pat my hair, checking for more bits of foliage.

"That was the only piece," he says. "But since we're unchaperoned, I thought it best to take it out before we leave the forest together. I don't want anyone's mind going where it shouldn't."

I clear my throat, uncomfortable. He's not wrong. If we'd walked out together with a bit of brush in my hair, it would have looked incriminating. "No, we wouldn't want that," I agree. "If any of the tributes think something happened between us, I'll likely wake up with a shaved head in the morning."

I'm serious. I've already been sabotaged once. I wouldn't put it past some of these tributes to do it again. But Prince Dryden thinks I'm joking and barks out a laugh. I can't deny it's infectious in a good way, one that makes me feel lighter, despite myself and the circumstances.

"You have lovely hair," he says. "It reminds me of spun gold."

Hmm. Maybe I am the prince's type after all.

"It would be a travesty to lose it," he goes on, "so let's hurry back before anyone gets suspicious."

I don't mean to, but I find myself smiling up at Prince Dryden. The male is an enigma. Just when I think I have him figured out, he changes like a shifter, becoming someone altogether different. And this lighter version, I'm surprised to learn, I happen to like.

When we make it back to the grove, all eyes are indeed on us. Prince Dryden is quickly swarmed by the tributes, so I take the opportunity to slide away from him and head toward one of the carriages. I catch Princess Primrose watching me as I pass, her gaze sharp and calculating. I'm sure she's figured out I was the tribute the prince was looking for. I just hope she doesn't realize I overheard her conversation with Princess Tori.

Rather than trying to get Prince Dryden's attention like the rest of the tributes, Princess Tori is standing off to the side, frowning over at him.

I try to remember what I can about the Fire Kingdom, where Princess Tori is from. I don't know of any discord between the Ember and Fire Kingdoms. The Fire Kingdom holds great strength and influence. Not as much as the Ember Kingdom, of course, but their volcanic soil is rich in minerals and excellent for water retention. Their warriors may no longer be able to shoot flames from their palms at their adversaries, but that hardly matters in our now mostly peaceful society. Their production of flame-root, crimson grain, volcanic wine, and fireleaf tea has proven far more beneficial, leaving me at a loss for an obvious reason why they'd want harm to come to Prince Dryden.

As I keep an eye on Princess Tori, she reaches into her reticule and pulls out a small pocket mirror. I'm in the middle of wondering if she already has a plan in place to bring about the prince's ruin when the mirror catches the sun and my mind goes blank.

I need that mirror.

Changing my trajectory, my feet start me in the direction of Princess Tori rather than the carriages, my hand twitching with the desire to grab that pocket mirror.

I just need to get another look at it. That's all.

I'm only a couple of body lengths from her when Shayla steps into my path.

"Were you just alone in the forest with the prince?" She loops her arm in mine and starts leading us back toward the carriages.

I sneak another peek over my shoulder at Tori and her mirror, but she's placed it back in her handbag. The desire to have it lingers, but less intensely now that I can't see it anymore, which is a relief.

"Greer?" Shayla prompts, and I shake my head to clear it.

"Yes, I was. Or rather, he found me there and escorted me back."

"And that's all?" she asks, her face alight with interest.

"I'm afraid so. In fact, it was quite embarrassing," I say, and she leans in closer to hear why. "He caught me after I'd relieved myself."

She gasps, then covers her mouth when a laugh sneaks out. "He didn't!" she says.

"Oh, but he did. If I wasn't forced into this courting season, I'd never show my face to him again."

We laugh about it as we climb into our carriage together. With any luck, Shayla will let the other tributes know of my embarrassing interaction with the prince to keep their animosity from me.

When we settle into the carriage, I peek out the window, not searching for Prince Dryden, like most of the other tributes are, but for Princess Tori. I spot her climbing into another carriage in front of ours—Princess Primrose on her heels. My gaze immediately zooms in on her reticule, imagining the handheld mirror within. I decide then and there I have to find a way to get into her room.

Princess Tori is hiding something, and I have to find out what it is.

Chapter 18

FOUR DAYS GO BY AND I'M NO CLOSER TO FINDING Princess Tori's secrets. Two more princesses are sent home: Princess Tien of the Grassland Kingdom and Princess Sonjai of the Silk Kingdom. I try not to let the seemingly random cuts get to me, but it's in the back of my mind that I could be next.

With Princesses Tien and Sonjai gone, that still leaves twelve tributes, and the only princess I feel confident ruling out is Princess Willow, and not because she looks too innocent to be our assassin or because of her incessant chatter whenever I get within a few feet of her, but rather because of what I found written in the journal she accidentally left in the solarium one day. The last few entries were all about how she's already half in love with Prince Dryden. She's practically planning their wedding. She had a whole page devoted to writing both their names together inside of hearts. It was creepy, to be sure, but not the calculated mind of a potential assassin.

Prince Dryden has started courting a few of the tributes more seriously than the rest of us. He spent chaperoned one-on-one time with Princesses Primrose, Meer, and Pluma—three of my top suspects, since they all are known for either their cunning or might. My interactions with the prince have been minimal since our incident in the forest, and I'm as glad I'm still here as I am that I haven't been asked to spend one-on-one time with the prince. But the strangest thing is, I've caught him watching me from afar from time to time during our group excursions. His gaze ranges from curious to speculative, and I can't shake the feeling that the dark-haired heir is trying to figure me out. It unnerves me. What if he suspects the truth?

Keeping a close eye on Tori, I notice that her moods are indeed erratic. More than ever, I'm convinced she is hiding something. She's at the very top of my list of suspects, but despite my best efforts, I haven't been able to find a way into her rooms to check for clues or incriminating evidence. Nor have I seen Neo or Bram to give them an update.

I've held back from sending a note to Olette to arrange a check-in, because besides the conversation I overheard between Primrose and Tori, I don't have any evidence. I'm prepared to reach out anyway if another day goes by, but then a second letter arrives first thing in the morning, slipped under my door with nothing but a time: one a.m. The same as before.

My heart stutters at the familiar bold script, but there's no time to linger on it. The day ahead is packed enough with activities all around Everlight that are sure to leave my feet aching by nightfall, including a visit to the botanical gardens, browsing the Crystal Archives, and a stroll through Artisan's Row. So I hide the note in my trunk before Eilowyn arrives to help me dress for the day.

After breakfast in the solarium with the other tributes, we pile into carriages bound for town. At each stop, I try to socialize with the quieter princesses I'm still not sure about, namely Princesses Lakelyn and Pluma. Both are careful with their words. By the end of the day, I still can't tell if that's simply their nature, a product of royal training, or a calculated effort to be evasive.

I return to the palace frustrated that I can't cross names off my list as easily as I'd expected. Talking has gotten me nowhere, which means I'll have to find proof somewhere else. But I don't have time to plot because I immediately have to change into evening wear for a dinner party with Prince Dryden, King Darius, and some of the highborn elite.

I spend the entirety of the evening appeasing the highborns and still keeping an eye on the remaining tributes for suspicious behavior. It's a level of mental acrobatics that leaves me exhausted at the end of the long evening. And it's not even close to being over.

I struggle to keep my eyes open while Eilowyn takes down my hair and helps me into my bedclothes. She leaves and I start drinking sablethorn tea, hoping it will revive me, but as the hours tick by toward one a.m., my lids get heavier and my mind fogs.

A little before one, I give my bed one last loving glance before padding quietly into the hallway. The lumestra stone and map Neo gave me are both tucked into the pocket of my robe, but I don't pull them out until I'm behind the portrait of King Drake and Queen Teresa.

With the soft glow of the stone to guide me, I navigate the hidden passageways and stop in front of the secret room. I lift my hand to softly knock, but before I have a chance, the door swings open. Neo stands there, his blue gaze spearing me, causing a shiver to trickle down my spine and goose bumps to pop out on my arms.

Without uttering a word, he reaches forward and loops an arm around my waist, dragging me toward him. I'm pressed up against his chest, breathless, when he shuts the door behind us. I blink up at him, my mind in a different type of fog now, but just as quickly as he grabbed me, his arm melts from my back and he steps away, putting a proper distance between us.

"Was there anyone else out there?" Bram asks, startling me. I didn't see him standing off to the side in the dim room.

Neo shakes his head, then plows a hand through his hair. He seems off tonight. His hair is disheveled, and there are dark smudges under his eyes. I want to ask him if he's okay, but when I open my mouth to speak, he talks over me. "Were you seen?" he asks, a worry line between his eyebrows.

I shake my head. "No."

"Are you certain?"

"I don't think so, but I suppose I can't be certain. I didn't hear or see anyone, though." I don't admit to him that because of exhaustion, I probably wasn't being as watchful as I should have; he already looks wound too tight.

Neo relaxes a fraction, his shoulders dropping slightly. "Good. Good."

"What's going on?" I ask, glancing between the two of them.

"We heard movement in the tunnels before you arrived," Neo explains.

"Someone else is using the passageways?" I ask, surprised. "Who else knows about them?"

"Besides the fae in this room? Not very many," Neo admits. "When we leave, I'll make sure you get back to your room."

When I nod my agreement, I detect a note of relief in Neo's gaze. Bram lights another lantern, giving the room a bit more light, and so I stow my lumestra stone back in my pocket. When we've settled around the small table, I launch into a recap of events since I last saw them, explaining what happened at the picnic and my suspicions about Princesses Tori and Primrose. When I finish speaking, Neo and Bram both look thoughtful.

Bram glances at Neo. "Our relationship with the Fire Kingdom is calm, but it's worth looking into."

Neo rubs two fingers over his lower lip, his gaze miles away. He nods. "I agree."

"I want to search her room," I cut in. "But I haven't been able to find an opportunity. Especially in the daytime with so many guards walking the palace corridors. The croquet game is tomorrow. I think I can slip away without anyone noticing, but it still leaves the issue of how to get into her rooms."

"I have a way for you to get into her room undetected," Neo says. He shoves out of his chair and goes over to the shelf across the room.

"Neo," Bram says, a clear warning in his voice that Neo ignores as he rifles through the small stash of books. Pulling one down, he returns to the table with a thin, leather-bound book in his hand.

It's small, the size of a journal rather than a novel or textbook. The cover is cracked and faded, making me think the book is either very old or used often.

Setting it on the table between us, Neo starts to open it, but Bram places his hand on top of the cover.

"Neo," Bram says again. "Are you sure this is wise? You know what you'll be giving her access to?"

I don't know what's in the book, but it must be something secretive if Bram is hesitant to show me. I try not to be offended by his reluctance but still feel a little sting. I brush it aside easily. I've been treated worse. Bram is right to be cautious.

Neo pulls the book out from underneath Bram's hand and addresses the older fae. "I know what I'm doing." Turning his head, he looks at me, his blue gaze steady. "I trust her."

The words steal my breath. They're simple words. *Trust.* A sentiment that most fae take for granted. But even though I'm dressed and polished to look like a real princess, underneath I'm just a thief. Something Neo is keenly aware of. But despite that, he still trusts me, and it hits me to my core.

I break eye contact and glance down at the book in the middle of the table, worried that if I don't, I'll do or say something that betrays my emotions. It's silly that Neo's trust means so much to me. I don't want them to know.

"I can search the girl's room instead," Bram offers, but I quickly shake my head.

"No, it needs to be me. I've been studying Princess Tori. I think I'll be able to search her room more efficiently. And I also know how to do a sweep without anyone knowing I was ever there."

I don't mention that if Bram goes instead of me, I won't ever find that pocket mirror. Days later, I'm still thinking about it.

"I agree," Neo says. "This is exactly why we looked for someone like Rowan to begin with. She has more experience in this area. If Princess Tori is the one we are looking for, we don't want to tip her off that we are on to her."

Pressing his lips together, Bram nods. I can tell he's still hesitant about me seeing whatever is in the book, but he doesn't protest this time as Neo flips the cover open.

It's not a normal book with multiple pages one can flip through. There are large, folded sheets of paper tucked within. He unfolds the first sheet, and when it's fully out, it's four times the size of the book, but still bound to it in one place.

"It's a map," I say, and glance up at both Neo and Bram.

Neo nods. "A map of the hidden passageways throughout the palace." He quickly folds up the sheet and opens the next. "Each sheet is a different wing, and a different floor. With this map, you could get almost anywhere in the palace undetected. Many of the rooms have direct access to the passageways, so with any luck, we'll be able to get you right into Princess Tori's room."

Leaning forward, I track all the lines and symbols on the page in front of me. At the top of the page is written East wing, third floor. I glance up sharply, my eyes wide. "These are the royal family's rooms." I point at a spot on the map. "These are the prince's rooms." I move my finger to another place. "These are the king's. And these are the queen's."

Bram leans back in his seat, crossing his arms over his chest. "The veritable keys to the kingdom," he says, nodding at the map, and I instantly understand why he was reluctant for me to see this. And he was right to be. With this map, I can gain access to the royal family when they are most vulnerable.

Neo folds the map back up and hands me the book. "Guard this with your life," he says, and I nod as I carefully take it. "Look through it and figure out if you can access Princess Tori's room."

"I will. Too bad I wasn't placed in a room that had direct access to the tunnels."

"That was by design," Neo says, and I lift my eyebrows. "We wanted direct access to as many of the other tributes as possible."

That makes sense, but it still would have been nice to be able to come and go from my room without having to worry about running into a palace guard.

After that, we talk a little while longer about strategies to get me closer to some of the other princesses and then wrap up our meeting. After I say goodbye to Bram, Neo and I leave the room, but before we go, Neo tells me not to take out my lumestra stone.

"If there is someone in these tunnels, I don't want them knowing we're coming."

"But how will we get back if we can't see?"

"I've been traveling in these passageways for as long as I can remember. I know them better than I know my own face. I don't need the light." He takes my hand, his familiar calluses brushing against my palm.

"So, you grew up in the palace, then?" I whisper as Neo tugs me forward.

It's a beat before he quietly answers, "I did."

I wonder, and not for the first time, how Neo is involved in all of this. Olette, being the prince's aunt, makes sense to me. But who really is Neo? Is he somehow related to the prince as well? Or just a loyal subject to the crown? Where's the connection, and why is he so secretive about it?

We fall silent as we slip through the passageways. I never lose awareness of Neo's warm hand wrapped tightly around mine. It's almost pitch-black, but his steps are sure as he guides me back to the portrait entrance. Even though I can't see him, I sense the tension in him with every step we take. He's alert, ready to jump into action at a moment's notice, and although I take pride in being able to defend myself, there's something comforting about knowing that Neo would fight to protect me.

When we reach the portrait, Neo finally lets me take out my lumestra stone, although he cautions me to keep it low so no one sees me sneaking back to my room. I'm about to turn to leave when I pause, looking into Neo's tired eyes.

"Are you all right?" My question seems to startle him, but he recovers quickly.

"Of course. I'm fine."

I frown, taking in the dark smudges under his eyes and the weary lines on his face, all visible even in the low light. He looks as exhausted as I feel.

"It would be okay if you weren't," I say, giving him permission to let the façade drop. It's just the two of us in this small space. There's no one here he needs to keep up a front for. It's just me.

Neo sighs, running a hand through his hair. "It's been . . . a stressful time. But I promise I'll be fine. We just need to find this assassin and then I'll sleep easier at night."

I nod, understanding. "I'm doing my best. We just have to hope

I can ferret her out before the prince grows bored of me and kicks me out."

Neo's eyes soften as he gazes down at me. Something in that look makes my heart beat faster. "I'm sure the prince is fully enthralled with you."

I huff out a half laugh, thinking about the last time I had a real conversation with the prince and told him I was relieving myself in the woods. "Oh, I very much doubt that."

Neo tilts his head, his eyes tracing over my face, soaking in each dip and curve. "You don't see it, do you?"

"See what?"

"How exquisite you are."

The breath catches in my throat. I can't seem to form words. I'd brush off his comment as false flattery, but the intensity of his stare makes me think he's being honest. I duck my head, unable to look at him anymore, but he puts two fingers under my chin and lifts my face.

"It's true," he says. "You may not have been born a princess, but you're worth far more than any of the preening peacocks running around the palace trying to snare Prince Dryden. One day, should you desire it, you will make one fae the luckiest male in all the kingdoms."

I let Neo's words roll over me slowly and sink in past flesh and bone to my very soul. No one has ever spoken to me like this before. The way he still stares at me, like I am this priceless and unattainable creature, rocks me to my core.

I open my mouth to say something—what, I'm not yet sure—and Neo's gaze drops to my lips, unveiled longing in his eyes. My heart thumps against my chest and I sway toward him, knowing that his desire is surely mirrored in my eyes as well.

The fingers under my chin start a slow slide up my jaw until they reach my ear. They brush lightly over the shell, ringing up over the pointed tip and back down again, causing a delicious shiver to dance down my spine.

"Neo," I say, his name not much more than a whisper.

His gaze travels back to mine. My stomach hollows and then fills with butterflies.

Neo leans forward, his hand still traveling over my sensitive skin, brushing against the nape of my neck as he urges me to tip my head back farther.

My eyes have just fluttered shut when suddenly there's a creak from deeper in the hidden passageways. Neo twists quickly, shoving me behind him, his hand going to the weapon sheathed at his side.

We stand frozen, my heart hammering against my chest for a whole different reason this time, my head a muddled mess of emotions.

Seconds tick by and only silence greets us. Without looking over his shoulder, Neo whispers for me to get back to my room. His brisk command stings a little considering the intimate moment we just shared, but I try not to let it bother me.

With a nod that he can't see because his back is to me, I slip out from behind the portrait, catching only a flash of his blond hair over my shoulder before I snap the hidden door closed behind me.

Chapter 19

THE NEXT DAY, I WAIT UNTIL ALL THE TRIButes and the prince have selected their croquet mallets and started the game before begging off, claiming a sudden headache. Prince Dryden sent Princesses Juniper of the Tide Kingdom and Laurel of the Coral Kingdom home this morning. It was the most public of the dismissals so far and became a rather awkward affair when both princesses cried.

It was clear that the prince was uncomfortable and didn't expect such a reaction when he tried to have a private conversation with both of them over breakfast. But now with two more tributes gone and only ten of us left, it will be that much harder to slip away without being noticed. Even so, I have to take the chance.

Telling the princesses closest to me that I'm going to go lie down and will join them again after the match, I turn to leave, noticing Prince Dryden glancing at me from across the field as I do. I feel his gaze warming my back as I make my way across the green and up the steps to the palace, but when I glance over my shoulder, his attention is on Princess Octavia of the Desert Kingdom. She flips her butter-yellow hair over her shoulder as he tries to show her how to hold her mallet, and it hits him in the face. I put a hand over my mouth to hold in my laugh just as I slip inside the palace.

I hurry back to my room to grab the book of maps. Once inside, I close the door firmly behind me and rush to the trunk, throwing it open and pulling up the false bottom to reveal all my treasures. A touch of shame rolls through me as I look down at the small bounty. Princess Octavia's silver chain bracelet lies beside the book Neo and Olette let me keep from the pub where we had our secret meeting. I've also amassed a bud vase from the solarium, a jeweled comb that I deftly plucked right from Princess Sonjai's hair before she was sent home, and silver cream and sugar bowls from my tea set, and after searching Princess Tori's room, I might be able to add her compact mirror to the bounty.

I hope that when this is all over, Neo and Olette never find these items. It's not that I truly wanted to steal them, but that I couldn't help myself. I had to. Apparently, even being free of that life, I can't shake the compulsion to steal. I've thought about returning them, but each time, nausea roils in my gut and I can't bring myself to give the items up. I can only pray that when I leave the Ember Kingdom to make a new life for myself, the impulse to pinch items stays here. I want a fresh start, free of my past transgressions.

Taking a breath, I reach into the trunk and pull out the small book of hidden-passageway maps that's nestled between the vase and tea set items. I flip the book open to the wing of the palace where all the tributes are housed, running my finger along the path that I already mapped out that morning and trying to commit it to memory.

The closest entry point from my room is not actually the portrait of the former king and queen, but a false door at the back of a linen closet just down the hall. It's a short trip to Princess Tori's room, just three turns once I'm in the passageway, but just in case,

I grab a purse and shove the book into it. The purse is good because it's large enough to fit some other small objects as well, in case I need to take anything from Tori's room as evidence.

Or in case I find the mirror and can add it to my collection.

Shoving that errant thought from my mind, I grab my lumestra stone too, knowing the hidden passageways will be dark even in the daytime, and hustle to the door. Peeking out, I make sure the hallway is clear. I have to wait for a footman to turn the corner at the end of the hall, then I hurry toward the linen closet, my feet soundless on the padded carpet.

After I shut the linen closet door quietly behind me, I lift the lumestra stone, looking for the hidden entrance to the passageways. It takes me a few minutes to realize it's under a shelf in the back. I have to stow the lumestra stone and get on my hands and knees to push a panel back, which slides to the side, and then I crawl into the passageway.

When I get to my feet, I slide the panel back into place. The dress I'm wearing today is dusty pink, and when I get the lumestra stone out again and allow it to shine light in the space, I can see that I've gotten it messy. I have to hope I don't run into anyone before getting back to my room, because I'm not sure how to explain the dirt and dust smudges over my knees.

Without pulling out the map, I make the twists and turns until I'm standing in front of what I believe is the hidden door to Tori's room. There's a large wood panel with a small hook around where a knob should be that I think will allow me to pull the door open. I press my ear against the panel, listening carefully for the sound of talking. When only silence greets me, I give the hook a strong tug and the panel pops open to reveal a row of dresses.

The door must lead to the back of Princess Tori's armoire. Putting the lumestra stone back in my pocket, I carefully push some of the dresses aside so that I can squeeze through. When I open the armoire, I find myself in a bedroom similar to my own, with a main sleeping area and a smaller antechamber, except her rooms are draped in red and gold, the Fire Kingdom's colors.

The croquet game will probably take at least another hour, but on the off chance Princess Tori's lady's maid walks in, I want to get this done as quickly as possible. I start by checking the trunk at the end of her bed, considering that's where I've been hiding the items in my own rooms. Her trunk is littered with books and sentimental objects like miniature portraits of her family members and childhood mementos. There are also hair and jewelry accessories and some blankets. Nothing that pegs her as the assassin.

I check under her bed and the love seat in her antechamber, then inside the two nightstands and small writing desk in the corner, hoping for any incriminating evidence, but I come up empty. The only thing I find is a letter she hasn't yet sent to her mother, overflowing with how amazing the prince is, how wonderful the palace is, and how she's sure he's going to pick her to be his bride.

In other words, complete lies.

But something is a little off. When I overheard Primrose, she made it sound like it was Tori's parents who ordered her to do something. If that something was kill the prince, why would Tori be sending such flowery and complimentary letters about the prince back to them? Maybe the letters are coded?

I go to her vanity next, and as I'm looking through her makeup, I come across the small hand mirror I spotted the day of the picnic. With hardly a thought, I tuck the prize in my purse and keep searching, a feeling of satisfaction settling over me.

Once I've checked the obvious places, I move on to the unlikely ones: the fireplace, inside the flower vases, behind the drapery . . . and still come up empty. I stand in the middle of her antechamber, my hands on my hips, and huff in frustration. At the very least, I thought I'd be able to find a weapon of some sort, or perhaps some poison vials, but my search so far hasn't turned up a single useful thing.

A bolt of fear shoots through me when the door handle rattles. Thinking quickly, I slip behind the thick curtains right before the door swings open. I squeeze my eyes shut and hold my breath as someone pours into the room in a fit of giggles. I pray that whoever it is doesn't notice the slight lump in the curtains.

More giggles sound on the other side of the fabric, followed by hushed whispers. I cock my head, my eyebrows drawing together as I try to decipher what's going on out there. Their voices muffle and I can only hear heavy breathing, realizing with a start that they are kissing.

Did the maid bring a male with her, hoping to have a tryst in her mistress's room while she's out today? That's beyond risky, bordering on stupidity. The maid should know better. More than just her position is at stake if she gets caught.

"My love," a male voice says. "Forget this charade and run away with me."

Charade? What charade?

There's a sigh. "You know I would, but my parents . . . they'd never forgive me."

I try to smother my gasp but only half succeed.

That's not Princess Tori's maid. That *is* Princess Tori.

The couple falls silent, and I put a hand over my mouth and hold my breath to keep from making noise.

"Did you hear that?" Tori asks.

"It was nothing. Probably someone passing in the corridor," the male says, and relief floods my chest.

They start talking in low tones again between kisses, but I only pick up words here and there. Eventually, I can tell by the direction of their voices that they've moved to Princess Tori's bedroom. I don't hear the door click shut, but I think they've at least partially closed it, as I hear the squeak of hinges.

The door out of Princess Tori's chamber is just a few feet to my right. Every second I stay here is another second I might get caught. But is it too big of a risk to try for the door? I don't know.

Ever so carefully, I shift to the side and peek out from behind the curtains. I was right; the door to Tori's bedroom is mostly closed but not fully latched. I can't see anything through the crack in the doorway, but I can hear her giggle in the other room.

The exit is *right there*, so I decide to go for it.

I tiptoe out from behind the curtains, stepping carefully to keep quiet.

My hand is on the knob and the door is open a few inches when the door to Princess Tori's bedroom squeaks behind me. There's a gasp, and I freeze.

"Princess Greer?"

Spinning, I find Tori standing in her bedroom doorway. Fully dressed, thankfully, but her hair is askew, and a bit of lipstick is smeared on her bottom lip. Her eyes are wide as she stares at me, at a loss for words.

"Oh, I, ah . . ."

The fae with her steps into view, his cravat untied and hair mussed, and he freezes as well. His startled gaze bounces between me and Tori, a look of horror on his face. Recognition hits me, and I realize it's the same guard Tori was arguing with during the opening ball. The pieces all fall into place. Princess Tori isn't our assassin; she's having a secret love affair with this guard.

I almost laugh with the realization, but I'm still in a precarious position. My mind scrambles for some explanation to give her as to what I'm doing in her room.

"I was just coming to see if you were going to rejoin us and, um . . ." My gaze shifts to the guard. "When I realized you were busy, I tried to leave," I explain, trying to make her believe the false narrative.

Princess Tori rushes me. I quickly shift to the side, ready to protect myself, but she only slams the door shut again and then takes my hands in between hers.

"Please," she begs, gripping my hands so tightly my fingers start to go numb. "You can't tell anyone. The scandal. I'd be disowned." She glances over her shoulder at the guard. "And Roland would be punished. You mustn't tell anyone."

I realize then that no matter how bad it looks that she caught me in her room, it's far worse for her if I let the prince, or really anyone else in the palace, know about her and Roland.

"I—" I start, but Princess Tori cuts me off.

"I love him," she says, and I see Roland's gaze soften as he watches her.

"If so, why are you still here?" I ask, genuinely confused. "Can't you just talk to the prince and explain that you aren't interested in marrying him?"

Horror fills her light green gaze, and she shakes her head. Her grip on my hands gets impossibly tighter, making me wince.

"There's no way I can do that," she all but wails. Tears well in her eyes. "I would dishonor my family and my kingdom."

"But what if the prince picks you?"

"He won't. I know he won't. He's only keeping me here because our kingdoms have a strong trade agreement. It's political, nothing more."

"And it gives me time to figure out how to support Tori and myself at the end of the season," Roland says, speaking for the first time. Stepping forward, he slips a hand around Princess Tori's waist, and she practically melts.

She finally, *finally*, lets go of my hands in order to fall into his embrace. I have to open and close my fingers to get feeling back.

"We're in love," Roland says, looking over Princess Tori's head at me. "We don't yet know what we are going to do, but we're going to figure it out. I refuse to live without her."

Princess Tori lifts her tearstained face to him. "I feel the same way," she says, her smile wobbly but sincere.

They look so wrapped up in each other again, I consider leaving while they are distracted. The moment I take a step, both their heads swing to me.

"You'll keep our secret, right, Greer?" Tori's eyes are filled with hope when she looks at me. Roland, however, looks like he's bracing himself.

I nod. "Yes, of course. I won't tell anyone."

A huge smile breaks over her face. "Thank you. Thank you so much. And I'll do anything for you. I know so much about Prince Dryden. I can help you in your pursuit if you'd like. I noticed you've been hanging back, making yourself somewhat of a mystery to him. It's not a strategy I would have tried, but I think it's working. I've caught the prince staring at you more than once. I'm convinced that at the very least, he's intrigued."

"Well, that's nice," I say awkwardly, not knowing what else to say. "For now, should we both return to the game so we don't drum up any more suspicion?"

"Oh, yes." She nods.

"You might want to . . ." I say, gesturing toward her hair.

She reaches up and pats her head lightly. Realizing she's a bit disheveled, her face turns a light shade of pink. "Yes, yes. Of course. I may need a few minutes. Oh, and your dress is soiled," she says, her gaze fixed on my dirty skirts.

"Right, I tripped. I should get cleaned up as well. I'll see you out there," I say, then flee without waiting for her to agree.

It takes less than a minute for me to reach my room. I burst inside, slamming the door behind me and leaning back up against it. I shake my head. Of all the scenarios I ran through, I never would have imagined the one that just unfolded.

With a nervous chuckle, I go to my own armoire. After checking the back for a false door—just in case—and finding none, I store the book of maps, the lumestra stone, and Tori's mirror in my trunk. Before I replace the hidden panel, the book Neo let me take from the pub catches my eye. I run my fingers over the black leather cover, which for a moment I think feels warm to the touch, but then the sensation passes.

I shake my head, telling myself it was nothing, and quickly change dresses and then rejoin the tributes. By the time I return, Princess Tori is already there. She catches my eye and gives me another thankful smile, to which I nod. Princess Primrose catches our silent exchange and scowls.

Without bothering to grab a mallet, I go over to Shayla, who's in a small group with Princesses Willow and Soraya. Apparently, they're doing so poorly that they've given up playing, opting to sit and watch the rest of the game instead.

Princess Shayla welcomes me back with a warm smile, asking how I'm feeling. I let her know that my headache has passed and fall into an easy conversation with the three of them.

Today didn't turn out at all like I'd expected, but at least a couple of good things came out of my misadventures. I can cross Princess Tori off my list, and I think, surprisingly, I just made myself an ally.

Chapter 20

I CAN'T SLEEP.

I punch my pillow like it's to blame, then roll over for what feels like the millionth time.

"It's too quiet," I grumble, shifting again, searching for that one perfect position that'll finally lull me to sleep—if it even exists.

I force myself to stay in bed, stubbornly keeping my eyes closed and my body still, even though I know it's useless. My mind is as active as if it were midday instead of the middle of the night.

Another handful of minutes crawls by at the pace of a lame tortoise before I finally snap.

With a grunt of frustration, I throw off the covers and sit up, mumbling obscenities as I slide from the bed and fumble around my nightstand for the tinderbox to light my bedside candle. A particularly foul curse slips from my lips as, in my agitation, I knock the candle to the floor.

Abandoning the tinderbox and candle, I feel my way to the foot of my bed. A dim flicker from the dying embers in the hearth in my antechamber barely lights my way, and I slam my toe into the trunk at the foot of my bed, swallowing the fresh string of curses that rise in my throat.

Breathing through my nose, I wait for the sharp pain to fade as I sink to my knees, splaying my hands across the smooth wood of my trunk and focusing on the items inside that are truly to blame for my sleeplessness.

Ever since I laid my head down this evening, my secret treasures have called to me. Softly scratching at the edges of my mind, persistently refusing to be ignored. One item in particular hasn't given me rest since the moment I brushed my fingers over it earlier in the day.

The black leather-bound book.

For weeks, it sat unnoticed, all but forgotten in my room at Autumnburn Manor, then hidden away in my trunk here at the palace. But as if I'd awakened it through touch earlier, it remained at the periphery of my thoughts throughout the day and clawed its way to the forefront at night. Knocking. Insistently. And I know, with a bone-deep certainty, I won't get a moment of sleep until I answer its call.

But that doesn't mean I'm happy about it.

With a huff, I throw open the trunk and dig through the blankets. Once I reach the false bottom, I remove the panel and feel around for the smooth lumestra stone, curling it into my palm the moment I find it. Just like every time before, the stone slowly warms up, casting a gentle glow until it reaches the brightness I desire.

I resist the muted lure of the other treasures and reach for the book that's taken over my thoughts. Turning it in my hands, I sit back on my heels, wondering what mysteries the deceptively innocuous thing might hold.

I finally crack open the cover for the first time since grabbing the book in the pub, and flip to the first page. There are no words, only a drawing. The ink is faded, the lines so faint I can barely make out the image. It could be a sigil or a constellation. I can't quite tell, but there's something about it that makes me pause.

Whatever it is, it seems important. Purposeful. As if it were meant to be understood by those who knew how to look.

The parchment beneath my fingers is rough and thick as I carefully flip through the pages. It reminds me of the unicorn skin of my indenture contract, which causes a shiver to run down my spine. This book doesn't just contain history. It *is* history.

I catch writing on some of the pages. The script itself is ornate and flowing, every letter a delicate swirl of ink that looks more like art than language. Beautiful, but completely indecipherable to me.

The mysterious book is written in Faelith, a language very few, if any, living still know how to read, let alone interpret. As the first fae dialect, the words themselves were said to hold a touch of magic. And when magic began to fade in Vaeloria, so did Faelith, slowly disappearing from the culture and the minds of the fae like mist in the morning sun.

I skim through a few more pages, stopping on a ghostly sketch of creatures in battle, their snarling muzzles and elongated claws captured mid-motion. Fae are scattered throughout the scene, seemingly fighting on both sides. Some aiding the beasts with claws, others standing beside their fanged enemies.

The air feels heavier as I will the lumestra stone to brighten, its glow casting sharper light over the illustration as I study it more closely. My fingertips tingle where they graze the parchment. I know it's probably just nerves or my overactive imagination, but it feels as though the book is watching. Waiting. Calling.

Beneath the drawing is a line of Faelith text I originally mistook for decorative borderwork. I squint, studying the unfamiliar script. The swirls and sharp angles blur together, but something about the arrangement tugs at the edges of my understanding. It doesn't make sense—I can't read Faelith. And yet . . .

My lips part of their own accord, and before I can stop myself, I whisper foreign words aloud. The syllables feel strange in my mouth, like they don't quite belong, but still they slide off my tongue with surprising ease.

The moment the last word leaves my lips, the temperature in the room drops. A strange pressure builds behind my eyes, and the room around me vanishes.

I gasp as my bare feet land on icy ground, the shock of it stabbing up my legs. I'm no longer sitting in my bedchamber, but rather standing in the middle of an open field.

I stagger back, but there's nowhere to escape. Cold wind bites at my exposed skin, ripping through the thin fabric of my nightgown. And all around me, war rages between two monstrous factions.

One side moves in blurs of motion, pale figures with glowing eyes and extended fangs that flash with every snarl. Some fight barehanded, tearing into opponents with terrifying speed, while others wield elegant, dark-hilted swords that slice through them with deadly precision. Blood stains their mouths like war paint across their cheeks and chins.

On the other side, twisted, half-shifted beings growl and snap, their yellow eyes glowing like embers, claws glinting in the moonlight. Patches of coarse fur streak their arms and bare torsos, and their faces stretch into wolfish shapes without fully transforming. Their movements are jerky and primal, their bodies barely containing the raw power within.

Otherworlders.

The clash of steel and claws rings out in deafening bursts. Screams, some raw and animalistic, others tinged with anguish, pierce the air and mingle with the wet, meaty *thud* of bodies colliding.

And amid the chaos, fae are everywhere.

Their magic crackles like lightning, sizzling through the air before detonating in bursts of flame or ice. Some wield glowing weapons, blades trailing fire or pulsing with light. Others hurl elemental magic across the battlefield, arcs of lightning, vines that lash like whips, and shards of crystal spinning like blades. They fight on both sides, their allegiance split between the two factions of otherworlders.

My chest tightens as I take it all in, frozen in terror, yet awestruck. I never imagined magic could be so fierce, so beautiful, so devastating. This is power unbridled. Raw and ancient.

A gust of wind kicks up, and the stench is overwhelming. Ironrich blood, singed hair, damp earth, and the animal musk of sweat and fur fill my nostrils. I try to move, to back away, but the battle stretches in every direction.

A half-shifted creature barrels straight through me, leaving only a rush of wind and the lingering heat of its body in its wake. I stagger, my heart thundering, the ground cold and wet beneath my feet.

But as I'm forced to watch the scene unfold around me, a different kind of horror starts to settle within me.

There is something off about the way the fae move. The way they look. Their strikes are fierce, but they lack the conviction of warriors fighting for something they believe in. Their eyes—when not trained on a target—betray something else entirely. Resignation. Desperation.

I spot the faint glint of glowing iron shackles at the ankles of some. Others bear scorched brands above their collars, just visible through the grime and blood. And it hits me . . .

They are not here of their own volition.

They have been forced into this war, controlled by the very otherworlders they fight beside.

Suddenly, the violence feels even crueler. The magic crackling through the air, the blades carving through flesh, the fire and ice and blood. It is all being wielded by those who aren't given a choice.

The ground lurches beneath me, and in the blink of an eye, the battlefield is gone.

The cold, blood-soaked earth vanishes, replaced by the solid, rug-covered floor of my bedchamber.

A strangled breath escapes me at the abrupt return, leaving me dazed and queasy. The lumestra stone slips from my fingers, clattering to the floor beside the book I must have dropped as well.

My stomach twists, nausea hitting before I can even process the return to reality. I fumble through the dark until my hands find the edge of the chamber pot and I retch violently, emptying what little is in my stomach, the image of shackled fae and blood-slicked weapons still burned behind my eyes.

When the heaving stops, I sink back on my heels, trembling, my nightgown clinging to my clammy skin. My gaze drifts to the leather-bound book, its cover seeming darker now, as though it absorbed the weight of what it just showed me.

That's the real reason why the fae retreated to Vaeloria. Why we turned our backs on the otherworlders. Not out of cowardice, or even to protect our lands, but because we were being used. Forced to fight wars that weren't our own.

A shudder runs through me.

I've never been more thankful for the ember crystal's barrier. For the magic that keeps Vaeloria safe and separate.

My eyes land on the book again, and a knot pulls tight beneath my ribs.

Never again.

I don't care what mysteries it holds. I am never opening that book again.

Chapter 21

PUSHING THE DISTURBING VISION OF THE BATtle to the far corners of my mind, I force myself to focus entirely on the task at hand: finding the assassin.

Over the next few days, Prince Dryden takes Princess Willow on a boat ride on the small lake in Greenbriar Park and invites Princess Soraya for a midafternoon tea in the queen's rose gardens. And last night Princess Shayla accompanied him to the opera.

Shayla stopped by my room before she left, wearing a stunning red dress that flattered her olive complexion and gray eyes. Her hair was curled and cascaded down her back in a river of black waves. She was exquisite, and I couldn't help but think she and the prince might make a striking pair. Yet after she departed, an ugly knot sat low in my gut for the rest of the evening.

Just because I haven't been spending time with the prince and the tributes in group activities doesn't mean I've been idle. Using the book of hidden passageways Neo gifted me, I managed to sneak into Princess Soraya's room when she was on her outing with Prince Dryden.

I know it's risky to enter into the princesses' bedchambers, but searching their things proves to be fruitful. In Soraya's room, I found letters back and forth from her parents coaching her on how to attract Prince Dryden and reminding her how useful an alliance with his kingdom would be. If they're pushing their daughter so hard to win the prince's heart, I feel confident that they wouldn't want harm to befall him, and I mentally cross her off my list.

I also attempted to check Princess Primrose's bedchamber, but just before I popped open the mirror that hid the secret door, I heard voices within the room. I don't know if it's simply because I don't like Princess Primrose or not, but she's the one who I'm most suspicious about.

Today, all the remaining tributes are getting together to have a luncheon hosted by the dowager queen, King Darius and Prince Dryden's mother. I was surprised when the luncheon was announced, considering the dowager has hardly been seen since her husband, King Drake, passed. I've yet to even see Queen Teresa in passing since the courting season began.

As a group, we are escorted to the wing of Whitespire where the royal family lives. The queen's receiving room is, like everything else in Whitespire, exquisite. The ivory walls are decorated with hand-carved gold filigree. A crystal chandelier hangs from the middle of the two-story ceiling, casting rainbows around the space. Delicate settees and chairs are placed strategically around the room to allow for small group conversation. Along the back wall, a table draped with a cream tablecloth is set up with food for our luncheon—a pleasant array of finger sandwiches, fresh fruit, salads, and tea cakes.

The queen, however, is nowhere to be seen.

Shayla comes up next to me, looping her arm through mine. "And how are we this fine day?"

I glance over at her, wondering if the smile on her face and the pep in her step have anything to do with her outing with the prince the night before. From the very first day, she said she wasn't interested in Prince Dryden, but that all could have just been an act, or spending time with him could have changed her mind.

"I'm doing well," I answer, then ask with a smirk, "How was your evening?"

Shayla rolls her eyes. "A bore, if you must know."

I raise my eyebrows. I was not expecting that. "You didn't enjoy the opera?"

Shayla scrunches her nose. "I could barely keep my eyes open. I almost fell out of my chair once when the singer hit a particularly high note. I was half asleep and she startled me awake."

An unexpected laugh bursts out of me, drawing the eyes of more than one of the tributes. "Well, what about the prince's company? The other tributes have done nothing but gush about how well-spoken and attentive he is on their outings."

Shayla sighs. "He was cordial enough. The opera doesn't leave much time for chitchat, though. We mostly just sat next to each other in silence." We find a pair of seats by the window and settle into them. Then Shayla goes on: "I'll be the first to admit that Prince Dryden is pretty to look at. But he always seems distracted. Like he's saying and doing all the right things but is only half there. Haven't you noticed that as well?"

"Honestly, I've had very little interaction with the prince," I admit. "The few short conversations we've had haven't been particularly deep."

By design.

I've avoided him since he caught me spying on Princesses Primrose and Tori, knowing more interaction would only make it likelier that I'll be sent away early. But I am increasingly unsettled by the way his gaze lingers during group events. I can never tell what the prince is thinking, and I fear he sees through me. If he pierces the façade Olette and Neo helped me build, I won't just be sent from the palace. My life could be at risk.

But even though I've done my best to avoid the prince, I understand what she's talking about. The smiles he puts on never seem to reach his eyes, and for a prince who is considered roguish, he has been surprisingly reserved.

Shayla shrugs and I smile on the inside, loving how she's the one princess who doesn't seem to care about sticking to the rules of how a princess should behave. If she wants to shrug, she shrugs. She unapologetically speaks her mind and treats the staff the same as she does royalty. She's impossible not to like.

"I'm just saying he's difficult to get to know." Another shrug. "Perhaps that doesn't matter in the end. Marriage to a royal is more transactional than romantic. But I would have preferred he took me shopping instead of to the opera. At least then I would have some pretty items to show for my time."

"You're incorrigible," I say with a smirk.

"I should hope so," she answers, and we share a light laugh.

A footman offers us both a glass of punch that we accept and thank him for. I glance around the room as I take a sip. Taking a quick head count, I realize we're one tribute shy. "Princess Octavia isn't here."

Shayla scans the room. "You're right. She isn't. Do you think she's the most recent to be sent home?"

Feeling rebellious, I shrug too.

Every time a princess is sent home, it's one fewer I have to worry about. With any luck, the prince will accidentally send the assassin home, and the courting season will just pass without a hitch as it always should have.

"Queen Teresa of the Ember Kingdom," a footman announces loudly. The tributes, Shayla and myself included, stand and turn toward the doors on the far side of the room.

They open slowly to reveal a stately older female in a voluminous mauve silk gown. Her black-and-white-streaked hair is piled high on top of her head, and she's dripping in jewels.

Queen Teresa stops in the middle of the room and glances at the tributes before her. Even if it weren't for her dark hair and green eyes, I would have immediately noticed the resemblance to her sister, Lady Greyblossom. But where I'm used to warmth and a touch of mischief in Olette's gaze, there's only lingering sadness in the queen's.

"Thank you for coming," Queen Teresa starts. "Not only to this luncheon event, but also for leaving your kingdoms and traveling to our own for this courting season. We are humbled by your presence, and I truly hope you've all enjoyed your time in the Ember Kingdom so far."

Never the one to miss an opportunity, Princess Primrose steps forward, dropping into a low curtsy. "On behalf of all the tributes, it's our honor to be here," she says, her voice full of false reverence.

Out of my peripheral vision, I catch Shayla rolling her eyes.

Princess Primrose straightens and starts a conversation with the queen. A few more of the tributes drift over to them to meet Prince Dryden's mother, no doubt hoping to make a good impression.

Princess Tori comes up beside me and whispers in my ear, "The queen's favorite dessert is chocolate wyldberry mousse, and she has a special fondness for stringed instruments."

When I glance over at her, she smiles at me conspiratorially. She's trying to help me, either out of appreciation for me keeping her secret, or fear that I won't. I give her a grateful smile and she drifts over to the buffet table and starts placing items on her plate.

"What did she want?" Shayla asks.

"Nothing important," I answer with a polite smile, hoping she doesn't press the issue. "Should we go introduce ourselves to the dowager?"

Shayla sighs dramatically. "If we must."

I loop my arm through hers, pulling her with me. "That's the spirit."

A small crowd of tributes rings the queen, so Shayla and I have to wait a few minutes before we get the opportunity to speak with her. I have to bite my lip to keep from laughing at all the praise they are raining down on her.

"Your gown is exquisite. Is it made from the Silk Kingdom's famous fabric?"

"Whitespire is the most magical palace I've ever visited."

"That is the perfect shade of purple for your complexion. Just perfection!"

"These peach and juniper scones are the most delicious. I must talk to the cook to get the recipe."

I remind myself to be kind. These princesses are only trying to make a good impression. But even so, I have to cover a giggle with a small cough when Princess Willow announces to the queen that she had a dream last night that she and Dryden had four children with black curly hair.

The queen herself seems to struggle to keep a straight face as well, telling Princess Willow "How nice," before turning to someone else.

Finally, the last few tributes in front of us drift off to get refreshments, and the queen moves her attention to Shayla and me. We both dip into a small curtsy, but when I drop my gaze, it snags on a charm of a dragon with a red ruby clutched in its clawed feet hanging from an elegant chain wrapped around her waist.

I didn't notice the bauble when she first came in; it was on the other side of her body. But now that I'm almost nose-to-nose with it, I can't take my eyes off it. And not just because it's beautifully crafted, which it is, but because a familiar itch and twitch starts in my fingers and runs up my arms.

I want that charm. I need it.

Shayla nudges me with her elbow, and I realize she's already risen while I'm still stooped. I straighten quickly, ripping my gaze from the bauble hanging from the decorative chain at the queen's waist.

Shayla and Queen Teresa are staring at me expectantly. Shayla must have already introduced herself, and so I say, "I'm Princess Greer of the Glacier Kingdom. It's truly an honor to meet you, Your Majesty."

Something sparks in Queen Teresa's eyes when I tell her who I am, giving them a little life that wasn't there a moment before. "Princess Greer," the queen says, and I force my eyes to stay on her face rather than dropping to the dragon charm hanging at her side. "I've heard a bit about you already." The smile that curves her mouth tells me what she's heard amuses her in some way, although I can't fathom what she's talking about.

My confusion must show on my face, because the queen laughs lightly. "Don't worry, my son hasn't confided in me about any of the tributes. He tends to know his own mind. But I heard about your performance at the opening ball and have been curious to meet you ever since."

A blush rises to my cheeks. That evening was filled with embarrassing moments for me.

"You're as lovely as I've been told," she says graciously, then turns to Shayla. "You both are."

Shayla dips her head in acknowledgment and thanks the queen, who then asks after Shayla's parents, who apparently the queen is acquainted with. As they fall into an easy conversation, my gaze drifts back to the dragon charm and the red jewel that winks up at me.

My mind goes a little fuzzy, and without realizing it, I note where the charm's clasped to the chain and how to quickly remove it. I could easily take it and slip it into a pocket. The queen wouldn't feel a thing, but I'm coherent enough to realize that there are eyes all around us, most of them directed at the queen.

There's a crash, and the queen and the rest of the room glance over to see that Princess Willow has knocked over her plate. Without thought for the consequences, I quickly and easily detach the charm and slide it into my pocket before the queen has even turned back to Shayla and me.

Tears well in Willow's large blue eyes as several footmen rush over to clean up the mess she made.

"Please excuse me," the queen says, turning back to Shayla and me. "I should go let the poor dear know it's no problem."

"Yes, of course," Shayla says, and I nod in agreement.

With a kind smile, the queen goes over to Willow, ducking her head to address the princess quietly. Willow gives Queen Teresa a wobbly smile and swipes at a tear that's escaped. A swell of guilt rises in me as I watch the queen give Princess Willow a small hug.

What have I just done?

I can't do this. I can't steal something that belongs to the queen. Perhaps the charm is just one of many baubles she has in her collection, but what if it has sentimental value? She's lost so much already, and even though everything in me wants to squeeze the dragon in my hand and make a run for it, I force myself to take slow, measured steps toward Queen Teresa. I won't let my compulsion rule me anymore. I'm not the same person I was two months ago. I don't want to steal.

Just before I reach the queen, I sink to my knees, pretending to pick something off the ground when I'm really pulling the charm out of my pocket.

"Oh dear," Queen Teresa says, turning toward me. "Are you all right?"

I rise, holding the dragon in my open palm. My hand trembles a little, but I hope she doesn't notice. "I think this must have fallen off you, Your Majesty."

Queen Teresa lets out a small gasp, her hand going to the spot where her charm was hanging from the chain. "Why, yes. That is mine."

She reaches forward to take it from me, and I lock up to keep from wrapping my fingers around the piece of jewelry and shoving it back in my pocket. Sweat dampens my skin with the effort to control myself. It's physically painful when the queen grabs it and hands it to one of the footmen, asking him to bring it to the royal jeweler to check the clasp.

I can't look away from the footman who has the charm clasped in his hand until he reaches the door. There, my eyes connect with Prince Dryden's cunning gaze instead.

How long has he been standing there? What did he see?

He's frowning, and his gaze is calculated, like he knows I took the charm to begin with. A spear of fear pierces my chest, driving straight into my heart.

If Prince Dryden realizes I've tried to steal from his mother, the whole façade about me being Princess Greer could start to unravel. What princess would also be a thief?

"Thank you so much, Princess Greer," Queen Teresa says, and I snap my gaze back to her. "King Drake gave that to me after Dryden was born. It's dear to me. I would have been very upset to have lost it."

I nod, not able to form words; part of my mind is still on the charm, the other part is filled with fear that Prince Dryden knows I tried to take it.

Reaching forward, Queen Teresa lays a hand on my shoulder. "Are you all right? You look flushed."

"Oh, oh, yes," I say, finally pulling myself together. "I do feel very warm, though. Perhaps I should go back to my room and lie down?"

Queen Teresa looks worried for me. "Yes, I think you should." She turns to one of the footmen and asks him to have a selection of the luncheon foods delivered to my room for me when I finish a rest.

I give the queen a wobbly smile and tell her how lovely it was to meet her, and then head straight for the door—where Prince Dryden is, unfortunately, still standing.

"Leaving so soon?" he asks as I near.

I force a pleasant smile. "I hate to miss the rest of the luncheon, but I'm afraid I'm not feeling quite myself." I start to pass him, but he turns with me.

"Allow me to see you to your room," he says, falling in step with me.

Glancing over my shoulder, I catch more than one of the tributes frowning in our direction. "Oh no, I couldn't ask that of you."

"You didn't," he says. "I offered."

"Truly, I'm fine on my own."

"I do get that impression, but I feel compelled just the same."

My stomach drops. Does he want to get me alone to ask about the dragon charm? Or are his intentions, as he says, to see me safely to my room?

A nervous energy shoots through me, and when I peer at Prince Dryden, he's studying me. Is that disappointment I read in his eyes?

"How are you finding the weather here?" he asks as we travel down the hallway.

I blink over at him. "You want to know how I feel about the weather?"

The prince looks back at me with a neutral expression on his face, not a hint of the calculation I saw there only moments before.

He nods. "Yes. It's my understanding that it's snowy most of the year up in the Glacier Kingdom. I'm curious to know if you miss the chill, or if you are enjoying our milder weather."

In truth, I've never even seen snow before. The Ember Kingdom does have four seasons, but the temperature doesn't shift much here in Everlight. The mountain region near our northern border sees more severe climate changes with each of the seasons, getting snow in the winter and flowers in the warmer months.

"I find the weather here very pleasant," I say with a smile, counting the steps until we reach my room. I just need to get down two more long corridors without saying anything I shouldn't.

"Do you prefer one over the other?"

Why are we still talking about this? Is the real Princess Greer known to have a particular fondness or hatred for the snow and cold weather? I'm not sure. "They both have their pluses and minuses," I answer impartially.

Prince Dryden opens his mouth, and to stop the inquisition over my climate preferences, I quickly speak up: "Did you enjoy the opera last night?"

"You want to know about my time with one of the other tributes?" he asks, sounding amused.

"Well, um . . . I've become rather close to Princess Shayla, and she said she had a marvelous time," I lie, and from the look on Prince Dryden's face, I think he knows it.

"Did she, now?"

I nod. "I'm sure all the princesses have had a wonderful time with you."

He lets out a self-deprecating half laugh. "I think you give me far too much credit."

Probably, I think, but instead say, "Oh no. Every tribute has gushed about how . . . how . . ."

Dryden stares at me expectantly as I fumble over my words, my mind going suddenly blank.

"How articulate you are."

Did I really just say that?

The prince's eyebrows shoot up. "Articulate?"

"I mean to say they've all expressed how much they've enjoyed the time they've gotten to spend with you. And how thoughtful and attentive you've been to them."

"Hmm," is all he says, and because I'm nervous, I keep babbling on.

"Like for instance, I'm sure you heard how homesick Princess Soraya has been, so you made a point to serve her favorite tea from the Spice Kingdom during your outing in the rose garden, which must have made her feel that much more at ease. Very thoughtful and attentive. And given how often Princess Willow talks about her love for the flowing rivers in her kingdom, I imagine that's what inspired you to take her on a boat ride at the park."

What am I even saying at this point?

Prince Dryden cocks his head, his intelligent gaze seeing much more than I want him to. "You seem to know quite a bit about your fellow tributes. If I didn't know any better, Lady Stormfeather, I'd say you were more interested in them than you are in me."

I laugh lightly, hoping it doesn't sound forced. "What a silly notion. The other princesses are, for all intents and purposes, my competition. Whyever would I be more interested in them than in you?"

He arches one eyebrow. "Why indeed?"

I swallow, wetting my dry throat as nerves start to bubble in my gut.

"You view this courting season as a competition with me as the prize, then?" he asks, catching me off guard. This is a dangerous topic of conversation. The prince may very well view that as an insult. I wish I'd never brought that word up.

"Well, of course not," I say, trying to backpedal.

"So you don't consider me a prize?" he asks, his eyebrows rising.

"Oh no. That's not what I mean. What I mean to say is that—"

"This is just a competition for you to win, that you don't actually want to marry me." He fills in the blanks for me.

"I, ah . . ." We've finally reached my rooms, and I'm utterly tongue-tied.

The prince waits patiently for me to answer, and I can't tell if he's angry or not, but I know I've botched this conversation.

The only way to recover is with a little touch of honesty for a change. "I think, Your Highness, that it's no secret an alliance with your kingdom would be advantageous for any of the tributes, myself included. And because of that, it's going to be difficult for you to get to know any of us beyond the surface, which is a disservice to everyone involved. But regardless of what you might think of me, I truly do hope that whoever you pick as your bride is not only for the good of your kingdom but for you as well."

He cocks his head, and a thick lock of hair falls over one eye. "I think you just might mean that."

"I do. If I've learned anything from being a princess, it's that sometimes we have to do what needs to be done to steal a little bit of happiness for ourselves."

A shadow seems to cross Prince Dryden's face, and I could kick myself for using the word *steal*.

"Well, thank you for walking me back to my room. Very gallant of you," I say. I'm starting to turn when his voice halts me.

"A word of caution, Lady Stormfeather. The palace is filled with eyes, and not much goes unnoticed." His gaze drops to my skirts, roughly where my side pocket is, and then rises back to my face. When I look at him, there's a darkness in his eyes. Anger brews in the depths.

There's no doubt about it. He saw what I did. And he's furious.

Blood rushes to my head so quickly that I sway a little. Prince Dryden's arm shoots out to steady me.

"I would take care if I were you." He lets go, his eyes never warming. "I look forward to seeing you at dinner tonight," he says, his cordial words at odds with the hardness of his face and the ice in his voice.

With that, he turns on a heel and strides back the way we came, his spine straight and his long steps determined. I watch him until he turns the corner, then I throw my door open and flee into my room.

Chapter 22

I LEAN BACK AGAINST THE DOOR, MY HEART BEATing like I've just run through the streets of Everlight with watchmen on my tail.

This is bad. So very bad.

I go back and forth for a few minutes about whether or not I should pull the plug on this whole thing—send Eilowyn back to Autumnburn Manor asking for my violet dress and then wait for someone to whisk me from the palace. But I manage to talk myself off the ledge.

Prince Dryden might have seen what I did, but he isn't going to throw a princess into the dungeon for having sticky fingers. At least . . . I don't think he will.

I can't assume that he's going to figure out I'm a fraud from this—maybe I'm just a princess with a bad habit—but in my heart I don't really believe that. Something in Prince Dryden's gaze said he knew more than I wanted him to, but I just don't know what.

There is one thing I know for sure: I need to talk to Neo.

Shoving away from the door, I rush to the small writing desk in the corner of the antechamber. My hands are shaking so badly I fumble when I pull out an inkpot and quill, almost dumping ink onto the paper and the rest of the desk. Closing my eyes, I breathe in for five counts, then breathe out for five counts. I can't lose my head now.

Sitting down, I scribble out a coded note to Olette, telling her that I think I might have been compromised and that I need to meet. I seal the letter with the Glacier Kingdom insignia and then call for Eilowyn. By the time she arrives, I've been able to compose myself, at least outwardly. I let her know that I need the letter delivered to Lady Greyblossom today and then I sit back and wait, hoping a messenger will return with news quickly.

I spend the rest of the afternoon and early evening hiding in my room until it's time for another awkward and dreaded dinner with Prince Dryden and the rest of the tributes. Shayla stops by after the luncheon to check on me, but I have Eilowyn send her away, saying I'm resting. I didn't eat a bite of the food the queen had sent to me, too nervous to get anything down, so by the time I'm dressed and ready for dinner, my stomach is sour from lack of sustenance.

I'm both ravenously hungry and unbelievably nauseous as I walk through the palace corridors to the formal dining room. My legs are shaky and I'm lightheaded, a dangerous combo when I need my wits about me. I don't know if Prince Dryden is waiting for an audience to send me home or call me out for thievery, but I can't imagine him just letting it go.

When I enter the dining room, I see that I'm the last to arrive; everyone has already been seated. Nine sets of eyes—eight tributes' and the prince's—swing to me as I stand self-consciously in the open doorway.

"Oh," I say. "I'm sorry. I didn't realize I was running late."

Prince Dryden stands from his chair, a friendly smile on his face that doesn't quite reach his eyes. "Did you not get the message that dinner was to start thirty minutes early this evening?" he asks as he tucks my hand around his elbow and leads me to the dinner table.

I shake my head.

"Well, never mind that. I've saved you a seat right next to me. We've not had much time to get to know each other."

I swallow as Prince Dryden pulls out the only empty chair, to the right of his at the head of the table. Most of the other tributes glare at me, with the exception of Shayla and Tori. The former looks a touch confused, and the latter pleased.

"Thank you," I say. "That was very kind."

Prince Dryden gives me a chilly smile that reminds me of a wolf baring its teeth, and sits.

Conversation around the dinner table takes a few minutes to start flowing. I allow the other princesses to engage with Prince Dryden as my stomach twists in knots. Servers bring out the first course, setting a watermelon and feta salad in front of every princess and the prince, except me.

I glance around, trying to figure out what is going on, when a server finally brings me a plate as well. A pungent smell wafts up from the dish in front of me. Princess Pluma to my right makes a choking sound and then puts a hand up to cover her nose.

"What *is* that?" asks Princess Meer, who's seated across from me. She leans forward to get a better look but rears back when the smell reaches her.

I stare down at the food, having no idea what it is or why I've been given it. It appears to be cubes of whitish meat, some tinged with pink, sitting on a bed of lettuce. It looks innocuous enough, but the smell is nothing short of offensive. Like a combination of sweat and urine.

"Hakarl," Prince Dryden says next to me. "A particular favorite of Lady Stormfeather's." He looks over at me. "I believe you said your mother used to make it, correct?"

It comes to me then. *Fermented shark.* I'd gotten the dish confused with another from the Glacier Kingdom and accidentally told Prince Dryden it was my favorite the first night we met.

"Yes. You have a good memory," I say with a tight smile.

Nausea roils in my gut, threatening to move higher. I know where this is going, and I'm not sure I can do it.

"Well," Prince Dryden says, an expectant look on his face. "Aren't you going to try it?"

I place a hand on my stomach. "I'm not quite feeling myself today. Hakarl is such a strong dish. I'm not sure it will agree with me this evening. Although I do appreciate your thoughtfulness."

"Nonsense," he says with a wave of his hand. "It's your favorite dish. I want to see if our chefs' skills measure up to your mother's. If not, I might have to send one of them to the Glacier Kingdom to brush up on their culinary technique."

Prince Dryden isn't going to let me out of this. From the look in his eye, he sees my discomfort, and either doesn't care or is enjoying it. There's no doubt in my mind that he saw what I did today and is making me pay. And if he's making me pay in this way, that means he knows I don't like hakarl. And if he knows I don't like rotten fermented shark, then he knows I lied. And if he knows I lied about that, what else does he know I've lied about?

I'm in trouble.

Not feeling like I have a choice, I pick up a fork and spear one of the chunks of shark flesh. The whole table has stopped what they are doing to watch me eat. Without pausing to think about what I'm about to do, I open my mouth and pop the whole cube in, forcing myself to chew while keeping my face neutral. It's one of the hardest things I've ever done, but at this point it feels like my life might be on the line, so I stop myself from gagging by sheer force of will alone.

The texture of the hakarl isn't that bad. It's akin to a piece of cheese, but the flavor is hands down the most rancid thing I've ever had the misfortune of tasting. And that's saying something, because there were days I ate rotten food that had been thrown into the back alleys behind pubs to stay alive. Both before and after I indentured myself to Sinclair.

It takes longer than it should, but I eventually manage to swallow the piece. My stomach rebels the moment it hits bottom, and I have to clamp my mouth shut and breathe through my nose to keep it from coming back up.

"So," Prince Dryden says, leaning forward with a smirk on his stupidly handsome face. "How does it compare?"

I glance at him with a forced smile, the shark having left an aftertaste of urine in my mouth. Before answering, I pick up my glass of faewine and take a delicate sip, resisting the urge to swish it around my mouth before swallowing. I can't say that the flavor of faewine and urine is much better together than it was alone, but I make sure that doesn't show on my face either.

"Delicious," I say. "But not quite as good as my mother's. The flavor is a little less potent than I'm used to, but for people not of the far north, your chefs did well."

Prince Dryden leans back in his seat, a gleam in his eye that if I didn't know better, I'd say was respect.

Spearing another chunk, I hold the fork in his direction. "Here, Your Highness. You must try some for yourself. It is one of our kingdom's delicacies, after all."

I don't believe for a moment that Prince Dryden is going to take me up on my offer, which is why I almost drop the fork when he leans forward and bites the cube of rotten shark off the end. I have to hold back a laugh as I watch him struggle to control his face as he forces himself to chew. At one point, his tanned skin takes on a greenish hue, but he powers through and swallows.

He clears his throat and then takes a hearty swig from his own glass. "Well," he says, his eyes watering, "that was, no question, the vilest thing I've ever eaten." And then he bursts out laughing as he wipes his eyes.

The tension in the dining room immediately breaks. The princesses all laugh along with him. The knot in my chest doesn't unravel, but it does loosen as Prince Dryden reaches in front of me and grabs the dish, handing it off to Princess Meer next to him.

"Here," he says. "You have to try this. It's absolutely disgusting."

Princess Meer's eyes widen. It's clear she doesn't want to but also doesn't feel like she can refuse the prince.

"It's an acquired taste," I offer. "You should hold your nose. It will help that first bite go down easier."

Princess Meer daintily holds her nose as she brings a small piece to her mouth. Squeezing her eyes shut, she takes a bite and chews only twice before swallowing. A shudder racks her frame, and the prince and other tributes all chuckle at her reaction.

She scrunches her nose and shakes her head, reaching for her wine.

"I wouldn't do that," the prince warns. "It actually makes it worse."

After that, it becomes a game; the hakarl plate is passed around the table, each tribute trying a bite and the rest of us laughing at their funny reaction. Princess Willow, the poor thing, actually gets up and runs out of the room instead of swallowing. By the time the plate reaches me again, there isn't a single piece left.

"My apologies, Lady Stormfeather," Prince Dryden says. "We've eaten the whole dish and left none for you. The shark was imported, so I'm afraid there's no more."

Thank goodness for that. I don't think I would have been able to choke down another piece. My stomach is still rebelling from the bite I did have.

"Oh, that's quite all right," I say with a pleasant smile. "It was just nice to be able to share a piece of my home with everyone."

Some warmth has returned to the prince's gaze, and it confuses me. I would have bet coin that Prince Dryden was out to unmask me, but now the look he gives me is full of a fondness that I'm not used to seeing from him. It's as if he's two different fae entirely. It has me twisted in knots and turned upside down.

It's maddening. He's maddening.

The atmosphere around the dining room table becomes quite lively. At the opposite end of the table, Tori and Shayla reenact their expressions from when they ate the hakarl, and the princesses around them howl with laughter. The first course is cleared, and the upbeat mood continues throughout the meal, as if the hakarl broke some sort of ice that had kept the tributes in check. Everyone looks to be enjoying themselves, including the prince, for once.

I do my best to play the part of an unconcerned tribute, enjoying the evening, but it's not without difficulty. I force down food, laugh lightly at the appropriate times, and spend most of the evening overanalyzing Prince Dryden's reactions. By the time the meal is over, some of the tributes convince the prince to join a game of cards, but I beg off, claiming I'm still recovering from my bout of light-headedness earlier in the day, and rush to the relative safety of my room.

I've already decided that if I don't have a letter from Olette waiting for me, I'm going to brave the hidden passageways to look for Neo and Bram myself. But I spot a sealed note with her family signet pressed into the wax seal lying on a silver letter tray the moment I enter the room. Eilowyn is there waiting to help me out of my gown and into my bedclothes, and I don't even wait for her to leave before tearing into it, my body sagging in relief when I read that Olette has arranged for me to meet with her outside the palace the next day.

Eilowyn chatters on as she helps me get ready for bed, and I respond appropriately, but even after she leaves and I climb under the covers and lie down, one thought keeps circling in my head.

I don't think I can do this anymore.

Chapter 23

"I DON'T THINK I CAN DO THIS ANYMORE."

Olette blinks back at me, not having gotten a chance to utter even a single word since I stormed into the back room of the tavern she's reserved for us.

It's almost midday, but I've been awake since before dawn. Even though Prince Dryden's behavior seemed to shift after the hakarl episode last night, I'm still convinced he suspects something. What if he starts looking into me and discovers I'm a false princess?

I pace, and Olette stands from her padded chair and comes over to me. She steps in my path to stop me and gently lays her hands on my shoulders. "Calm down, Rowan. I'm sure everything is going to be all right. Tell me what's upset you."

Her gaze is steady and clear as she looks into my eyes, but her peaceful demeanor doesn't rub off on me. If anything, her green eyes just remind me of her nephew's, and it makes my heart rate spike.

She doesn't understand. She doesn't know what it's like living in the palace day in and day out, constantly fearful you're going to be discovered as the fraud you are. Constantly worried your lies will be uncovered.

"He knows. I know he does," I say, and a pleat appears between Olette's eyebrows.

"Who knows what?" she asks.

"The prince," I all but wail. "He knows I'm not Princess Greer. Or at least he suspects something. Even if he doesn't know who I am, he's going to send me home soon."

Olette's face softens again, like she's relieved, when in fact she should be just as alarmed as I am. If I'm discovered now, they won't have a spy among the tributes anymore.

She squeezes my shoulder, then takes my hand and leads me over to the table she was seated at when I burst into the room. There's a pot of tea and three teacups set out.

"Come, sit," she says, trying to coax me into a chair, but I'm too amped up to do so. "Rowan . . . dear, I can see that you are very agitated, but I can promise you that the prince won't be an issue. Please just sit down and have some tea. It will calm you."

"Why does everyone keep telling me the prince won't be an issue?" I say, resisting the urge to stomp my foot. "Of course he's an issue. If the prince finds out I'm not actually Princess Greer, he could have my head, and there's nothing you or anyone else could do about it."

Olette looks back at me with a blank expression that I can't interpret. She opens her mouth to say something, but the door opens behind me. I glance over my shoulder to see Neo stride into the room. His presence immediately makes me feel better.

"I wasn't sure if you'd be able to get away," Olette says, going over to greet him.

He kisses her on the cheek and then gives her a lopsided smile. "I figured it out. But I shouldn't be gone for too long."

"Right," she says with a nod. Then they both look over at me.

Neo's gaze drops to where I'm wringing my hands, and guilt

flashes across his face. "Olette," he says. "Can I have a few minutes with Rowan alone?"

She raises her eyebrows; her gaze shifts between us before she says, "Of course." With an encouraging smile in my direction, she leaves the room, closing the door gently behind her.

Tension that's never existed before hangs in the air between me and Neo, heavy and unspoken. Something's off. He's visibly uncomfortable, and I can't shake the feeling that it has something to do with what happened between us in the hidden passages. I can still feel the phantom brush of his fingers against my jaw, the memory sending a shiver through me. But what if it's something he regrets?

Instead of saying anything, we just stare at each other from across the room. Finally, Neo releases a small sigh and walks over to me. "I understand that you are a little distressed right now."

"Distressed?" I let out a bitter laugh. "I'm a little more than *distressed*."

"You needn't be. I promise that everything is going to plan."

"Going to plan?" I parrot, in disbelief over what I'm hearing. "It was your plan for the prince to hate me? If so, then yes, it looks like things are going swimmingly."

Neo runs a weary hand down his face. "The prince does not hate you."

I'm a little high-strung at the moment, but I have good reason to be, and his blasé attitude is really starting to make me mad. "Yes, I can assure you he does," I say. "And I know for a fact that he's on to me. Otherwise he wouldn't have issued me a veiled threat yesterday after the queen's luncheon."

At the mention of the luncheon, something dark flicks across Neo's features, but I blink and it's gone.

"Everything is going to be fine, I promise," he says, but his placating doesn't help, and I start wringing my hands and pacing again. I can't understand why he and Olette aren't more alarmed. Am I that disposable to them?

All my hard work and weeks of training to become Princess Greer will be for nothing if the prince discovers I'm a fraud and takes my head for the deception. I really thought I was past all this self-doubt, but being in the palace is so much more intense than playing the part in front of Lady Greyblossom's house staff.

"Rowan," Neo says, irritation clear in his tone. "You need to calm down."

I stop pacing and face Neo. "Calm down? *Calm down?*" I take a few determined steps until I'm poking my finger into his chest. "You aren't the one putting your neck on the line. You aren't the one living under scrutiny from royals and tributes and palace staff almost every minute of every day. You don't know what it's like, so don't tell me to calm down."

Neo glances down at my finger and then back up at my face. "Actually, I know precisely what that's like."

I make a very unladylike sound in the back of my throat, and Neo lifts his eyebrows.

"I highly doubt that," I say. "You hide in the shadows doing all your shadowy spy things. You aren't parading in front of the entire court on a daily basis."

Neo starts laughing. Caught off guard, I do nothing but blink back at him for a few seconds before finding my voice.

"This isn't funny," I snap.

Neo rubs his mouth to control himself and then looks down at me. "You're right, it isn't . . . but also, it is." He sighs. "Can you not just take my word for it that the prince won't pose a problem?"

I stare back at him in disbelief. "No. Of course not. You don't even know what he pulled last night."

The corner of Neo's mouth jumps before he straightens it again. Did he hear about the hakarl incident?

Neo sighs again, and it makes my blood boil. I need his help right now, and he's acting like my fears are unreasonable when I know they are anything but.

"I think it's time you knew, but the question is what you're going to be angrier about: the truth or the lie."

My stomach drops at the realization that there's something big being kept from me. "What are you talking about? You aren't making any sense."

"I know," he says, and runs a hand through his hair, brushing back the light strands. He suddenly looks nervous. "Just don't scream or run."

Scream or run? I furrow my brow, confused.

"Do you promise not to do either of those things until I've had a chance to explain?"

I don't know what to say, so I just nod.

Neo goes to the door and flips the lock. I'm nervous about being in a locked room with him. I don't understand why he did that. I keep my mouth shut, waiting for him to explain his odd behavior.

Instead, he comes to stand in front of me and then closes his eyes. The air around him gets wavy, like heat from a fire. I take a half step back, not understanding what's happening as right before my eyes, Neo's features start to change and shift.

His long hair starts to shorten, like it's retracting into his skull, and darkens in color. Then his face changes—his jaw sharpens, his cheekbones move higher, his nose narrows slightly and straightens, except for a small bump on the bridge. His ears lengthen and become more pointed.

I stop breathing, not able to process or believe what I'm seeing. Am I hallucinating? Is this a dream?

But his transformation isn't complete. As the space around him still vibrates, Neo's body narrows and he grows an inch or two taller. He opens his eyes, and I gasp because I'm not looking into Neo's bright blue gaze anymore; his eyes are now green.

I stumble back and bump into the table behind me. The teapot and cups rattle, but I don't pay them any mind because the air around him starts to clear, and it's no longer Neo standing in front of me but Prince Dryden himself.

My brain clunks along slowly as I try to make sense of what just happened, but I can't. I don't understand.

Fae don't just turn into other fae. It's not possible.

"Who are you?" I ask, fear making my voice tremble. "*What* are you?"

Neo, or Dryden, or whichever fae now stands in front of me, winces at my questions, and a prick of guilt pierces my chest.

"It's still me. Neo," he clarifies, but the timbre of his voice is different from Neo's—slightly deeper and a touch more refined. He doesn't just look like Prince Dryden; he sounds like him as well.

He starts to move closer, but I throw up a hand and he halts.

"But you look like the prince. Why? And how?"

The fae runs his tongue over his bottom lip, seemingly trying to find the right words. "I'm Neo, but I'm also the prince."

I shake my head, feeling like I'm going insane. "I don't understand."

"I know," he says, a look of remorse, or even perhaps guilt, sliding over his features—a look I'm not used to seeing on the arrogant prince.

He runs a nervous hand through his hair, a gesture I've seen from Neo but not Prince Dryden. It makes my head spin. He's acting like Neo but looks and sounds like the prince. I don't know what to do with that.

"I have a very specific type of magic," he finally says. "It's called glamour. It allows me to change my physical appearance. From what we've uncovered, many fae in the Ember Kingdom once possessed this type of magic, though full transformations like mine were rare, even when magic was prevalent."

I blink back at him, trying to process his words, and a completely inappropriate giggle bubbles up in my throat. I have to slap a hand across my mouth to make it stop. He looks at me like I might be losing it, and he's probably not wrong.

Fae just can't *do* that. Yes, magic used to be part of our culture, but we no longer have the ability to wield it like we used to. The only magic that still exists is in some relics and objects, like an indenture contract or a lumestra stone. And even then, it's a watered-down version of what used to be. The magic he's claiming to have was lost centuries ago.

But I just saw him transform before my own eyes.

An image of fae using their magic in battle flashes through my mind, reminding me how powerful they once were.

"I don't understand how this is possible," I say, feeling both overwhelmed and oddly numb at the same time.

"I'm not sure how it is either," he admits with a shake of his head. Strands of dark hair fall onto his forehead. Prince Dryden usually has his hair expertly styled, and I get the strange urge to push the hair back into place. "As far as we can tell, this is magic I was born with. My mother says that when I was little, there were a few times my hair seemed to darken or lighten, but she and my father explained it away as a trick of the light. When I was eight, I changed my appearance completely. They thought someone had broken into my rooms and tried on my clothes, but it was just me."

"Which is the real you?" I ask, and I don't have to explain what I'm asking. He knows.

"This is my true form," he says, and my heart drops.

It's not that Prince Dryden isn't handsome. He is, probably even more so than Neo to the objective eye, but it feels like in an instant I've lost Neo, and that makes me confused and upset.

"This whole time, from the first moment we met, it's always been you? Crown prince of the Ember Kingdom?"

He nods, and a cold truth hits me like a punch to the gut.

If Neo is actually Dryden, then that means my life is tied to his. If the prince dies, so do I.

"You linked my fate to yours when there's an assassin stalking you? How could you not tell me this sooner when it isn't just your life on the line, but mine as well?"

He shakes his head and tries to reach for me, but I step out of range. "Rowan, I don't intend to die anytime soon."

A bitter laugh starts to choke me. "Is that supposed to reassure me?"

Death is a thief, stealing what's most precious to us without regard for our beliefs or plans for the future. Dryden may have power as a prince, but not over death.

"I promise, I won't let anything happen to you," he says with so much conviction that I almost believe him.

As I stare at Dryden, I can't keep my mind from spinning, wondering what parts of him beyond the physical are true and which are the deception. Is the male standing before me the empathetic and protective fae I know as Neo, or the distant and arrogant Prince Dryden?

Is his real personality a mixture of both, or is one of his personas a complete lie?

A memory from the night before trickles through my mind, immediately sparking my rage.

"You made me eat rotten shark flesh," I grit out, my fists clenching.

His mouth twitches. "Yes, well . . ." He rubs his mouth, trying to hide his smile. "That was perhaps too far."

"Too far? *Too. Far?*"

He puts his hands up in front of himself in a gesture of peace. "In my defense, you did try to steal from my mother. After seeing that, I was a touch angry with you, but perhaps my actions yesterday were a bit too hasty."

Too *far*? Too *hasty*?

For a whole day, I've believed I might be discovered and sentenced to death. He'd terrified me. He'd been playing with me the entire time, and for what? Because he was angry about the charm that I gave back to his mother? That's diabolical.

With a muffled scream, I grab the thing closest to me, which ends up being a teacup, and hurl it at him, my anger over his deception and the wild emotions running through me fueling my actions.

He ducks out of the way, his eyes flaring wide in surprise. But my anger isn't spent yet, and as the teacup smashes against the floor, I come at him with my fists.

I'm a good fighter, scrappy, and it's only because of his fast reaction and the fact that I get tangled in my ridiculous skirts that I don't manage to connect with his nose. My knuckles graze off his cheekbone.

I try to right myself and take another swing, but he twists me in his arms, trapping me against his chest. He holds me captive with my back pressed against his front and his strong arms banded around me, keeping my arms trapped at my sides.

I growl and try to break free, hurling insults at him that are more befitting a pirate than a princess, but he just tightens his hold on me, making it impossible to move. It takes several minutes, but eventually I tire myself out and stop thrashing.

Dryden dips his head, his warm breath fanning my neck, causing my stomach to flip. "Are you quite done?" he asks, but before I can answer, the doorknob rattles and my gaze snaps to it.

Someone tries the knob again, but he locked the door, so they can't enter.

"Is everything all right in there?" Olette asks softly. "I heard something smash."

The air around me goes warm, and Dryden's hold on me shifts. "We're all right. Just give us a few more minutes," he says, and my breath catches at hearing Neo's voice instead.

I crane to look over my shoulder and see that he's shifted into Neo. Our faces are only inches apart, and blue eyes stare back at me. It's enough of a shock to melt what remains of my anger.

"Let go," I order. "I won't attack again."

He frowns, but his arms loosen, and I quickly step out of his grasp. I feel a measure better after the physical exertion, but now that my rage is spent, hurt fills its place.

It doesn't help that he's shifted back to Neo. It's harder to be mad at him when he looks like that. As Neo, he'd managed to burrow past my shields. As much as I hate to admit it now, I liked Neo, trusted him. Feelings had started to develop, but now I feel betrayed, and I want answers.

Crossing my arms over my chest, I ask, "So you acted the way you did yesterday because you were mad at me?"

A touch of sadness creeps into Neo's gaze. "Yes, and I'm sorry. When I saw you take my mother's charm, it angered me. It was an immature way to act. But I'm very protective of my mother."

A bolt of shame and guilt spears me, and I look away from Neo. I know I did the right thing giving her the charm back, but I never should have taken it in the first place. I should be able to control my compulsion to steal. I'm embarrassed that sometimes I can't.

"I gave it back to her," I mumble.

Neo sighs. "I know. I'm sorry. I shouldn't have reacted the way I did. I just felt . . . betrayed."

I nod. Not that I condone how he treated me, but I wasn't faultless.

"Why did you look at me with such disgust the first time we met at the opening ball, before I'd even performed?" I ask, seeming to startle Neo a little.

"Disgust?" he says, his eyebrows shooting up before he lets out a short, humorless laugh. "Let me assure you, that was not the emotion I felt when I first saw you enter the ballroom that evening. But you were supposed to blend in, and in your gown, looking the way you did . . ." He blows out a breath as he runs a hand through his hair again. "Let me just say that you failed miserably at that task."

"I can't breathe or walk in the high fashion the elite of our kingdom prefer." I gesture to my skirts, reminding him of how they just tripped me up. "I thought it was clever to mix the designs of the Glacier Kingdom and the Ember Kingdom," I say defensively.

His expression softens. "It was very clever," he admits. "And for the record, you looked lovely. It just caught me off guard is all. It was either look at you with disdain, or . . ."

Or?

But he doesn't finish his sentence.

I cross my arms over my chest, not quite mollified, but the comment about me being lovely does help smooth my hackles.

"Were you expecting me to show up in a day dress and my hair down?"

"Of course not." He sighs. "This is all much more complicated than I assumed it would be."

"You assumed finding someone off the street to impersonate a princess and placing her in the palace to uncover a potential assassin, all the while pretending you were two different people, would be simple?"

Reaching up, he rubs the back of his neck. Another familiar gesture that makes my chest tighten with emotion. "I didn't exactly find you off the street."

I shoot him a look that says, "Yes, you did," and he drops his hand.

"But at the time, yes, it seemed fairly straightforward to me. I suppose I didn't think through all the possible complications."

I shake my head. Males. They can be a simple lot, even princes.

"You should have told me the truth," I say quietly. "These last couple weeks have been . . . difficult. It would have been so much less stressful if I'd known it was you all along."

Neo takes a step closer but then stops himself. "I'm sorry I didn't tell you sooner. But no one outside of my mother, my brother, Aunt Olette, and Bram knows about my magic."

And now me.

I want to stay mad, but with so few people knowing about his ability, it's a big deal that he revealed himself to me.

"Why the secrecy?"

"Magic like mine is unheard of nowadays. We don't know how the kingdom would react if they knew. They might react in fear, which could be dangerous for me. And we've been keeping this secret for so long . . ." He lifts his hands and shrugs, but I think I understand. Different isn't always accepted. "Plus, this magic has its perks. It allows me a sense of anonymity that I wouldn't otherwise have."

That also makes sense. I'm not saying they have it as hard as others, but if the last month and a half has taught me anything, it's that life as a royal comes with its difficulties. And speaking of . . .

"Aren't you supposed to be out with the tributes right now?"

I'd had to get out of one of the outings myself, faking a wardrobe emergency that required a visit Madame Larkfire to skip a trip to the royal vineyard.

Neo smirks. "The tributes were sent to the vineyard without me. They believe the prince is recovering from food poisoning from last night. I thought that would be fairly believable considering how vile that hakarl was." Neo puckers his lips and shudders.

"That was disgusting," I say, remembering how the taste of urine lingered in my mouth throughout the entire meal.

He chuckles. "I was very impressed with how well you choked it down, though. Your acting skills are second to none."

I shake my head, but a small smile sneaks through. If Neo only knew what I've forced myself to eat in order to stay alive. But even rancid meat and fruit furred with mold wasn't as disgusting as that hakarl.

"Where do we go from here?" I ask, feeling suddenly lost.

"Our goal is the same. To ferret out which of the tributes means me harm. Now you just don't have to fear that Prince Dryden is going to out you or send you home."

"That is a great relief."

He smiles, and there's a light knock on the door. Neo goes over and opens it for Olette, who slips back into the room.

"Is everything all right?" she asks.

"Yes. We've gotten the situation under control," Neo answers for the both of us.

Olette glances between us, then down at the broken cup, understanding dawning in her gaze. "You told her," she says, looking a touch surprised.

"Technically, I showed her. It wasn't fair to keep her in the dark any longer."

Olette nods, but concern tightens her features. I try not to let it hurt my feelings. I'm not Bram, and I'm not family.

"I won't tell a soul. I promise."

Olette smiles at me, the worry falling from her face. "Oh, I know, my dear. It's just . . ."

I wait for her to go on, but she just waves a hand through the air. "Never mind. Since we're all here anyway, let's use the time we have. Tell me about these princesses."

✦

I SPEND ANOTHER hour with Olette and Neo, or rather, Prince Dryden. At first, it's a struggle to concentrate on our conversation. I keep stealing glances at him, expecting him to morph right in front of me, which, of course, he never does. But I really start paying attention when he announces that he sent Princess Lakelyn home earlier that morning. He also confesses that getting his brother's approval to send princesses home was a hard-fought battle, and that there are some he's not allowed to send home early for political reasons—namely, Princesses Tori, Willow, Shayla, Meer, and Primrose. Over half the tributes are still part of the courting season, leaving myself, Soraya, and Pluma as the only ones he has the option of sending home early.

It feels strange talking about the tributes with him now, knowing that he'll be picking one of them to be his bride at the end of the courting season, but it also makes it easier to whittle down the list. I tell him how I don't believe it's Princesses Willow, Tori, or Soraya, and the reasons why. He seems particularly uncomfortable when I tell him about Soraya's scheming with her parents to snag his affection and surprised by the revelation that Tori is involved with one of his palace guards, but he promises to keep the secret.

The rest of the tributes still can't be ruled out, but we all agree our top suspects are Primrose, Meer, and Pluma, so we decide to focus our attention on them over the next week. Neo says he can take them out individually or as a group to give me time to search their rooms for clues.

On a whim, I ask about the potential otherworlder attacks, and his face turns grim. Since I saw him last, there have been two more incidents. Just like before, fae were found drained of their blood. But this time, it happened within the Ember Kingdom's borders, and so his brother has finally started taking the incidents more seriously and dispatched investigators to look into it.

Neo tells me not to worry about it, that I should keep my mind focused on both of us getting through the next couple weeks. I agree, but I don't know how to push something like this out of my mind. Drained blood sounds like a vampire attack, and the implications of that are almost too great to consider, especially after the book showed me those horrific images from the past, the way that fae were used by both the werewolves and vampires in their seemingly endless war for supremacy. The thought that we could somehow get dragged back into their feud is chilling.

"I should probably get back to the palace," Neo finally says, rising from his chair. "I already begged off the midday activity. I need to return for the ball tonight."

The Summer Eve Ball. I'd almost completely forgotten about it. It is the annual celebration that marks the changing of the season. A night of music, spectacle, and carefully calculated encounters between fae elite. Highborn, as well as tributes and the Ember Kingdom royalty, will be in attendance. Olette will be there as well. Eilowyn is probably already wondering where I am and fretting that she won't have enough time to get me ready.

Neo glances at me, and for probably the fifteenth time in the last hour, I have to remind myself that he's Prince Dryden. "You best return as well," he says. "And this time, please take it easy on my feet when we dance."

I feel heat rise to my cheeks. "My apologies," I say tartly. "My teacher wasn't very good."

Neo barks out a laugh. "Just remember not to overthink it."

Chapter 24

"I'M SORRY THAT IT'S NOT MORE INTRICATE," Eilowyn says in the mirror behind me as she wrings her hands. Her brows pull together in concern.

"Nonsense," I tell her, turning my head from side to side. My hair is mostly down in soft honey waves, but with braids crisscrossing the crown and small pale green and purple flowers tucked among the plaits. "I love it. You have a true skill."

I mean it. Eilowyn smiles shyly, pink coloring her cheeks at my praise.

I stand; layers of my skirt as light as gossamer trail behind me as I walk. The theme of the Summer Eve Ball is "enchanted garden," and the gown Madame Larkfire made for me is light and airy for a change. The sleeves are off-the-shoulder, but the sheer fabric drapes down to my fingertips. The bodice is fitted and decorated with hand-sewn lavender flowers atop a frosty green base. The drop-waist skirt is voluminous, but doesn't feel cumbersome because the layers upon layers of glossy green fabric atop the lavender underskirt are as delicate as butterfly wings.

I feel like a woodland nymph in the gown, and the knot of anxiety that usually sits heavily in my gut before an event such as this isn't there. Instead, a touch of anticipation bubbles inside. I tell myself the fluttering of butterflies in my stomach has nothing to do with eagerness to see Neo . . . er, Dryden, that evening. It's just the immense relief I'm feeling because I don't have to worry about being sent home or discovered under the prince's watchful gaze anymore. Tonight, the prince is an ally in the ballroom rather than a potential threat, and that thought makes my steps light as I hurry out of my rooms and down the corridor.

The ballroom has been completely transformed and is now almost as beautiful as the solarium, with leafy vines curling around the banisters and crawling over the curved staircases. Trailing wisterias line the walls and hang from the chandeliers. Guests walk and dance on grass rather than hardwood, and potted trees have been placed strategically throughout the room. Tea lights hang suspended over the dance floor, creating a romantic and intimate atmosphere as couples weave in and out of the trees and foliage.

Enchanted garden indeed. It's awe-inspiring.

At the far end of the room is a raised dais where King Darius sits on a throne of twisted branches and trailing flowers, talking with some of his nobility as he oversees the festivities. I barely spare him a glance. Instead, I scan the crowd, picking out the other tributes one by one the same way I'd pick marks in a crowded market.

All the tributes are wearing nature-inspired gowns, like I am. Princess Primrose wears a dress that is obviously inspired by her namesake. It looks like someone has sewn together thousands of delicate blooms to make her gown. The color starts as purple on her bodice but fades into red, pink, orange, and finally cream. All colors of primroses.

Princess Pluma is dressed in a cream gown that has vine embellishments that crawl from her skirt up the side of her dress. Red blooms dot the vines. The color is striking against her bronze skin.

Princess Meer's dress is a structured gown of various shades of metallic gold and yellow fabric, theatrical in its size and color. If she's going for drama over everything else, I'd say she accomplished it. But objectively, with her shiny brown hair slicked back into a sleek ponytail and her tanned complexion, it's somehow still flattering. She will, undoubtedly, turn heads this evening, but my mind automatically goes to what she might be hiding under the folds of her gown. Weapons, perhaps? Is tonight the night she makes a move against Prince Dryden?

The thought sends a sharper chill through my chest than it ever did before I knew Neo and the prince were one and the same. I shove the feeling aside, channeling it into focus rather than letting it shake me.

Princess Shayla's gown is by far my favorite. The base color is cream, but the bottom of the bell skirt is covered in sewn green foliage and dotted with multicolored flowers that creep upward. Her bodice is covered with more fabric flowers, and the braiding on her cap sleeves is meant to look like trailing ivy. Her hair is down, her midnight curls cascading almost to her waist. She looks lovely.

And will look striking next to Prince Dryden, I think without meaning to, and something knots in my gut, suddenly making me feel queasy.

As I glance around the room, I notice that Princess Soraya is missing. When I ask Tori about it, she tells me the princess was cut right before the ball, and I can't help but think it's because I told Neo earlier in the day about her scheming. So now we are down to seven. Less than half the number that started just two weeks ago.

"Here we are again," Shayla says as she slides up next to me with a mischievous smile. "Do you think the prince might do us a favor and just announce his choice tonight so we can end this silly charade?"

I smile back at her, something loosening inside me as the nausea fades. She really couldn't care less about being Dryden's bride. Either that or she's a fantastic actress. Unfortunately, despite how much I enjoy her company, I don't really know her well enough to figure out which it is. That's why I haven't ruled her out as a suspect yet.

"I don't think you'll find such luck tonight," I say. "It seems to me that Prince Dryden is determined to take his time picking his bride."

Shayla rolls her eyes and groans.

"Do you blame him?" I ask with a light laugh. "It is a rather binding decision."

She lets out a very unladylike snort that makes me like her all the better, and waves off my words. "As if it truly matters who he marries. His life will be exactly the same no matter which one of us he picks."

I raise my brows, not knowing if she means that or not. But I wonder if she's right.

"It must be nice to be the prince of the most influential kingdom in Vaeloria," Shayla says, sounding a touch bitter, which surprises me. Shayla has always treated the courting season as somewhat of a joke, unflappable in her blasé attitude toward the whole thing. But am I finally getting a peek at her real feelings? Is she hiding resentment toward Prince Dryden? Resentment that would fuel an assassination attempt?

"How do you mean?" I ask, the knot re-forming in my gut. Have I let my affection for the Iron Kingdom's princess cloud my judgment?

Shayla flicks her hair over her shoulder, looking annoyed. "Just that he, at least, gets a choice."

She's not wrong. Prince Dryden is the one getting to choose

among the tributes, but now that I know Dryden is also Neo and vice versa, I can't help but feel a little more sympathy for him. Sure, he's been given the illusion of choice, but he is trapped in this courting season just as much as the tributes. At the end of the day, he's being forced into marriage for political purposes, not for love.

"In some ways, I think the prince is just as trapped in this charade as we are," I say, giving voice to my thoughts.

Shayla scrunches her nose as she scrutinizes me.

"What?" I ask, feeling self-conscious.

"I've never heard you defend the prince before. You've always seemed a little standoffish toward him, if I'm being honest. I've watched you purposefully move out of his orbit to avoid him. Has something changed?"

A spike of alarm goes through me. Shayla's been paying closer attention to me than I thought. I may not be in jeopardy of being outed by Prince Dryden anymore, but it would still be bad for any of the tributes to be suspicious of me.

"Changed? Not really," I say, trying to play it off, but when Shayla's gaze turns analytical, I realize I have to give her more than that.

I sigh, dusting off my acting skills. "Fine, if you must know, I'm really feeling the pressure. I received a letter from my parents today. They're encouraging me to make a better impression on the prince. To actually try. I'm sure I don't need to explain what a union with the prince would mean to our small kingdom. The chances of him picking me are low, but even so, I feel like I have to put in some sort of effort. For my kingdom, at least."

Shayla nods, traces of sympathy on her features that make my insides relax. "Yes, I know how that can be," she says. "A princess's cage may be gilded, but it's still a cage."

A sadness I've never seen before darkens Shayla's gaze, and I suddenly realize how good she's been at keeping up a front.

"But enough about all that," she says, and as she straightens her shoulders, the melancholy seems to melt right off her. A mischievous smile curves her lips when she leans in and says, "If you are truly trying to capture the prince's attention, may I make a suggestion?"

There's a twinkle in Shayla's eyes that makes me both curious and cautious. "I don't know if I want to hear this," I say with a laugh, and Shayla's smile grows into a full-blown grin.

"We need to find the most handsome male at the ball tonight for you to flirt with, right in front of the prince. That should get his attention."

"Or convince him that my affections lie elsewhere."

"Trust me," Shayla says as she loops her arm through mine. "Males are not that complicated. They want what they can't have. If he sees others finding you desirable, he will as well."

Shayla makes it her mission throughout the night to push me at any and every half-attractive fae she comes across at the ball. It's amusing at first, but quickly becomes tedious. Besides distracting me from watching the tributes for suspicious behavior, it's also exhausting keeping up small talk with different highborn fae.

Prince Dryden hadn't yet arrived when the tributes were announced, and I don't spot him until halfway through the evening, when he's twirling Princess Meer on the dance floor. An impressive feat considering the size of her skirt.

To go with the theme like the rest of the attendees, he's wearing a forest green coat over a darker green waistcoat. Gold embroidered vines with green leaves crawl up the back, over his shoulders, and down the front. Large dark purple petals cap his shoulders, broadening his already impressive figure.

I can't help my appreciative gaze as it trails over him, but my stomach sours when he smiles down at Meer, dipping his head to whisper something in her ear. I want to believe it's a fluke, but my stomach curdles each time I catch him dancing with a different tribute.

"What do you think?" the fae in front of me asks, shifting so that my line of sight to Prince Dryden and Princess Meer is cut off.

My stomach drops. I haven't a clue as to what he was saying. My attention was fully on the prince as I obsessed over the way his face lit up at something Princess Meer said.

What is wrong with me?

"Oh, I'm so sorry, Lord . . ." Oh no. I don't even remember his name.

The blond lord in front of me frowns, realizing I wasn't paying any attention to him.

"Lord Beaumont," he snaps.

"Yes, of course. My apologies. I haven't been sleeping well lately and—" I start, fumbling over an apology and excuses for my behavior, when Dryden's deep voice sounds behind me, sending an unwanted shiver down my spine.

"Excuse me, Lord Beaumont. May I steal the princess away for a dance?"

Lord Beaumont's gaze trains over my shoulder. "Of course, Your Highness," he says, and with a quick bow, leaves without bothering to acknowledge me.

Dryden arches a dark brow at me, the hint of a smirk on his lips. "He seemed in an awful hurry to get away. I'd go as far as to say he looked relieved by my intrusion. Whatever did you say to him?"

I smash my lips together, annoyed. Ignoring his comment, I hold out my hand for him to take and lead me to the dance floor.

He takes my outstretched hand, but rather than guiding me to the dance floor, he tucks it into the crook of his arm and steers us in a different direction.

"What are you doing?" I hiss at him as he leads me into an alcove, partially hidden by one of the potted trees and some hanging wisteria.

It's not that we're doing anything particularly scandalous, but if we are discovered, at the very least it will start tongues wagging. My strategy of convincing the other tributes I have no real interest in the prince has been mostly working so far. I don't want to see him ruin that.

"I'm trying to speak with you without having to fend off every male suitor in my court," he bites out.

"What are you talking about?"

Dryden glances over at me, annoyance clear on his face. "Only that you've spent half the night flirting with every eligible bachelor here. If I didn't know better, I'd say you were trying to snag yourself a highborn husband."

I'm angry that he'd think that of me . . . but also, a tiny seed of satisfaction burrows deep in my chest, and despite myself, the corners of my lips curl. I've spent most of the night thinking Dryden was ignoring me, but here's evidence that he's been just as observant of me as I've been of him.

"Why are you smiling?" he asks, a sour look on his face, and my smirk turns into a full grin.

Vexing Dryden is surprisingly fun. And surprisingly easy. If only I'd known that Neo and Dryden were one and the same from the beginning. Oh, the fun I could have been having these past weeks.

"Well, Your Highness," I say with a demure smile, "we both know that I'm not a contender for your hand, but there are *many* fine fae here tonight who would make wonderful husbands." I pretend to peek through the foliage at the guests and feel Dryden stiffen next to me.

"You don't mean that," he lightly scoffs, but I glance back at him innocently.

"Of course I do. I've had a taste of what it's like to be a highborn now. Do you really think I'm ready to give up this life of leisure?"

"You're not here to husband-hunt," he all but snaps, clearly struggling to keep his temper in check. "But besides that, you can't honestly expect to pretend to be Lady Stormfeather for—" He cuts himself off when a small laugh bubbles up my throat. He tilts his head, studying me, his gaze assessing. "You're jesting," he says flatly.

"Yes, of course I am," I say with another giggle. "I have no desire to tie myself to any of the spoiled and overinflated fae here tonight. You know my wish has always been to leave the kingdom and start a new life. Nothing about that has changed."

"Right," he says with a nod. "Yes, that's good. Leaving the kingdom is still the best course of action. Your cover as Princess Greer was never meant to hold up in the long run. If you tried to assume her persona indefinitely, you'd surely be caught."

A cold finger of dread scrapes down my spine at the thought of getting caught, but I shove it away. The likelihood of getting discovered is much less now that I know Dryden is an ally. I only have to make it a few more weeks and then I'll be free. With Dryden now on my side, I can't fail.

"I'm looking forward to the day I can throw off this disguise," I say truthfully. "If I've learned anything about the highborn from this experience, it's not to envy them anymore. On the whole, they are a miserable group of fae who only care about themselves. They are wretched."

"Do you think that of all of them?" Dryden asks, and when I

glance up into his green eyes, I get a little tongue-tied by how intently he's staring at me. He's not really asking what I think of the highborn fae, but rather what I think of him.

I lick my lips, and his gaze drops to my mouth before sliding back up to my eyes.

"No, not all of them," I admit, very aware of the fact that my hand is still looped through his elbow but that we're now face-to-face rather than side by side. The position is infinitely more intimate than it was a moment ago. Or at least it feels that way.

One side of his mouth turns up in an irresistible crooked grin. "I'm glad to hear that."

"I've even become particularly fond of one," I say, watching Dryden's eyes light with interest. "Lady Greyblossom is one of the kindest souls I've ever met. I wouldn't lump her in with the rest."

Dryden's mouth quirks. "I'm glad you think highly of my aunt. I agree, with the exception of my mother as well. They're the only two highborn of value."

"Not including present company, I assume?" I ask with an arched brow.

"Oh no. I'm one of the worst offenders in the bunch. I'm sure you will be as relieved to flee from me as you are from the rest of high society."

"My, my, you're being quite hard on yourself."

"On the contrary," he says. "I've worked diligently to build up that rakish reputation. I get a great amount of pride knowing that it's standing up to scrutiny."

"I don't know . . ." I say with a smirk. "From what I've seen so far, I think Prince Dryden's reputation has been blown completely out of proportion. The behavior I've observed over the last couple weeks, albeit exceedingly arrogant at times, has been nothing but completely gentlemanly. Perhaps you are losing your touch?"

"Is that what you think? That I'm a gentleman?" he asks with a devilish spark in his gaze that gives me pause, but then I nod. I may have been wary of Prince Dryden before because I didn't want him discovering my secret, but he's been the picture of the perfect prince since day one.

"Yes. I've not seen anything to make me think contrary."

"Hmm." He makes a noise deep in his chest like he's considering my answer. The sound absolutely does not cause light shivers to break out on my arms. "Perhaps I'm getting rusty?"

He shifts slightly, his gaze straying from my eyes to brush first over the contours of my face and then trace the line of my neck down to the hollow of my throat and over my collarbone. He takes his time before his stare drifts, almost lazily, back up to my face and latches on to my mouth.

My mind knows that Dryden and Neo are one and the same, but the way he's looking at me right now makes me forget how comfortable I've become around him, and a flurry of butterflies takes flight in my stomach. Their delicate tickling sends a burst of sensation straight to my chest. My heart pounds, pumping blood through my veins, causing my breathing to labor even though I've done nothing exerting.

What's happening to me?

The longer Dryden's gaze stays fixed on my lips, the more sensitive they feel, until I can't help but dart my tongue out to sweep over the bottom and then the top. His gaze flares, and I notice his pupils have taken up so much of his eyes that only a thin ring of forest green remains.

He leans in, finally tearing his gaze from my mouth as his head dips down so he can whisper into my ear. "For the record," he says, his breath caressing a sensitive spot behind my ear I never knew existed. "You never needed lessons in seduction. Even had I not been the prince, I've no doubt you would have managed to enthrall any male, putting him fully under your spell."

His words are as intoxicating as his scent, which goes straight to my head, muddling my thoughts and making me completely forget about the activities swirling outside the alcove.

When Dryden straightens, his gaze stays locked with mine. "You're looking a little flushed, Princess Greer," he says. "Are you quite certain I've lost my touch?"

Like a soap bubble popping, so does the seductive spell Dryden has so easily woven upon me.

"That was an unnecessary demonstration," I bite out, yanking my hand from his arm and taking a step back.

He doesn't look at all put off by my anger. It seems to amuse him, so of course that just angers me more.

"You called into question the validity of my reputation as a rake. I had to make sure I hadn't truly stooped so low as to be considered proper and honorable." He gives a fake shudder.

"You *are* a cad," I say, calling him all sorts of other vile names in my head that should never be uttered by a proper princess. If he continues to push me, I'll let them fly. I am, after all, not a proper princess, so why should I hold back?

"I should certainly hope so," he says with a grin.

I make an annoyed grunt, and Dryden's smile widens.

"Why did you want to haul me over here anyway?" I ask, not able to keep the sharpness out of my words. But not really trying either. I'm annoyed at him, and I don't care if he knows.

"Can you not believe I just wanted some time alone with the most beautiful fae in the room?"

I roll my eyes, no longer letting his easy smile and pretty words work on me. "No, I don't believe that. Not for a moment."

Thinking he's just messing with me, I pick up my skirts to leave, but before I can escape, Dryden captures my hand, halting me mid-turn. I glance back at him with a question on my face. He brushes his thumb over the back of my hand, and I hate that it sends a tingle of awareness up my arm.

"My apologies for my previous behavior," he says, looking sincere despite the flash of humor hiding in his gaze. But then he turns serious. "There are times with you that I find I can't hold myself back as I should."

I furrow my brow. What is that supposed to mean?

I'm opening my mouth to question him when a voice breaks through. "Have you seen the prince? I've been looking for him for a quarter of an hour, and I swear he's disappeared into thin air."

Princess Pluma.

"I last saw him speaking with Lady Stormfeather," comes another voice. Princess Willow, I believe.

There's a scoff and then, "I don't even know why she's still here. It doesn't matter how lovely she is, as if Prince Dryden will ever align himself with such a small kingdom. All she's doing is sucking up the time *we* should have with the prince. I wish he'd send her home already."

Ouch.

Princess Pluma may not have warmed up to me yet, but her words are cutting. Even though I know I'm not the real Princess Greer, nor have I ever been a contender for Dryden's hand, I can still feel my cheeks heat.

When I glance at Dryden, his face radiates annoyance.

"The prince is free to choose whoever he desires as a bride," Princess Willow says. "He may decide to forgo a political alliance for a love match."

Princess Pluma lets out a condescending laugh. "If you believe that will happen, you're just as delusional as Princess Greer. King Darius will never allow his brother to marry for *love*."

She says "love" like it's a diseased word, and I can't keep my gaze from drifting back to Dryden. His mouth is pressed into a hard line, and his eyes have taken on a distant look.

As off-putting as Princess Pluma is, her words ring true. At the end of the courting season, Dryden will have to pick a bride. He won't have the option *not* to marry one of the tributes if he finds that he doesn't feel affection toward any of them. He will have to marry regardless, that much is clear.

A swell of pity washes away the last remnants of my annoyance toward Dryden. As privileged as he is, when all this is said and done, I'll have more freedom than he does.

Princesses Pluma and Willow continue their conversation, switching topics to which of the kingdoms would be most beneficial for the Ember Kingdom to align with. Their voices grow stronger, and I realize they are drifting closer to our hiding place. I spot them through the decorative foliage in front of us. If they were to turn, they could easily see Dryden and me.

My eyes widen in alarm, and I glance over at the prince. The last thing I want is for any of the tributes to discover us. Dryden reads my face, and with a quick squeeze of my hand, he slips from behind the foliage.

"Your Highnesses," he says smoothly. "Just the lovely ladies I was looking for."

Princesses Pluma and Willow giggle at his flattery as Dryden deftly steers them toward the dessert table and away from where I'm still concealed.

I breathe a sigh of relief at not having been discovered. Feeling like I've given it the appropriate amount of time, I'm about to return to the ball when I hear more voices and halt, pressing myself back into the flowered ivy and foliage decorations.

"I'm going to do it tonight," says a voice that I recognize as Princess Primrose's.

I peek through the foliage and see her and an elderly female I don't immediately recognize whose silver hair is coiffed into an elaborate updo. Both are completely oblivious to my presence.

I shift, hiding myself as best I can behind the leafy decor.

"No," the elderly fae says. "It's too dangerous."

"I don't care. I've waited long enough," Princess Primrose snaps back. "I'm ready for this to be over already."

"But you could get caught," the other female hisses back. "It's not worth the risk. Just be patient." I catch a glimpse of her side profile and realize it's Princess Primrose's adviser. I saw them talking in the private room before all the advisers were sent away the night of the opening ball.

"I'm not going to get caught. I know where the prince's room is, and I paid a maid to give me the guard's rotation schedule. At two a.m., I'll have an opening and be able to sneak in. I only wish I'd thought to do it sooner. But—" Primrose suddenly cuts herself off when Princess Meer appears and joins them.

I put a hand over my mouth to smother my gasp. Primrose is going to sneak into Dryden's bedroom tonight? Why? To try to kill him?

Primrose carries on a conversation with her adviser and Princess Meer as if she was never talking about breaking into the prince's bedroom only moments before. My heart beats so loudly I'm half worried the trio will hear and discover me eavesdropping. I hold my breath, waiting for them to move on, which, after what feels like hours but is only a fraction of that time, they finally do.

I force myself to count to two hundred before slipping out of the alcove. As soon as I do, I start searching for Dryden.

I have to tell him. Warn him. Princess Primrose might try to kill him this very night.

But Dryden is nowhere to be found, and it's so late into the evening, the ball is winding down. Even so, I spend the remaining time dodging suitors Shayla sends my way as I search for the prince.

I finally spot him on the dance floor with Princess Primrose and I am determined to cut in, even if it isn't socially acceptable for females to do so, but Lord Sylvan slides in front of me, blocking my way. When I try to sidestep him, he shifts with me.

"Excuse me," I say sharply. "I need to—"

Reaching out, Lord Sylvan snatches my hand and tucks it in the crook of his arm and steers me in the other direction. I try to yank from his grasp, but he wraps his fingers around my wrist, keeping me from pulling free.

"Lord Sylvan," I snap, while still speaking quietly as to not attract attention. "Let me go *immediately*."

He squeezes my wrist painfully. Forget decorum.

I go to twist out of his hold, gearing up to punch him square in the face, when he hisses, "Be a good girl, *Lady Stormfeather*, and keep a pleasant smile on your face so that we can have our conversation in private. I can assure you that you don't want anyone overhearing what I have to say."

The emphasis he puts on my title, and the threat that he has information I won't want anyone else knowing, is enough to keep me from lashing out as he leads us to the edge of the ballroom, away from the remaining guests.

Peeking over my shoulder, I catch Dryden twirling Primrose on the dance floor before another couple blocks my view. A streak of panic runs through me, but I remind myself that Princess Primrose said she wasn't going to do anything until late into the night. I still have time.

When we finally pause, Lord Sylvan lets go of my wrist and I rear away from him, not caring who sees.

"How dare you manhandle me?" I spit at him as I rub my sore wrist.

He narrows his eyes, not looking even a bit regretful. "I'd apologize, *Lady Stormfeather*, but in truth, I don't really care."

"When I tell the prince—"

"You'll say nothing at all to the prince," he says, cutting me off. "Because if you do, I'll reveal what I know."

I clamp my mouth shut, not giving him the satisfaction of asking what he's talking about.

He takes a step closer, and I backpedal to keep distance between us. "Don't you want to know what I'm talking about?" he asks, an oily smile on his face.

"I've had enough of you," I say, and turn to walk away.

"If you walk away now, I'll make sure the prince and everyone else in the kingdom knows you aren't Princess Greer."

I halt, my feet planted to the floor as if they have roots. The blood in my veins freezes to ice.

What does he know? How does he know?

Composing myself, I slowly turn to face Lord Sylvan again. Taking in the smug look on his face, I make sure none of the panic I'm feeling shows on mine.

I let out a laugh I hope doesn't come across as forced. "Of course I'm Princess Greer. Who else would I be? Perhaps you've had too much faewine this evening?" I make a show of leaning forward and peering into his eyes as if I'm looking to see if they are bloodshot from too many spirits.

He crosses his arms over his chest and tips his chin up, looking down his nose at me. "Nice try. What I want to know is, if you aren't Princess Greer, then who are you?"

That was a mistake, for him to reveal that he doesn't know who I truly am. It makes me think he doesn't actually have any evidence of me not being Princess Greer. Perhaps it's just something he suspects.

It's time to see just how good of a liar I really am.

Mustering every bit of training I received from Olette and Neo, I straighten my shoulders and channel as much regal authority as I can into my body language and voice. "I don't know what you are going on about, but I've had enough of this conversation."

"I talked to the harbor master," he says casually. Too casually.

I place my hands on my hips. "Why does that concern me?"

A slow smile appears on his face, chilling me. "Because he said that there's no record of a Lady Stormfeather having arrived on any vessel, let alone a storm-battered one that almost sank. In fact, he said that there hasn't been a single ship to sail upriver from the Glacier Kingdom in six months."

I roll my eyes, trying to look unaffected by Lord Sylvan's revelation, when in reality, I'm racking my brain to figure out what gave me away. I don't know what I did. I was the perfect princess in front of Lord Sylvan. I didn't mess up any of the details of Princess Greer's life. I behaved exactly as I should have. The only reason I can think for him having looked into me was that his pride was hurt by my rejection and Dryden's dismissal of him. And in that case, he didn't just stumble across something, he was actively searching for dirt on me.

I give him a patronizing look. "Well, then there's obviously been a mistake, because I arrived six weeks ago."

He shakes his head. "No, I don't believe a mistake was

made. I think you aren't actually Lady Stormfeather. You are an impostor."

"Your accusation is preposterous," I say. "I know it, and you know it. What did you even hope to gain by accusing me of something so ridiculous?"

"You will do whatever I want you to, or I'll go to the prince with this information," he growls, losing his temper because I'm not cowering in fear or groveling for him to keep my secret like he expected.

Thank goodness I now know Dryden is Neo. One day ago, that threat would have terrified me. Now it is laughable.

"Fine. Go to the prince with your suspicions," I say, calling his bluff.

For the first time since Lord Sylvan dragged me into this conversation, his confidence slips, and I smile.

Taking a step forward, I go in for the kill. "I only wish I could be there to see how foolish you are going to look in front of him." I allow a mocking smile to shape my mouth.

His nostrils flare, and I know he now has his doubts. I start to brush past him when he grabs my arm, stopping me.

"I sent a letter to King Silas yesterday. How do you think he'll react when he finds out someone is impersonating his daughter?"

I mentally calculate the time it will take for a letter to make it all the way up to the Glacier Kingdom and then for a message, or a small army to arrest me, to make it back. It's cutting it a little closer than I'd like, but I should be okay. Besides, if it turns out our assassin is Princess Primrose, tonight might be my last carrying out this charade.

"I told you not to touch me again," I say right before I grab his thumb and bend it backward.

There's a *snap*, then Lord Sylvan curses loudly and snatches his hand back, cradling it to his chest.

"You broke my finger," he spits, his face turning red. How I ever considered him handsome, I have no idea. Standing in front of me now, he looks like a child on the verge of a temper tantrum.

"Touch me again and I'll break far more than that," I warn.

"How dare you threaten—"

"That's not a threat, it's a promise," I say, and without giving him another look, I take off to resume my search for Dryden.

When I return to the edge of the dance floor, both Dryden and Primrose are nowhere to be found. I discreetly ask some of the partygoers if they've seen the prince, but no one knows where he went, and I eventually give up looking, assuming he left the party. But finding Dryden and letting him know what I overheard can't wait, so I'm only left with one option: to use the map of the palace and get to his room before Primrose does.

Chapter 25

I STARE AT THE GRANDFATHER CLOCK IN THE corner of the room while Eilowyn puts away my dress. I've already changed into a nightgown, but I haven't brushed out my hair or washed my face.

It's 1:23.

I still have over a half hour, but what if Princess Primrose decides to sneak into Dryden's room early? I'm antsy as Eilowyn putters around the room, chatting excitedly about everything she heard about the ball. The decor. The dresses. The attendees. I don't really hear much of it over the clock ticking down in my head.

"Eilowyn," I finally say, "it's so very late and I'm so tired. Would you mind if we left the rest until morning?"

"Oh, I'm so sorry," she says, then sets the brush back down on the vanity. "Of course you're right. Ring me when you need me in the morning. Otherwise, I'll let you sleep in a bit."

With a curtsy, she smiles and leaves. The second the door closes behind her, I rush over to the trunk, yanking the false bottom out. The book of the palace's hidden passageways is just where I left it. I quickly flip through the pages until I find the map I'm looking for. The one of the east wing, where all the royals' chambers are.

Trailing my finger over the route I need to take to Dryden's room, I do my best to commit it to memory. The last thing I want to do is to get caught with it, so I have to leave it behind. But one wrong turn and I could end up popping out in King Darius's or Queen Teresa's chambers, and that would be disastrous. If I were to be caught in either of those rooms, I don't think even Dryden could help me.

The trickiest part of this whole endeavor is going to be getting access to the hidden passageways on the other side of the palace. I can't just enter them from the access linen closet in my corridor. The tributes' rooms are in the west wing, whereas Dryden's and his family's rooms are in the east wing. The hidden passageways don't connect the two wings, so I have to go over to the east wing first and then slip into the tunnels through a false door in the library.

Shutting my eyes, I recite the route in my head for once I enter the passageways through the library entrance. *Take a left and then the second right. Go up two flights of stairs to get to the third floor, then make two left turns and there's a door to Dryden's room hidden behind a tapestry.*

I take a deep breath just as the clock chimes on the half hour, letting me know I'm running out of time.

My blood is rushing through my veins. I have to leave now.

After I return the book to the trunk and replace the false bottom, I listen at the door for guards. Not hearing anybody, I peek out, checking the corridor in both directions. It's clear, so I jut out of the room, keeping a brisk pace as I hurry down the hall. It's not until I'm halfway to the library—after already ducking into an alcove to avoid a guard—that I realize I should've grabbed my lumestra stone. Moonlight pours in through the windows at the end of the corridor, making it fairly easy to see, but it will be another story once I'm in the hidden passageways. I was in a rush to get to

Dryden, but how could I have been so thoughtless? Now I'm going to need to use my hands to guide me.

I have to stop and hide twice more before I reach the library in the east wing—once when a night guard is making his rounds, and again when a lady's maid leaves her mistress's room, yawning as she heads back to her room to get a few hours of sleep before her workday starts again.

Both pass by without realizing I'm there, but it slows my progress. When I finally reach the library, I shut the doors behind me and rush to where there's supposed to be an entrance to the passageways. I catch the time on a mantel clock as I brush past. Fifteen minutes until two a.m. I'm cutting it too close.

I can't keep the image of Princess Primrose stabbing Dryden as he lies asleep in his bed out of my mind. My hands are frantic as I pass over books and shelf decor, looking for the button that is supposed to open the door. I finally find it hidden behind a row of thick books on the history of Vaeloria. There's a click and the bookshelf pops open. I quickly slide through the opening and pull the bookcase closed behind me. As expected, the passageway is completely dark.

"Take a left," I whisper to myself, remembering the route. With one hand trailing over the wall, I move forward, my steps both tentative and hurried.

I recite the rest of the route over and over again until I've made the appropriate turns—at least I think I have—and am standing in front of the hidden door that leads to Dryden's room. I don't have time to hesitate, yet I'm halted by fear.

Please be Dryden's room. Please let me not be too late, I think to myself before carefully pulling open the door. There's a thick tapestry hung in front of the entrance, just like the map indicated there would be, and I breathe a sigh of relief.

Sliding the tapestry aside, I slip soundlessly into Dryden's room with my heart in my throat.

The room is dim. There aren't any lit lanterns or candles, but moonlight peeks through a crack in Dryden's curtains, giving off a sliver of light. Since my eyes have already adjusted to the darkness, the moonlight is enough for me to make out some of the space.

The first thing I notice is that Dryden's room is huge. Easily four times the size of the one I'm staying in, but that makes sense as, until his brother has a child, he's the heir to the throne and therefore the second most important fae in the kingdom.

The next thing that catches my eye is the huge four-poster bed across from where I'm standing. The moonlight doesn't reach the bed, so I have to get closer to check it.

Holding my breath, I tiptoe forward, hoping that all I find within it is Dryden's sleeping form. As I take careful steps, my mind conjures all sorts of sordid and morbid images. Dryden's stabbed and bleeding out, him battered and lying prone and near death on the mattress.

I can't make out anything until I'm almost pressed right up against the side of the mattress. Even then, I need to lean forward to make out Dryden's shape in the middle of the bed. He's on his back, lying with the sheet pulled up to his waist and an arm flung over his head. But the knot in my gut doesn't disappear. I can't hear him breathing, and he seems unnaturally still.

Gingerly, I put one knee on the mattress and hoist myself onto the bed. I slowly crawl forward, my whole body tense as I look for signs that he's uninjured. It's not until I'm practically hovering over him that I detect his chest, his very bare and naked chest, moving up and down.

I breathe a sigh of relief. He's just asleep. Oh thank—

A small yelp slips out of me when Dryden surges forward. Wrapping an arm around my waist, he hauls me close and I slam into his bare chest. Before I even realize what's happened, he's rolled, twisting us both in the sheets, which puts him on top and me trapped beneath him. Quick as a snake, he grabs my wrists and pins them on either side of my head, then blinks down at me.

"What are you doing here?" Dryden asks, his sleep-laden voice filled with confusion. The gruff sound makes my stomach flip and my heart thump.

"I was checking on you," I say, wiggling beneath him. But he doesn't roll off me.

"Why?"

"I thought someone might be here," I explain.

Dryden pulls back a little so he can look me more fully in the eyes, and it's only then that I absorb how closely we're pressed together. We've never been this close, even while dancing. His hands are still holding me down against the bed, and his whole body is draped over mine from foot to mid-chest. I trail my gaze from his face over his exposed skin, skimming his shoulders and the visible part of his chest. You wouldn't think a pampered prince would be hiding that many muscles, but you'd be wrong. So wrong.

My mouth goes dry and heat rushes to my face.

"Someone? As in one of the tributes?" he asks, and I snap my gaze back up to his face to see him staring at me with a furrowed brow.

I clear my throat. "I overheard Princess Primrose talking about how she was going to sneak in here tonight. I tried to find you at the ball, but I got sidetracked and . . ." I shrug. Now that I'm here, and it's clear he's alone, I feel a little silly for worrying.

Dryden's features soften, and in the dim light I see a lazy smile curl the corners of his mouth. "And you were planning on coming to my rescue?"

Yes. "No. I just wanted to witness one of them cutting you open to see if my suspicions about Primrose are correct."

We both know that's a bold-faced lie. I'd never stand by and watch someone kill him. At least not while our lives are still linked through my contract and his death would mean mine as well.

That's not the only reason, my mind whispers, but I tell it to be quiet.

His grip on my hands loosens. He swipes his thumb over the sensitive skin on my wrists, soothing the area he squeezed so tightly.

"I think—"

The doors to Dryden's outer chamber suddenly open, the hinges creaking loudly, and both our eyes go wide.

"Your Highness?" comes a deep male voice from the other room.

"A guard," Dryden whispers.

I need to hide before I'm discovered, but Dryden's body is still heavy upon me, pressing me into the soft mattress.

"Get off," I hiss, but he doesn't even so much as shift so I can squirm away from him.

The look on his face is resigned, and a ball of lead forms in my gut when he whispers, "Rowan, I'm sorry about this."

"Sorry about wh—?"

His mouth descends on mine: warm, soft, and insistent. I gasp and he takes advantage of my lips parting to deepen the kiss, swiping his tongue over my bottom lip before touching it to mine.

The sensation of his mouth pressing and moving against mine is like nothing I've ever felt before. A blossom of heat forms low in my belly, and the thought of pushing him away doesn't even enter my mind. His lips are more intoxicating than faewine, and when his hand drifts down my arm and over my rib cage to land on my hip, I'm convinced I must be drugged.

Of its own accord, my leg shifts to the side and lifts to hook around his. A needy sound rumbles in the back of my throat when he sucks my bottom lip into his mouth and bites down gently on it.

I've been kissed before. I had a crush on the baker's son and used to visit him at the end of the day. He'd give me leftover treats from their shop that hadn't sold that day, and we'd talk. One day he asked if he could kiss me, and I said yes. No sooner had his lips pressed up against mine than his mother caught us and pulled us apart. She called me trash and said she'd call the constable on me if she ever saw me lurking behind their store again. The next day I still came back, but he never came out to see me again. I passed him on the street a month later, and when our gazes connected, he turned and walked in the opposite direction.

Even so, I never regretted that first kiss. That kiss had been nice. Sweet. But there's nothing *nice* or *sweet* about what Dryden is doing to me right now. He is devastating me, ruining me for every nice or sweet kiss in the future, and I can't say that I mind.

A throat clears and then a male voice says, "Your Highness, I apologize for the intrusion."

Like a bucket of cold water poured over my head, the spell Dryden cast on me with his kisses and light touches is broken instantly. The room isn't dark anymore, and I tense when I realize how entwined the two of us are.

My leg is still wrapped around him, and he must have released my wrists at some point, because I'm gripping his biceps. One of his hands cups my jaw, his fingers tangled in my loose hair, and his other is on my rib cage, his thumb dangerously high.

I'm fully clothed, but Dryden clearly isn't. I can tell some of the bedding has shifted and I don't even want to look to see how much of him is now exposed.

Dryden seems completely unconcerned by all of this and takes his time, his lips rubbing against mine twice before he pulls back. His gaze is half lidded and sultry as he scans my heated face before turning his head to glare at the guard standing next to the bed. There's a lantern in the guard's hand, and it registers that is where the light is coming from.

"What are you doing here?" he asks the guard, his tone as cold as a chilly winter day.

"I heard a commotion and wanted to make sure you weren't in danger."

Dryden lifts a brow and looks down the length of our entwined bodies. "Do I look in danger to you?"

The guard clears his throat. "Not at present, Your Highness. No."

"Then your services are not required." It's a clear dismissal.

"Yes, Your Highness." The guard shifts on his feet, obviously uncomfortable. "Would you like me to escort the princess from your chambers, or . . . ?"

Dryden sighs. "If I'm to choose a bride, it's only natural I'd want to sample their goods before committing to a purchase. I've not yet had the opportunity to do so because of your interruption. So no, I do not want you escorting her anywhere."

Instant heat shoots to my cheeks.

He really said that.

I know he's putting on a show for this guard. Playing the part of the playboy Prince Dryden to keep his carefree image intact, but still. *Sample my goods before committing to a purchase.*

Ew.

Under the blankets I pinch his side, hard, and he twitches away from my hand. I don't feel bad about it at all.

"Um, yes. Yes, of course, Your Highness. Since there's not a threat, I'll leave you now."

"Please do so."

The guard turns to leave, but Dryden stops him before he exits the bedroom. "Call for extra guards at the door," he says. "And of course it goes without saying that I expect your discretion."

He nods once. "Yes, Your Highness." And with that he's gone.

Once we hear the doors to Dryden's suite close, he rolls off me, twisting the blankets to cover his lower body as he sits up with his back to me and his legs over the side of the bed. He plows a hand through his hair and then shakes his head. "I'm sorry about that. There wasn't time for you to hide and—"

"Yes, I know. You were creating a feasible reason for me to be in your room." *And in your bed.* I clear my throat as I sit up. My lips are still buzzing, and my body's overheated.

Dryden groans. "By morning, the entire palace will have heard of this."

It takes a moment for his words to settle in. "But you asked the guard to be discreet. Surely he will honor his prince's wishes."

"Gossip is as much a currency here at court as coin. I would have thought you'd realized that by now." He sighs and glances over his shoulder at me. "You know what this means, right?"

I shake my head. My brain is still struggling to switch gears. Many of the intricacies of fae court life still baffle me.

"Our game plan has to change. We can no longer keep our distance and feign disinterest in each other."

Scooching to the edge of the bed, I sit next to him, leaving at least two feet between us as I pretend nothing physical just happened. "Do you mean I have to flirt with you?"

I scrunch my nose at the thought. Flirting was never part of my training, and I'm horribly bad at it. Even when Dryden, as Neo, tried to give me pointers, I still failed. Why did everything have to get so complicated?

Dryden chuckles. "I'm afraid it's much worse than that. Tomorrow I'll have to start courting you properly."

Chapter 26

DRYDEN DOESN'T LET ME LEAVE HIS ROOM FOR another full hour, claiming that his reputation will take a hit if I go any sooner. I want to be irked by that, but I'm too busy reeling from that kiss. It's a strange sort of torture to be sequestered in the room with him for that long after the intimacy we just shared. I do my best to appear unaffected, but I'm not sure I'm that good of an actress. At least Dryden doesn't comment on the fact that I can't seem to meet his eyes, even after he pulls on a shirt and pants.

Despite the awkwardness, the extra time alone gives me the opportunity to let him know what I overheard with Princess Primrose—and also my interaction with Lord Sylvan. He seems thoughtful when I'm talking about my suspicions about Princess Primrose, and downright furious when I tell him about Lord Sylvan.

"He put his hands on you?" he asks, his voice cold and sharp.

I nod.

A change comes over him. Even beneath his clothes, I can tell he's tensing his muscles. He tells me he'll take care of Lord Sylvan, and there's such venom in his voice that I sneak a peek at his face to see his eyes practically glowing with barely contained rage.

I change the topic to Primrose, which feels like safer ground. Thankfully, it works, his anger dissipating quickly.

"Princess Primrose is definitely a suspect, but . . ." He trails off.

"What?"

He rubs his hand over his mouth. I think it might be to cover a smile. "There's every chance that her intentions of sneaking into my room tonight weren't quite as nefarious as you interpreted them to be."

"What do you mean?" I ask with a tilt of my head.

"Just that her motivation might have had more to do with the courting season and its outcome than wanting to hurt me."

It dawns on me then what he is tactfully trying to tell me. "You think she was trying to enter your bedchamber to seduce you." It's not a question.

He starts to chuckle when he sees the look on my face, but then quickly stops and clears his throat. "I'm just saying it's an option. You'd be surprised at the lengths the tributes have already gone to in order to get my attention."

I want to ask, but I clamp my mouth shut, refusing to go there. "I see," is all I say.

By the time I leave, it's well past three, and Dryden has four guards stationed outside his door just in case Princess Primrose does make an appearance. I want to leave through the tunnels, but he insists I go out the door so one of his guards can escort me back to my room. I start to argue, but then he asks if I want the guards thinking I spent the whole night in his room. He has a point, so I relent.

The guard who walks me back to the west wing doesn't utter a word as we make our way through the palace. For that, at least, I'm grateful. When we reach my room, the guard gives a slight bow before departing. I don't miss the once-over he gives me, or the smirk on his face before he turns to leave. It makes my cheeks heat, but I hold my head high as I reenter my bedchamber.

Exhausted, I fall into my bed, face-planting on the pillow, too drained to even bother getting under the blankets. It's just as well, because I feel strangely hot anyway.

Even though my body is worn from the long and eventful day, my mind won't quiet. I lie in bed, waiting as my mind and body battle it out. I absolutely do not think of Dryden's lips or the feeling of his weight on top of me. The way that it felt when he nuzzled my neck. His fingers brushing over my sensitive skin. As I finally drift off to sleep hours later, it isn't to thoughts of Dryden and the way that he said my name. Nope. Not at all.

✦

BY THE TIME I wake the next morning, the entire night before feels like a dream. Despite only getting a few hours of sleep, I'm still surprisingly refreshed.

Raising my hands over my head, I stretch leisurely.

"Oh, Lady Greer," Eilowyn says as she enters the bedchamber, stopping when she sees me. "I didn't expect you to be awake this early."

The way she says it makes me think that it's not long after dawn.

"What time is it?" I ask as I swing my legs over the side of the bed and slide off the mattress.

"Just past nine o'clock," she says. "I'll ring for some tea. I didn't think you'd need any yet."

I stop, my brow furrowing as I look at Eilowyn. Nine o'clock isn't very early. Why is she acting like she expected me to sleep half the day away? Yes, the festivities stretched into the night, but not nearly as late as the opening ball.

I say as much to her, and she shrugs as she pulls a dress out for me. It's pale blue and frothy, not one of the overskirt dresses, but I don't complain.

"It's just that you had such an eventful night," she says, and glances at me with a small smirk and a twinkle in her eye.

"Yes, I suppose the ball was exciting."

She giggles, and it makes me think that I'm missing something, but I have too much on my mind right now to work it out.

After I get into my day dress, Eilowyn offers to ring for breakfast, but I tell her not to bother. Breakfast is served for the tributes every morning until ten in the solarium. I don't always attend, but I'm anxious to see how Primrose is acting this morning.

Once I'm dressed and Eilowyn pins my hair up, I head to the solarium. I'm expecting to slip into the room unnoticed like I always do, but the moment I enter the breakfast area, all conversation halts and multiple heads swivel my way.

I stop in my tracks and glance over my shoulder, sure their reactions can't be because of me, but there's no one else there. Tentatively, I pick up a plate next to the buffet that's been set out this morning.

As I take my time placing food on my plate, hushed conversations eventually resume, but more than one hostile glare is still directed at me. What is going on?

When I finish filling my plate with food that I have no appetite to eat, I turn and my gaze immediately connects with Princess Primrose. The look she's giving me sends a chill through me. It's not just envy or even simple hate I read in her eyes; there's also calculation there. And that, more than the petty emotions I see leaking through, makes the fine hairs stand up at the back of my neck. My gut says she's the one we're looking for, and I'm going to make it my mission today to ferret out her true intentions, one way or another.

"You dirty little liar," someone hisses in my ear, startling me.

Breaking eye contact with Primrose, I look over to find Shayla standing next to me.

My heart jumps into my throat. How does she know? What does she know?

"What are you talking about?" I ask, making sure to speak quietly.

"And here you had me convinced you weren't interested in the prince," she says, placing a hand on her hip, but with a twinkle in her eye.

"I'm not," I say a little too loudly, and a couple of heads swivel in our direction again. Clearing my throat lightly, I lower my voice so we're not overheard. "I'm not," I reiterate. "Why would you think that?"

Dryden warned me gossip would circulate through the palace quickly, but it couldn't have gotten around so fast. Could it? It isn't even midday yet.

Her brows rise. "Come now. We all know."

Dread starts to swirl in my gut.

"Know what?" I ask, worried I know what she's going to say, and that it's not much better than the truth.

She glances over my shoulder at the other princesses behind me, then sets her plate down, lightly grabs my arm, and pulls me off to the side, still within eyesight of the hostile tributes, but definitely far enough so they can't hear us.

"You spent last night with the prince, didn't you?" she asks. In contrast to the aggressive looks most of the other tributes have sent my way, Shayla just looks curious, if not a touch amused.

"No," I say, shaking my head.

"No?" She cocks her head, confused. "But that's the buzz around the palace this morning. That one of the guards barged into Prince Dryden's room last night to find you there with him."

With a groan, I set my plate down on the table next to us and then rub my forehead. This is a nightmare. And exactly what Dryden said was going to happen.

What to do? What to do?

My face heats. "It's not what you think," I start.

The grin appears on her face again. "You must tell me *everything*," she says. "Starting with how big—"

The door to the solarium swings open and footsteps sound on the stone floor, cutting Shayla off. We both glance over as a footman enters the cavernous room, carrying a letter on a silver tray.

Murmurs rise as the remaining tributes perk up, their eyes fastened on the fae as he weaves through the room toward us. A letter delivered via a footman has become the typical way Dryden asks one of us to spend time with him, so the air fills with anticipation as we wait to see who the recipient is today.

The excitement leaks out of the room like a deflated balloon the moment the footman stops in front of me and holds out the tray. Placed on top is a folded piece of paper with Lady Stormfeather written across it.

Even though I don't glance around the room, I still feel the chilly gazes of the other tributes. If glares were daggers, I'd be riddled with stab wounds right now.

"Your Highness," he says with a small bow, waiting for me to collect the note. But I just stare at it as if it's a poisonous snake about to strike.

Seconds tick by and I still don't pick up the letter. The footman shoots me a veiled but still clearly annoyed look, and Shayla nudges me. With a resigned sigh, I gingerly grasp the paper.

Unfolding it, I quickly read it to discover it's a formal invitation to an outing with Prince Dryden this afternoon. The note is short and to the point. He asks for the pleasure of my company and gives me the time.

I furrow my eyebrows as I try to work out a way to decline. I know he's only asking me because of the rumors, so maybe it's something I can find a way out of. It's not as if I'm worried about hurting his feelings or being asked to leave anymore. And really, what I need to be doing this afternoon is figuring out a way to search Princess Primrose's room more thoroughly, not waste the time away putting on a show with Dryden.

The footman clears his throat and I glance up to see him staring at me expectantly, waiting for my answer, which for the most part is just a formality. No one actually expects me to decline.

I smother a groan.

Why did Dryden have to invite me on an outing when there were so many witnesses? If all the remaining tributes weren't staring at me right now, I could easily come up with a way to decline, but since it's obvious to all what's written on that note, it means one thing and one thing only: I'm going to have to spend the afternoon with the prince.

✦

"I UNDERESTIMATED YOU." Coming from behind me, the words echo down the hall as I'm on my way to meet Dryden for our courting sham.

I recognize the pitch and tone immediately, and dread forms a tangled knot in my chest as I whirl around. Princess Primrose is the last person I want at my back.

I wasn't able to find a way into her quarters today. Shayla kept me in the solarium the rest of the morning. When I finally got back to my room, right as I was going to try to sneak out and use the secret passageways, Eilowyn arrived with lunch and then fussed over getting me ready for my outing with Dryden, insisting I wear just the right thing and that my hair and makeup be perfect. No matter how hard I tried, I couldn't hurry her along. When she finally finished, there simply wasn't time.

I scan the corridor for the pink-haired princess, my gaze darting over the seemingly empty hallway, until I spot a swath of pink taffeta peeking out from one of the window alcoves. She's tucked into the window well, most of her body hidden behind the thick red and yellow curtains.

I must have walked right by her without even knowing. I remind myself to remain sharp. Pretending to be a pampered princess has obviously dulled my senses.

"Princess Primrose. You startled me," I say with false levity and a forced chuckle as she stands and reveals herself.

I lay a hand over my heart as if I'm trying to steady it. In reality, I'm taking her in, checking for weapons and categorizing what level of threat she poses. Something I used to do by instinct every time I came across someone, but I stupidly stopped assessing fae that way in the last couple of weeks.

That was a mistake.

Primrose appears weaponless, but seeing the cold hatred in her eyes reminds me how dangerous it is to let my guard down. She might not be carrying a dagger, but that doesn't mean she's not a threat. I already know she'll go to great lengths to get what she wants. The question is, how far?

Her feet pad soundlessly over the carpeted floor as she takes measured steps toward me. My hand twitches, wanting to reach for the dagger I used to carry before all of this started. I force my limbs and face to relax, putting on a show for her.

The best offense I have with the possible assassin in front of me is to make her believe I'm blissfully unaware of who she truly is and what her plans are.

"I'm surprised you didn't notice me," Primrose says, cocking her head to the side in a way that reminds me of a bird.

"Well, you were partially hidden by those thick curtains," I say, holding a polite smile.

"Hmm. It's just that you always seem so aware of your surroundings. Of who is in the room with you and what they are saying."

"I don't know what you mean," I say, feigning ignorance, but on the inside, the knot in my chest tightens. This princess is observant. Too observant. It strengthens my suspicions about her being the one we're looking for. Just as I've been watching her, she's been watching me.

"I think you know exactly what I mean," she says, moving forward and into my space.

I take a step back to keep our distance, and there's a flash of satisfaction in her eyes, like she enjoys intimidating me, and that brings my inner fighter to the surface.

When she shifts closer again, I don't retreat this time. Instead, I stand tall and stare her down. The polite smile drops off my face as I dare her to come at me.

"There you are," she says on a whispered hiss. "I'm glad to see you aren't hiding anymore. That little mouse act you've been feeding everyone doesn't become you. I want to have this conversation with the real you, not the fake one you've been desperately trying to get everyone to believe. It's time we *both* shed our façades."

My alarm bells blare.

"I don't know how, but you knew of my plans last night, didn't you? You knew what I was going to do and you stopped me." I open my mouth to lie and tell her I don't know what she's talking about, but she doesn't pause to let me answer before going on: "But it doesn't matter, because all you did was push off the inevitable. You didn't actually stop anything."

This is it. She's going to confess her malicious plans and then try to kill me. But I'm not easy to kill. If I were, I'd never have made it this far.

I'm about to shift into a defensive position when Primrose gets in my face and says, "The prince might be momentarily distracted by your charms, but know that he will never choose you to be his bride."

Wait. What?

"Your kingdom is small and useless," she goes on. "The Ember Kingdom would never align themselves with such a weak ally. The fact that you are here is a joke. This kingdom needs what the Bloom Kingdom has to offer. What *I* have to offer."

Well, even I know that's overstating her kingdom's value to the Ember Kingdom. The Bloom Kingdom is wealthy, but mostly from exporting frivolous luxuries—perfumes, teas, and essential oils—all recently popular among Vaelorian highborn. Their only truly useful export is medicine derived from their abundant flora. To suggest a union with Dryden would benefit the Ember Kingdom is the real joke.

She lifts her finger, pointing it right at my face. "So, I'm here to tell you whatever pathetic plans you have to trick Prince Dryden into marrying you won't work."

I'm confused. I expected threats on my life. Confessions of her murderous plans for Dryden, but instead I get this?

Clarity slams into me. The only reason she's in my face right now is to warn me away from Dryden so she can have him for herself. She's threatened by me, not because she suspects I'm standing in the way of her killing him, but because she's worried I'll somehow win Prince Dryden's hand instead of her.

The knot of dread that was twisting in my chest unfurrows. The urge to laugh in her face tickles my throat, but I manage to hold it together in order to play the part of an offended princess. Primrose still needs to believe I'm here to compete for Dryden.

"We shall see," I say, lifting my chin in defiance.

She narrows her eyes. "You really don't want to go up against me." Her words carry a clear threat.

"No," I say, rising to my full height, which is sadly still a few inches shorter than her. "*You* don't want to go up against *me*."

I take a step forward, and she's forced to shift back. Concern flashes across her face, but she chases it quickly away, replacing it with a look of utter disdain. If she's expecting that to faze me, she's going to be disappointed. Years of being looked down upon have made me immune to the opinions of others.

"If you'll excuse me," I say with a condescending smile. "The prince is waiting for me." With a swish of my skirts, I turn away from her and start back down the hall.

"We're not done here," she calls after me. I can practically hear her teeth grinding as I walk away from her, and it brings a satisfied smile to my face.

"Oh, I can assure you," I say without stopping or looking back, "we most certainly are."

"He will never be yours," she growls just as I round the corner and leave her behind . . .

. . . and an unexpected pain stabs me in the heart, because she's right.

Prince Dryden, Neo, will never be mine. He'll always belong to this kingdom, never a gutter fae like me. But that truth has been clear since the day we met, so it shouldn't affect me now.

Yet for some reason, it does.

Chapter 27

I CAN'T LOOK DRYDEN IN THE EYE AS HE TAKES my hand and helps me into the carriage. He was right about the whole palace gossiping about us. It wasn't just the tributes at breakfast this morning, but the palace staff as well. After leaving Primrose sputtering in the hallway, I passed a group of maids who couldn't stop giggling and exchanging looks with one another as I neared. You'd think they'd be a little more inconspicuous about it. And now I know why Eilowyn was odd this morning. She's clearly heard the rumor, too.

After helping me into the carriage, Dryden follows me inside and closes the door behind him. He raps on the ceiling twice to let the coachman know we are ready, and we're off.

"Where's the chaperone?" I ask, taken a little off guard to be in the closed space with him alone. We've never required a chaperone before because this is our first one-on-one outing, but from listening to the other tributes, a chaperone is always present.

Although if I'm honest, it's not the missing chaperone that's throwing me off, but rather the thickness of the air that swirls around us and the weight of his stare from across the short distance between us.

I clear my throat, shifting in the seat from annoyance at myself. I've been alone with Dryden both as Neo and as himself. This shouldn't be any different.

But it is.

The corner of Dryden's mouth quirks up. "I asked her if she'd ride up front with the coachman to give us some privacy."

"And she was okay with that?" The chaperones have been notoriously vigilant in their tasks. I heard Princess Soraya complaining after her date that the chaperone was practically breathing down her neck during her walk with Dryden in the gardens.

Dryden's smile is wicked and does wicked things to my belly. "She said she didn't expect there was anything I could do to you in the carriage that probably wasn't already done to you last night."

My mouth drops open. "No, she didn't say that . . . ?"

Dryden chuckles. "She did, actually."

"Well . . . I . . . That's . . ." I'm at a loss as to what to say to that, so I clear my throat and change the subject.

Dryden proceeds to try to engage me in simple conversation, but I still can't meet his gaze and I don't seem to know what to do with my hands, so I end up fidgeting with my shawl until the fabric is twisted so tightly around my hands and fingers that I have to tug them free.

"Why are you acting so strange?" he asks bluntly.

I huff and force myself to finally meet his eyes. Amusement flickers in his gaze, turning my own hard.

He thinks this is funny, does he? Why should I be the only one squirming? "Well, you *did* actually kiss me last night," I say boldly, hoping to shock and embarrass him, but as I wait for him to look away or at least have some reaction to show his shame, the hint of a smile appears on his face instead.

My blood starts to boil in the not-fun way. I swear, if he laughs, I'll deck him.

"I did," he agrees. "Was it so awful and unbearable that you can't stand my presence anymore?"

"No, it wasn't awful. Well, what I mean to say is that it wasn't unbearable, per se, or rather—"

"Would you feel more comfortable if I were to assure you it won't happen again?"

His question causes an unexpected thorn of disappointment to pierce my chest. I clear my throat and shift in my seat. "I don't think that assurance will be necessary."

He tilts his head, his gaze sharpening. "Do you mean to say that assurance isn't needed or isn't desired?"

"I hardly think what I desire is important in this situation."

Dryden leans forward, his presence seeming to take up too much of the air in the small space. "On the contrary, I find myself becoming increasingly interested in your desires."

My cheeks feel warm, and I have to swallow before speaking. "Can we please not talk about my desires?" The request comes out barely louder than a whisper.

Dryden's gaze brushes over my face. I have no idea what he reads on it. After what feels like several minutes, but is probably only a handful of swift seconds, he leans back, folding his arms over his chest. "I would wager no one has bothered to ask about your desires before, and that's a true pity."

The added space between us helps me gather my wits. I know Dryden is hinting at more than just my carnal desires, and it's a little unnerving how easily he reads me sometimes. It makes me feel exposed in a way I'm not comfortable with. But I can't deny there's a thrill in finally feeling seen by someone.

"You saw how I lived. Very few people have bothered to ask

anything about me. I'm more accustomed to being ordered than asked."

He frowns. "When this is all over, that will change. You'll have the life you always should have had."

I look away from him and out the window. We've left the city proper and are ambling down a dirt road, headed into the countryside outside of Everlight. Flower-dotted fields stretch out in front of me.

Dryden's right. When this is all over, I'll have a new life in a new land with all new people. For the first time since freedom was offered to me, the thought of never seeing anyone from this life again fills me with sadness.

✦

DRYDEN TAKES ME to a peach orchard for our outing. We unhurriedly stroll through the rows of trees under the guise of fruit-picking before a picnic, but in actuality, now that I've gotten over my awkwardness, we're using the rare alone time to plot.

Dryden plucks a peach from a tree and puts it into the basket at my feet. "So, you think Princess Pluma is sincere?"

I scoff, thinking of Princess Pluma's biting words about me at the ball the night before. "I didn't say that. She's one of the more closed-off princesses. And her obvious skill with blades is a cause for concern. I need to get into her room."

Dryden nods, his expression thoughtful as we leisurely amble through the orchard. Our chaperone, coachman, and guards remain at the edge of it, far enough away that our conversation won't carry to them.

Not having to worry about the chaperone hovering has worked out in our favor. We've been able to speak freely, in the carriage and now out in the open. I hate to admit it, but maybe the whole debacle in his room last night was actually a blessing in disguise. Yes, I'm embarrassed, and poor Princess Greer's reputation is certainly tarnished, but it's allowed us the privacy we needed.

"You seem close with Princess Shayla," Dryden says conversationally, but I can't help but notice how carefully he watches me each time he brings up a different princess. I'm assuming he's searching for my true reaction. I have, after all, spent more time with the tributes than he has. But when he mentions Shayla, I can't hold his gaze anymore and turn to the peach trees next to us, taking a step closer to inspect a fuzzy piece of fruit larger than my fist.

"Shayla is . . ." I start, but then have to swallow past a lump in my throat as it hits me how real this courting season is to him.

The goal of the courting season has always been to find Prince Dryden a bride, but *my* focus has been thwarting an assassination attempt on his life. I never wished Dryden ill, but I also didn't think too deeply about him marrying one of the princesses at the end of all this. Now that I know Dryden and Neo are one and the same, it hits me differently than it did before.

Dryden comes up beside me, patiently waiting for me to go on. I glance over at him, my gaze halting just below his face as a riot of emotions threaten to rise up. I shove them down with effort, telling myself they mean nothing, that I'm just confused because of what happened the night before. Anyone in my position would feel the same.

Forcing myself to look up into his green eyes, I ignore my body's involuntary reaction to the way his gaze sweeps over me like the lightest of caresses.

I give myself a mental slap.

Yes, I'm here to help avoid an assassination, but barring his murder, on the other side of this whole ridiculous charade, he will be expected to take a bride. The truth of the matter is that I've grown to care for him, and I'm in the unique position to not only keep him safe but also offer him some valuable insight into these females. There's no reason to withhold any information that might help him make a more well-informed decision about who he should pick as his bride.

Right?

I clear my throat and glance back at the pudgy peach right at face level. Reaching up, I pluck it from the tree. I can't make myself say the next words while still looking at him. "I think you and Shayla would get along well," I say honestly, even as a knot forms in my gut from the confession. "She's lovely, and a free thinker. She would challenge you, keep you from getting bored."

The more truth I admit, the worse I feel. "I think she'd be a good companion for you . . . if it turns out she's not the assassin, of course."

Dryden makes a sound that rumbles deep in his chest like he agrees with me. I swivel to look at him and find him staring down at me.

"You think she's a good choice?" His gaze is searching again, stripping my layers away in a manner that makes my heart start to race.

I swallow and then wet my lips. "She'd be perfect for you," I say, hating that it might be true.

Dryden's gaze darkens, his green eyes filling with intensity. Grasping my arms, he takes two steps forward, forcing me to retreat until my back is pressed up against the peach tree trunk, out of sight of the chaperone or any guards who may be able to see us down the row of trees.

Dryden releases me but cages me in by grabbing the branches on either side of my head.

"Tell me," he challenges.

"Tell you what?" I ask, the words coming out no louder than a breathy whisper.

"Tell me how the other princesses are perfect for me. Tell me which one you think I should wed. Which one I should take to bed." His voice is hard, his gaze punishing as it holds my own.

"I—"

"I want to hear you say it. I want to watch the words come from your mouth as you tell me how I belong with someone else, so I know exactly what you look like when you lie."

I gasp, my eyes going wide, and something about the sound ignites Dryden.

His mouth comes crashing down on mine. Not out of necessity this time, but out of pent-up passion that will no longer be denied.

Our mouths move together as if that's what they were made for. He kisses me deeply, branding himself on my lips in a way that I never knew was possible.

I know there's a world outside of the two of us, but it doesn't exist. Not right now. Not to me. The only thing that exists is Dryden and this perfect moment in time.

He nips at my lower lip, and the sensation makes my stomach bottom out and my head light. His hand dives into my hair, and I don't give a thought to the pins he's knocking free or how it's going to look later.

Dropping the peach, I paw at him, my arms wrapping around his neck and pulling him impossibly closer.

He moans, and we're pressed so close together that I can feel the deep sound as it resonates in his chest. He rips his mouth away from mine, only to place a trail of kisses from beneath my chin and down my neck. One of his hands has dropped out of my hair to my throat, and his thumb is brushing lazy circles on the sensitive skin at the base of my neck, making my head spin.

I didn't know it was possible to feel like this.

"Dryden." I say his name on a heated whisper.

"Your skin tastes like honey," he says, his breath fanning my ear. "So sweet. I'll never get enough."

I'm burning up inside.

He pulls back so his face is directly in front of mine. I'm taking in big gulps of air, and he's not breathing much easier himself. He starts to speak, and when he does, his lips brush up against mine with every word, setting fire to my already heated blood.

"When I said that wouldn't happen again, I lied. I've been holding myself back for so long, but as soon as I tasted you, Rowan, I knew there was no going back."

His confession kindles something inside of me that blazes brightly, warming not only my body but my heart as well. And since we're being honest . . . "When I told you I didn't want it to happen again, I lied as well."

As soon as I say the words, his mouth is on mine again, taking everything and leaving me with nothing in return.

Suddenly, Dryden pulls back and then freezes. I blink up at him, still lost in a bit of a haze as he goes unnaturally still. Like a predator who senses prey.

A spike of trepidation runs through me. Something's not right. "What's wrong?"

"It's quiet," he says, the words rumbling in his chest, which is still pressed against mine.

"Um, yes?"

"Too quiet."

He steps away from me, his gaze alert and his head on a swivel as he scans down the row of trees. "The guards are missing. The chaperone, too."

I take a shaky step forward, trying not to focus on how unsteady I am from what just happened. Or how unaffected Dryden seems to be. "Could they just be giving us privacy?"

"Maybe." But his gaze darts about, and his frown says he doesn't think that's it.

I'm not sure I do either.

The only sound is the wind blowing through the trees. Fingers of unease start a slow trek down my spine.

"Come on," Dryden says. Grabbing my hand, he tugs me forward, positioning himself in front of me as we rush down the row of trees back toward where the carriage should be waiting.

When we reach the edge of the orchard, Dryden suddenly throws his arm out, halting me. I slam into his forearm and then he spins toward me. The look in his eyes makes my blood freeze in my veins, because what I see in them is something I've never seen in Dryden, as himself or as Neo.

Fear.

Chapter 28

AS QUICKLY AS THE FEAR APPEARED, DRYDEN wipes it from his features and a mask of determination slams down in its place. He tries moving me back in the direction we came from, but I peek over his shoulder to see what caused the color to leach from his face.

The chaperone, the driver, and the two guards who accompanied us to the peach orchard are sprawled out on the ground. I only get a glimpse of the macabre scene before Dryden is pulling me down the tree-lined path once again, but a glimpse is more than enough for me to know that they are dead.

Red was splashed across their faces, necks, and chests. The chaperone, whose name I don't even remember, still had a dagger protruding from her. Her eyes stared lifelessly up at the sky while her mouth was twisted open in a silent scream.

The guards looked like they'd had their throats cut, maybe with the same dagger that was still embedded in the chaperone's chest. As long as I live, I'll never be able to scrub the image of that scene from my mind. I'm going to see it when I close my eyes at night and before I open them again in the morning.

Nausea rolls in my gut, but now isn't the time to fall apart. My life, *Dryden's* life, depends on me keeping my head right now.

My feet pound into the soft grass, and I send up a silent thanks to whoever is listening that I chose to wear slipper-like footwear today instead of something with a heel. The shoes I have on aren't as good as boots, but at least I can still run.

But where exactly are we running? The horses and carriage are in the other direction, and we can't run all the way back to White-spire. The city is miles away.

"Where are we going?" I ask Dryden without slowing my stride. Years of running in the slums has conditioned me to move and move fast, so I'm not yet winded.

He glances over at me. His hair, mussed from either my hands or the wind as we flee, is wild, but the look in his eyes isn't. "There's an abandoned caretaker's cabin not far from here." His gaze only briefly touches me before he's back to scanning the orchard for the threat we know is hiding somewhere. "I'm getting you out of here. Somewhere safe. And then I'm going back to look for the murderer."

My stomach bottoms out. "Absolutely not."

Dryden's grip on my hand tightens as if he anticipates having to drag me to the cabin, but other than that, he doesn't respond.

"Dryden," I growl. "You're not going back there alone."

He opens his mouth to respond, but the words never make it out before he's roughly shoving me away from him.

As I fall, something whizzes by my cheek, close enough to pierce the air where my head just was.

My teeth snap together when I slam into the ground, my shoulder and hip taking the brunt of the fall. A coppery tang fills my mouth and I realize I've bitten my lip.

"Stay down," Dryden yells just as another projectile rips through the low-hanging branches above me and sinks into the soft earth five feet away.

I swing my gaze across the open row to where Dryden is hunkered next to a peach tree. There's a small cut high on his cheek that's leaking blood down the side of his face. He's too far away for me to see how deep it is, but just the sight of the wound causes fury to bubble up inside me.

I start to scramble to my feet, but Dryden holds up an arm. "No, stay where you are," he commands. "Use the tree for cover."

Another arrow rips through the branches, but this time it's meant for Dryden, finding its target and punching into his shoulder. Dryden grunts and twists his body so that he's hidden the best he can behind the narrow peach tree trunk.

I'm up and moving before I realize I've made the decision to do so. Dryden yells at me to stop, but I'm not listening as I sprint across the narrow row, my gaze locked on him.

An arrow rips harmlessly through my skirts flowing behind me as I move. I dive into a roll right in front of Dryden. When I pop back up into a crouch, the expression on his face is half relieved, half furious.

Ignoring the look, I quickly assess his wounds, dismissing the cut on his cheek immediately. It's bleeding a lot, but that's common with head wounds. I know right away it's not deep. The arrow in his shoulder, though, that's a problem. There's a growing bloom of red soaking through his clothes.

Another arrow streaks by us, and I peek around Dryden to try to see who is shooting at us, but the same branches that are helping conceal us are hiding the archer.

"We have to get out of here," I say, and Dryden nods. Already some of the color has left his face, but determination glints in his eyes.

"The caretaker's cabin is that way," he says, gesturing with his hand. "We need to run through the rows and then cut up toward the far end of the orchard. If we can make it, we can bar ourselves inside and wait for the palace to send guards out to look for us."

I nod. Dryden starts to rise, but I stop him with a hand on his good shoulder. He can't run through these trees with this arrow sticking out of him.

Without giving him any warning, I grasp the shaft of the arrow in both hands and quickly snap it as close to his wound as I can, wincing when Dryden swears.

I know enough to leave the point where it is until we have time to pack the wound. I'm sure it's painful, but right now it's partially stanching the flow of blood.

"A little warning next time," he pants.

I huff out a half laugh that's more nerves than anything. "Sorry."

Taking hold of the fabric of my heavy skirts, I rip the stitches until I'm free of the material, left in just my long-sleeved fitted top and pants. I've never been happier about incorporating the pants and overskirt dresses into my wardrobe. "Let's go," I say to Dryden, and he nods.

We're up and running again, but this time ducking branches and trunks as we sprint straight through the rows of peach trees rather than down them. The archer is dogging our steps; arrows pierce the air around us. But to keep up, he's forced to run as well, impairing his aim.

Dryden tries to reach for me with his injured arm, but when a streak of pain tightens his face, he drops his hand. "This way," he calls to me, and we take a sharp turn back up a row.

Fear takes hold of my heart and squeezes. I expect the archer to pop out in front of us at any moment, but as we near the end of the orchard without a confrontation, I can see a small stone dwelling down a slope in front of us.

My feet get heavy. There's no cover between us and the cabin. If this archer is any good, we'll never make it there unscathed. But we don't really have another choice.

Both Dryden and I race toward the caretaker's cabin as fast as we can. We're halfway there when a streak of fire cuts its way across my arm and I cry out. I don't need to look down to know that I've been grazed.

Still sprinting, Dryden grabs me and shoves me in front of him, using his body as a shield. There's no time for me to argue that he's the prince and I'm a nobody, so I push myself to move as quickly as possible. Our only chance is getting inside that cabin before one of the archer's arrows finds its deadly mark.

We're almost there, just a few more steps, when Dryden releases a grunt of pain and then his body slams into me, shoving me forward into the closed door. The knob presses into my gut, but I manage to squeeze a hand in front of me and turn it. When the door swings open, both of us tumble into the house, falling to the dusty ground.

Dryden shifts just enough that I'm able to drag myself out from under him. Another arrow cuts through the air, thudding into the floorboards an inch from my hand, and I gasp.

Staying as low as possible, I rush back to the door to shut and lock it, stopping the onslaught of projectiles.

I get a single glimpse of our attacker as they loose another arrow, which sticks in the door the instant it slams shut.

I should have known who it was the moment the first arrow struck the ground.

Princess Shayla.

Chapter 29

FROZEN IN SHOCK, I FINALLY SNAP OUT OF IT at Dryden's grunt of pain. I turn to find him on the floor where he fell, two new arrows sticking out of him. Arrows that might have been embedded in my flesh if he hadn't shielded me with his body. One in the back of his thigh and the other in his lower back just above his hip.

My heart seizes at the sight and then almost stops completely when he tries to struggle to his feet.

"No, stop," I say, rushing to him, crouching in front of him. "Don't move. You have more arrows in you. Two of them."

Dryden huffs a sound I think is supposed to be a laugh, but it isn't filled with even an ounce of humor. "Unfortunately, I'm acutely aware of that fact." His gaze moves from me to the locked door visible over my shoulder. "Did you happen to get a look at who was shooting at us?"

I nod. "Princess Shayla," I say around the knot of betrayal lodged in my chest.

"Are you sure?" he asks, looking surprised.

"Yes."

I may not have seen her face, but I know it's her. She's wearing her kingdom's purple and black colors, and I saw her unmistakable red bow clenched in her hand before I slammed the door.

Grim resolve settles on Dryden's face. "Did you see anyone else with her?"

I shake my head. "It was just her."

"Well, at least we have that going for us."

I don't bother mentioning that her bow negates any two-on-one advantage we might have.

Dryden tries to get to his feet again, and rather than wasting time trying to stop him, I loop his arm over my shoulder to help as he struggles to stand. Sweat mixes with the blood on his face, his coloring pale beneath the red smeared on his skin.

He glances at the door. "The lock should keep her out, but we need to find weapons to defend ourselves in case she finds a way inside."

I look around the room. The windows I see are small and covered with barred wood shutters. There are two doors that lead to somewhere else, but I can't worry about that just yet.

"We *need* to dress your wounds or you're going to bleed out."

"I'm fine," he insists, even as his clothes soak up the blood leaking from his injuries.

The cabin door rattles and we both freeze, watching the knob turn. I hold my breath until the lock catches, keeping Shayla from entering. She gives it a couple more tries, rattling the door aggressively before it falls silent again.

I glance at Dryden; his nostrils are flared and his mouth is pressed into a hard line. Every sharp edge and bunched muscle across his face and body radiates fury as we wait to see what happens next.

My mind keeps repeating the same phrase over and over again, trying to get it to sink in.

Shayla is the assassin.

Our interactions over the last weeks flood through me. The conversations, the meals, the private jokes. The friendship I thought we were building. I always knew she could be the assassin, but I'd never really believed it.

She was too genuine. Too real. The only one of the tributes who didn't feel like they were putting on a front.

Yet this whole time, it was her. Always her I was looking for, hiding in plain sight.

What did I miss? Could I have known? Should I have?

From the other side of the door, we hear Shayla sigh loudly, then the door shudders once more. My guess is she kicked it, but after that, the only sounds are our ragged breaths.

Dryden tries to take a step, but his injured leg gives out on him, almost taking both of us down. We manage to get him over to a weathered table to lean up against and he growls in frustration. "We need to find a weapon."

He's right, but so am I. If I don't stop the bleeding, or at least slow it down, he's going to lose consciousness. Or maybe even bleed out. And I need to make sure the cabin is secure.

There's a broken wood chair on the floor. Slipping out from under his arms, I grab a large piece of it that has a pointed end. It's not much of a weapon, but if Shayla gets close enough, it could be used to bludgeon her, or with enough force, stake her.

"Take this," I say, and hand the shard of wood to Dryden. "I'm going to check the other rooms and look for something to wrap those wounds."

"It can wait—"

"No, it can't."

"I told you that I'm fine."

"Do I need to remind you that if you die, I die too?" I snap back. He's still my contract holder, a fact he must have temporarily forgotten.

"Rowan—" he starts, and I know he's just going to argue with me, so I tell him, "I'll be right back," and leave before he can try to stop me.

The only other rooms besides the main one are a single bedroom and a windowless bathing room. The windows in the bedroom are also small and barred by thick wood shutters. I don't think they're large enough for someone to fit through.

I find what I'm looking for in the bedroom. A sheet. After ripping the dusty and dirty sheet from the partially collapsed bed, I rush back into the main room only to find that Dryden's somehow managed to hobble over to the small open kitchen on his own. With two arrows still sticking out of him, he's opening and closing drawers with his good arm as he searches for a weapon. And it appears he's been successful, in part, because I spot a rusted table knife clenched in his hand.

His leg buckles but he catches himself on the counter with his uninjured arm, staying standing through sheer willpower alone.

With a gasp, I run to his side, bringing the sheet with me. I don't even bother arguing with him. If we make it out of this alive, I intend to let him know how he's the most infuriatingly stubborn fae I've ever met, but right now I'm on a mission.

"I found a knife," he says, his voice weak.

"Good," is all I say as I lead him back to lean against the table.

I start ripping the sheet into long strips. As Dryden watches silently, I finish the task quickly, then go to the kitchen, where I find a small bowl. Placing it under the semi-rusted faucet, I hold my breath as I twist the knob. Something makes a clunking sound in the pipes, which I'm sure haven't been used for years, but eventually water that appears clean starts flowing.

Returning to Dryden, I crouch down in front of him, inspecting the back of his thigh where one arrow is embedded, thinking that will be the easiest to wrap. Without waiting for permission, I rip a bigger hole in his pants, feeling like there's a clock ticking in the back of my mind.

We're certainly safer inside than we were out in the open, but it doesn't mean I feel safe. I'm not sure how Shayla could get through the door to reach us, but I don't believe for a second she's going to leave us be.

"It doesn't look too deep. I'm going to pull the arrow and then dress the wound."

I inwardly cringe. It's not only going to hurt, but ideally this wound would be sewn and wrapped with sterile dressing. Instead, I'm going to have to pack and wrap it with filthy makeshift bandages.

Dipping a piece of sheet into the water, I do my best to clean around where the arrow is lodged in his leg. Once that task is done, I take hold of the shaft. Knowing it's going to be painful, and the bleeding will worsen, I pause before yanking it out.

Over his shoulder, Dryden looks down on me. His face doesn't betray any of the pain he must be feeling. "Do it."

With a curt nod, I fix my gaze on the injury and pull the arrow free in one swift motion.

Dryden grunts as blood starts flowing in earnest from the hole in the back of his thigh.

With deft fingers, I pack the wound by pressing a balled-up piece of sheet into it. His body tightens, but he doesn't make a sound. Once it is in place, I take another strip of sheet and wrap it around Dryden's leg as many times as I can to create a tourniquet over the open wound to slow the loss of blood.

One down. Two to go.

I stand to inspect the arrow embedded low in his back. The

head went in at an angle, the entry point low on his hip. I'm not a physician, but I think it's just embedded in muscle, which has to be better than an organ. Since the arrow went through more than one layer of clothes, I need a better look to be sure.

"We need to get your clothes off," I tell Dryden, and even in his weakened condition, he glances over his shoulder at me with one dark eyebrow quirked and a look that makes my cheeks heat.

"Is that so?"

I duck my head, busying myself with trying to gently rip some of the fabric away, definitely not because I can't bring myself to look in his eye. "So I can see the entry point. It's gone through your jacket."

"Oh, Rowan," he says. My name feels like a caress, and a small shiver runs down my back that's completely inappropriate considering the circumstances. "You never need to explain why you want me to disrobe. I'm happy to oblige."

"I can't believe you're flirting right now," I grumble.

His low chuckle does nothing to defuse the situation. "I can think of no better time."

I roll my eyes and gingerly help Dryden slip out of his overcoat. I ripped a hole big enough that I can slide it over the arrow once it's off his arm, but when I jostle the shaft, he tenses.

"Besides," he says, and I hear the strain in his voice this time. "Flirting with you keeps my mind off what you're doing."

I bite my lower lip, my heart tweaking for him and the agony he must be experiencing. The arrow is sticking out right above the waistline of his pants. His shirt is saturated in blood around the area. The front of his shirt is also covered in blood, so at this point it's just in the way.

"Can we take this off too?" I ask, plucking at his shirt.

"What did I already tell you about taking off my clothes?" The lightness is back in his tone, and I know he must be forcing it. "Be my guest."

Slowly and carefully, making sure not to knock the arrow piercing him, I untuck the shirt from his pants before moving to stand in front of him to unbutton it. I feel Dryden's gaze on me, but instead of looking up, I concentrate on my task.

Once his torn and bloody shirt is hanging open in front of him, I do my best to slide it off his injured shoulder without hurting him. The arrowhead is still embedded in his flesh, but since I already snapped off the shaft, it's relatively easy to get his shirt off that arm.

Without meaning to, I make a small noise in the back of my throat when I see the wound. It's not bleeding as badly as it could be, but the whole arrowhead is sunk into Dryden. It must be unimaginably painful. How is he still conscious?

I shift to go around him and tend to the wound on his lower back first when he reaches up and tugs my bottom lip free with his thumb. I hadn't even known I was chewing on it.

When I release my lip, he slowly runs the pad of his thumb back and forth over it. I can't help looking up at him then.

I see the pain shining in his eyes, but that's not all I see. There's something else there, deeper and more potent than the pain he's fighting through. Something my mind can't process right now except to acknowledge that it's a look that calls to me, demanding I answer.

Taking a step back, I break the physical connection between the two of us. Dryden's pupils are blown out, and his breathing seems fast. I don't know if it's from the pain or something else, but I'd be lying if I said my own rapid heartbeat was only out of fear.

A trickle of blood leaks out of the wound on his shoulder, sliding over his pec and down the defined ridges of his stomach. The sight knocks some sense into me, and I pull away, swiftly moving behind him and focusing on the long shaft of the arrow lodged in his back.

Now that his shirt and waistcoat are removed, I can see the entry point more clearly. The wound is just as intimidating as the others, an angry gash where the arrowhead is embedded that's steadily leaking blood onto his pants. It needs to be stitched, but I don't have anything to work with here besides the linens I pulled off the bed.

"Just yank it out," Dryden says through clenched teeth.

I press my lips together and make sure that I have a wad of cloth to pack the wound, as well as a strip of the bedsheet to wrap around his waist, ready to go. Without warning, I grab the arrow and yank. Dryden grunts in pain but doesn't cry out. The muscles in his back are bunched as I press the cloth into the wound to stanch the flow of blood. I then start winding the sheet around his body the best I can, wrapping my arms around him at times to accomplish the task quickly. At one point, I have to pull his pants down a little to fully cover the wound, and I get a glimpse of the top of Dryden's backside. My cheeks flush even as I dutifully avert my gaze.

Dryden chuckles lightly. "I must admit," he says, sounding almost normal. "I did not anticipate you pulling down my pants as part of this outing. What a lovely turn of events."

I snort. "You're probably the only one who didn't foresee that, considering all the rumors of us now floating around the palace."

The laugh that bursts out of Dryden sounds sincere. "Good point."

I tie off my makeshift bandage, making sure it's as tight as I can get it, and then coax the prince to lean back against the table.

"Last one," I say softly, inspecting his shoulder wound.

This one is the trickiest because I'm not exactly sure how to wrap it. Circling the strip of bedsheet over his shoulder and under his arm is going to be the best I can do, but I'm not confident it's going to be enough pressure against the wound. Maybe I should just leave the arrowhead in this one?

Reaching up, I gently prod the arrow and Dryden sucks in a sharp breath of air.

I wince. "I'm sorry."

When I look up, sweat has dampened the hair framing Dryden's face, and although it's clear he's trying to hide it from me, pain and exhaustion pull at his features. The cut on his cheek isn't bleeding anymore, but blood, dirt, and sweat are smeared across his face.

"I'm not sure I should pull this one."

Dryden rolls his other shoulder. "It has to come out. My arm is useless with it in."

"I'm worried I won't be able to stop the bleeding. You've already lost too much."

"I'm fine," he stubbornly says, when he's clearly not.

When I don't move to pull the arrow out, Dryden makes a frustrated sound in the back of his throat and then reaches up and over. He's already gripping the broken piece of the shaft when I realize he intends to yank it out himself.

"Dryden, no!" I shout, but it's too late. With a grunt of pain, he yanks the arrow from the wound and a fresh flow of blood pours from the hole.

"Bloody hell," he cusses, and with a gasp I slap a wadded piece of sheet against the injury. It gets saturated before I can even start to wrap it.

My eyes are wild; my heart feels like it's beating hard enough to crack a rib as I order the stubborn and stupid prince to put pressure on his wound.

Grabbing the remaining bedsheet, I tear off a larger piece and quickly prepare it to pack into the bloody injury. I slap Dryden's hand away, not caring about being gentle anymore, and after pulling off the saturated cloth, I replace it with a new makeshift bandage, using what strength I have to press against the wound.

Clearly in pain, Dryden cusses again and grits his teeth, but my primary concern is no longer how much agony I'm causing him. It's stopping the blood loss. I may not be a doctor, but even I know there's only so much he can safely lose.

My hand is shaking as I press the cloth to his wound, watching to see if it's going to fill with blood as quickly as the last one, when Dryden's hand comes over mine. I glance up into his green eyes, reading the pain he's trying to suppress there.

"I'm f—"

"If you try to tell me you're 'fine' one more time, I'm going to pick up one of these arrows and use it to punch another hole in you."

He must read the sincerity—or the panic—in my eyes, because he doesn't make a joke. He only nods.

"I can help keep the pressure on it so you can wrap it."

Blood hasn't leaked through this time, so with a shaky nod I carefully slip my hand away, letting Dryden hold it in place.

It's slow going, but I eventually get the wound wrapped up like the other two, only satisfied that he's not going to bleed out after checking all of them twice to make sure they aren't leaking. My handiwork isn't pretty, but it seems to be getting the job done.

As I stand in front of him, my limbs weaken as my body starts to crash. Without meaning to, I sway, and Dryden immediately reaches out with both arms to steady me, wincing slightly with the movement. When I regain my footing, he removes his hands, only to notice that one of his palms is covered in blood.

It's not until that moment that the shallow wound on my bicep starts to sting. I'd completely forgotten that I was grazed.

"Your turn," Dryden says, trying to get me to sit on the table he's been propped against. He's moving easier than he was with the arrows sticking out of him, but he's still proceeding carefully.

I shake my head. "No, I'm f—"

He stops me by placing two fingers against my mouth, but it's the look on his face that keeps the protests from returning. It's as if he's begging me without words to let him take care of me.

Taking a shaky breath, I nod, and he removes his hand. After I sit on the table, he moves to my side, gently picking up my arm. The injury is on my right bicep. My sleeve is ripped and partially soaked in blood, but it's nowhere near as saturated as Dryden's clothes. Now that I'm focused on it, the ache has intensified, refusing to be ignored, but I try not to let it show. The cut is the least of our worries right now.

Grabbing the forgotten kitchen knife, Dryden uses it to cut the sleeve off my dress, ripping it first at the seams and then down the middle so that he doesn't have to peel it over the wound.

I look away when the injury is exposed. I'm no stranger to cuts, or worse. I have the scars to prove it. But I've seen my fill of ripped flesh for the day.

Dryden is quiet as he cleans the wound. He's gentle, his fingers tender as he carefully runs the wet cloth around the torn skin. "It's not too deep. You'll probably still need stitches when we return to the palace. But it's not bleeding very much anymore."

I nod, if only to let him know that I'm listening.

The wet sheet brushes against the wound, and I flinch involuntarily at the spike of pain.

"Sorry," he says, and I shake my head.

"It's fine. It just surprised me."

He sucks in a lungful of air through his nose. "No. It's not fine."

The hard edge to his voice makes me glance over at him. When I do, fury is written across his face, but his touch remains light and careful as he wraps a strip of fabric around my arm.

As he finishes, he has to pull the cloth tight so it holds when he ties it off, and I can't stop my arm muscles from spasming. He jerks his gaze to me quickly, reading my face, which I keep purposefully blank.

Dryden releases a heavy sigh. "This shouldn't have happened."

Even though he's done with wrapping my wound, he doesn't release my arm. He gently brushes his fingers over the wrappings on the back side of my arm, his calloused fingertips sweeping over some of the exposed skin as he does, ramping up my awareness of our closeness.

"It's basically a scratch," I murmur, hoping it helps smooth the worry lines on his face, even though we both know it's a lie. It will scar, but I'll live, and that's what is really important.

"I was wrong to drag you into this mess. You could have been killed today."

Dryden's head is bowed, obscuring my view of his eyes. Reaching over with my free hand, I tentatively brush the tips of my fingers over his cheekbone. His breath catches, but he still doesn't look up at me.

"You didn't force me. You gave me the option of walking away," I remind him.

He shakes his head. "I didn't really. I offered you a lifeline with strings attached. It was like waving a steak in front of a starving person. Of course you were always going to accept. What I did was wrong."

I press my lips together, thinking back to the night we first met and the bargain he offered me. Stay and pretend to be Princess Greer and I would earn not only my freedom, but money to live a comfortable new life. He's not wrong. There was no way I would have turned that down. But for the life of me, I can't be angry at him for it. Despite the danger, I wouldn't have traded what I've gained these last weeks for the promise of safety.

"I have to tell you something," he says. "Something I should have told you before but didn't. Because I was selfish. And a coward."

Dryden still won't look at me. I've never heard him speak like this before.

"Okay, what is it?" I ask, almost scared to know what he's about to say.

He takes a breath and then says, "You won't die tonight if I do. I've already freed you from your contract."

My body goes hot and then cold.

He nullified my contract? I'm no longer indentured?

The very air feels like it stills as Dryden's confession sinks in.

"What?" I ask, but he doesn't respond. He knows I heard him.

I've lived so many years under the weight of my servitude, it's hard to believe I'm actually free.

"But . . . when?"

Shouldn't I have felt the moment I was released? Surely something of this magnitude couldn't have happened without my knowledge. I always thought I could feel the weight of the contract, but perhaps that was always just in my head.

"After our last dance lesson at Olette's. Before you even set foot in Whitespire." He runs a hand over his face, and I hear the regret in his voice. "If I had told you then like I should have, you never would have gotten caught up in all of this. You'd be somewhere far from here right now. Safe. But instead, I selfishly dragged you into this mess, putting your life at risk."

He promised me freedom from the start, but all this time I almost didn't dare hope for it. In truth, I'd been so caught up in being Princess Greer that part of me had forgotten what it was like to be Rowan, an indentured servant from the slums. But with the mention of my contract, it all comes back to me, along with the impact of what it means to be free.

Finally free.

"Dryden, you freed me . . ." Tears spring to my eyes as a wave of gratitude smashes into me. "Thank you."

He shakes his head, and even without looking into his eyes, I see the guilt and shame splashed across his face. "No, don't thank me. I should have freed you from your contract the moment I took it over from that vile fae. I never should have forced you to pretend to be Princess Greer. I was too obsessed with my own goals to see how wrong that was. To see the danger I was putting you in."

He's right, he could have released me from my contract earlier. It would have been the moral thing to do, to give me the choice from the very beginning, but I can't bring myself to regret everything that's happened since. These past weeks have changed me.

He probably thinks I hate him right now, but how could I when I'm suddenly so happy?

I run my fingers over the tip of his ear, then slide my hand into his hair—something I've been secretly aching to do for longer than I'm willing to admit even to myself. The strands are as soft and silky as they look.

He rests his forehead on my shoulder as I continue to run my hand through his hair, silently soothing him.

So quietly that I have to strain to hear him, he says, "I'm so sorry."

I nod, even though he can't see the gesture. "I forgive you," I whisper, because I think he needs to hear it.

He finally lifts his gaze, and when I look into his eyes, I see brokenness there that makes my heart ache. "Truly?"

"Of course. You did what you thought was right at the time."

"But without regard to what was right for you."

"You got me away from Sinclair. You gave me a chance to be something other than what I was. I'll never be sorry for that."

He sees the tears in my eyes, and he lifts his hand to wipe them away. "I caused these. I'm so sorry. I never want to make you cry."

"I'm not sorry," I say with a wobbly smile. "Happy tears. They're the best tears I've ever cried."

Carefully, like I'm made of something delicate and precious, he folds me in his arms and lets me continue to cry. And I do, until all the broken pieces of me are washed away with my tears.

Chapter 30

"REINFORCEMENTS SHOULD HAVE ARRIVED BY now." Dryden paces in the small space, limping slightly.

The light in the cabin was already bad, but hours have passed and the sun's rays are no longer seeping through the cracks in the shutters, leaving the room dim and visibility low. We found a couple of candles and lit them with matches from a discarded matchbox hidden within one of the kitchen cabinets, but they do little to bring true light into the space.

I stand from the chair I was seated in, stepping into Dryden's path and forcing him to stop. It's not that I disagree with him—someone should have come looking for us by now—but pacing isn't doing him any favors. And he needs to get off his injured leg.

"You need to rest." Gently taking his uninjured arm, I try to lead him over to the dusty couch, but he won't move.

When I glance up into his eyes, he's staring down at me with a haunted look. "Something is wrong."

I want to deny it, but pretending he's wrong won't do us any favors. I sigh. "I know."

"If guards haven't been dispatched to look for us yet, that means there's most likely someone else at the palace aiding Shayla."

What's scary about that thought is that if he's right and Shayla isn't acting alone, that means her accomplice is powerful enough to keep the palace guards from looking for their prince. Who has that amount of power but has been able to hide in plain sight?

"If no one is coming for us, we're going to have to get out of this ourselves. We have to leave the cabin and try to make it back to the carriage. We can take it back to the palace."

"But we don't have any idea where Shayla is," I argue. "What if her plan at this point is just to wait us out? Once we set foot outside this cabin, we're sitting ducks."

Dryden plows a hand through his hair, shoving the black strands off his forehead. "You're not wrong. But if Shayla is working with someone else, if we wait much longer, we may be up against more than just a princess with a bow and arrow. She could be waiting for her own reinforcements to arrive. What I'm most worried about is being injured and outnumbered with only a rusty kitchen knife to defend ourselves."

I chew on my bottom lip. There are no good options. Stay, and we may just be waiting for death. Leave, and we might be walking straight into it. It's a gamble either way.

Dryden's restlessness tells me he'd rather take his chances in the open than wait it out in the cabin. But is that really prudent? And if we leave the cabin, we're going to have to move fast. Is Dryden even capable of that? He has three arrow wounds that could start bleeding again if he moves too much.

I'm opening my mouth to tell him that I don't think we should chance it when a crash comes from the bedroom. We both spring into action. Dryden grabs my arm and propels us toward the front door. Throwing the lock, he shoves the door with his uninjured shoulder and pushes me through and out into the open just as someone bursts through the bedroom door, proving I was wrong about the windows being too small to fit through.

In the low light, I still can't see Shayla's face. She has a cloth wrapped around her mouth, and with her hood pulled low over her brow, the rest of her features are hidden in shadows. What's clear is the gleam of the arrowhead when she lifts her bow and points it toward us.

Toward Dryden.

Just as she looses her arrow, I dive for the prince, shoving him to the side and out of the open doorway. The sharp hiss of the arrow splits the air as it whizzes by my ear. Too close.

Dryden grabs my hand, and we run up the small hill toward the orchard. The tree cover isn't far, but until we get to it, we are completely out in the open. Just as we're about to reach cover, Dryden grunts and then stumbles to his knees, yanking me down with him. I spot the rusty kitchen knife in the grass next to me. He must have dropped it. Snatching the blade, I pop to my feet and twist back toward the cabin.

Shayla's backlit figure fills the doorway below, another arrow nocked and pointed in our direction. The knife is sailing out of my hand toward the princess before I've even made the conscious decision to throw it. I know I've hit my mark when she cries out and hunches over, dropping her bow to clutch at her thigh.

This is it; we have to escape now before she picks up her bow.

Turning back to Dryden, my heart stumbles when I see he's still on the ground with another arrow protruding from his back. He's still.

I drop to my knees, fearing the worst, but he rouses and tries to stand. With my help, he struggles to his feet.

He tries to take in a breath, and I hear the wheeze in his chest. Did the arrow pierce his lung?

"Do you think you can make it back to the carriage?"

Dryden nods. "I'm okay," he says weakly.

A lie, but we have to go. Another arrow sails through the air but goes wide. When I look back toward the cabin, it's to see the bow back in Shayla's hand and her limping to reach us.

Dryden and I take off, zigzagging through the orchard in the direction we think the carriage is, with just the moonlight to guide us. The only good thing about the lack of sunlight is that it will be hard for Shayla to see us.

At first Dryden is able to keep up with me, even with a fresh arrow sticking out of his back. But as we dart in and out of the rows of trees, he begins to flag, eventually stopping to lean against a tree trunk.

Each breath he takes sounds both wet and weak. "You have to go without me."

I'm already shaking my head before he finishes. "No. It can't be that much farther. We'll make it together."

The telltale whistling of an arrow piercing the air sounds to our left. I don't know which direction it came from, but it was far enough away that I don't think Shayla knows exactly where we are. She's probably shooting blindly in hopes it causes us to give away our position.

Dryden shakes his head and tries to push me away from him, but he's so weak he can't make me budge.

Another arrow whizzes through the air, this one closer than before.

Not willing to stand here and argue with Dryden, I sling his uninjured arm over my shoulders and tug him forward. He grunts in pain but doesn't pull away.

His limp has gotten worse. His body is probably too weak from blood loss to compensate for the injury to his thigh. I don't even want to think about what damage that arrow is doing in his back right now.

As we stumble-run through the orchard, his breathing worsens until he's gasping for air. I urge Dryden on, knowing the only thing that can help him now is medical attention. I can feel the strain in every step he takes, but I force myself to ignore his pain as I all but drag him forward. All of my focus needs to be on finding that carriage and getting him back to Whitespire, where he'll be tended to by the best physicians in the kingdom.

We finally break through the maze of trees, and I spot the carriage, as well as the carnage Shayla left, not far away. Maybe a hundred feet. Despite the slaughter decorating the ground around them, the horses are grazing peacefully.

"We're almost there," I say to Dryden, but he doesn't even have the energy to answer.

My heart slams against my ribs when we reach the carriage. I throw open the door and start to help Dryden into the cab when an arrow sinks into the gilded wood to the right of my head.

"Get in," I order him, and he basically tumbles the rest of the way into the cab. I slam the door behind him and swing around, looking for Shayla, but I don't see her anywhere.

I rush to the front to climb up on the driver's seat, hoping that last arrow was another blind shot that got lucky. Then a second arrow whistles through the air, sinking into one of the horses' necks.

No. No!

Both horses rear up, whinnying and beating the air with their hooves in fear. The uninjured horse tries to bolt but is held back by the other, which sinks to its knees as blood pours from its neck wound, staining its white coat.

My heart cries for the animal, but there's nothing I can do. It will be dead in moments.

The hard truth sinks in, burning my hopes to ash: We can't flee in the carriage anymore.

Our only chance is to get the remaining horse unhitched and ride him back to Everlight. But how can I free the horse and get Dryden mounted while dodging Shayla's arrows?

A figure steps out of the orchard only about fifty feet away, limping slightly. Even with the moonlight backlighting her, I can make out another arrow nocked and ready to aim.

As I watch her raise the bow, fear and panic fall away and rage surges through me, burning the lesser emotions away.

I'm injured and bleeding, Dryden's close to death, and she just killed an innocent animal.

I'm done acting like prey. I've been that my entire life. It's time to fight back.

Shayla looses her arrow, but I'm already moving, so it misses its mark. There are several discarded weapons left over from the murdered fae littering the ground around the carriage.

Swooping low as I run in Shayla's direction, I grab a loaded crossbow without breaking my stride. In one fluid motion, I lift the weapon, aim, and pull the trigger. It's not a weapon I'm particularly used to, but the bolt comes close enough to my attacker to make her flinch.

I don't know how to reload the crossbow, so I toss the weapon aside, hitting the ground a moment later to dodge another arrow. There's a fallen guard lying beside me, his lifeless eyes staring straight up into the starry sky.

Another wave of anger rushes through me. All these fae, needlessly killed.

Reaching across his body, I pull a dagger sheathed at his waist and pop to my feet. I may not be proficient with a crossbow, but I'm well acquainted with daggers. I'd go as far as to say they're the only reason I'm still alive. They are light and easy to conceal, and there was a time I'd never be caught without one.

Life as a make-believe princess has softened me, making me forget that dangers lurk around every corner. But never again.

There must be something written across my face, or in my stance, because as I come at Shayla with the blade, she backpedals even though I'm still several body lengths away.

Not giving her a chance to nock another arrow, I whip my arm and send the blade flying toward her. She tries to dive to the ground to avoid the dagger but isn't fast enough, and the blade cuts a path across her upper arm. The wound doesn't appear deep but starts bleeding immediately.

As she struggles back to her feet, I search the ground for another dagger, spotting two sheathed at the waist of the other fallen guard behind me. Turning my back on my enemy, I sprint to the bodies, grabbing the weapons as fast as I can, and then spin back toward Shayla just in time to catch her running into the orchard for cover, limping and holding her newly injured arm.

Right before she ducks into the tree cover, she glances back at me, and the moonlight illuminates her face. I catch a spark of fear in her gaze right before she disappears. But it must be a trick of the moonlight or the distance between us clouding my vision, because in that brief flash, I could have sworn her eyes were blue, not gray.

Chapter 31

FUMBLING WITH THE STRAPS AND HARNESSES, I unhook the fidgety horse from the dead one and then from the carriage. I don't know if Shayla has fled for good or if this is only a temporary reprieve, but either way, I have to move fast. Dryden is in dire need of medical attention, and one more well-aimed arrow could be the death of either one of us.

Once I've disconnected the horse, I lead it around to the other side of the carriage, quickly securing it to the bench seat up front so it can't flee. I can only hope that the boxy cab will give us some cover in case Shayla doubles back and starts shooting at us again.

Yanking open the carriage door, I find Dryden lying face down on the floor. Each breath he takes rattles in his chest. How am I going to get him up on the horse and keep him there if he's unconscious?

The arrow is still sticking out of his back, and I know that's going to be an issue, but I also know I can't pull it out until it can be treated.

Reaching forward, I snap the shaft like I did before, leaving the arrowhead in place. Dryden jolts and he cries out, and as much as it hurts me to see him in so much pain, I'm relieved he's conscious again.

"Dryden, get up. We have to go."

He gets to his hands and knees, his body shaking from the effort.

How am I going to ask him to mount a horse like this?

But I don't have a choice. Shayla could attack again at any moment.

Using the carriage steps, I'm somehow able to help get Dryden up on the horse. Untying the reins, I mount in front of him.

"Hold on to me," I say as I guide his arms around me.

He leans heavily against my back, but his arms clamp around my middle. I nudge the horse with my heels, urging it into a gallop as quickly as possible, terrified that Dryden is going to pass out and fall off any moment.

Just as we're about to clear the orchard entirely, another arrow whizzes by us, missing its mark. A scream of frustration pierces the air as we pound down the street, leaving the orchard and the would-be assassin behind.

✦

DRYDEN'S HOLD AROUND my waist loosens the closer we get to Everlight and Whitespire. His weight against my back feels heavier, and I know he's fighting to stay conscious.

A battle I fear he's losing.

"We're almost there," I call over my shoulder as we reach the outskirts of the city.

Dryden mumbles something that I can't make out even though he's speaking close to my ear.

My heart is thrashing against my ribs as I point the horse toward Greenbriar Park, intending to ride straight through because it's the most direct route to Whitespire.

Dryden's hold on me is precarious at best, but there's nothing I can do except get us to help as quickly as possible. He's slumped forward, leaning against my back. I feel his warm, sticky blood from his shoulder wound seeping through my top.

How much blood loss can one fae survive?

We make it through the park and gallop through the narrow city streets. The faces of the few fae we pass along the way are blurred as we race past them at breakneck speed. If Dryden slips off now, the fall alone could kill him.

"Hang on," I whisper, even though I know he can't hear me.

I risk taking one hand off the reins and place it over Dryden's. He turns his hand in my palm and squeezes my fingers, letting me know he's still with me. Returning to grasp the reins in both hands, I spur the horse on.

We aren't far from Whitespire now, but the last few blocks before the palace's gates come into view feel like an eternity. I don't slow the horse; instead I start screaming to the guards up ahead that I have the injured prince and to open the gates.

The shock on their faces is clear as they scramble to make way for us. I only slow the horse after we pound through the palace's gates, approaching the stone steps that lead to the front entrance.

The moment the horse skids to a halt, Dryden's arms slide away from me and he tips from his seat, falling onto the pea gravel below.

With a gasp, I jump down, rushing to where he lies face down, the arrow nub still embedded in his back. The stillness of his body sends a bolt of sheer terror through me. I'm only able to turn him on his side before we are swarmed by palace guards.

The next few moments are chaos. Suddenly I'm being pushed aside as Dryden is lifted and rushed into the palace. I yell after them that he was attacked by Princess Shayla and that they need to send guards out to apprehend her, but I'm barely given a passing glance.

I go to follow Dryden and the group of guards carrying him up the stairs and into the palace when a pair of uniformed fae move into my path, halting me. I go to sidestep them when I'm roughly grabbed by the arm, right over my bandaged injury. I cry out in pain, but he doesn't let go.

"You need to come with us," he says, jerking me forward.

I don't understand what's going on, but I'm not going to allow anyone to keep me from Dryden. Swinging with my free arm, I punch the guard square in the face, the crunch of bone sharp as his nose collapses against my knuckles.

He immediately releases me, howling as he brings his hands up to his face. The other guard lunges forward, but I dart to the side, avoiding his hands, and race up the stairs.

By the time I enter the palace, the hallways are clear. Dryden has already been taken somewhere, hopefully directly to the palace physician, but I don't know where that is.

Shouts from behind draw my attention, and I glance over my shoulder to see not only the guards who tried to detain me running up the steps, but a half dozen more.

Without thinking, I take off in the direction of my room, where I have weapons stashed. I lost the fallen guard's daggers somewhere during the frantic ride to get Dryden back to Whitespire. It's clear these guards are not simply looking for an explanation of what happened to their prince. If they were, they wouldn't have manhandled me. I don't understand why I'm being pursued, but I know I don't want to face off against them unarmed.

If I'm to go down, it won't be without a fight.

Sprinting as fast as I can, I reach the corner before the guards enter the palace behind me, leaving them guessing what direction I took and buying myself a few precious extra seconds. My rooms in Whitespire Palace are deep in the west wing. If I can reach them before being discovered, I can grab not only a weapon but also the book of hidden passageways. If I make it into one of the passageways, I'll be able to search the palace for Dryden from there.

I'm assuming they took Dryden to either his rooms or some sort of medical facility in the palace. I don't have it memorized, but the maps are so detailed, they'll probably give me an idea of where to go if he's not in his rooms.

I take the last corner without slowing and skid around it. My room is only a few doors up, and I race toward it, almost overshooting it in my haste.

Bursting into the room, I slide to a stop, thinking I've entered the wrong one. Clothes are scattered everywhere; furniture is upended and overturned. I'm still blinking, trying to make sense of what I'm seeing, when Princess Primrose, her rosy hair plaited and twisted into an updo without a single strand out of place, steps out of my sleeping chamber and into the sitting room. The smug look on her face falters when she takes in my disheveled, bloody state, but then she gives her head a small shake, as if to dismiss it as unimportant. Her mouth curves into a smirk that sends a chill running through me, but then she lifts her hand, and I see what she has grasped in her fingers. My blood runs cold.

Octavia's silver bracelet.

"Gotcha," the princess says, her smirk blooming into a full grin.

I'm frozen for half a second and then I spin, but I only get a half turn before my hands are roughly clamped behind me by a guard I hadn't realized was there. He must have been standing to the side of the door when I burst into the room. But it's only one guard. I can take him.

Twisting, I break his hold easily and duck under his arm in one fluid motion before kicking out, sending him stumbling forward. Instead of waiting to watch him fall, I scramble to the door. Primrose's shrill shrieks as she yells at the guard to get up chase me the entire way.

Throwing the door open, I dart into the hall, only to be met with a wall of dark blue–uniformed guards, including the one whose nose I broke. Blood covers the lower half of his face, and rage shines from his eyes. At least a dozen guards form a semicircle in front of me, blocking my way, their hands poised on the hilts of their swords in a clear warning that they will use their weapons if necessary.

I back up a step, trying to think through my options. I can handle a couple guards, but not this many. Behind me are only a single guard I've already bested and Princess Primrose. They're no match for me, but even if I best them and barricade myself in my room, I'd still be trapped. I'm three stories above the ground. There's nowhere for me to go.

A familiar guard steps forward. He's the other one who first tried to bring me in. I hesitate for just a second. He has kind blue eyes and blond hair that suddenly reminds me of Neo. "You're under arrest," he says.

I don't bother asking him for what when it's clear from the bracelet in Primrose's hand that my stash of stolen goods has been discovered. Most likely the map as well, damning me further.

It's ironic that as a princess I'm still being arrested for thievery.

The blond guard takes another step forward. Reaching behind himself, he pulls out a pair of shackles, causing me to take a step away from him.

"There's nowhere for you to go, so it's best if you come quietly.

If you continue to put up a fight . . ." Rather than finish his sentence, he arches an eyebrow and nods to the guards around us, ready to pull their weapons at a moment's notice.

"I need to see Prince Dryden," I say, proud of myself that my voice comes out clear and steady.

There's a snort behind me and Primrose shoves past me, still holding the silver bracelet. "If I have anything to say about it, you'll never see the prince again," she sneers.

The thought of that coming true, of never seeing Dryden again, fills me with a sense of panic so acute it steals my breath.

Never see Dryden again. Neo's blue eyes flash through my mind, followed by Dryden's flirtatious smirk, and a spike of pain hits me.

The wise thing would be to surrender, to hold my hands out and let the guard with the kind eyes shackle me and then wait for an opportunity to escape or somehow get word to Dryden. But Primrose's comment about not ever seeing him again has stolen my ability to think rationally, leaving me with nothing but raw emotions and the burning need to find Dryden.

Without thought or intention, I rush the guards blocking my path to freedom. The first to go down is the one holding the shackles. I catch the surprise in his eyes just before I deliver a jab to his Adam's apple.

He drops the shackles to clutch his throat, gasping for air. A spike of guilt shoots through me, but I don't think I hit him hard enough to collapse his windpipe. I don't have any room to hold on to the guilt, though, with my fear and panic over Dryden coursing through me.

The row of guards in front of me are only just pulling their weapons when I reach them. Dropping low, I swoop my leg out, causing the first guard to drop to the floor. Shouts ring out around me as I throw myself over the fallen guard, tucking into a roll before popping to my feet again.

I catch movement out of the corner of my eye and duck just in time to feel the *whoosh* of a blade as it sails over my head. I don't have time to process how close I just came to death before a hand snags my arm, swinging me to the side. My momentum causes me to smash into the wall, bouncing painfully off the immovable object. A portrait of a past queen shakes loose and falls to the floor in front of me.

Fiery determination courses through me as a body slams into me, sending us crashing to the carpet. I try to wiggle out from underneath him, but the guard's heavy weight keeps me pinned in place.

He lifts off me, but before I can move, two sets of hands clamp around my biceps and haul me to my feet. I bite down on my lip to stifle a cry as pain flares from my arm injury.

The guard with the broken nose steps in front of me, rage as well as his blood painting his face. He raises his arm, his sword in hand, and I think this is it. This is the moment I die. But right before he swings downward, he twists his hand, pointing the blade away from me.

A scream gets caught in my throat as the hilt of his sword comes toward me, and then everything goes black.

Chapter 32

I SUPPOSE AT THE BACK OF MY MIND I ALWAYS believed I'd end up in this situation.

Arrested.

Thrown in a cell.

Hopeless.

Alone.

When I regain consciousness, I'm lying face down, my cheek pressed against an icy stone floor, my body numb except for the throbbing on my head where I must have been struck. I moan and try to blink my eyes open, but nothing happens. It's only when my muddled brain realizes that my eyes *are* open that true terror crawls into my throat and squeezes.

I'm in complete darkness.

I bite my lip to keep from whimpering as I roll over and sit up. I can only guess that I'm in the palace's fabled dungeon. I have no idea what time it is or how long I'm going to have to wait here until someone comes for me.

Without daylight for reference, the moments slip by at an excruciating pace, each second feeling like the slow drip from a leaky faucet.

Pulling my knees tighter against my chest, I wrap my arms around myself, doing what I can to stay warm. If hell were a frozen nightmare rather than a blazing inferno, I'd think that's where I am. The cold is unrelenting as it seeps straight through my clothes and into my bones, chilling me from the inside out. The only plus is that I'm so cold, I no longer feel the wound on my arm.

Something scurries across my foot, and the yelp is out of my mouth before I can stifle it. Jumping up, I shuffle in total darkness to what I think is the other side of the cell. I've only taken two steps before I slam into a jagged stone wall, my shoulder taking the brunt of the impact.

I pace around the perimeter of the cell to keep myself awake. I find a small bucket of rancid water in the corner, and I'm parched enough to drink from it, but after it goes down, it takes an effort to keep it there.

It's not long before I grow weary. I'm tired. From lack of food. From fear. But I don't dare sit back down with whatever creature is sharing the cramped cell with me.

More time drags by. I can't feel my fingers or the tip of my nose anymore. My legs are weak, so I use the sharp wall at my back to keep myself standing. I think my eyes have drifted shut, but it's also hard to tell because open or closed, I see the same thing: black nothing.

Time is irrelevant when you're swallowed by darkness, and after a while I can't even guess how long it's been since I regained consciousness in this midnight abyss.

One day. Two?

From the hollowness in my stomach, I think maybe two.

I try not to wonder why someone hasn't come for me yet. I always told myself if I was captured or discovered, I'd be on my own. But deep inside, I'd held on to a shred of hope that if the worst happened, someone would rescue me: Olette or Bram.

Dryden.

A sharp pain has me curving my shoulders and hunching into myself, taking slow breaths until the pain subsides to a dull ache in the middle of my chest. I've tried to avoid thinking of him, but his image keeps coming to me.

The way he grinned at me as Neo. The way he watched me as Dryden.

The way he held me. The way he kissed me.

I've had a lot of time to consider why Dryden hasn't either come to me himself or sent someone to release me. I refuse to believe everything he said to me in the orchard was a lie, so the only explanation that makes sense is that he's so gravely injured, he's physically unable to.

Or that he's dead.

I drive myself near crazy as I wonder if he succumbed to his injuries, or if Princess Shayla returned to finish the job.

My knees buckle, but I catch myself before sliding to the floor. I don't know how much longer I can remain standing, and I wonder what will go first, my mind or my body. Already pieces of me feel like they've broken off and floated away, forever to be buried in the bowels beneath Whitespire, forgotten along with the rest of me.

I think I'm touching on insanity when I start to be able to pick up details around me. First, it's the shape of a rock jutting from the cell wall beside me, before more of the wall starts to appear. After only a few moments, I can see well enough to look down my body all the way to my feet and the uneven floor below me. It's not much, but suddenly I can see something rather than nothing.

It's both a relief and a shock, and I'm not convinced it isn't my mind playing tricks on me until I hear the unmistakable stomping of footsteps.

I snap my head toward the front of the cell. The bars, strips of black against a swath of gray, get lighter by the moment. It isn't long before the soft, flickering glow of a flame casts shadows and illuminates the details inside my cell. And then a figure appears, holding a lantern at eye level.

I know the light isn't very bright, but after being in the dark for so long, I still flinch away from the sharp sting it causes, blinking as my eyes water.

My eyes don't want to adjust quickly, but I force my gaze back to the cell's entrance, unable to make out who is holding the lantern with it so close to their face. But when they reach over and hang the light on a hook and step back, a gasp rises in my throat.

It's the king. I don't know who I was expecting to see, but it certainly wasn't him.

I had a plan. When someone finally showed up, I would plead my innocence, and if that didn't work, I'd demand my release, threatening them with my position as Princess Greer.

Yes, they found my stash of stolen items, but surely no one's figured out I'm not Lady Stormfeather. Right? So even if they don't believe I'm innocent, they can't hold a princess in the dungeon for something as frivolous as petty theft.

If I was truly a princess of the Glacier Kingdom, this imprisonment would be an outrage, triggering some sort of retaliation, if not full-out war. But with the king standing in front of me now, assessing me with hard, cold eyes, the words stick in my throat.

If there is anyone in all of the Ember Kingdom who won't be intimidated by me, it's King Darius.

I'm trying to work out what he's doing down here when he finally speaks: "You're wondering why my brother hasn't been down to rescue you yet, aren't you?"

His blunt question jolts me, sending a shock of icy fire through my system that's sorely needed. It gets the blood pumping in my veins and clears some of the fog from my mind.

I push off the wall and take a shaky step to the center of the cell to stare at King Darius. I'm trying to work out if I should admit that he's right or not, but he doesn't wait for my answer.

"He won't, you know. Rescue you."

Fear makes my fingers tingle and my gut clench.

"Is he all right?" I ask, my throat tightening to the point that it's hard to push out my next questions. "Has something else happened to him? Did you find Princess Shayla?"

I have to hold myself back from rushing to the bars and begging King Darius to answer my questions.

As if he knows how hard it is for me to wait for his response, King Darius pauses before answering. Tilting his head as he watches me, amusement dancing in his dark eyes. "Nothing else has happened to my brother . . . yet."

That word, *yet*, echoes in my mind, threatening to snap my sanity, but I clamp my mouth shut, waiting for King Darius to go on.

"You see, no one has seen you in two days, since you showed up and dumped a half-dead prince in front of the palace."

"That's not what happened," I say, anger rising in my gut, but King Darius only shrugs.

"Regardless, the only thing anyone in the palace knows is that you disappeared that night."

"Disappeared?" I all but scoff. "I was attacked by palace guards and thrown in this cell," I say, waving my hand in front of me to indicate my current predicament. One that he's clearly aware of, since he's standing in front of me.

He shakes his head while making a *tsk*ing sound. "You see, when staff went to check on you that next morning, they found your rooms in shambles. You'd ransacked the entire place, taking some of your belongings and leaving the rest. It's clear to all that you fled in order to escape punishment for stealing from your fellow tributes and the palace."

A knot of unease tightens in my gut. "Dryden would never believe that I fled."

His eyebrows hike up in mock surprise. "Wouldn't he? You were caught with stolen items from the other tributes, as well as the royal family, in your possession. Rather than face judgment for your crimes, you ran."

I shake my head, trying to convince myself as much as King Darius that Dryden wouldn't believe that I'd just up and run away.

"No. He'd know that wasn't true," I argue, conviction I'm not sure I believe ringing in every word. Because Dryden does know that I'm a thief, and I did take those items from the palace and other tributes. If he found out about that, would his faith in me be so shaken as to believe that I've fled?

Maybe?

It's clear the king doesn't want Dryden or anyone else knowing that I'm still at the palace. He created a scenario that I'd fled to explain my absence. I doubt it took much to get the guards to stay quiet, or to convince Princess Primrose to play along. She wouldn't care a lick what happens to me as long as I'm finally out of her way.

But why go to all this trouble? Why the deception when he could just let everyone know the truth, that I'd been arrested?

Was it because King Darius feared retaliation from the Glacier Kingdom for holding one of their princesses prisoner? I was going to try to use that as a reason to be let go, but the truth is, the Glacier Kingdom is one of the most inconsequential in all of Vaeloria, so that's unlikely to concern him.

If this ruse has nothing to do with my status as a princess, could it have something to do with Dryden instead? Did the king pick up on our connection and fear his brother would choose me for his bride? This feels like extreme measures to keep that from happening.

"Would he, though? Know that wasn't true?" King Darius asks, echoing my secret fear. "Especially considering your past. It's not as if stealing is out of your character."

My muscles lock.

Dryden explicitly said that his brother didn't know about our arrangement, so King Darius can't know the truth about me. Can he?

Taking a measured breath, I school my features and voice, trying to look and sound innocent, when in reality my heart and mind are racing. "What are you talking about?"

King Darius takes a step forward. The lantern's flame casts sinister shadows on his face, darkening half of it while lighting the other. "I know who you are. Or rather, who you are not."

How? Did Lord Sylvan go to him instead of Dryden?

Even though it feels like the floor drops out from underneath me, I force myself not to react. At least, not in the way he might be expecting. Lord Sylvan's evidence against me was flimsy. Maybe I can still fake my way out of this.

I force a light laugh from my chapped lips. "Of course you do. I'm Lady Stormfeather, princess of the Glacier Kingdom."

He *tsks* but doesn't refute me. Instead, he reaches behind himself and pulls something from a hidden sheath.

A dagger. A familiar one.

The light glints off the blade of Neo's silver-hilted, black-bladed dagger and captures my attention immediately. King Darius twists the blade back and forth, letting the lantern's light dance over the shiny surfaces, entrancing me.

Just like the other times I laid eyes on this dagger, I want it. I need it.

My hands are already wrapped around the cell bars before I realize I've stepped forward. The feel of the cold metal on my palms shakes some awareness into me and I retreat again. But putting distance between myself and the dagger takes effort.

When I tear my gaze from the blade to glance up at the king, there's a self-satisfied look on his face. He shoves the dagger back into the sheath, and even though I still long for the blade, not having it in view helps my mind clear.

A slow smile breaks on King Darius's face, causing a slimy feeling to rise up inside me.

I should have been frightened when he pulled the blade, but instead I was mesmerized. My hands itch in a familiar way when I see something I have to have. And it's clear King Darius noticed my reaction.

"Just as I suspected," the king says. "You, my dear, are turning out to be a very unexpected but welcome surprise."

I shake my head, not understanding what he's talking about.

The king's eyebrows rise and then narrow. He cocks his head. "Is it possible you don't even know?"

"Don't know what?" I snap, no longer caring that he's the king and that my life is in his hands. Everything he's done and said since appearing has been half riddles, and I'm ready to speak plainly. There's some purpose in him being here, and I want to know what it is.

He chuckles, and the sound rolls over me like a horde of spiders stampeding across my skin. "It seems I know much more about you than you know of yourself."

I purse my lips but keep my mouth shut, crossing my arms in front of me.

"I see you don't believe me. Allow me to prove it to you."

"I don't know what you think—"

"You are not Princess Greer of the Glacier Kingdom."

"Yes, of course—"

"You are, in fact, Rowan of nowhere except the slums of Everlight. Indentured to my brother and the known criminal Sinclair before him."

I should be denying it. I'm just so shocked that he truly knows who I am that even though I open my mouth to respond, no words emerge.

"I've known since the beginning."

I remain speechless for a moment before blurting, "How?"

"My spies are far better than my baby brother's. It was clear he wasn't going to drop the report he heard about one of the princesses coming to kill him. I knew he would try to pull something, so I just had to be patient, wait, and watch."

I rear back. "Pull something? He was trying to save his life. The threat he uncovered turned out to be very real. If you'd taken it seriously, he'd never have had to go to such lengths."

"My orders to my brother were to stand down, yet he continued to defy me. I allowed this little charade he cooked up because I knew what he was doing the whole time. At a certain point, it was easier to monitor what he was doing than try to control him outright."

I take another step back, suddenly wanting to put as much distance as I can between myself and the king.

"Why wouldn't you want your brother protected?" I ask, half scared I already know the answer.

From the beginning, that never made sense to me. Even if King Darius didn't believe the threat, what's the harm in looking into it a little?

Unless . . .

The king gives me a pointed look, one that makes it clear he thinks I'm daft. "Have you really not figured it out by now?"

"You knew Princess Shayla would try to kill your brother and you sat back and let it happen." My voice is no louder than a horrified whisper.

"Not exactly," he says, and my eyebrows jump. If he tries denying he was aware of the situation, I won't believe him.

"You see, it's not that I sat back and let it happen, but that I planned it from the start."

Realization slams into me, leaving me frozen.

My fear for Dryden increases tenfold. This whole time Dryden's brother has been plotting his death, and he almost succeeded. Could still succeed, because who is there to stop him? King Darius can leave here and order Dryden's death with a snap of his fingers, all while I'm trapped behind these bars, unable to warn him.

"Why?" I choke out. "Why do you want your brother dead?"

King Darius sighs, almost as if I'm boring him, and I clench my fists, practically vibrating with the desire to lash out at him. "Many reasons, but you'll be pleased to know that my plans have changed." A tiny spark of hope comes to life in my chest. It's smothered the next moment when he says, "At least temporarily. And my brother has you to thank for his borrowed time."

"Me? What do you mean?"

"If my brother dies, so do you. I can't have my brother killed until your contract is transferred over to me."

So he doesn't know everything like he thinks he does. Because if he did, he'd know that Dryden released me from my contract, setting me free. I'm not about to offer up that information, especially if that's what's keeping Dryden breathing for the time being.

"And why do you even care if I die?" I whisper, unable to keep the question to myself, because it doesn't make any sense.

I'm only a gutter fae who Dryden and Olette cleaned up well enough to fool the elite. Why should he care if I live or die?

King Darius steps close enough to the cell to wrap his long fingers around the bars as he peers at me. "Oh, my dear. I've been waiting for someone like you for a long time. I don't intend to give you up anytime soon."

+

I'VE GONE OVER King Darius's revelations a thousand times since his visit. He left me with more questions than answers. I've turned his words upside down and inside out, trying to fill in the gaps and holes. How long has he been plotting against his brother and why? How long does he intend to keep me trapped beneath the earth? And what possible use can I be to him?

Nothing makes sense. I don't think he wants to use my thieving skills. I'm good, but there are plenty of others just like me in the city. And who knows why he wants Dryden dead. To elicit sympathy from his subjects or the other kingdoms? To secure his place on the throne?

The questions keep coming with no answers, so I grasp for anything to stop myself from spiraling. I learn the dimensions of my cell in the dark. Two and a half strides, fourteen hands, and eight of my feet from one wall to the other. Three steps, twenty hands, and twelve of my feet from the back wall to the bars. Ten bars separating me from freedom. Twenty-six stone blocks making up the back wall of my cell and thirty-six on each parallel wall. I even count the cobblestones on the floor by feeling them with my hands, twice. Eighty-six.

I search for anything to keep my mind from the one truth it doesn't want to absorb.

King Darius wants to kill Dryden . . . and there is nothing I can do about it.

Not while I'm still trapped in this godforsaken cell.

The light pad of footsteps echoes off the dungeon's stone walls somewhere in the distance, and I hurry to the corner of the cell farthest from where the light will appear. Flopping down on the ground, I ready myself to face the king again.

I have a plan. To pretend to be injured, forcing King Darius to unlock the cell door to check on me. Once he's in the cell with me, I'll overtake him and escape.

Nausea roils in my gut as I think about my poorly thought-out strategy. I know it's not a good plan, but it's all I've got.

The icy bite of the stone beneath my cheek barely registers as I wait for King Darius to appear. As the footsteps get louder, echoing off the stone walls, the cell starts to brighten. I close my eyes, lying in wait for the king to spring my trap.

It's only a few brief moments before a gruff male who is very much *not* King Darius barks, "Stop fighting."

"This isn't right," a defiant female voice answers. "There has to have been a mistake."

"No mistake," the male says, and the hinges groan on what I assume is the cell across from mine as it's being opened.

"You can't do this!" she cries.

It sounds like there's a struggle before she's thrown into the cell across from me. I can hear the impact as she hits the stone. I'm itching to flip over and see what's going on, but I remain where I am. It may not be King Darius who's traveled to the bowels of the dungeon, but my plan is the same: get my cell door opened so I have a chance at escape.

"Please," she begs, a note of fear in her voice, one that's starting to sound confusingly familiar, but I refuse to check and ruin my plan. "I didn't do anything. You can't just leave me here."

Her protests fall on deaf ears. The cell door slams shut, followed by the telltale click of a key turning in a rusty lock.

Panic claws at me. Is he just going to leave without checking on me? But then a different male says, "Hey. Do you think she's all right in there?"

I didn't realize there were two of them, but that's okay. I still like my odds.

Someone takes a few steps, and then I think they may be holding a lantern through the bars to get a better look at me, because brightness shines through my closed eyelids.

I stay perfectly still, holding my breath so it appears I'm not even breathing.

Come on. Just open the cell door to check on me.

"Is she bleeding?" one of them asks. It's hard to tell them apart because they both sound so gruff.

"Naw," the other answers. "Or if she is, the wound isn't fresh, so who cares? We were told not to interact with the other prisoner. Let's go. I'm hungry, and my dinner is most likely getting cold."

The other one makes a bit of a grunt and then says, "Sally made mutton tonight, didn't she? That's my favorite." And then their retreating footsteps echo.

Bastards.

With a silent growl, I sit up just in time to see a familiar face and pair of frightened gray eyes staring from the cell opposite mine before her features are obscured by darkness.

Just who I thought.

Shayla.

Chapter 33

"YOU!" I SPIT. THE WORD COMES OUT AS A GROWL.

"Greer, is that you?" Shayla asks, a tremor in her voice.

Is she scared now that she doesn't have a bow and arrow? If she's expecting sympathy, she's delusional. My clothes are still stiff with my blood and Dryden's. At the thought, the wound on my arm starts throbbing again, despite the numbing cold of the dungeon.

What I wouldn't give for a weapon, preferably a dagger; even in the pitch-black I think I'd have a shot at hitting her. Her cell can't be more than a body's length from my own. A bow and arrow would be a sort of poetic justice, but I'd even welcome that rusty kitchen knife right now.

I surge to my feet, rushing toward the cell bars even though we can't see each other in the dungeon's eternal darkness. There's a rustling in her direction, and I imagine her standing as well.

"We need to get out of here," she says, her words falling over each other in a babbled mess. "They said I have to wait here for a trial, but I don't even know—"

"Stop the act," I snap, and Shayla gasps.

"Wh-what are you talking about?" she asks, sounding convincingly confused.

"I don't know what kind of game you're playing, but I still have the prince's blood crusted under my fingernails. And without closing my eyes, I can see the moonlight gleaming off one of your cursed arrowheads. If you think I'm just going to forget how you tried to kill Dryden and me, you're delusional."

Shayla gasps. "Kill you? Kill him? I would never!"

What sort of fool does she think I am?

"Don't even try to deny it. Back in the orchard. You shot at us. I *saw* you," I spit back, my hands itching to wrap around her throat and squeeze.

"No, no. Whatever happened, it wasn't me," she protests. "Greer, listen to me. I'm your friend. I would never hurt you."

"Just stop. King Darius already confirmed you're working with him to kill Prince Dryden. I know it was you."

There's a clanking sound; I think Shayla grabbed her cell bars. "I don't know what the king told you, but he's lying. Why would I want to kill Prince Dryden? That doesn't even make sense. I'm here to try to *marry* him. What purpose would killing him even serve?"

"Some advancement to be gained by King Darius's favor, I assume."

"My kingdom is small, yes, but we're strong. We don't rely on the favor of other kingdoms to thrive. Even this courting season is silly. I only came because it would have been a slight if I hadn't. I don't really care about being Prince Dryden's bride."

"Of course you don't care, because you have been plotting to kill him all along."

"No!" she shouts. "You're not hearing me. The Ember Kingdom doesn't have anything we need, so there's nothing King Darius could have offered us to do something as despicable as assassinating the prince."

I open my mouth to start to refute her paltry denials, but I hesitate.

The pair of blue eyes that I thought was a trick of the moonlight flash through my mind. Shayla's eyes are gray, not blue. What if . . .

"Just think about it a minute. Nothing adds up. If I was working with King Darius in some sort of insane plan to kill his brother, why would he throw me in here? I'm being framed. You have to believe me."

I don't yet, but I'd be lying to myself if I said her denials weren't casting some suspicion in my mind. However, there's more evidence than just King Darius's word. "When we were attacked, I recognized your red bow, and you were wearing your kingdom's colors: purple and black."

"I haven't seen my bow since last week. I thought I'd just misplaced it, but my maid and I haven't been able to find it since. Maybe someone stole it to make you think that it was me. And everyone knows those are my kingdom's colors. Of course someone would dress in them if they were trying to frame me."

Shayla's arguments give me pause. There's logic there, but I can't fit all the pieces together. It's a stretch to believe that someone would impersonate her. But then again, if Shayla was working with King Darius to kill his brother, she's right, why would he throw her in the dungeon? Could this all be a setup to not only kill Dryden, but also frame Shayla for the murder?

So many lies. So many deceptions. Where's the truth?

I shake my head, even though she can't see me. "That's not enough evidence to prove it wasn't you. Especially when I saw you attack me. I faced off against you."

"How much of this archer did you see?" she asks. "Her face? Her hair? Because if you didn't see her face, how can you be sure it was me?"

The lower half of her face had been covered in a scarf, and the top hidden in shadows. The only half-decent look I'd gotten at her was in that one sliver of moonlight.

"Greer, I know it's only been a couple of weeks, but we're friends." Her voice breaks. "You know me. I wouldn't do something like this."

I'm confused, so confused. I don't know if she's starting to make sense because she's telling the truth, or if it's what I want to be the truth. Because she's right, we were friends, and I did think I knew her.

Shayla is quiet for a few seconds, and then she says, "How many shots did they get off?"

I scoff. "I don't know. I wasn't exactly counting as I was running for my life."

"Was it more than one?"

"Of course."

"Well, then, you know it wasn't me."

I sigh. "And why's that?"

"Because I don't miss. If it had been me, one would have been enough."

✦

SHAYLA TELLS ME she's been locked in her room for two days, not allowed to leave or see anyone except a palace guard. She had no idea that I was arrested and hadn't heard the story about me fleeing that King Darius is telling everyone. She also hadn't realized the prince was injured. She claims to be completely in the dark as to what has been going on, and even why she's in the cell across from me. As she continues to talk, I start to believe her.

It doesn't make sense that King Darius would imprison an ally, but it does make sense that he might be trying to frame her and her kingdom. The Iron Kingdom is a coveted land in Vaeloria. Just because the kingdoms are living in relative peace now doesn't mean it's always been that way or will remain so. If King Darius wanted an excuse to invade the Iron Kingdom without giving the other kingdoms a reason to retaliate, murdering his brother would work. And as Shayla pointed out, why would she put her kingdom in a vulnerable position like that?

"We have to get out of here," I say. I don't know everything, but I do know one thing for sure: Dryden is in danger, and I have to warn him.

"How?" Shayla asks.

How indeed? "Do you have anything on you?"

"Like what?"

"A weapon, perhaps?"

"No."

I think for a moment. What might one of us have on us that can help us escape? I'm an expert at picking locks, which is done mostly through touch and sound rather than sight. I know I'd be able to pick these locks if I had the right tools. If only—

"What type of dress are you wearing?" I ask, suddenly having an idea.

"A day gown, why?"

"Is it a structured bodice? Like a corset?"

"Yes."

"Perfect. I need you to rip off the top of your dress and throw it over to me."

"Excuse me?" Shayla says, sounding more shocked than outraged.

"If I can find a thin enough piece of boning in the bodice, I can pick the locks," I explain.

"You know how to pick locks?" she asks, her question laced with confusion.

Right. Shayla still knows me as Princess Greer, the upstanding and highborn royal from the Glacier Kingdom. "It's just something I picked up for fun," I say, cringing at how unbelievable that sounds. "You know, there's not much to do during the winter months on the isles."

"I guess," she says, not sounding convinced, but a moment later I hear a ripping sound. "I'm going to put it through the bars. Can you reach it?"

I stretch my own arm through the bars, waving it around in the darkness, trying to find Shayla's dress. "Got it. You can let go."

When she does, I pull the fabric into my cell and start feeling around for the boning, praying it's thin enough to insert into a lock.

"Luckily, this dress is worn with a chemise, or I'd be very cold indeed," Shayla jokes, but there's a tremor in her voice. Chemise material is paper-thin. She has to be freezing.

As my fingers trace the patterns of the corset top, I think I've found a strip of boning thin enough for my purposes. Using my teeth and fingers, I rip at the material, tearing the stitching until I can pull a long piece free.

Even though it's delicate and thinner than the regular strips, I'm still worried it's too wide for my purposes. But it's the best I have to work with, so I'm going to try anyway.

I feel my way along the cell bars until I find the lock, breathing easier when I discover it's just a standard lock, nothing overly complicated about it. If I had some regular lock-picking tools, it would take me less than a minute to break out of this cell.

Crossing my fingers and toes, I insert the thin piece of boning into the lock, relieved that it fits. I move it around, trying to scrub the pins, but quickly realize I need a tension wrench to hold the lock in place. Going back to Shayla's corset, I remove another thin strip and get back to work.

It takes several tries and a handful of long minutes, but eventually there's a soft *click* as the lock disengages and then the cell door swings open with a rusty squeal.

"Did it work?"

I cross the narrow space between our cells. "It did. Now reach your arm out. Your right one."

I think Shayla is telling me the truth, but I have to make sure. I cut the archer when I threw a blade at her. If Shayla is innocent, she won't have a wound.

"What?" she asks.

"I just need to feel your arm."

"Ah . . . okay."

The skirts of her dress rustle as Shayla shuffles to her feet, then her arm bumps into me. Reaching through the bars to her shoulder, I make sure it's the right arm, and then work my way down to her bicep. In only her sleeveless chemise now, I can feel along her goosebumped flesh.

There's no wound.

It wasn't her.

Letting go of her arm, I sigh in relief. I already knew in my heart that she was innocent, but I want to be able to tell Dryden that I checked, because he doesn't know the princess like I do.

"What was that all about?" she asks.

"Nothing, I was just checking something," I say, and start feeling around for her lock. I've only just located it when Shayla's hand closes over mine. Her fingers are like icicles as she grips my hand.

"Thank you," she says.

"For what?" I ask. "I haven't freed you yet."

"For believing me. I swear to you it wasn't me who attacked you and Prince Dryden. I promise to help you find the person responsible."

I already know the person responsible. King Darius.

"There's nothing to thank me for," I say. "You're as much of a victim in this scenario as I am. I already know who is responsible, and I intend to make him pay."

"How?" Shayla asks, but before I can answer, voices echo down to us from somewhere else in the dungeon.

"Someone is coming," she whispers. "You have to go."

I shake my head even though she can't see me, and quickly insert my makeshift picking tools into the lock, furiously trying to disengage the locking mechanism. "I can't. I haven't freed you yet."

"No, you have to leave now or you'll be discovered."

"I can't leave you down here," I whisper-hiss back.

"You have to. The only chance both of us have right now is if you can tell the prince what's going on. He needs to know I wasn't the one who attacked him and that his life is still in danger. Just please . . . don't forget me down here," she says, and my heart breaks.

She's right. I know she is. I hate the thought of leaving her, but I'm weak. If I don't go now, I'll probably be overpowered and thrown back into the cell, and that wouldn't benefit either of us, and least of all Dryden.

Rushing back to my cell, I feel around the ground for Shayla's corset and then dart back, shoving it through the bars to her along with the pieces of boning I pulled out. "Try to put this back on and hide the damage from the guards so they don't know what we used it for. I'll warn Dryden and either send someone to free you or be back for you myself."

I wish I had something else to offer her. Even some extra material to keep her warm down here, but I don't.

The voices are still faint but getting louder. I can hear them well enough now to recognize the gruff utterings of the guards who brought Shayla down here. No light has penetrated our part of the dungeon yet, but I know it will soon enough. By the time it does, I'll need to have found somewhere to hide for when the guards pass by.

Shayla says, "If you follow this tunnel straight, you'll eventually come to stairs that lead up to a cellar, and then a path to the surface. The tunnel will curve, but don't go down any of the side tunnels, and you'll find your way out." I'm thankful for the information. I was unconscious when I was brought to the cell. "Now go, quickly," she urges.

I find her hand clenching the bar and give it a squeeze. "I won't forget you," I promise, then take off, trying to keep my footsteps light. I trail a hand along the wall to keep from running into something in the darkness.

The tunnel starts to lighten just as I pass one of the turns. Ducking around the corner, I flatten against the wall because there's nowhere to hide, praying that the guards will pass by without looking back and noticing me.

Despite the cold, sweat dampens my bodice as I wait for the guards. As they draw nearer, their voices echo off the tunnel walls. They're arguing, but about what I couldn't care less.

When they finally reach the tunnel that I'm hiding in, their lanterns light up the surrounding area. There's nowhere obvious to hide, and as they march past me, all they have to do is turn their heads to the side to see me plastered against the wall, hiding in plain sight.

I hold my breath, trying not to make a sound. The pounding of my heartbeat in my ears drowns out their voices, turning them to gibberish.

It feels like they're walking in slow motion, each step an eternity, until they finally move farther down the tunnel toward Shayla's cell and my empty one. It's not until they've rounded a bend that I allow myself to breathe again. My limbs are weak with relief, and I slump against the wall in the dark, taking a moment to assure myself I'm all right. But the reprieve doesn't last long, and I jolt when the roar of one of the guards' voices echoes throughout the dungeon tunnels.

It sounds like, "Where is she?"

They've already discovered I'm missing.

Using my hand for guidance, I move as quickly as possible in the darkness, tripping over my own feet as often as the uneven stone floor as I race through the dungeon, searching for the stairs.

My footfalls echo off the walls as I run, giving me away, but I can't slow. Even now the guards' shouts are getting louder as they search the dungeon for me. The darkness has become a strange comfort, because it means they haven't caught up to me yet, so when I start to be able to pick out murky shapes, panic rouses in my gut.

Still moving, I glance over my shoulder. The warm glow of a lantern is brightening the tunnel walls just before the bend in the passageway. The guards' voices are louder as they shout at each other to keep looking, that I must be hiding somewhere.

I have to get out—

I tumble forward, my hip slamming into the ground just before my shoulder, and then my head, crash against hard stone. I'm disoriented at first, especially since the ground is so uneven. It isn't until I can see the stairs I'm sprawled across that I realize I've reached the exit I was looking for.

"There she is," one of the guards yells, and I twist, glancing behind me to see both guards charging. The light from the lanterns they're holding casts shadows on the tunnel walls as well as on the stairs that bruised me.

Scrambling to my feet, I ignore my body's protests and sprint up the winding staircase. After the first curve, I lose the light and have to use my hand against the wall as a guide once again. I fall twice, banging my shins and knees against the unforgiving stone steps.

From somewhere beneath me, the out-of-breath guards shout for me to halt. Their voices ricochet off the walls, making it feel like they are right behind me even though I know they aren't moving up the staircase as quickly as I am.

I reach the top landing, skidding to a halt right before I face-plant into the door. My hands fumble over the rough wood until I find the handle and then shove it open, spilling out into a cellar of some sort. The walls are stacked stones with curved arches. A few lanterns hung on the walls cast dim light, but it's more than enough for me considering I've been suffering in almost total darkness.

The guards have stopped ordering me to halt and instead are yelling threats at me as they scramble up the stairs. I start to take off when I see the wood bar leaned up against the wall. Grabbing it, I slam the door shut and slide the bar into the brackets on either side, locking the guards in.

Not more than two seconds pass before they ram into the door, unable to break through the thick slab of wood.

I place a hand over where my heart slams against my ribs, trying to slow its beats. The guards pound their boots against the door, but it only shudders in its frame.

I did it. I made it out. But I'm not in the clear yet.

Turning my back on the dungeon and the ruckus the guards are making, I stride forward with a single goal burning in my mind.

Find Dryden.

Chapter 34

I EXPECTED THE DUNGEON TO BE UNDERNEATH Whitespire Palace, but after twisting and turning through the cellar and then going up another short set of stairs, I finally emerge from what looks to be a relatively nondescript outbuilding in the wooded area behind the palace. Although still technically on palace grounds, the dungeon is set apart from the main structure.

Even though it's dusk, my eyes water and I squint, blinking to adjust to the low light. Through the trees, the sky overhead is a mix of dark purple streaks cast over a lighter lavender backdrop. The very brightest of stars peek through in the early evening, and it may be because I've been deprived of daylight and fresh air, but I think they're the most beautiful things I've ever seen.

A horse brays and I jerk toward the noise to find the stables to my left. In front of me, the upper portion of the palace's single white spire is visible through a break in the trees.

I'm familiar with the palace and its surrounding grounds. Before the first day of the courting season, I made it my job to know the area. Out of paranoia and self-preservation, I plotted the fastest route for escape more than once. Through the trees in front of me are the gardens, and then, farther on, the palace itself. Behind me, deeper into the wooded area, is the wall that runs around the palace and grounds. And beyond that is the city of Everlight.

The possibility of escape flashes through my mind before I have the chance to reel it in.

The wall is patrolled—but not heavily so. Full night is approaching, when the shadows will steal visibility from the night guards. If I make my way to the wall now, I could wait for a break in the patrol and be up and over it quickly, just another shadow in the night before blending into the city.

Dryden's released me from my contract. Now I could be free. Truly free.

But that would be leaving Dryden to the mercy of the brother he doesn't know betrayed him. Not to mention leaving Shayla to pay for a crime she didn't commit.

There's no doubt in my mind that if I flee now, running toward the one thing I've always desired, Dryden will die, and an innocent will be blamed for it.

My gut tightens with the thought, and I already know the decision has been made. It was never really a choice to begin with. Heading back into the palace will most likely mean my demise, but somewhere along the way, the arrogant, infuriating, flirtatious prince's life became more precious to me than my own. And I should be scared of that. Alarmed, at the very least, but instead all I feel deep inside is grim resolve.

Resolve to save the prince.

Resolve to clear Shayla's name.

Resolve to see the king toppled from his throne.

I cast a glance over my shoulder toward the wall, hidden somewhere behind the thick trees. I won't lie to myself and say I'm not tempted, but it turns out freedom isn't worth the price I'd have to pay for it.

+

SNEAKING INTO THE palace is harder than I thought it was going to be. Even though the two guards who know I've escaped are still locked in the dungeon, there are more guards on patrol than usual. By the time I'm able to slip past two of them and enter the palace through the solarium door, it's dark enough that every star is out, twinkling down on me from above.

I immediately move into the belly of the solarium, using the thick foliage for cover. The closest entrance to the hidden passageways that lead to Dryden's rooms aren't too far from here. I don't know where the prince is right now, but that's my best guess. My memory on how to get to his rooms is a little murky, but I'm going to figure it out. I won't let myself fail.

I'm sliding between two leafy trees when the tinkle of feminine laughter reaches my ears. Peering through the greenery, I spot the remaining tributes seated at a table, seemingly enjoying a before-dinner aperitif. The back of Princess Primrose's pink head is to me, and I clench my fists. Just the sight of her makes my blood pressure spike.

Just because Shayla is innocent doesn't mean all the tributes are. I don't know if King Darius used his own assassin to attack Dryden and me in the orchard, or if it was another one of the princesses pretending to be Shayla. That still leaves five suspects in total: Primrose, Pluma, Meer, Willow, and Tori.

Out of all of them, Primrose seems the most suspicious to me, considering she's played along with the king's charade about me having fled the palace. Part of me hopes it's her because I'd love an excuse to plow my fist right into her perfect nose.

I'm forced to move closer to the group to reach the solarium exit, so, carefully, crouching as low as possible, I inch forward, moving from one cover to the next.

"Well," Princess Primrose says haughtily, "she's a filthy little thief, and I for one am glad she's gone."

I press my lips into a thin line. Of course she's talking about me.

Even though I shouldn't care, I still pause to hear the other princesses' responses. A swell of affection rises in my chest when Tori immediately comes to my defense.

"I don't believe it," she says. "It doesn't make sense. The Glacier Kingdom is small but by no means poor. What would a princess even need with small trinkets?"

Primrose leans forward. Having moved, I'm now viewing her from the side, but even without a direct line of sight, I don't miss the way she stares Tori down. "You weren't there. I saw her *collection* for myself. The little sticky-fingered thief has been nicking items since day one. And that lumestra stone alone is probably worth her whole kingdom's yearly income. King Darius told me that it was the prince's. A gift from his father on his twenty-first birthday."

I have to swallow a gasp. Could that be true? Did Dryden give me something his late father had gifted to him?

Tori shrugs. "Maybe he gave it to her as a gift. We all noticed his attachment to her. It was clear as day. And who's to say you aren't just lying?" she accuses boldly, shocking everyone. "There's not a tribute here who doesn't know that you'd do or say anything to win Prince Dryden for yourself. Maybe you made the whole thing up to get your competition out of the way?"

Princess Willow, seated between Tori and Primrose, gasps, placing a hand to her chest as she looks back and forth between the two tributes. For once, speechless. Princesses Pluma and Meer haven't said a word either, but Pluma shifts in her seat uncomfortably and Meer's brows are pinched tight.

Tori and Primrose have been close since the beginning, so it's surprising to see Tori stand up to her. I feel humbled that she would defend me, but also guilty because I did actually take her pocket mirror.

Primrose's gaze narrows. "You, out of everyone, should know how trustworthy I am."

Tori's eyes go wide and she seals her lips. I'd forgotten that Primrose knows about Tori's relationship with the guard, Roland. It's what I overheard them talking about during the first group outing at the Eldergrove, when I assumed they were talking about killing Dryden instead. One word from Primrose, and Tori would be in a world of trouble.

"Would anyone like a goat cheese fig?" Princess Willow asks, gesturing to a dish in the middle of the round table in front of them. "I had one two days ago, and they are just divine. We have something similar in our kingdom, but it's dipped in honey. I don't know which one I prefer, but these are truly delicious, and . . ."

Princess Primrose shoves away from the table while Willow is still nervously chattering and rises to her feet. "I think I'm done here. Ladies, let's go," she says, clearly addressing everyone *but* Tori.

With a flip of her hair, she storms toward the exit. The remaining princesses shoot Tori looks of apology before scurrying off after Primrose. The moment the doors click shut behind them, Tori releases a sigh and slouches back in her chair. Pinching her nose, she grumbles, "How much more of this circus will I have to put up with?"

I'm about to sneak past her when a thought occurs to me. It's taking a chance. Tori could still be the assassin. And even if she isn't, she may not help me, especially if she discovers how much I've been lying to her since we met. But having her as an ally right now could make all the difference.

Searching my heart, my gut tells me that she can be trusted. And that's all I have to go off of right now.

After making sure there's no one else in the solarium, I take a fortifying breath and stand. I've only taken a single step toward Tori when her gaze snaps in my direction, spotting me quickly even as I weave my way through the thick foliage.

"Greer?" she says, coming to her feet.

Wincing, I cast a glance around to make sure there's no one nearby to hear. Putting my finger to my lips, I indicate she should be quiet. Someone could enter the solarium at any moment.

A furrow appears between Tori's eyebrows, but she nods and walks toward me.

When we reach each other, Tori shocks me by pulling me into her arms and hugging me tight. "You're still here," she says, confusion clear in her voice.

It's only when she pulls back that she finally looks at me. Her gaze travels from my rat's nest of a head of hair down my body, taking in my ripped and bloodied clothes along the way, and back up again.

I haven't seen myself since before I left for my outing with Dryden. I'm sure I look awful. Seeing me has to be a shock to Tori, but to her credit, she takes it in stride. She's clearly confused, but she hasn't gone running screaming to a guard yet, so that's good.

"I never left. I've been here the whole time. Well, at least since Dryden and I returned from the orchard."

The pleat between Tori's eyebrow grows. "What's happened to you? We were told they found some stolen items in your room and that you fled."

"That's not exactly true," I hedge, unsure how to explain this whole mess.

"Of course it isn't. Because you are still here. I didn't believe for a second you'd done the things they said you had. Why would a Vaelorian princess have need to steal?" She laughs lightly, like the very thought is so preposterous, but her smile fades quickly as her gaze sweeps over me again. "But something has obviously happened. Is that dried blood?"

Leaning in, she brushes some of the hair off my forehead and I flinch. Her eyes go wide at what she sees.

I'd almost forgotten about the head wound that knocked me out. I haven't seen it yet, but there's a lump, and I've had a headache since I woke up in the dungeon.

Tori steps back, patiently waiting for me to explain . . . but where do I even start?

I open my mouth to spill the details from the last several days, but a sound spooks me and I crouch down, hiding behind a large fern. After a few moments, it's clear there's no one there.

I glance up at Tori, who doesn't look like she knows what to make of the situation. "Tori," I say, "it's bad, and Prince Dryden is in danger. I need your help."

+

TWENTY MINUTES LATER, Tori pokes her head out of the solarium door to check the palace's corridors for me. While I wait for her to give me the all clear, I lift the hood of the borrowed cloak she gave me up over my head. The heavy black material does its job of covering me from head to toe, concealing my absolutely ruined outfit as well as most of my face when the hood is up.

Will I look utterly suspicious strolling through the palace's halls swallowed in the cloak?

Yes.

But is it better than walking around exposed in the torn and bloodied remains of my gown?

Absolutely.

Darius has spent the last few days weaving an intricate web of lies. The remaining tributes were told I'd fled the kingdom after the stolen items were discovered. They had no idea Shayla was first under house arrest in her rooms, let alone now sitting in the dungeon. They thought Shayla was simply staying in her rooms because she was ill.

After I gave Tori an abbreviated version of everything that had happened over the last few days, including being attacked during my outing with Prince Dryden and then thrown into the dungeon afterward, she insisted on helping. She took it surprisingly well when I explained that the king has been plotting to have his brother killed and intended to frame Shayla for it.

I asked her if she could try to get a message to Shayla's parents, explaining that their daughter needs help, and she agreed. She asked a few questions but seemed to know that time was of the essence.

One thing I didn't tell her was that I wasn't, in fact, Princess Greer. I meant to. I wanted to. But when the time came, I just couldn't get the words out. I didn't want to see the look on her face when she realized that I was exactly what Princess Primrose had declared me to be: a filthy little thief.

After a couple of tense seconds, Tori waves me over. I told her about the hidden passageways throughout the palace and where the closest one was that I remembered.

After leaving the solarium, we have to head toward the palace's main entrance. It's not far, but it's also not right across the hall. The other tributes will be finishing up their dinner soon and then making their way back to their rooms for the night. I need to leave now, or else wait until everyone has gone to bed. It would be safer to move about in the middle of the night, but something tells me I need to get to Dryden before then. If King Darius learns I've escaped, every guard in the palace will start looking for me.

No, it has to be now, or it might be never.

Tori grabs my hand when I come up next to her. She gives me one hard look and then nods, telling me I've got this and she's with me with that one concise look and gesture. A mixture of appreciation and guilt swirls in my gut, but I push the feelings down. I can't let myself be distracted right now.

Without another word, we sweep out into the hallway. My head is on a swivel as we rush down the empty corridor, our feet soundless against the padded carpet and our ears sharp, listening for any sounds.

We make it down two hallways without running into anyone, and as we round the final bend, I think we're actually going to make it—until laughter echoes from up ahead.

The entrance is so close. I can see it. It's another painting that swings out like the one of King Drake and Queen Teresa, but this one is a Vaelorian landscape.

"Go," Tori whisper-hisses to me. "I'll distract them." With that, she takes off without waiting to see if I'll agree.

I fumble with the picture frame, hearing Tori's voice around the corner as she detains whoever almost discovered us. The painting of the king and queen I usually go through has a latch that pops it open, but I can't find anything on the edges of this frame. New voices sound from the other direction, and I flick my gaze to the side, looking down the long hallway. There's no one there, but from the sound of it, several fae are about to turn the corner and discover me.

I don't have time to fiddle with this stubborn entrance, so, gripping the frame, I tug with all my might. Something cracks, then the painting swings wide open. I duck into the hidden passageway, pulling the painting back into place. And not a moment too soon, because the voices are louder, and after only a handful of seconds, the group passes on the other side of the hidden door.

I wait until I don't hear anyone else before I breathe a sigh of relief. When I let go of the door to venture farther into the passageway, it begins to swing open behind me. I must have broken whatever mechanism allowed the hidden door to open and close, and now it's not closing properly. I can't just leave it like it is, gaping open for anyone to see.

There isn't any light in the passageway, and I don't have my lumestra stone to guide me. The only bit of light is what's shining through the cracks around the picture frame. Holding the painting closed with one hand, I start patting around the wall, feeling for anything that might help keep the painting from swinging open. Something sharp rakes across my palm, slicing into my skin. I pull my hand back with a hiss, realizing I've cut it open on an exposed nail.

"Could everything that could go wrong please not?" I grumble as blood drips from my palm to the dusty tunnel floor.

Using my uninjured hand, I reach under Tori's cloak and rip off some fabric from my sleeve and begin to clumsily wrap it around my hand, and it gives me an idea. Quickly, and sloppily, because I still have to keep a hand on the door to stop it from popping open, I tear the rest of both my sleeves off, and then what's left of the overskirt still clinging to my hips. It takes longer than it should, but I manage to tie the pieces together and then wrap one end around the handhold on the back side of the painting. Gingerly feeling along the wall, I find the nail that ripped into my hand and secure the other end to it. Holding my breath, I let go of the ripped fabric, and when the door doesn't pop open, I call it a win. It's not a permanent fix, but it's the best I can do considering the circumstances.

Turning away from the painting, I face the darkened passageway. Nothing but blackness yawns in front of me, immediately reminding me of the dungeon. I hope Shayla is okay.

I ignore the knot tightening in my gut, and the warnings screaming at me to turn around, and plunge forward into the abyss.

Chapter 35

I'VE BEEN ROAMING THE HIDDEN PASSAGEWAYS for hours. At least I think it's hours. My memory of how to get to Dryden's room isn't as sharp as I hoped it would be, not to mention I only have my hands to guide me in the dark, so I've hit dead ends and almost popped out of the passageway in the worst places—including the royal family's private dining room and what I think is a guard break room. I'm running low on faith and energy as I force my feet to keep moving, listening at walls whenever I hear voices, desperately hoping I catch Dryden's, or Neo's, familiar timbre.

As I hit what I think is another dead end, I chastise myself for not bringing a lantern with me. I might have already passed the entrance to Dryden's room more than once. The only thing I'm sure of is that I'm on the right floor, because it was easy to track going up and down stairs.

Turning around, I head back the way I came. At least . . . I think I do. I might've missed a turn I couldn't see. At this point, I'm so disoriented that it's fair to say I'm just blindly wandering the passageways.

I don't realize the hallway veers until I walk straight into a wall, smashing my nose against a wooden beam. Stepping back, I rub at the sore spot, trying to convince myself not to curl up into a ball on the ground and give up. I'm exhausted, and my empty stomach is trying to eat itself. I'm cut and bruised and bleeding, and I would do very bad things for a baguette and a bath right now.

I'm so caught up in my own self-pity that I don't hear the heated conversation make its way through the passageway wall to me until it's almost over. Halting, I cock my head, listening and picking up a pair of male voices.

Familiar voices.

Backtracking the best I can, I feel around until I find a passageway entrance. Putting my ear to the hidden door, I try to make out the voices.

"I've looked everywhere for her," a male says.

"You haven't looked everywhere, because you haven't found her yet," another male snaps back.

My heart jumps into my throat. It's Dryden. I'm sure of it. And the first voice is probably Bram.

My eyes start to water. I found him, I actually found him. I want to throw the door open and rush the room, but I stop myself. I have to make absolutely sure it's Bram with him and that they're alone before I enter.

"I've searched through every nook and cranny in Whitespire," the one who I think is Bram says. "I even walked all the passageways, thinking she may be hiding there. I'm telling you, she's not in the palace. If she were, I would have found her by now."

If he knows the passageways, it has to be Bram.

"Well, if she's not in the palace, what about Lord Sylvan? Did you check his country estate, too?"

Lord Sylvan. His threats feel laughable now compared to what I've faced the past few days.

"As much as I despise that despicable excuse for a fae, I don't believe he has her. I had both his city *and* country estates searched already. And when I questioned him, a punch to the jaw and a few choice threats had him blubbering like a baby. He would have told me if he had her."

Dryden makes a frustrated sound that's closer to a growl than anything else. "She couldn't have just disappeared into thin air. She has to be somewhere."

Giddy with relief that I've found them, I'm about to enter the room when Bram says, "Have you considered that she may have left like everyone assumes? The evidence of what was found in her room is quite damning, after all. I know you want to believe there's a reasonable explanation for what was found, but what if the most obvious explanation is the right one?"

King Darius did a wonderful job making it look like I fled the kingdom. And I inadvertently helped him build the narrative by actually stealing all those items. But despite how it looks, I want to know what Dryden thinks. No one else's opinion in this kingdom matters to me but his. With the evidence stacked against me, it would gut me, but I wouldn't blame him if—

"I don't care if she stole every bloody trinket in the entire palace. She didn't flee," Dryden says, the tone of his voice sending a chill down my spine. It's cold. Deadly. A tone I've never heard him take before, let alone with Bram. "Something has happened to her, and if you can't find her, I will."

"Are you daft?" Bram all but shouts. "You're still healing—"

"I'm fine," Dryden grits out.

"You were shot with four arrows. You are anything but fine. If you really believe she's here, I'll keep looking."

"No," Dryden says, and I can almost see the stubborn look on his face. "I'm well enough. You know my abilities help me heal fast. It's been three days. I'm not sitting in this room a moment longer."

Footfalls sound across the rug, and, worried Dryden is leaving, I shove open the secret door, batting the tapestry in front of it out of the way.

The telltale sound of a sword being pulled slices through the air, and when I emerge from behind the tapestry, Bram's blade hovers a hairsbreadth from my neck.

His eyes go wide. "Rowan?"

I glance down at the blade. "Do you mind? I think I've bled enough in the last few days."

He's already lowering his sword when Dryden's hand lands on Bram's shoulder and he's forcefully shoved out of the way.

I see relief splashed across Dryden's face the split second before he pulls me into his arms. He holds me painfully tight, but I don't mind. For the first time in days, I feel like I can relax.

His arms feel so right wrapped around me, holding me close. I never want him to let go. A sob threatens to crawl up my throat, but I don't let it. Instead, I bury my face in his chest.

"You're here. You're safe," he mumbles, his lips brushing the shell of my ear, causing a delicious shiver to run through me.

He smells so good. Too good. Like cedar and cinnamon. It reminds me how long it's been since I've bathed or worn fresh clothes, and I tense in his arms. Feeling me go rigid, he pulls back. His green gaze dances over my face, no doubt picking up all the filth and dried blood, and he goes still as well.

He gently brushes the hair off my forehead, where I was struck. I want to duck, hiding myself from him, but I force myself to stay put. When the tips of his fingers just barely skim over the sore spot, I flinch and his eyes darken.

"Who did this to you?"

I just shake my head, not knowing where to start.

Rather than pressing me, he steps back and lets his gaze trail down my body, which is mostly covered with Tori's cloak. Lifting his hand, he undoes the clasp that's holding the cloak together. The heavy fabric slips from my shoulders. I feel like I'm laid bare before him, but I let him inspect me.

He starts at my feet, his gaze running over every dirty, soiled, and bloody inch of me. I notice he pays particular attention to the fresh wound on my palm and the crusted blood on my forehead, injuries I didn't have the last time I saw him.

For my part, I'm glad to see that he appears well. There are dark smudges under his eyes that speak of a lack of sleep, but there's color in his cheeks, and he seems to be moving with ease. It's a relief, but with each cut and scrape he discovers on me, his eyes darken more until, when he's finally done taking me in, his face is a mask of barely controlled rage.

"Bram," Dryden says, addressing his friend without taking his eyes off me. "Find her something clean and comfortable to wear. And bring up some food from the kitchen. Something bland but hearty. I don't think she's eaten in days."

At the mention of food, my stomach growls, confirming I'm half starved, and I feel my cheeks warm.

Bram nods, then turns and leaves Dryden's bedchamber. When the antechamber door clicks shut behind him, Dryden gently takes my elbow and leads me to his private bathing room. He doesn't say anything as he guides me to sit on a stool next to his bathtub and crouches in front of me.

Carefully, he picks up my injured hand, holding it palm up in one of his own. With his other hand, he reaches for a basket off to the side, dragging it closer. It's filled with clean rolls of bandages and what look like jars of ointments. With his head bent before me, he starts to unravel the torn and bloodied fabric I hastily wrapped around my hand.

"Dryden," I start, feeling like there's so much I have to tell him, but he shakes his head, silencing me.

"I'm not ready to hear yet. Just let me take care of you first. I need a few minutes to . . . get control of myself." I can hear the strain in his voice, and I nod, even though he's not looking up at me.

Once the makeshift bandage is removed, he turns the knobs on the tub and fresh water starts to run. Digging through the basket, he pulls out a small washcloth and wets it. The cut on my palm isn't deep and has already stopped bleeding, so Dryden uses the washcloth to wipe away the dried blood and then gently clean the wound.

I stare at the top of Dryden's head as he tends to me, at the dark and wavy strands that I know feel like silk. I want to touch them, and because my tired brain can't come up with a reason not to, I do just that, grazing the tips of my fingers over the glossy strands.

At first, Dryden doesn't say or do anything. He cleans my palm and then covers the cut with some of his ointments. When he starts to rewrap the wound with fresh bandages, I get bolder and dive my fingers deeper, letting the locks run between. He pauses and tips his head so he can look up at me.

What am I doing?

I snatch my hand back, heat burning my cheeks, but Dryden shakes his head and says, "Don't stop. It feels good."

Tentatively, I start to reach forward again, but catch sight of my hand. Dirt is caked on my knuckles. The nails that aren't broken have filth and dried blood crusted under them. I'm appalled that I touched him with such disgusting hands.

Looking anywhere but at him, I try to tuck my hand away, but he catches it and brings it forward. I feel, rather than see, his soft lips press against my filthy palm.

I try to snatch my hand away. "Don't. I'm gross."

He holds tight to my wrist, and, bringing it to his cheek, he rests his face against my palm. "You're not gross. You could never be. Especially to me."

A knot of emotion clogs my throat. I don't know what it is about this simple gesture that breaks me apart, but I shatter in that moment. All the pain and stress and despair from the last few days falls on me at once, and sitting on a stool in his bathing room with the prince stooped before me, I crumble.

A sob racks my chest, and before the first tear can fall, Dryden has pulled me from the stool and is cradling me against his chest. He rubs circles on my back and whispers soft words in my ear—that I'm safe and that everything is all right—as I cry in his arms.

When my tears finally run dry, I'm practically boneless as I sag against him.

Knowing I can't stay like this forever, I gather whatever small vestiges of energy I can find and push against his chest. I feel his reluctance as he lets me sit up, putting some space between us.

When I glance at him, there's a question in his eyes. Even without tears left to cry, I'm not ready to talk about it. He needed time to regain control—and now I need the same to piece myself back together.

Seeming to understand, Dryden sets me back on the stool. Cupping my face between his hands, he asks if he can dress the rest of my wounds, and I nod.

He moves on to the arrow wound on my bicep next. It's long since stopped bleeding, but I haven't checked it since he first dressed the cut back in the cabin. When he goes to pull the fabric away, it sticks to me. Using his washcloth, he tries to separate the fabric from the wound, but it's stubborn, so he finally has to pull it away, taking some of the healing scab with it, reopening the cut.

"This needs stitches," he mumbles, but I just shrug.

"Do you have any needle and thread in that basket?" I ask.

He shakes his head.

"Didn't think so."

"I'll do my best until we can get a palace physician to get a proper look at it."

With the mention of a palace physician, a bolt of fear runs through me. "No," I say, the word just shy of a shout, surprising Dryden enough that he looks away from his task and up into my eyes. "No one can know I'm here, so just take care of it yourself. I'm sure I'll be fine."

I can see he's confused, but he nods.

It's silent in the bathing room except for the noise of the faucet turning on and off, and him rummaging around in his basket for bandages and supplies, so I startle a little when he finally says, "Shayla was found and arrested. She's awaiting trial in the dungeons. I know she isn't the only one who did all of this to you. I'll kill whoever else hurt you." The venom in his words tells me he means them.

I don't know how Dryden will react to hearing his brother wants him dead. He'll be hurt and angry, of course, but we never talked much about their relationship, so I have no idea how deep the truth is going to cut.

"We need to talk," I say, but Dryden suddenly surges to his feet. "Bathe first, then we can talk."

"But I'll get the fresh bandages wet," I argue.

He gives me a soft look. "I'll just rewrap them."

Right. Yeah.

Bending over, he puts a stopper in the tub. He rolls back his sleeves, and I can't tear my gaze from his forearms as he adjusts the water to the right temperature. Once he's satisfied that the water is warm enough, he says, "One second," and then turns, leaving the bathing room.

I don't know when Bram got back, but when Dryden returns a moment later, he's carrying a stack of fresh clothes. He sets them on a short bureau next to the tub.

I stare at him in wonderment as he opens the bureau drawers and pulls out towels for me, and then oils, which he drips into the filling tub. It isn't long before the small room fills with the smells of cinnamon, amber, and bergamot. The scents are a little more masculine than what I'd pick for myself, but right now anything is better than the odor of blood and sweat clinging to me.

When the tub is filled and the air is heavy with steam, he shuts the water off. For a moment, I think he's going to stay to watch me undress and get in. My face must give my thoughts away, because a small blush tints his high cheekbones. Clearing his throat, he takes a step back.

"You should have everything you need. Take your time. When you're done, you can eat and we can talk." Dryden turns to leave, but I catch his hand, stopping him. He glances over his shoulder at me, a small furrow between his brows.

"Don't let anyone know I'm here."

"Of course," he says with a tilt of his head.

"*No one*," I emphasize, needing him to agree before I can relax.

He nods. "Not a single soul. I promise."

With that assurance, I let my fingers slide through his. With one final look at me, Dryden leaves the bathing room, shutting the door quietly behind him.

Chapter 36

RATHER THAN SAVORING THE DECADENT BATH that Dryden drew for me, I work quickly, scrubbing myself as fast as I can while still taking care with my scabbed wounds. After I feel somewhat fae again, I dunk my head under the water and then use the bottle of soap and conditioning oils on my hair until I can run my fingers through it.

All in all, it's an arduous task that takes longer than I would have liked. But I wasn't just dirty—I had layers of grime and blood caked on me. I also took care not to dip my injured hand into the water more than necessary, which slowed me down. It was impossible not to get the bandages wet, but I managed to clean around them well enough.

By the time I emerge to dry myself off, the aroma of beef stew reaches me from beyond the closed door, which urges me on. Going to the bundle of clothes Bram secured, I slip on the loose shirt and pants. I don't know where Bram found the outfit. Maybe a stablehand? The simple garments remind me of the clothes I would have worn before all of this started, and I find that comforting. It's a welcome break from the heavy skirts and corsets I've been forced to wear for almost two months now.

Besides the emptiness in my gut, I feel halfway normal again as I emerge from the bathing room. There's a small table in the corner of Dryden's bedchamber where he and Bram are sitting and waiting for me. I think I've interrupted some sort of heated conversation. They're leaned in toward each other, and Dryden slashes his hand through the air at the same time as he says, "Absolutely not."

I clear my throat, and their heads swivel in my direction. They stand immediately, Dryden coming to my side while Bram hangs back. Dryden's eyes sweep over me in an almost clinical way.

I lift my hand, showing him the damp bandage. "I tried to keep it dry."

He waves me off. "I'll re-dress them after you've eaten."

Food. Yes, please.

My gaze travels past him to the table, where there's a loaf of bread, butter, and a small pot of stew. My mouth starts watering and I can't look away.

Leading me over to the table with him, Dryden seats me in a soft chair between his and Bram's. I'm too hungry to wait for an invitation to eat and instead dive right in, breaking off a hunk of bread from the loaf and shoving it in my mouth. Dryden ladles some of the stew into a bowl and places it in front of me. After I swallow, I take a spoonful of the thick broth. The flavors of roasted meat, carrots, onions, and potatoes, along with whatever spices were used, explode in my mouth, and I can't help the low moan of approval that escapes me.

Dryden's brow shoots up, and Bram chuckles.

"Good?" Bram asks.

I nod and take another bite. "The best."

There's warmth in Bram's eyes as he watches me shove bite after bite into my mouth, but I don't miss how his gaze sweeps over my injuries. Particularly my forehead and hand.

Bram and Dryden stay quiet while I eat. I don't miss the pointed looks they exchange with each other, but I just don't care, because this stew is the best thing I've ever eaten in my entire life and it's taking all my concentration not to make more weird moaning noises with every bite.

Eventually, my stomach starts to fill and I slow down. Bram leans forward in his seat, placing his forearms on the table in front of us. "What happened?" he asks, diving right into it.

"Bram, don't rush her," Dryden says sharply. "Let her finish her meal first. She's obviously starving. We can get to what happened in a bit."

Bram scoffs at the prince. "Stop coddling the girl. You know her well enough by now to know she's tough. Something's happened, and we need to know what."

Oddly, Bram's words give me confidence. I like that he sees me as tough. I know it's not that Dryden doesn't, but seeing me bloodied, bruised, and dirty obviously shook him, and he's still struggling.

"You're right. Something has happened to her," Dryden says, deceptively calm. "And perhaps she isn't ready—"

"It's fine," I say, cutting him off. I lay down my spoon, knowing what I have to tell them is going to sour my gut. "Bram's right. A lot has happened, and I have information that you need to know."

Dryden glances at me, and I can tell he's wrestling with himself. Perhaps part of him doesn't want to hear what I have to say, because his intuition is telling him it's bad. And it *is* bad. Once I tell him what I know, his life will change forever.

"Maybe start with where you've been the last couple of days," Bram says carefully, his gaze flicking over to Dryden to gauge his response. The prince holds himself still, as if he's bracing for what comes next.

I'm staring at Dryden when I answer Bram. "The dungeon."

Dryden freezes, except for the flash of shock in his eyes. I'm about to go on and tell them about King Darius and Shayla when he suddenly erupts out of his seat. His hands open and close into fists as he paces back and forth.

Bram stands too, holding his hands out in front of him as if he's trying to approach a wild beast. "You need to calm down and let—"

"Calm down? *Calm. Down?*" Dryden bares his teeth at his friend in a savage snarl. "Did you hear what she just said?" Bram doesn't get the opportunity to answer before Dryden turns to me. "Who put you in the dungeon? I want names," he grinds out, and he's so fierce I have to remind myself that his anger isn't directed *at* me, it's *for* me.

I pause, not knowing what's going to happen after I reveal the truth about his brother. I can't see that revelation defusing this situation. Perhaps now isn't the time to tell him that truth. Dryden is unhinged in a way I've never seen him before. Even as I stare up at him, there's a telltale ripple over his features as if he's lost control of his magic and is about to shift forms.

For the second time tonight, Dryden drops down in front of me. His voice softens, as if he knows he's frightening me, but despite his tone, his words are no less vicious than before. "Tell me who did this to you. Just say their name and I promise you, they won't live long enough to see the sunrise."

My heart is beating a furious cadence. His gaze burns into me as he waits for my answer. I don't know if I'm doing the right thing or not, but all I have to offer him is the truth.

"King Darius."

✦

I WATCH THE light dim in Dryden's eyes the moment I utter his brother's name. The rest of the story comes tumbling from my lips in a rush, each word tripping over the others, starting from the moment Dryden was carried into the palace and the guards tried to arrest me, to showing up in his private chambers.

Dryden doesn't interrupt me once. He returns to his seat, and it is like talking to a shell. He nods at the appropriate times and stares in my direction, but the look of shocked disbelief stays on his face. Bram interrupts me a couple of times to get clarification or ask a question, but Dryden never says another word. He lets me get every sordid detail out without a flicker of reaction.

When everything is finally out, I feel drained—wrung out like a wet rag without a drop left to give. Bram looks thoughtful. Concerned, but thoughtful. As I stare at Dryden, I can't tell if he believes me. His face is blank, devoid of any real emotion.

"Do you . . . believe me?" I ask, wondering if he's shut down because he thinks I'm a liar. Wondering if he's seeing me for the thief that I am.

Dryden's gaze meets mine, and I finally see a spark of life. He lifts his hand and tenderly brushes his thumb over my cheekbone. "I do."

"We have to do something about this," Bram says, and Dryden drops his hand, his gaze traveling past me to Bram.

Dryden seems to be considering something, and then, without a word, he slides out of his chair. Going over to his nightstand, he opens the drawer, pulls out a dagger and a belted sheath, and secures them around his waist. He walks right past us and heads through the antechamber toward his door.

Bram and I exchange a startled look, then both of us pop out of our seats to follow him.

"Where are you going?" Bram demands.

Pausing, Dryden glances over his shoulder at Bram, then his eyes slide to me. "Don't leave this room. I won't be gone long."

Panic spikes in my chest. "No, you can't go out there! Didn't you hear what I said? Shayla wasn't the assassin. I checked her arm for the dagger wound. The real assassin is still out there somewhere."

"She's right," Bram chimes in. "Have you also considered that at any moment your brother could find out Rowan's missing? Where do you think is the first place he's going to look for her?"

I hadn't thought about that, but he's right.

"Bar the door when I leave. Don't let anyone in except me. Protect her with your life. If I'm not back within an hour, go to the hidden room and wait for me there."

No, this can't be happening.

Dryden reaches the door and I rush forward, prepared to beg him if I have to.

"Your brother still wants to see you dead. You can't just go walking around unprotected."

"No one will know it's me," he says, and then before my eyes, the air around Dryden turns wavy. I've seen him do this one other time, but watching him change forms is still shocking. Especially when his raven hair lightens to a familiar shade, his shoulders broaden, the bridge of his nose flattens, and his jaw squares. After only a few more moments, it's not Dryden's green eyes I'm looking into anymore, but Neo's blue eyes.

The breath catches in my throat. It's been so long since I've seen him in this form. I'd forgotten the exact shade of his eyes and curve of his cheekbones in the time I've spent with him as Prince Dryden.

It's a strange mix of emotions that flood me, because my relationship with the prince started when he was in this form. It's where we forged friendship and trust. He looked like this when my feelings started to deepen for him, and even though Dryden and Neo are one and the same, seeing him as Neo still confuses me.

"I'll be fine," he says, sounding different than he did a moment before. "None of the guards know about my ability. They won't know it's me."

"But the king does, right?" I ask, remembering that he once told me his family knew of his glamour. "How do you know he hasn't told his guards to be on the lookout for you in this form, or any other form he knows you prefer to take? Or just to detain anyone in the palace who they don't know?"

Dryden pauses and it seems like my words are finally getting through to him. "That's unlikely."

"But possible," I argue.

A fist pounds against the door, startling both of us. No one says anything, and the banging starts again.

"Your Highness," comes a male voice. "We've had a prisoner escape. We're here to check your room and then stand guard."

Dryden glances over my shoulder at Bram, who stares back with a grim look on his face. The three of us retreat from the door, lowering our voices so we can't be heard by the guards on the other side.

"He knows I'm gone," I whisper, and both of them nod their agreement.

Dryden tries to hand me off to Bram. "Take Rowan to the hidden room."

"Come with us," I plead.

There's another bang. "We were sent here by the king. If you don't open the door, we've been instructed to break it down." After a pause, he adds, completely unconvincingly, "For your own safety."

I give Dryden a pointed look as if to say, "You see?" and he nods sharply. "All right, let's go."

Bram and I rush to the hidden door while Dryden grabs some things from his room. Bram and I are only just slipping behind the tapestry when we hear something much heavier than a fist ram against Dryden's door.

"Time to go," Bram says as he pops open the door and tries to usher me through it.

"Wait," I say, digging my heels in as he tugs me forward. "Dryden's not here yet."

"I'm right here," Dryden says, appearing suddenly with a bag slung over his shoulder and small lantern in his hand. *Smart.*

There's another loud bang, and this time it's accompanied by the sound of splintering wood as the guards breach the door.

My eyes go wide, and I let myself be pulled into the passageway with Dryden right behind me. Dryden quietly shuts the door just as the guards rush into his rooms. Multiple pairs of feet stomp over the floor and start searching for the prince, and presumably me. From the ruckus they are making, I'd guess it's at least ten, if not more.

"There's no one here," someone says on the other side of the hidden door.

All three of us move closer, pressing our ears to the wall to listen.

"Make sure," the head guard snaps back.

The guards proceed to move through Dryden's rooms, tossing furniture to search for us. I hold my breath, worried they are going to rip down the tapestry and find the hidden door, but they never do. When it's clear we're not there, they finally stop rampaging through Dryden's rooms.

"The king is going to be furious," the head guard grumbles. "He was very clear on his orders to find the girl and secure the prince in his rooms."

"Well, there's nothing we can do if they aren't here," another answers.

"Since when do you know King Darius to be reasonable?" he asks, then sighs loud enough for us to hear through the wall. "At least find the contract. That might mollify His Majesty."

My gaze shoots to Dryden, who looks back at me with wide eyes. Are they talking about my indenture contract? They must be. King Darius already confessed that he planned to own me.

There's a pause before, "We can't find that either."

Something smashes against the wall we're all pressed up against, making the three of us jump back. The guard must have thrown a chair in anger, and now one of the legs has punched through the wall completely. If any of the guards pull the chair out and look through the hole, they'll figure out there's a passageway back here.

Dryden grabs my hand and pulls us down the corridor, away from his room. With Bram following, we flee as quietly as possible, but as we turn the corner, I think I hear one of the guards ask what's behind the wall. We don't stay to see if he's figured it out.

✦

I CAN'T REMEMBER the last time I slept. In fairness, I never knew what time of day it was when I was trapped in the dungeon, so figuring it out would be near impossible. But from the way my body feels, I wouldn't be surprised if it's been days. I know I haven't had a *decent* night's sleep since before I went to the orchard with Dryden. Dryden, still looking like Neo, has dark smudges under his eyes that are visible even in the low light, suggesting it's the same for him.

"Sit down already," Bram barks as Dryden paces back and forth in the cramped hidden room. "You're giving me a headache. We're never going to figure this out with you wearing a hole in the floor."

Listening to the older fae, Dryden stops and sits down heavily in the seat next to me.

I'm tired, even more so now with a full belly, and cranky, and don't have time to beat around the bush anymore. "Why would your brother want you dead?"

If Dryden's surprised by the bluntness of my question, he doesn't let it show. Rather than answer right away, he flicks his gaze past me to Bram. The lift of Bram's brows says, "I told you so." Dryden sighs and shakes his head.

"What am I missing?" I ask, glancing between the two of them.

Dryden shoves a hand in his hair, pushing the blond strands off his forehead that stubbornly fall right back where they were. It reminds me of when I ran my fingers through his dark hair in the bathing room, and I can't help but wonder if Neo's hair is just as soft. A completely ridiculous thought considering the situation.

"Ever since my brother took the crown, he's been . . . different. Some of his decisions have been . . ." Dryden leans back in his chair, seemingly trying to find the right words.

"Unhinged," Bram supplies.

"Secretive," Dryden corrects him. "I wouldn't go as far as to say 'unhinged,'" he says, and Bram snorts. "But certainly confusing, and seemingly erratic at times. His decision to throw me into the marriage market is a prime example. Although now it makes some sense if he was going to use it as a way to have me killed. But it hasn't just been the strange decisions. There's been a shift in his personality, too."

"How so?" I ask. I never met the king before the first day of the courting season, and we've had very little interaction since.

Dryden shrugs. "At first, I thought it was just him getting used to his new rule; my father's death took all of us by surprise. The mantle of ruler will change anyone, so when Darius's decisions became more erratic and his personality sharpened, it was easily explained away by circumstance."

Bram huffs, crossing his arms over his chest. "*Power hungry* is what he's become. I've been telling you for months now to watch your back."

"That still doesn't explain why he would want you dead. He's already king of arguably the strongest kingdom in Vaeloria. It's not like you're standing in the way of that."

Dryden and Bram exchange another look, but Dryden shakes his head. "He didn't even know about it," he says to Bram.

"Do you really still think that?" Bram asks, exasperated. "Because that right there is a motive."

"What are you talking about?" I cut in, annoyed they are having a conversation over my head.

Bram glances at Dryden, who gestures to him to go ahead and tell me.

"A week before King Drake passed, he told Dryden he was going to name him as his successor."

I'm momentarily stunned. The line of royal succession follows the oldest heir. It's only ever been circumvented in extreme cases a time or two throughout history, and even then, it caused civil unrest in the kingdom. For King Drake to want to pass the throne to his second-born son rather than his first is no small thing.

"But why would he want you to be king?" I blurt, only to wince once the words are out of my mouth because of how insulting they sound.

"Mostly because of my magic," Dryden says, seeming not offended by the question. "One of my father's obsessions was uncovering why magic in Vaeloria has dwindled to almost nothing. He got it in his head that me being born with magic was a sign that I should be king. That somehow magic would be restored because of me."

"How?" I ask, and he shrugs.

"Maybe something to do with my glamour magic. I never did get the full story out of him before he passed, but he was adamant. I told him I didn't want to be king, and I thought that was the end of it. As far as I know, he didn't share this desire with anyone else."

"But if your brother found out . . ."

Bram nods. "If he found out, Dryden would be a threat on his birthright."

A horrible thought enters my mind. If Darius is willing to kill his brother to keep his crown, are there any lines he won't cross?

I turn to Dryden, looking into his tired and sad eyes. This can't be easy to talk about, but it's necessary. "How did your father die?" I ask gently.

Officially, King Drake died suddenly and tragically. The details surrounding his death were never divulged to the public. I can't help but wonder if the circumstances of his death were more nefarious than most of us in the kingdom realize.

Dryden hesitates, and I say, "I'm sorry. If it's too painful to talk about, I understand."

"It's not that," he says with a light shake of his head. "My father was found in his bedroom, decapitated and drained of his blood."

My body goes hot and then cold. "Drained of his blood? Like the attacks that have been happening around Vaeloria?"

Dryden nods. "The murderer was never found. We don't even know how he entered the bedchamber. The guards stationed at his door that night heard nothing, and the secret passageway to and from his room was locked from the inside. In order to avert a panic in the kingdom, his cause of death was kept secret."

"And still your brother refused to investigate the reports from the Coral Kingdom?"

He nods again.

"I can't make all the pieces fit, but it's clear something's not right here."

"That's an understatement," Bram says.

"Do you think it's possible . . . ?" I let the question hang in the air because it's almost too horrible to say out loud. But even so, Dryden knows exactly what I was getting at.

"That my brother killed our father?" he asks bluntly, and I nod. He runs a weary hand down his face and rubs the scruff on his jaw. "If you had asked me yesterday, I would have said there's no way. But now . . . perhaps it's possible."

"Possible?" Bram scoffs. "I think you mean probable."

Dryden sighs and then nods. I watch his face as he looks straight ahead, staring at nothing. I can't imagine what it must be like for him to take all of this in.

"So, one theory is that Darius finds out that his father wants to put Dryden on the throne instead of him and has him killed. If he was still threatened by you, why not kill you then too?"

"I'd like to say it's because of the affection he has toward me, but we all know that's not true. Perhaps it would have looked too suspicious if I died right around the same time? What I can't work out is why go through all this trouble? It makes sense to me that it would have raised some suspicion if I'd died at the same time as my father. But he didn't need to orchestrate this whole courting season just to have me assassinated. At any time, he could have staged an accident. Yes, it would have been seen as a tragedy to lose the king and a prince in the same year, but he would have gotten away with it."

I think about Shayla and her kingdom. "It must be a strategic move. He's framing Shayla for a reason. We just don't yet know what that is. Shayla thought it might give him a reason to try to take over their kingdom, so maybe that's why? The Iron Kingdom is a wealthy one. Maybe he saw the courting season charade as a way to kill two birds with one stone." When Dryden shoots me a dry look, I wince. "Sorry, poor choice of words."

"Whatever his reasoning," Bram says, "we're not going to figure out anything tonight. You two need sleep." He nods over to the small bed pushed up against the wall. "I'll stand watch. Once you've both rested, we can talk about what's really important."

"And what's that?" I ask.

"How we're going to get that crown off of King Darius's head and onto Dryden's. Because as long as Darius remains king, he's not going to stop until his brother is dead."

Chapter 37

THE SINGLE BED IN THE HIDDEN ROOM ISN'T large enough for two bodies. At least not unless we intertwine ourselves to fit, something that makes heat rise to my cheeks just thinking about it.

Over the years, I've spent more nights sleeping on the floor than not, and I'm practically asleep on my feet right now anyway, so I offer to take the floor. Dryden won't hear of it and insists I take the narrow bed for myself. With only a flat pillow, he settles himself on the floor next to the bed.

I should be able to fall asleep right away, but I don't. It's quiet, even with three bodies packed into such a tight space. The windowless room is dark, but the lantern casts a dim glow around the space. I don't realize how comforting that low light is until Bram gets up, telling us he's going to stand watch outside the room to keep an eye on the surrounding passageways, and takes the lantern with him.

The moment he leaves, the room goes pitch-black, and a small bud of panic sparks to life in my chest. I've never been afraid of the dark before. Even when I was a small child, I didn't have fears of monsters that lurked in the dark. I knew well enough that monsters existed in the daylight, too. In truth, for most of my life, the darkness has been my friend, helping me conceal my less-than-legal activities. But my time in the dungeon seems to have changed all that, because as I lie rigid atop the thin mattress, tendrils of unease start to slither around my heart.

I shut my eyes tightly, trying to ground myself in this moment. I force myself to notice that the air isn't bone-chillingly cold, how the bed beneath me isn't a stone floor, but instead a soft, albeit lumpy, mattress.

I'm safe. I'm not trapped in the dungeon. I'm safe. I'm safe, I chant to myself, but the utter blackness still triggers panic deep inside me that I can't wrangle.

Slight tremors rack my frame, and I clamp down on my lower lip, trying in vain to stop these unwanted feelings from pulling me under, but it's no use.

"Rowan?" Dryden's voice pierces the darkness, and even though he's lying on the floor right beside me, it sounds like he's very far away. "Rowan . . ." He says my name again when I don't respond. "Are you okay?"

I nod, then realize he can't see me. "Yes, I'm fine," I say, and then lick my dry lips, tasting the coppery tang of blood on my tongue. I must have split my lip when I bit down on it, but I hardly care.

Something brushes my shoulder and I let out a small yelp and curl into a ball, thinking of the furry bodies of the rats in my cell.

"Whoa, easy. It's just me," Dryden says. "I'm sorry. I didn't mean to scare you."

I want to laugh it off and tell him it's nothing, but I can't make my throat work properly. I can't even force myself to stretch back out again, so instead I stay huddled in a ball pressed up against the wall, shaking.

I'm not in the dungeon, but my body doesn't seem to realize

that, and the longer I stay like this, the more the panic sets in, making my breaths come out in shallow pants. Goose bumps break out over my skin even as sweat makes the fine hairs stick to my forehead.

"Rowan, you're not fine," Dryden tells me, sounding a little panicked himself. "What's going on? How can I help?"

He doesn't touch me again; he's probably scared to, considering how I reacted to his hand on my shoulder just a moment ago.

"Rowan . . ." he says quietly, trying to get a response from me.

I try to form words, but I can't make them come out.

I feel the bed dip, and I think he might have moved to sit on the edge. "You're having a panic attack," he says, keeping his voice level and smooth. "I'm going to touch you now. If you don't want that, please let me know."

I don't know what I want. Half my mind is stuck in the past, making me incapable of fully rational thought. Even though I know it's warm, I start shivering in earnest against the dungeon's phantom freeze, and the mattress's lumps start to feel like unforgiving stones, bruising my hip and shoulder as I lie upon them. And just like when I was stuck in that dark abyss, my fingers and toes go numb and the wounds on my head and bicep start to ache.

When Dryden's hand brushes against my shoulder again, I hardly feel it, too lost in the nightmare taking place in my own mind, but eventually the slow movement of his palm as it circles my back breaks through and I'm able to force a few words out in way of an explanation.

"The dungeon . . . was dark." My voice is small, but I know he hears me because the hand stroking my back stills for a moment before he starts up again.

"Does it feel like you're still there?" he asks gently.

I nod, even though he probably can't see me, as I shiver against the cold that only truly exists in my mind. "Can't get warm."

His hand disappears from my back and then he's shifting on the bed behind me, his body practically swallowing me as he curls around me, enveloping me in his warmth. "If this isn't okay, just tell me," he whispers into my hair, and a shiver dances down my spine that has nothing to do with being cold.

Sliding an arm around my waist, he drags me closer so my back is flush against his chest.

"Breathe with me," he gently orders, then takes a long, slow breath through his nose and releases it through his mouth. His chest moves behind me with his breathing. It takes a few tries and some more gentle coaxing, but I manage to slow my breathing enough to match his.

When my breathing levels out, he whispers things to me as he holds me tight, how I'm safe and that he has me, he won't let anyone hurt me like that again. His whispered promises bring tears to my eyes and an ache to the center of my chest.

It takes a while for me to come back to myself, but eventually my heart slows, the goose bumps disappear, and the feeling returns to my fingers and toes. It's only then that I become fully aware of how intertwined I am with Dryden. He positioned one arm bent under my head so I'm resting on his bicep. His other arm is wrapped around my middle as he holds me in place. I'm still curled in a ball, but the rest of his body is curved around me.

And it's not just his body that's surrounding me, but his fresh and wild scent as well. I wonder if he realizes that he smells slightly different as Neo than he does as Dryden. I'm certainly never going to confess that truth, but as Neo his scent is woodsy, and as Dryden it's spicier. If pressed, I wouldn't be able to pick which one is more appealing, which is another thing I'll never confess.

He's still whispering soft words of encouragement to me when I clear my throat and shift a little. His arm clamps down around me to keep me from moving. It should probably make me feel panicky or smothered, but it doesn't. It makes me want to burrow into him even more, although at this point, I don't know how much closer we could be.

Much to my hidden disappointment, he loosens his hold a moment later, going as far as to pull his arm from around my middle and scooch back far enough that there's a sliver of space between us. He leaves his arm under my head, but I feel the loss of our closeness immediately.

I felt comfortable in his arms. Safe. Protected. Wanted.

Dangerous feelings I'm scolding myself for having in the first place. I'm getting too comfortable with Dryden, and that's stupid. Because no matter how much I wish he was just Neo, the handsome yet mysterious fae who so brazenly pulled me from my life of indentured servitude, he's not. He's the crown prince of the Ember Kingdom, and if we make it out of this catastrophe alive, there's no place for me in his world.

"Are you feeling better?" he asks softly next to my ear. It's physically painful to keep myself from turning my head to look at him. I imagine that if I twisted just right, our mouths would be perfectly—

I clear my throat again, lightly, to stop my wayward thought. "Yes. I'm better now." And it's the truth, because Dryden helped chase away the fear.

"Good." He starts to shift away from me, sliding his arm out from under my head, and panic shoots through me again.

By instinct, I reach back for him and grab his arm, trying to keep him in place. He freezes.

"I'm sorry," I say, embarrassed. "The dungeon was so dark, and when Bram left with the light, I just went back there, I guess." My cheeks heat and I'm suddenly glad for the lack of light. I force my hand to release him, but he catches my fingers, interlacing them with his own.

"Do you want me to stay?" he asks, almost shyly. Shy is one thing I've never seen Dryden be, as a prince or as Neo.

I bite my lip, trying to find the courage to say yes even when it would be better in the long run if he moved away now.

When I don't answer after several heartbeats, he starts to move away again, but I tighten the hand he's holding and he understands. I want him to stay, but I'm not brave enough to utter the words.

He settles again behind me but doesn't wrap his arm around me this time. He places our joined hands lightly on top of my hip. But the most distracting part is when his thumb starts to take lazy swipes over my knuckles.

Why does such a light and innocent touch feel so good?

"I'm sorry I didn't find you," he says quietly. "When I regained consciousness, I demanded to see you right away, but no one would listen to me. I couldn't do anything the first day. They wouldn't let Bram or Olette visit, and I was too injured to do anything about it. I've never felt so helpless," he confesses.

"It's not your fault. You couldn't have known," I say, meaning it. I don't blame Dryden for not finding me before I escaped. It's not his responsibility to protect me. It's my own.

I feel him shaking his head lightly. "It *is* my fault. I brought you into all of this. To think you spent days there with no one even tending to your wounds. I'll never forgive myself."

I don't want him blaming himself, but I also don't know what to say to get him to stop. It was a horrific experience I hope never to go through again. "The important thing is that I got out."

We fall silent, and in the stillness, I start going over the last few days. With Dryden so close, the panic doesn't return, but it still causes a knot of anxiety to twist in my gut.

"Tell me something," I ask.

"Like what?"

"Anything to keep my mind off of the last few days."

He's silent for a few moments before saying, "Did you know when I was young, I had a lisp?"

It's such a random thing to say, I can't help the snort-laugh that bursts out of me. "What? No, you didn't." In no world can I imagine the smooth prince with a speech impediment.

"I did," he says, and I can almost hear the smile in his voice.

Dryden goes on to tell me about his lisp, and how he struggled with simple words such as *sauce* and *sleep*, making me laugh lightly when he imitates how he used to pronounce each word. He said his father hired a speech specialist who was a young female fae Dryden instantly developed a crush on. Even after he overcame the lisp, he pretended to have it around her so he'd still get to see her.

"How old were you?" I asked.

"Eight or nine."

"And your instructor?"

"Probably in her twenties."

I gasp, feigning shock. "So scandalous."

He chuckles. "What can I say? Some of my reputation is well-earned."

Dryden goes on to fill my head with stories of his childhood. About how he used to sneak into the kitchen to steal his favorite dessert and then try to blame his imaginary friend when he was caught. About his first pet, a brown-eyed mutt he found abandoned in the gardens, and how he insisted on keeping it even after it was discovered that his brother was allergic. He even tells me about the time Bram saved his life, when the family was at their country estate and he slipped into the river while playing near the edge. The current was strong, and he was too small to fight it. Bram dove in and pulled him out before anyone else realized he was missing. Dryden says it like it's nothing, but there's a weight in the words. After that, Bram wasn't just a royal family guard. He was his. The one person who would always come for him.

I don't stop him when my head starts getting foggy with sleep, and so I drift off to his voice in my ear and the rumbles of his chest pressed against my back.

✦

"WE HAVE TO go."

I think someone is saying something, but I'm still locked in that delicious space between sleep and wakefulness, reluctant to leave. The presence cocooning me is making me feel things I haven't felt in a long time: warm, safe, protected. It's only when I try to turn into it that I realize there's a body pressed against my back and an arm wrapped around me, holding me in place.

A zing of awareness rushes through me.

Dryden.

Still not fully awake, Dryden grumbles at the intrusion and buries his face in the back of my neck, his lips brushing against my skin and sending sweet warmth throughout my body.

"Sorry to break things up when you two look so cozy, but we have to get going. The passageways are crawling with guards. They're scurrying around like mice in a maze. If we don't leave now, one of them is going to eventually find us."

With a gasp, I rip myself from Dryden's arms and sit up. I glance down to see Dryden sprawled out on the bed next to me. Or at least as much as a large male can sprawl in such a small space. He's back to his true form now, and his black curls are mussed in such a way that makes him look more innocent than I know him to be.

His green eyes blink open, still heavy with sleep, and he stares up at me. The weight of everything comes crashing down on me at once.

His brother wants him dead. We're hiding for our lives, and we don't have a real plan for what to do next. Memories of my breakdown the night before creep in along with Dryden crawling into bed to calm me and staying here because I asked him to.

Heat rushes to my cheeks as he wakes and grins lazily, as if he doesn't have a care in the world. As if his brother wasn't trying to kill him and enslave me. As if he's just a boy and I'm just a girl, and life is as simple as that.

It's not.

"Up and at 'em, Your Highness," Bram says in a mocking tone. He tosses Dryden's bag onto his stomach. Dryden huffs from the impact and runs a lazy hand through his unruly hair.

I look up at Bram, my blush deepening. "We were just . . . or rather, I—" I stumble over my words.

"Don't care. Doesn't matter," he says, but I can see the smile he's trying to hide. "But like I said, we've gotta go."

With a nod, I crawl over Dryden to get out of the bed. Or at least I try to, because the moment I swing my leg over his hip, he sits up. The bag Bram threw to him starts to slide off his lap, falling to the floor. He shifts to grab it and it throws me off balance, and I pitch forward, landing my face right in his chest.

Rearing back, I try to just roll off him, but my legs are tangled in the bedding, so all that does is twine Dryden and me further.

I twist to the side, trying to free myself, but with my legs still trapped, my upper body is the only part of me that rolls off Dryden, and I head face-first straight for the floor.

Dryden reaches for me, trying to pull me back up, but doesn't have the leverage he needs and ends up tumbling off the bed with me, somehow managing to take the brunt of the fall.

I end up sprawled over him again, our upper bodies uncovered by the blanket, but our legs a tangled mess in the bedding. Mortified, I start squirming, trying to slip free of the bedding.

"Please stop moving," Dryden says, sounding like he's in pain.

I freeze. "Oh, shoot, am I hurting you?"

Propping myself up and off his chest, I glance down at him. He pulls a face I can't decipher. "Not exactly," is all he says.

"Not the time for that, you two," Bram mock-scolds, and when I glance up at him, he's standing over us with whatever weapons he was able to find, a huge grin on his face despite the fact he told us guards could bust in on us at any moment.

"Just let me get it," Dryden says, and I nod.

Once I let him take the lead, he has us untangled and on our feet in less than a minute.

"Thanks," I mumble to him, embarrassed by the whole ordeal.

"Oh, it was my pleasure," he says, chuckling now that we're both free. When I sneak a peek at him, he quirks a cocky brow at me. "It was a memorable way to get out of bed."

I shake my head, huffing. Only Dryden would try to flirt at a time like this.

I'm ready in seconds, only needing to pull on my boots.

"As far as I can tell, the guards have only made it to the western passages," Bram says, and Dryden immediately becomes serious. "If we take the southern route toward the back of the palace, we may be able to slip out and use the wooded area for cover."

"We're leaving the palace?"

Dryden nods and sits to pull on his own boots. Bram leaves, saying he's going to do a quick check of the nearby passageways to make sure the coast is clear. He leaves the lantern with us.

"Where are we going to go?" I ask when the door closes behind Bram, not knowing where we could go that would be safe. At least not in the Ember Kingdom. Who would we even trust?

"My aunt," Dryden says. "I need to fill her in on what is going on anyway. It might be one of the places Darius looks for me, but Aunt Olette would never give me up."

I believe that. The bond between Dryden and his aunt is strong. If there's anyone we can trust besides the three of us in this room, it's Olette.

"Okay, so we go to Olette's. Then what?"

Dryden runs a hand through his hair, a lot less relaxed than he was a few minutes ago. "Then we flee the kingdom."

"To regroup?"

He shrugs. "Perhaps." He straightens and slings his bag over his shoulder. His gaze turns penetrating as he stands in front of me. "Or perhaps we just leave and live our lives."

The breath catches in my throat. Dryden's thinking of just fleeing and abandoning it all?

A smile lifts the corners of his mouth but doesn't reach his eyes. "Why do you look so surprised? You were always planning on leaving anyway. Now you'll just have a couple of travel companions."

"Yes, I was always planning to leave. But . . . what are you saying?"

He lifts a hand and tucks a strand of hair behind my ear, letting the tips of his fingers trail down my cheek and then slide around the base of my neck, gently pulling me closer.

"I'm saying that there are options on the table right now, and not being the crown prince anymore is one of them."

My eyes go wide. "You would abandon your kingdom?"

"Does it count as abandonment when the king wants me dead?"

I don't have words. I just assumed that Dryden would do something to fight back against his brother. It never crossed my mind that he would give it all up and just start anew.

I shake my head lightly, trying to clear it. "You would, just . . . what? Go to another kingdom and pretend to be a commoner? Why would you want to do that?"

"You mean besides to stay alive?" he asks with a cockeyed smile. But then he sheds the humor and takes a half step closer. Lifting his other hand, he cradles my head, his fingers tickling the back of my neck in a wholly distracting way. "Can you really say you don't see why that life would appeal to me?"

He's telling me something with his eyes that is almost too much for me to believe.

Something tickles the back of my mind, other reasons why we can't just flee the Ember Kingdom and start a new life, but as Dryden dips his head, his mouth aligning with mine, my mind empties except for the singular focus of having his lips on mine again.

The door creaks and I rear back, expecting to be rushed by royal guards, but it's just Bram. "Sorry to keep interrupting, but we really do have to go now. Guards are about to cut off our path of escape."

"Right," Dryden says, "but before we go, I should change."

I'm about to tell Dryden we don't have time for him to put on something else when the air starts to ripple around him in the now-familiar way that tells me he's using his magic. The physical changes are more subtle than when he shifts between Dryden and Neo. His hair shortens. His face becomes leaner, his nose sharper, but there's still a striking resemblance to Dryden.

The last part of him to change is his eye color, and when the dark brown fully swallows the green in his irises, it's no longer Dryden standing before me, but the king himself.

A shiver of fear runs through me. Even though I know it's Dryden looking back at me, seeing him with the face of his brother is unnerving.

"In case we get stopped," he explains, and I nod, understanding why he transformed to look like this.

Bram douses the lantern, plunging us back into darkness after explaining that it's safer to move through the passageways without it; he doesn't need light to get us out of the palace. A tendril of panic swirls in my gut until Dryden grabs my hand, anchoring me. With a comforting squeeze, he tugs me forward and out of the hidden room. We move as silently as possible through the dark passageways toward freedom.

Chapter 38

WE SNEAK THROUGH THE HIDDEN PASSAGEWAYS without being caught, but there are two close calls. When we finally get to the exit, I'm ready to shove through the door and make a run for it, but Dryden stops me to check for patrols. And it's a good thing, because if he hadn't, I would have run right into one of King Darius's guards. We move forward only after the guard has passed.

When we step out of the passageways, I blink against the brightness, my eyes watering after not being exposed to the sun for so many days. But even with the discomfort, I don't mind. Seeing the blue sky up above is glorious.

Bram, Dryden, and I hide behind one of the queen's rosebushes, waiting for another guard to pass to make a run for the wooded area. I scan the surroundings, watching for anyone else who might appear. The gardens are quiet, and we're in a spot we think is protected from anyone looking down from a window in the palace. The stables are up ahead, and just beyond them are the trees we need to reach for cover.

As my gaze tracks over to the stables, the tickle in the back of my mind I felt when Dryden was telling me of his plans to leave the Ember Kingdom for good turns into a thunderous roar. I smother a gasp.

Shayla.

How could I have forgotten about her? Shame and guilt settle in my bones.

"We can't leave yet," I whisper-hiss to Bram and Dryden.

Bram's gaze remains on the guard he's tracking, but Dryden glances over his shoulder at me and I purposefully avoid looking directly into his fake dark gaze. "What do you mean?" he asks, a deep furrow creating a groove between his brows.

"Shayla. I told her I would come back for her. Promised her I would."

Understanding dawns on his face.

Bram releases a quiet grunt up ahead. "We can't help her."

I can tell from the conflict and then guilt that flash across Dryden's features that he's going to agree with Bram. But they don't understand. They don't know what it's like in the dungeon.

He starts to say something, but I cut him off. "I can't just leave her. She's my friend, and as much of a victim in all this as we are."

Dryden presses his mouth into a determined line and nods once. "You're right. The dungeon isn't usually heavily guarded because its entrance is so well hidden. We can make a detour to get her."

Bram makes a sound of displeasure but doesn't argue. Another minute passes, then our way is clear. As a group, we run toward the trees. When we make it across the open space, Dryden takes the lead, guiding us toward the dungeon entrance. By the time we finally stop in front of the unassuming building that leads to the dungeon, my heart is pounding.

"Bram, stand guard. You're the least recognizable. Don't let anyone come in after us."

Bram gives a sharp nod in response to Dryden's order.

Dryden jerks his head to indicate I should follow him, then pushes through the door. I take one step after him, but I can't get my feet to go any farther. A cold sweat breaks out on my brow.

Seeing me falter, Dryden pauses, watching me over his shoulder. Understanding dawns on his face and he returns. "You don't have to do this. You can wait out here with Bram while I go and get Shayla."

He's giving me an out, and I appreciate it, but I need to do this. I'm the one who insisted we rescue Shayla. My fear of the dungeon is valid, but conquerable.

I shake my head. "I'm coming with you."

Pressing his mouth into a straight line, he nods, seeming to understand why I have to do this. He grabs my hand, intertwining his fingers with mine, and the feeling of his palm pressed against my own grounds me.

"Let's do it," I say, and he tugs me forward.

"If we're not out in thirty minutes, leave without us," Dryden tells Bram. "Go to Olette and tell her what's happened, and then get yourself safe."

Bram looks like he wants to argue, but he nods.

With that, Dryden shoves open the door and pulls me back into hell.

"Hold on," he says when the door shuts behind us, then with a ripple of magic, he starts to turn back into himself.

Tension I didn't even realize I was holding while he was glamoured to look like his brother eases the moment the green bleeds back into his gaze.

"All right. Let's go," he says once the transformation is complete, but I stop him.

"Why did you change back?"

Dryden looks down at me, a serious expression on his face. "Once we reach Shayla, I won't be able to change without her knowing about my magic. It's better if I just appear as myself."

Dryden has kept his secret from almost everyone his entire life, so I can understand his hesitancy to reveal himself to Shayla. I want to tell him that my friend would keep his secret, but I can't say for certain that's true, so I just nod, respecting his decision.

Grabbing a lit torch from the wall, Dryden holds it in front of him, lighting our way as we travel deeper into the cellar. I keep reminding myself that I'm all right and safe. The light is helping. The last time I did this, I didn't have a torch. But the closer we get to the door that leads to the dungeon's tunnels, my muscles threaten to seize up. I force myself to keep moving, my feet pounding against the packed dirt to keep up with Dryden.

We reach the cellar, the true entrance to the dungeon. The door I locked the two guards behind is smashed to pieces. The guards must have had to hack at the thick wood with their swords to get out.

I don't want to go down there, I really don't. But I'm going to because Shayla is somewhere in that darkness, all alone.

I'm coming, I silently say to her.

Dryden shoves the remaining pieces of the door out of the way so we can pass, dropping my hand to grab a thick shard of wood roughly the length and width of my arm.

"What's that for?" I ask.

"Leverage. To get the cell door open. I don't have the keys."

"Well, if that doesn't work, all I need is some corset boning."

He shoots me a half smile. "Is that so?"

I nod. "How do you think I escaped? I have lots of hidden talents."

He looks me up and down in a way that is highly suggestive. "I don't doubt it."

My pulse picks up, fighting off the chill that's coming from the open doorway.

"Come on," Dryden says with a wicked smile wholly inappropriate for the situation. "We have a princess to save."

Taking a deep breath in through my nose, I do my best to ignore all the conflicting feelings and sensations zipping through my body and plunge forward, following Dryden as we wind our way down the staircase to the underground tunnels.

When we reach the bottom, I take the torch from Dryden, leading the way as we jog through the tunnels. Having the torchlight helps me stay anchored in the moment rather than getting swept away in the memory of my escape the night before, but eventually the dungeon's chill seeps in. It isn't long before my teeth are chattering, but there's a curve in the tunnel that feels familiar. I think we're close.

It's less than a minute later that I'm skidding to a stop at the dead end. Two cells are across from each other. One was mine. The other is where they put Shayla. But it's quiet and I don't see her right away.

Did they take her somewhere else? Are we too late?

"Shayla?" I call tentatively, stepping closer to the bars, holding the torch out to see farther into the small space.

A sigh of relief escapes me when I see a body huddled in the farthest corner, her head of matted black hair tucked close to her chest. She lifts her dirt-streaked face and squints at me, blinking against the light she's not used to.

"Greer?"

"Yes, it's me."

Hope slowly brightens her gaze. "You came back for me." She says it as if she can hardly believe it.

"Yes. Of course. And we're going to get you out of here."

"We?" Shayla asks, getting shakily to her feet. She put her torn corset back on and is holding it together in the front over her chemise. When she gets close, I see that her lips are blue. She's freezing. Even though she's only been in the dungeon for a day, it's taken its toll.

"Prince Dryden's here to help as well."

Dryden steps forward into the light, and her eyes widen with surprise. Ever the true princess, she tries to fix her hair and stand up straighter. I'd chuckle if there were anything funny about the situation, but there's not.

"We'll get you out of here quickly," Dryden promises, and I step back to let him work on the cell door, ready to pick the lock if his plan doesn't work. But there's no need, because he wedges the piece of wood under the door at an angle, and with a single forceful downward shove, manages to pop the door off the hinges.

I look at Dryden in surprise. "That was easy."

He grins back. "You're not the only one with hidden talents."

I give him a slow once-over like he did to me and mirror his words: "I don't doubt it."

The look he gives me back isn't lacking in heat, and I can't help but remember how he stared at me in the hidden room when he said we could just leave and live our lives. That maybe he didn't have to be the crown prince of the Ember Kingdom anymore.

It's scary to admit, but the truth is, I want that. Desperately. Maybe it's selfish to want Dryden to leave this all behind, to not be a prince anymore and just be himself. For him to be free. Free to be with me. Now that that thought has taken root, my heart aches with how badly I want that future.

Dryden turns away first, forcefully pulling the door open enough so Shayla can exit the cell. She squeezes out of the opening, shivering, and I wrap her in a hug she tries to return, but she has trouble moving her arms.

She's frozen. I wish I had something to give her.

Pulling back, I try to rub some warmth into her arms. I'm not sure if it's helping, because she just sways on her feet.

From behind her, I catch Dryden's gaze, and it's filled with sadness. I know he's not thinking only of Princess Shayla, but of how I was stuck down here for days.

"Do you think you're going to be able to walk?" I ask Shayla, and she gives me a weak nod.

I glance over at Dryden with concern. "Let's go," he says. "She'll be fine once we can get her warmed up."

It takes longer to get back through the tunnels, and Dryden has to carry Shayla up the winding staircase to the cellar. I worry about his injuries, but he says he's fine.

"Just a little farther," I say encouragingly to her after Dryden sets her back on her feet. "Once we make it outside, we're going to leave the palace grounds by going over the back wall. We'll stay with someone safe who can help you get back to your kingdom."

With the mention of returning to her home, her face lights up; a small smile lifts the corners of her mouth for the first time since we found her huddled up in the cell.

"Whatever is going on, my father will help you," she says. "If you need somewhere safe to flee, you can both come with me."

I glance at Dryden, and he just tilts his head.

"It's not something we have to figure out right now," I say. "Let's get out of the palace first."

It takes another few minutes, then we've reached the door to the outside. I replace the torch, putting it back where Dryden grabbed it when we entered, while he checks to make sure the coast is clear. When he waves us forward, we slip outside, where Bram is still keeping watch.

Shayla blinks rapidly against the brightness but then tips her face upward, soaking in the rays like it's been years since she's been outside, rather than a day. From experience, I know a day in the dungeon can feel like years.

"Any trouble?" Bram asks Dryden.

He shakes his head. "You?"

"No. But we should go," he says, scanning the surrounding areas. "Something feels off. It's been too quiet."

"Maybe all the guards are busy looking for us in the palace?" Dryden suggests.

"Maybe," Bram says, looking unconvinced.

We head deeper into the wooded area, keeping an eye out for anyone lurking about. The farther away from the palace, the denser the foliage becomes, making it that much easier for us to hide as we make our way to the edge of the palace grounds.

"There," Dryden says, pointing ahead.

Through a small break in the trees, I can see the ivy-covered brick wall. The wall can't be more than a hundred feet away. The relief that hits me is staggering.

We weave through the trees and then the wall looms in front of us, shooting thirty feet in the air. Thick ivy with mature branches clings to the wall, making it scalable, but the ivy is cut so it doesn't trail over the wall. They don't want anyone to be able to climb up from the outside, so I don't know how we're going to get safely down once we've reached the top. I say as much to the group, hoping someone has a solution.

Reaching into his bag, Dryden pulls out a length of thin rope.

I don't know what made him think to grab that from his room, but I want to kiss him for it.

"Will that be long enough?" Shayla asks.

Dryden shakes his head. "I think it's going to be about ten feet short, but we'll have to make do."

Reaching down, Shayla starts tearing at her skirt. It only takes a second to realize what she's doing, then I help her pull strips of fabric until we have enough to extend the length of the rope. Dryden and Bram get to work tying the extra pieces together and then attaching them to the rope.

Bram takes it. "I can tie this to one of the thicker branches up top. You all can use it to help you up this side, then we can drape it over the other side to get down."

Bram loops the long length of rope over his shoulder and around his chest, then grabs some of the ivy, preparing to scale the wall. Then a branch snaps behind us.

I spin to find a pair of startled, doll-like blue eyes staring back at us that belong to the last person I would have expected to see.

Princess Willow.

Willow stands right at the trees' edge wearing a flowy pink dress. Her hair is pulled up into a bun with some bouncy ringlets pulled free, and a look of shock is splashed across her face.

I have no idea what the princess is doing this far from the palace. Maybe she's out foraging or having a picnic, considering the basket hanging from the crook in her arm. Knowing her, she's probably been conversing with the squirrels and chipmunks the whole time, so it's actually a little surprising we didn't hear her coming.

As Princess Willow's eyes bounce back and forth among us, my mind whirls with what to do. I have no desire to hurt the delicate princess, but we can't let her stand in the way of our escape or run to tell the guards she's found us. But then her gaze snags on Dryden and holds. Her eyes turn dreamy, and she gives him a nervous smile.

I shift a glance to Dryden, remembering the sappy entries she wrote about him in her journal. She thinks she's in love with him. Maybe we won't have to go to extreme measures to ensure her silence after all.

I catch Dryden's eye. I think he may be thinking the same thing I am. When he glances back at Willow, a smooth smile is on his face, one of his masks I can easily see through now.

"Willow, my dear. What are you doing this far from the palace?"

"I was just going for a walk and berry picking. I suppose I got lost?" Her gaze travels over all of us again, her smile melting, confusion clear on her face when she looks at Shayla and then me.

"We were told you fled back to your kingdom when you were caught stealing," she says to me, glancing over at Shayla. "And that you kidnapped the prince."

Kidnapped the prince. That must be what King Darius told everyone. I suppose he needed a reason to justify why his guards were scouring the palace for Dryden, and also to explain Shayla's sudden disappearance.

Dryden moves toward Willow, and it's silly, but I want to yank him away from her.

He shakes his head. "No, that's not true. I realize there's been some misinformation going around. But what you need to know is that I'm no longer safe at the palace, and so I need to leave."

Princess Willow gasps, lifting a hand to cover her mouth. "Are you saying you're in danger?"

Dryden nods solemnly. "I am."

She looks past him back to me and Shayla, the gears in her mind turning as she tries to figure out what we're doing here, no doubt. Dryden glances over his shoulder, following Willow's gaze.

"Princesses Greer and Shayla are assisting me. Their names have been besmirched in order to thwart any suspicion that they may be involved in my escape," he says, answering her unvoiced question.

"Escape?" Willow asks, her eyes going wide again.

"More like a temporary relocation for my safety," Dryden quickly explains. "You do want me to be safe, don't you?" His voice is silky smooth as he does his best to charm Princess Willow.

She nods vigorously. "Yes. Yes, of course I want that."

"Then I'm so sorry to ask you this, but I need you to not report any of this."

A small crease forms between her eyes, and she tilts her head. "You don't want me to tell the guards I saw you?"

Dryden shakes his head.

"What about King Darius?"

"Not even him," he says, and I hold my breath, waiting to see if Willow will believe Dryden's story or not.

"Will you help me by keeping this to yourself?" Dryden asks. "To keep me safe?"

Willow looks up at Dryden, and I swear there are hearts in her eyes. "Well, I guess if it's for your safety, then I won't say anything. Will you . . ." She chews on her bottom lip, tipping her chin down so she's looking up at Dryden from beneath her lashes. It takes physical effort not to roll my eyes at that practiced move. "Will you write to me when you're safe, so I know you're all right?"

Reaching out, he grasps Willow's fingers. "Your regard for my well-being truly touches my heart. Thank you. Of course I'll send word when I'm safe." For extra measure, he bows, pressing the back of her hand to his forehead before releasing it, and this time I can't hold back the eye roll.

Willow, however, has fully fallen under the handsome prince's spell. It looks like she might swoon.

"We have to go," he tells her, and she doesn't do much besides giggle and nod.

Turning away from her, Dryden gestures back to the wall. He comes up next to me just as Bram starts to climb.

"That was very convincing," I whisper to him, aware that Willow is still watching us.

Dryden tilts his head slightly as he regards me, a small smirk dancing at the corners of his mouth. "If I didn't know any better," he whispers back, "I'd say you sound a little jealous."

"Good thing you know better, then."

He chuckles. "Yes, good thing."

When Bram reaches the top of the wall, he quickly ties the rope to a sturdy branch and then tosses it down.

"Go ahead," Dryden says to me. "I'll be right behind you."

I shake my head. "No. Let Shayla go first," I answer, and then turn to Shayla beside me, ready to give her a hand, but the look on her face stops me cold.

Her eyes are wide in shock and her mouth is moving, but no words emerge. The color is leached from her face, and as she tries to take a step forward, she stumbles, knocking right into me.

I catch her, trying to help her stay upright, but horror runs through me as blood leaks from her mouth, dribbling down her chin onto the tattered remains of her clothes.

Over her shoulder, I see a blade embedded in the middle of her back, and I gasp.

Losing the strength to keep herself upright, Shayla drops to her knees, and I follow her down, cradling her in my arms. Tears form in my eyes. I know this isn't a wound she can come back from.

Dryden yells something, but there's a ringing in my ears, so I don't know what he says. The next moment he's standing in front of me, blocking me with his body.

Shayla looks up at me as she lies in my arms, dying. A single tear tracks out of the corner of her eye and makes its way over her cheek. She's trying to speak, but doesn't have the strength to get the words out.

No, not Shayla. Please, not her. She's too full of life, too kind, too real to die.

She tries to speak again, and I don't know what she's saying.

Sorrow crashes into me, and I get a flash of the first time we met at the opening ball. The way we secretly giggled together at the absurdity of it all. How easy it was to talk to her, and how I instantly felt like I'd found a friend, despite the circumstances.

"I'm sorry. I'm so sorry," I say over and over again as blood fills her mouth and she starts choking. It's a horrible wet sound that I'll never forget for the rest of my life.

Tears are streaming down my face as I stare down at her, completely unable to do anything to help her right now.

This isn't fair. This shouldn't be happening. She doesn't deserve this.

Even though I know it's not, this feels like my fault. Guilt and grief latch on to me, trying to swallow me whole.

"No, Shayla, please. Hang on," I beg. "You have to show me your kingdom. Remember you promised to take me riding in the mountains. You said it was the most beautiful country in all of Vaeloria and I didn't believe you. You have to stay to take me there."

With her last bit of strength, Shayla shifts her hand, twining her fingers with mine and giving my hand a weak squeeze.

She knows. I can see it in her eyes. She knows this is the end and she's trying to offer me comfort.

I've never felt more helpless in my life. All I can do is hang on to her and tell her how special she is, how much our friendship has meant to me.

Even though she can't talk back, I think she understands. And then, as suddenly as this all began, she stills. Her eyes turn glassy and unseeing and her chest stops moving. She's gone.

"Stay behind me," Dryden orders, and I lift my face, realizing he's trying to protect me from someone. A doll-like girl with a dagger in her hand and a smile on her face that's evil enough to freeze my beating heart.

It's only then that I realize what just happened.

Princess Willow murdered my friend.

Chapter 39

WILLOW GIVES SOME SORT OF SIGNAL AND A HORDE of guards materialize from the woods around us, surrounding me and Dryden. There must be at least twenty of them, if not more. How did we not realize they were there?

"What's the meaning of this?" Dryden snaps, princely authority ringing in his voice.

"Go after the other one; he can't have gotten far," Willow commands, and a group of guards start to scale the wall.

Bram!

I crane my neck, looking up the wall to see that he's gone. The rope we were supposed to climb is tossed over the other side. He must have escaped.

"Take them," Willow says next, flicking her hand in our direction, and the guards nearest to us move forward.

They ignore Dryden's commands to stand down as they form a shrinking semicircle around us. When they're close enough, two guards reach for Dryden. He pulls a dagger from his satchel and strikes out, carving into the arm of one before sinking the blade into the thigh of the second. Both guards wail in pain and stumble back, but two more take their place. Dryden's blade is still embedded in the guard's thigh, leaving him with only his fists to fight back.

I watch Dryden battle with a scary sort of detachment. A distant part of me screams to get up and fight alongside him. But so much of me is numb, watching the scene in front of me unfold as if it's a theater play rather than real life.

I have a vague notion that my reaction is not normal. I should be feeling something right now and acting on it, but I can't seem to make myself release Shayla. Her body goes cold in my arms even as her warm blood continues to stain my hands and clothes.

It's not until I catch a growing red bloom on Dryden's shoulder that I snap out of it.

Up until now, he's moved with such ease it was easy to forget he's still injured. Especially with more than one guard either limping away from their altercation or lying unconscious near his feet. But fast healer or not, that growing red mark means one of his old wounds has ripped open.

Just as I make up my mind to abandon Shayla and aid Dryden, a pair of guards get by him and lunge for me. I scream for them not to touch me, striking out at them even as Shayla's body is still draped across my lap, her black hair fanned over the grass.

I'm able to fight off the hands of the first few guards who approach, but as Dryden starts to tire, more guards make it past him, and I'm quickly overwhelmed. They tear me from Shayla's body, dragging me away from her.

I kick and punch, bloodying noses and feeling the satisfying crunch of bones breaking under my knuckles, but there are simply too many of them. Before long, my arms are bound behind my back, and I'm left panting and incapacitated. To my left, Dryden is similarly bound, being held between two burly guards. Blood dribbles down his chin from a split lip, and one of his eyes is starting to blacken. Seeing him injured again ignites a fire inside of me. I scream, battling against the guards even with my hands tied behind me.

I take a fist to the temple that has me falling to my knees and seeing stars. Dryden's outraged shouts reach my ears as I'm roughly hauled to my feet again. I blink several times before my vision clears, but when it does, the group of guards parts and Princess Willow steps forward.

It's only then that I notice the slight hitch in her steps. I cut my gaze to her arm to look for the second wound I inflicted on the archer, but she's wearing long sleeves, covering any injury that might be beneath. But I don't need to see the dagger wound to know it was her all along.

When Princess Willow stops in front of me, all I see is a fae I don't recognize. She still looks like a doll, but a deranged one. She has the same large blue eyes, round cherub face, and ringlet curls, but there's a cruelty in her gaze that chills me, distorting her once-familiar features into something warped and shadowed. A stranger carved from malice.

She makes a *tsk*ing sound as she looks over Dryden and me with fake compassion. "So dramatic," she says. Even her voice sounds different now. Darker. Deeper. Colder.

Dryden spits out a glob of blood, hitting the hem of her skirt. "You're one to talk," he says with a sneer.

She tilts her head like she doesn't know what he means.

"'Will you write to me when you're safe?'" he says, mimicking her words from earlier. "What was that whole act about? Why bother?"

Willow giggles, the sound just the same as before, which makes it all the more creepy. "Well, yes. I suppose you have me there. I couldn't pass up the opportunity to watch you struggle to charm me. I should tell you your act would have been more convincing if you'd been able to keep your eyes on me the whole time. But you kept sneaking peeks at your fake little princess over there."

Her gaze shifts to me, and I swear I see a touch of jealousy flash in her eyes. Why, I have no idea. She's clearly not in love with Dryden like I thought.

"So this whole thing has been an act?" I ask.

"Of course, you stupid girl. I've known who you are from the first day we met." She leans in, lowering her voice like we're sharing a secret. "Did you know I left that journal out for you to find?"

"So that I wouldn't suspect you," I say, as the pieces start to fall into place. "Because you're working with King Darius."

"That's right. Kill a prince, become a queen. Seems like a pretty good trade-off, don't you think?"

Kill a prince, become a queen? I don't know what she's talking about, nor do I really care. The bottom line is that she's the assassin we've been looking for this whole time, but we unmasked her too late.

"And you attacked us in the orchard," I say, fury building in my gut.

Rather than answer, she just smirks.

"Why?" I spit. "Why did you frame Shayla? Why did you kill her?"

Willow just sighs like I'm being tedious and she's had enough of me. "This is boring," she says. "We have somewhere else to be right now. It's rude to keep a king waiting." Glancing over at one of the guards, she makes a gesture that we should go and then turns to walk away.

"What about the body?" one of the guards asks, and Willow doesn't even pause as she shrugs like she couldn't care less if they take Shayla or leave her there to rot.

"You're a monster," I growl, and she glances over her shoulder at me and smirks.

"You have no idea."

✦

I DON'T SEE what they do with Shayla, and it kills me not knowing. She was a princess of Vaeloria, the only daughter of the king and queen of the Iron Kingdom. But besides that, she was a kind and good fae. She didn't deserve what happened to her. I'll regret not having been able to save my friend until the day I die.

I glance over at Dryden. He doesn't look like he's in good shape. He's covered in his own blood as well as that of the guards he fought. He has some cuts and bruises on his face, and it's clear that he's in pain. The guards on either side of him are practically dragging him back to the palace. I catch his eye, and despite his condition, he gives me one of his charming half smiles, trying to look like he's fine when I know he's not.

We pass the entrance to the dungeon on the way back to Whitespire, and terror snakes down my spine. I can't go back there. I'd rather die fighting, but there's every indication I won't have a choice either way.

After weaving back through the gardens, the guards march us up the back steps and into the palace. When we enter Whitespire, the hallways are empty. No staff hustling through the corridors. No tributes or other guests walking around. Since I arrived at Whitespire Palace, it's always been a busy place, but we don't pass a single other soul as Willow leads us through the halls and corridors. It's unnerving.

We take a turn I'm not familiar with and then travel down a long hallway toward a closed double door that's flanked by the king's guards. It's not until Willow flings both doors open to reveal a seemingly endless open spiral stairway that I realize where she's taking us: the tower.

I don't know what they keep in the oldest part of the palace besides the ember crystal; it's off-limits to most fae. I cast Dryden a curious glance. He looks confused and calls out to Willow, asking why we're going into the spire. Willow glances over her shoulder and again gives a smirk instead of answering, which only ratchets my nerves higher.

We start the ascent and climb, and climb, and climb. The stairs wind around the interior of the tower, leaving a space in the middle through which you can see all the way to the floor. I'm not used to heights, so I purposefully don't look down.

It feels like we're climbing forever before the stairs end on a platform that leads to a trapdoor to the floor above. Willow all but skips up that final set of stairs, opening the trapdoor and disappearing overhead. The guards force Dryden and me to follow after her into a large, cylindrical room. The moment I walk into the room, I'm immediately overwhelmed by a familiar urge, but a thousand times stronger than I've ever felt it before.

The room is filled with a seemingly random assortment of different objects. Books, gilded weapons, vases and jewelry, mirrors and paintings, even some articles of clothing.

As I glance around the space, my gaze bounces from one thing to another, not knowing where to land. My fingers itch, tingling to snatch one of the scattered items. I don't even notice the other fae around me until the king's voice cuts through my trance.

"If I wasn't sure of it before, this has confirmed it," he says, and I snap my head in his direction. He's standing across the room with Princess Willow at his side, a wrought iron spiral staircase behind him that must lead to an upper level. That has to be the room where the ember crystal is stored.

I have a hard time keeping my attention on King Darius. My eyes want to dart from one item to the next, but I force myself to ignore the pull and hold his gaze.

There's a pleased smirk on King Darius's face as he stares at me, and I read greed in his eyes. But it's when I catch Willow's expression that I really begin to worry. She's looking at me with something akin to fear.

I glance over at Dryden, and his eyes widen.

"What?" I ask, alarmed at the look.

Dryden swallows. "Your eyes. They're glowing."

"Glowing?" That can't be right. I have an unusual eye color, to be sure. But my eyes don't glow.

"Don't worry, my dear," King Darius says as he walks toward me. "It's just your magic finally coming to the surface."

His words don't make sense. My magic? I don't have any magic.

He turns from my confused gaze to his brother. The look on Dryden's face starts to morph from confusion to awe. "You spent all this time with her, brother, and you never suspected? Very short-sighted of you. Perhaps if you weren't so distracted trying to get under her skirt, you'd have figured it out for yourself."

"Stop," Dryden barks, and the king arches an eyebrow.

"Or what?" he says with a chuckle, taunting his brother. "Do you realize now what's been under your nose the entire time? She's a mystfinder."

Mystfinder?

A muscle ticks in Dryden's jaw as he clenches it. "What do you want with her?" he demands, but King Darius just makes a *tsk*ing sound with his tongue.

"You'll know soon enough."

"Why are you doing this?" Dryden asks, yanking against the hold the guards still have on him.

King Darius gives Dryden an unimpressed look. "Oh, you must have figured it out by now. At least in part."

"You're that threatened that I'll take your crown?"

King Darius shrugs. "I worked quite hard to get it. I'm not leaving anything to chance. Especially when your death will serve a purpose."

Anger simmers in my gut as Shayla's lifeless gaze appears in my mind's eye. "The purpose being to blame his death on Princess Shayla to give you an excuse to invade her kingdom."

King Darius looks at me. "Ah, good, so you are caught up."

"Why did you kill her?" I ask Willow. The River Kingdom princess, her initial shock at my eyes long gone, glares back without a trace of remorse. "The kingdom already believed she was guilty. She didn't have to die."

"Mostly just for fun," she says with a cool smile.

I go feral, thrashing against the guards holding me. Even with my hands bound behind my back, I nearly break free. Eventually, I lose steam and sag in the guards' grip. Panting in exhaustion and rage, I glare daggers at the king and princess.

A snake and a murderer.

"Now, now, my pet," King Darius says to Willow, going as far as to pat her on the head like she's his dog. Willow beams at him, soaking in his attention. The whole thing is sick. "You don't need to get her worked up. We're all going to be on the same side soon enough."

Her smile disappears at that, and the king shifts his attention back to me. With fake contrition, he says, "What Princess Willow said is not entirely true. I want you to know that Princess Shayla didn't die in vain. She was a loose end we were always going to have to tie up. Her death ensures her silence, and the way that it happened, well, you did us a favor there. It will be easy to convince my subjects, as well as the other kingdoms, that she was killed trying to kidnap the prince." His gaze tracks to Dryden, who's staring at him with utter disgust. "Who she tragically killed when she realized she wasn't going to be able to escape."

"You orchestrated this entire courting season for that? To frame an innocent and kill your brother?"

"I did," King Darius says with pride rather than remorse. "And now as the reward for their support, the River Kingdom will grow their lands when we and our allies help them take over the Iron Kingdom."

"And I get to be his queen," Willow says gleefully. "King Darius promised to marry me as well, uniting our kingdoms."

Willow misses the flash of disgust that crosses the king's face when she says she's going to be his queen. There's no way he's going to marry her. I might feel a touch of sympathy for her if I didn't hate her with every fiber of my soul.

"Shayla was more than a means to an end," I say, my heart broken for my friend.

"To my brother, everyone is a means to an end," Dryden says, chillingly cold. "Including our own father."

King Darius flinches but tries to cover it with a smooth smile.

"You killed him, didn't you?" Dryden accuses.

Darius shrugs. "I didn't kill him, but I suppose he *is* dead because of me."

"How could you do that to our own father?"

Darkness overtakes the king's face as he steps forward to stand in front of Dryden. "How could I *not*?" he asks, his words sharp and cutting. "He was going to steal my birthright out from under me."

"Did it ever occur to you that I didn't *want* to be king?" Dryden asks. "That regardless of what Father wanted, I would have refused?"

King Darius scoffs. "You like to think of yourself as a saint, don't you? But the truth of the matter is that everyone wants power. If the moment would have come for you to steal the crown, I don't believe for a second you wouldn't have grabbed hold of it with both hands."

"How did you do it?" Dryden asks. "The way that he was found. It looked like a vampire attack."

King Darius straightens, pulling his shoulders back as he reins in his temper. "Secure the two of them and leave us," he commands.

The guards shove me and Dryden into chairs, binding us quickly before filing out of the room.

"You too," King Darius tells Princess Willow, and her face falls.

"But I wanted to watch when—"

"Out!" he barks. She flinches but spins on her heel, pausing only to shoot me a glare, which I return without hesitation, before sweeping from the room.

Once the trapdoor closes above her, King Darius's gaze shifts to the window, where an unfamiliar male lounges on the sill with one foot propped casually on the ledge. I'd overlooked him completely, distracted by the two monsters in front of us and the odd, irresistible objects scattered around the chamber.

Even now, it takes effort to concentrate on anything other than the items in the room practically begging me to steal them.

"Would you like to answer that question?" King Darius says to the male, and without even glancing at Dryden, I can feel the tension coming off him. "It was, after all, your handiwork."

The male tips his head in acknowledgment to the king and then plants both boots on the floor, rising smoothly. He's large, roughly

Dryden's height, but bulkier. His simple clothes don't signify him as anyone special, but they strain against his chest and thighs.

Despite his size, there's a predator's grace in his steps as he moves across the room. He passes in front of me as he walks toward Darius, and with his sandy shoulder-length hair tucked behind his ear, I notice the tip isn't pointed, and shock ripples through me.

He's not fae.

He pauses when I gasp softly, and grins, showing off a pair of sharp canine teeth. When I look into his brown eyes, they flash yellow before returning to their normal color.

A memory slams into me from when the book dragged me into its vision. Creatures with beast-like features and glowing yellow eyes, tearing into their enemies with a brutality unlike anything I'd ever seen.

Sudden fear chokes me.

Werewolf.

"Are you mad?" Dryden explodes. "You've allowed a werewolf into our lands?"

"Not just *allowed*," the stranger says with a wolfish grin. "Invited."

"It was you," Dryden all but growls in anger. "You did something to allow otherworlders past the barrier. And now they are moving through Vaeloria and our kingdom, terrorizing and murdering our subjects."

"I did," Darius admits. "I've been disabling the barrier in intervals to allow groups of Prince Varek's troops onto the island."

I don't recognize the name, but the way Dryden's face leaches of color makes it clear he does. When he speaks, his words are dripping with disgust. "You let King Torin's eldest son, *the heir* to the werewolf ruler, *and* vampires into our lands? Did you just send an open invite to all of Lunaris and Drakhar?"

Darius's eyes narrow in annoyance. "There are no vampires in Vaeloria."

"But the reported attacks throughout this last year. And Father."

With a lazy flick of his hand, Darius says, "Werewolves are perfectly capable of making an attack look like one from their enemy."

Understanding dawns on Dryden, horror washing over his features. "Which is what happened to Father. You allowed these beasts to kill him and make it look like a vampire attack."

Rather than answer, Darius just inclines his head.

"Why are you doing this?" Dryden asks. "You already have control of the kingdom. What more could you want?"

"Vaeloria."

For a moment, Dryden seems stunned into silence. Then he says, "You *are* mad."

King Darius shakes his head. "Not mad. Ambitious."

"Even with an army of werewolves, you won't be able to take over all of Vaeloria."

The look King Darius gives his brother says he thinks he is naïve to believe that, and as much as I hate to admit it, I agree. Werewolves are vicious. Even if the fae numbers are greater, they might still prevail. In my vision, even with magic, the fae struggled against the werewolves' ferocity. What chance do we stand now without it?

"I think I like my chances with the werewolves," Darius says. "But I like to stack the odds in my favor as much as possible. I'm sure you realize I have allies throughout Vaeloria."

"No fae will stand with werewolves against their own kind," Dryden argues. "Do you not remember our history? The reason the barrier was put up to begin with?"

"Some already have," King Darius says. "The River Kingdom

has been harboring our werewolf friends for the last year, letting me build up our forces slowly. And as for the rest of the kingdoms, well, fear is an effective motivator. They'll align with me if they want to live."

Dryden scoffs, and I appreciate his bravado, but I'm rattled.

"Besides," King Darius goes on, "with all the vampire attacks that have happened in Vaeloria—"

"Attacks you orchestrated," Dryden cuts in.

"Well, the werewolves are our natural allies. The enemy of my enemy, and all that," he finishes.

From what I saw in the book's vision, both the vampires and werewolves were exploiting the fae. But the more King Darius talks, the clearer his overall plan becomes. "You've been sacrificing fae, making it look like vampires were responsible for the attacks so that the other kingdoms will be more likely to support you when they discover you've aligned yourself with the werewolves."

King Darius's web of deception is so much broader than I ever imagined. His plan is genius. Diabolical and horrifying, but genius. And I'm scared that it's going to work.

The look on Dryden's face says he's less sure now that the fae won't tolerate the werewolves than he was before.

"Do you really believe that the werewolves are just going to leave peacefully after you've conquered the kingdoms?" Dryden asks.

"I do," King Darius says confidently. "Because we have an agreement. They help me, and I help them."

"How?" Dryden asks, and both the king's and the werewolf prince's gazes land on me.

Chapter 40

"YOU STAY AWAY FROM HER!" DRYDEN YELLS, frantically trying to break free from the ropes binding him as King Darius and Prince Varek draw closer.

The covetous gleam in the werewolf's eyes makes me uneasy as he comes to a stop in front of me.

"Shall we see what she's capable of?" King Darius asks the werewolf.

Varek nods, and then, so fast that he blurs, he slashes down with his hand, slicing through the ropes binding me to the chair.

I gasp as the ropes fall away from me, staring up at both of them in surprise as Dryden continues to yell at his brother and the werewolf prince.

With a wicked gleam, Prince Varek holds up his hand to show the sharp claws that, even now, are retracting into his fingers. A bolt of terror runs through me. He's a nightmare come true.

"Pick something," King Darius orders.

"What?" I ask, disoriented.

King Darius gestures to the room. "Just pick something."

What is he playing at now?

I glance over at Dryden, still tethered to the chair next to me.

There's an edge of panic in his eyes. "You don't have to do anything he says."

"Oh, calm down, little brother," Darius says. "I'm not hurting her." Turning back to me, he says, "Just pick something in this room. Your choice. Anything."

I stay rooted in my seat as if I were still tied to it.

Darius tilts his head. "You can't tell me you haven't been dying to take a closer look at some of the items in this room." There's a knowing gleam in his eye. "Now's your chance. You can have anything here. What will it be?"

Now that he's brought attention to the bounty, I'm practically vibrating with the desire to grab something. To hold it in my hand and bring it close. Inspect every curve and angle.

I don't know if this is some sort of weird trap, but I can't stop myself from standing and walking toward the edge of the room, my gaze drinking in the objects with barely restrained hunger.

The room is silent behind me. Even Dryden has stopped yelling. I'm a little shaky as I draw closer to the treasure trove. The itch in my hands urges me to grab something and run.

I've never been in a situation before where I've felt such a consuming urge. It's hard enough to control myself when a single treasure calls to me, and there are multiple items in this room screaming for my attention.

Feeling a presence behind me, I glance over my shoulder to find King Darius standing close, an excited gleam in his eye. "Go on," he encourages.

I force my hands into fists at my sides as I step up to a table with objects piled high. Several of them stand out to me, and my eye catches on one jeweled necklace in particular. It's a round rose gold pendant hanging on a rose gold chain. A rare pink diamond sits in the center of the pendant, surrounded by smaller pink diamonds and aquamarine stones.

Without giving myself permission, I'm already reaching for the necklace. A fine tremor shakes my hand in anticipation of holding the pendant, but at the last moment, my gaze snags on another item, a bejeweled dagger to the left of the necklace.

The breath catches in my throat. The dagger calls to me just as strongly as the necklace, and on impulse, I grab the blade instead. Spinning, I swing the blade, aiming the tip at King Darius's temple.

The king's eyes go wide, but before the dagger can sink into his skull, a hand wraps around my throat and lifts me into the air. Claw-tipped fingers dig into my neck, cutting off my air supply, and I drop the dagger, bringing my hands to my throat to try to pry his fingers off me.

Dryden shouts in the background while I kick out at only air, frantic as my oxygen supply dwindles.

As I stare down at Prince Varek's impassive face, he squeezes tighter.

"Stop! You need her!" Dryden screams. "If you kill her, she won't be able to help you."

My vision starts to blink out, but before I lose consciousness, Prince Varek releases me. I drop to the floor in a heap, coughing as sweet air floods my starved lungs.

"Rowan? Rowan?" Dryden calls to me, and I lift my gaze to find his. I've never seen such fear on his face before.

"I'm all right," I croak.

"I'll try not to hold that against you," King Darius says with narrowed eyes, then reaches down and roughly hauls me to my feet. Once standing, I don't even see his hand coming until his open palm slams me across the face hard enough to split my lip.

Gasping, I put my hand against the burning part of my face.

"Try something like that again and I'll make you regret it," he says. A little bit of what looks like madness shines through his eyes.

"I will kill you for that," Dryden says, his voice icy, and when I glance over at him, his face is eerily wiped of emotion.

Cold. Resolved. Immovable.

Even I'm a little shaken by the transformation that has come over him.

Darius laughs at his brother, but I see the look of concern on his face before he does.

"Did the demonstration meet your expectations?" King Darius asks the werewolf.

Prince Varek's gaze is locked on me when he nods. "I'm convinced."

"Convinced of what?" I ask. I have to know what they want me for.

King Darius smooths back his hair; any anger on his face melts away as he slips on his kingly mask. "You are a very convenient find. In exchange for helping me conquer Vaeloria, I've promised the werewolves certain magical items to help them in their fight against the vampires. These items are very hard to find and even harder to detect, and that's where you come in. Because you, my dear little mystfinder, have a very unique skill. Especially in a world where magic is dying."

"What skill do you think I have?" I ask.

"You can detect the very thing I'm searching for. Magic. In objects," he says, waving toward the items in the room around us. "That compulsion you have isn't random at all. It's the magic calling to you."

I don't want to believe him, but I think about the feeling I get from some objects but not others. The compulsion draws me to steal even when I know I shouldn't. Even when I tell myself not to, like with the queen's dragon charm. I've always brushed it off as normal, a side effect of being a thief, but could it be something else altogether?

"How do you know that?" I ask.

King Darius crosses his arms over his chest. "It was the items that you stole from around the palace. Each one had traces of magic. I tested my suspicions by bringing a magic-infused dagger to the dungeon. You should have seen the hunger in your gaze when I pulled it out. Bringing you here was another test. The necklace you were eyeing, as well as the dagger you grabbed, are both infused with magic. Relics of an era long gone that we can reclaim once again."

My mind reels. Could what he's saying be true?

"With practice," Darius continues, "you'll be able to not only identify the magic in an object, but also learn how to use it."

I shake my head, because what he's saying is almost unfathomable.

In Vaeloria, the remaining magical objects and relics are coveted, but often merely as collectibles. Just because something held magic doesn't mean we know how to use it anymore. Many magical items remain dormant, useful only in the most basic sense, with their deeper power sealed and unreachable to a now-magicless fae. Detecting magic is one thing, but awakening it is something else entirely.

"Oh yes," he says with a nod. "Maybe you'll even be able to sense magic in fae and other species as well."

I glance over at Dryden, remembering the familiar feeling I got when we first met. But it faded quickly and never happened again, so I didn't think much of it at the time. Could that have meant something, though?

As I'm processing, King Darius turns to Prince Varek. "So, now that you've seen for your own eyes that we can fulfill our end of the bargain, are you ready to seal the oath?"

Crossing his arms over his chest, Prince Varek gives a curt nod. "We'll seal the oath, and then you'll bring down the barrier."

"Agreed," King Darius says, and I snap my gaze to Dryden in horror.

If they bring down the barrier, Vaeloria won't be protected against otherworlders. It's bad enough that King Darius has been fiddling with it to allow Varek and some of his werewolves in, but if it comes down completely, Vaeloria could be overrun with otherworlders, and the fae would be once again at their mercy.

"Brother, don't do this," Dryden begs.

"I need more troops to conquer Vaeloria."

"At what cost?" Dryden asks. "Letting otherworlders into Vaeloria will mean the death of millions of fae and lead to our people being subjugated again."

"I'm doing this to free our subjects," Darius snaps. "Once the barrier is down, magic will start to return to our lands. We won't need to fear otherworlders. We'll have the power to protect ourselves."

"What?" Dryden asks, mirroring my thoughts.

Darius nods. "The barrier might have kept otherworlders out for centuries, but it's been siphoning our magic to do so. The magic in our land, our people, is what has been powering the barrier. It's the reason our magic has faded. Once it's down, our magic will return and we can reclaim our former glory. We'll be the fae we were always meant to be, not the shells that we've become."

If what he says is true, it's a terrifying thought, because it means we traded our magic for protection. But as the images from the vision flood my mind—of the fae being forced to battle in the otherworlders' war, of fae being killed, slaughtered—I can't help but think that as awful as losing our magic was, maybe the trade-off was worth it.

Dryden, looking firm in his conviction, shakes his head. "You can't do this, Darius—"

Darius glances at Prince Varek as Dryden goes on, trying to convince his brother not to go down this path. "Can you shut him up? Without killing him, of course. I still need him alive, for the time being."

"With pleasure," Varek says.

"No!" I scream as Varek coldcocks Dryden in the temple, knocking him out with one hit.

"I will kill you for that," I say, parroting Dryden's words to his brother after he slapped me.

I lunge for the discarded dagger, the one I tried to bury in King Darius, but Prince Varek is faster. He kicks the blade aside and then shoves me to the floor. With a knee pressed into my back, he grabs a length of the rope—which was once used to tie me to the chair—and binds my hands behind me. I squirm and scream, trying to twist free, but it's no use. The werewolf is too strong. He secures my ankles next, leaving me lying sprawled and helpless on the floor.

Just like I saw Dryden do when he made a blood oath with Sinclair all those weeks ago, Prince Varek says, "You have my oath," and then uses the dagger to slice the tip of his finger, drawing his own blood. He hands the blade to King Darius, who repeats the same words and actions, and then the blood oath is sealed.

A ball of lead settles in my gut. I don't bother begging King Darius not to do this. If Dryden's pleas fell on deaf ears, mine are sure to as well. There's truly nothing I can do as they both head to the spiral staircase that leads to the ember crystal to bring down the barrier protecting Vaeloria.

They don't spare us a second look as they climb the stairs and disappear, leaving Dryden and me alone. The moment they are out of sight, I start worm-scooching across the floor. I may not be able to stop Darius from bringing the barrier down, but if I can get my hands on something sharp, I may be able to cut myself and Dryden free.

I've just managed to roll onto my stomach and am pushing up onto my knees when a blast of unseen magic blows my hair forward. Out the window, an iridescent ripple spreads across the land, shooting outward.

No.

Terror rips through me. He actually did it. He disabled the barrier. Vaeloria has no idea what's coming.

Footsteps sound on the iron staircase.

No! I need more time.

No sooner have I gotten to my knees than they both reappear.

"Trying to go somewhere?" King Darius asks, amused. I don't bother responding, and his gaze shifts to Dryden. "That means there's only one final thing to be done."

As King Darius stares at his unconscious brother, I swear I read regret in his eyes. Icy fingers take hold of my heart and squeeze because I know what's coming.

Dryden groans as he wakes and then gives his head a light shake.

"It's time, brother," Darius says. "I'm going to need you to transfer her contract over to me. I promise, if you cooperate, I'll make your death quick and painless."

My heart slams against my chest.

Lifting his chin, Dryden looks his brother square in the eye. "I'll never do that."

King Darius still doesn't know that Dryden's no longer my

contract holder. That's the only thing still keeping Dryden alive. As long as we keep our mouths shut, maybe there's a chance to stay alive long enough to figure a way out of this mess.

"We'll see," King Darius says, and then, going over to Dryden, he starts searching him.

I'm not too terribly worried about whatever Darius might find until I see the dread in Dryden's eyes. A smile spreads across the king's face as he pulls a rolled piece of parchment from inside Dryden's boot.

Dryden looks at me with an apology in his gaze, and horror washes over me.

My contract.

King Darius unrolls the parchment and quickly scans it. His eyebrows rise, most likely when he realizes it's no longer valid; he can kill his brother without killing me, too.

"Well, this is a surprise," King Darius says as he rips the now-useless piece of parchment in two and lets it flutter to the floor. "On the one hand, it takes care of the pesky problem of having to convince you to sign this over to me before I can kill you," he says to Dryden, then glances at me. "But on the other, I was looking forward to having a leash on you. Pity, but we'll still make do."

Bending over, Darius picks up the dagger I tried to use on him and Prince Varek. He tests the sharpness on his thumb, drawing blood easily, and then glances at his brother.

Ice floods my veins.

No. No!

I don't realize I've yelled out loud until King Darius turns to me, a bored look on his face. I frantically shuffle forward on my knees, putting myself between the king and Dryden the best I can.

"No, don't do this. Please, I beg you." Tears are already forming in my eyes.

I can't lose Dryden. I can't.

King Darius sighs. "I've been clear about what I think about loose ends."

"He's not a loose end. He's your brother," I cry. "I'll do anything. Just don't kill him."

"Rowan, no, don't say that," Dryden snaps behind me.

I crane my neck to look at him. He doesn't show fear, only grim resolve, which makes me even more scared. He looks like a fae who's come to terms with their fate and has submitted to it.

Well, I haven't come to terms with anything.

I turn back to King Darius. I don't stop to consider what a horrible idea it is before saying, "I'll sign a new contract with you, indenturing myself to you if you spare his life."

"No, she won't!" Dryden roars behind me, fighting against his bindings again, but neither Darius nor I pay him any attention.

"I can't just let him go," King Darius says. "At best he'd form a rebellion against me. At worst he'd bury a dagger in my back."

"That's right," Dryden growls. "If you release me, I'll make it my life mission to see your end. I won't rest until you're dead and this kingdom is mine."

My stomach drops.

King Darius gestures toward Dryden in a "See, I told you" manner.

Prince Varek breaks the silence he has maintained since he returned. "You could hold him prisoner rather than killing him. Lock him in your dungeon with around-the-clock guards. In fact, I'll spare some of my pack to make sure he stays there, since it's clear your security is a bit lacking," he says, probably referencing my escape. "Tell your subjects he was murdered and then lock him away. That way, he stays alive without being a threat to you, and you get all the control you want over the mystfinder."

Darius appears to be considering the idea.

"There's no other way you'll be able to control me," I say. "If you kill Dryden, I'll do whatever I can *not* to help you. I'll spend a lifetime trying to find ways to ruin you."

"You'll sign a contract that gives me full control over you?"

I nod, and it brings a chilling smile to the king's mouth. He turns from me to cross the room.

"Rowan," Dryden says behind me, his voice filled with emotion. "Please, I beg you. Don't do this." He echoes the words I just spoke to his brother, and even though I should ignore him, I can't help but glance back at him another time.

His face is filled with anguish. "Please," he says so softly it's almost a whisper. "I'm not worth your freedom."

"Contract or not, do you think I'll ever truly be free now?" I have a hard time pushing the words past the lump in my throat. To think, just mere hours ago I was filled with hope. Hope I'd be free. Hope that I might not only have a chance at happiness but a chance at happiness with him. But now I'm on my knees, offering my life, my hard-earned freedom, in exchange for Dryden. And not a single part of me regrets the trade. It will be worth it to keep him alive.

"Do you really think the life you'll be buying me will be worth living?" he asks, and my heart squeezes. "You spent a couple days in the dungeon. Do you want me to be there for a lifetime?"

A tear rolls down my cheek, and my vision goes watery. That's not a life I want for him, but if it's in my power to save him . . . shouldn't I? Could I live with myself if I didn't?

As his words penetrate my brokenhearted mind, I realize he's right. He wouldn't have a life at all. He would only be existing.

"Rowan . . ." he says again, so lovely and soft that it makes my heart ache. "This isn't what I want. Let me go."

I start to nod when I'm suddenly hauled to my feet.

Dryden yells at Prince Varek to let me go as I'm dragged to the other side of the room, where Darius is standing by a table, scrawling something on a fresh piece of parchment. He's writing up a new contract, and when we get close to Darius, and Varek releases me, I get a glimpse of what he's written.

Darius is cunning, and he's crafted a contract that is even more restrictive than the one I had with Sinclair. It strips away all my freedoms. If I sign this, I won't be a fae anymore, but rather an object, subjugated to the king's every whim.

And the terms are for life.

King Darius pricks his hand with the quill, using his own blood to sign the contract. The parchment sucks up his blood hungrily, accepting the offering. Grabbing my hand, he stabs me with the quill as well and then hands it to me, ordering me to sign.

As I look down at the contract, the dagger lies just off to the side, a reminder of what he can and will do if I refuse to sign.

With the quill clenched in my trembling hand, my mind is steeped in indecision. I glance up at Dryden, and he just shakes his head, mouthing the word "Please."

He's not begging for his life; he's begging for mine.

I close my eyes, my heart shattering.

I set the quill down, but King Darius snatches my hand before I can let go. My lids pop open in surprise, and I'm staring directly into the crazed eyes of the king.

"Let me tell you what will happen if you don't sign this contract," King Darius says. "Refuse to sign and I will pull my brother apart, piece by piece, making you watch every slice and cut. I'll start with his hands, ripping off his nails, before chopping whole fingers off, and then move my way up his arms. Once his arms are gone, I'll repeat the same with his toes, feet, and legs until all that's left of him is his head and trunk. Not only that, but I'll take my time doing it. He'll suffer for days, months. I'll make sure he suffers through every amputation, and that you're there the entire time, hearing his screams of pain and agony, knowing that it's your fault he—"

"Stop. Stop!" I yell, wanting to slap my hands over my ears.

Dryden is yelling again too, trying to sway me. I want to believe the king is bluffing, but I don't think he is. I don't know if he'd relish disfiguring his brother, but I do believe he'd go to any lengths to get what he wants.

King Darius releases my hand. I drop the tip of the quill to the parchment, the magical paper drinking up the tiny drop of my blood greedily, satisfying the blood portion of the contract. But it still needs my full signature for the magic to activate.

Dryden shouts at me not to do it, but it sounds like he's very far away. The roaring of my blood pumping through my veins drowns out everything else.

As my hand starts to drift, beginning the first curve of a letter in my name, a sudden commotion snaps my head up. Dryden has somehow broken free of his bindings. He charges forward, but Prince Varek intercepts him. They collide with a crash, snarls and shouts erupting as they trade brutal blows.

I lower the quill, ready to help, but the king snatches my face, pinching my chin between his fingers.

"Finish it," he snaps.

"Gladly."

Bringing my hand up, I swing for his face, stabbing King Darius through the eye with the sharp tip of the quill. I shove it in as far as I can before he yanks away. With the writing instrument sticking out of his ruined eye, he screams in fury and pain.

"What have you done?" he rages. Grabbing the shaft, he rips it free, and blood pours from the wound.

His face is a bloody mask of unfiltered hate and wrath. He lunges, his hands going straight for my neck. I rear back, but not fast enough. He crashes into me, scattering the contents of the table as we both fall to the floor.

King Darius lands heavily on me, driving the air from my lungs. Before I can suck in a breath, he wraps his hands around my throat and starts squeezing, screaming, "I'll kill you," as blood from his eye socket pours down onto my face and chest.

I need a weapon, something, anything, to fight, because he's too large and strong for me to push him off.

Somewhere across the room, objects clatter to the floor as Dryden battles the werewolf prince. The king's thumbs dig deeper into my windpipe, and I'm convinced he'll crush my throat before I even lose consciousness.

If I don't act fast, he's going to kill me.

A flash of gold catches my eye. Instinct takes over as my hand closes around the jeweled dagger's hilt. I swing without hesitation, driving the blade into King Darius's temple, where it sinks to the hilt.

His grip on my neck goes slack, and he collapses on top of me. Warm blood pools on my chest before I can summon the strength to shove his body off. I stagger to my feet, only to find Dryden all-out battling with Prince Varek.

They've both taken a beating, but neither holds back. Prince Varek slashes with razor-sharp claws, while Dryden counters with twin daggers he must have picked up amid the chaos.

I'm bloodied and bruised, but I have to help Dryden. I've only taken a step when the trapdoor bursts open, splintering in half with the force of whatever rammed into it.

Bram, sword drawn, charges up the steps, shoving aside the

broken wood. And he's not alone. At least a dozen soldiers pour in after him.

The commotion of Bram's entrance is enough to shatter the bloodlust gripping Dryden and Varek. They break apart, panting and bloodied. Despite the bruises on Dryden's face, relief flashes in his eyes when he spots Bram and the others.

Prince Varek, on the other hand, quickly assesses the scene, taking in not only Bram and the soldiers starting to circle him, but also me and King Darius's bloodied corpse at my feet.

He peels his lips back, revealing blood-slicked teeth and elongated canines. Spears aimed and ready, the soldiers close in, forcing the werewolf prince to retreat step by step until his back hits the edge of an open window.

Varek's gaze locks with mine, and I see desire flicker in his eyes. Not lust—something darker, more possessive that fills me with dread.

"This isn't over," he growls. His brown eyes flash yellow before he turns and leaps out of the window.

A collective shock ripples through the room, freezing everyone in place, until Dryden starts shoving through the soldiers, forcing his way to me.

He's a battered mess. One eye is completely swollen shut; there's so much blood on his clothes I can't tell what's from this fight and what's from reopened wounds. His shirt and pants are torn and slashed in multiple places from Prince Varek's claws.

But it doesn't matter, because he's alive. And somehow, even bruised and bloodied, he's still the most devastatingly handsome fae I've ever laid eyes on.

"Where are you hurt?" he asks, his gaze wild as he searches me from head to toe.

If Dryden's a mess, I'm twice as bad, drenched in his brother's blood.

I catch his hands as he runs them over me, searching for injuries.

"It's not my blood," I say, my voice rasping from being choked.

He stills, his gaze falling to my neck, where I'm probably already bruising. I point to the side, drawing his attention to his brother's corpse, the jeweled dagger still buried in his temple.

Even though Darius threatened to do worse to him, I don't know how Dryden is going to feel about me having killed his brother. I tense as his eyes shift, taking in the full, gruesome scene.

I open my mouth to explain what happened, but before I can get a word out, he pulls me into his arms. He buries his face in my neck, holding me so tightly I can feel the shudders racking his body.

Lifting my arms, I wrap them around him, holding on just as tightly. I try not to think about how close we both came to dying today, but instead focus on the feel of him, solid and alive, in my arms.

Eventually, he pulls back, and I reluctantly loosen my hold.

His gaze travels my face like he's trying to memorize it. "Thank the stars it was him instead of you. I don't know what I would have done if I lost you."

His words warm a place deep inside me, but before I can respond, someone clears their throat.

When we glance over, Bram is standing off to the side. "I hate to interrupt, *again*, but perhaps this isn't exactly the time for declarations." His gaze shifts and we follow it to see the soldiers in the room staring at us.

Dryden sighs as he drops his arms and steps back. I miss the feel of him already, but all the gore splattered over me is starting to gross me out. It's easy to ignore the blood in the heat of the moment, but now all I want is a bath and to sleep for at least three days.

After Dryden gives Bram the highlights, Bram explains that once he realized Princess Willow had betrayed us, he fled to Olette. She went straight to Dryden's mother, revealing everything they knew, along with some of their suspicions, including those surrounding the king's death. Suspicions that we now can confirm are true.

Even the king can't order the execution of the crown prince without a trial, which gave the queen authority to act. She summoned the royal soldiers—those who serve the Ember Kingdom as a whole, not just the king's personal guards—and ordered them to find and secure us.

My heart aches for her. Not only did she lose her husband this year, but soon she'll know definitively that her oldest son orchestrated his death, and that she lost that son, too. The queen is strong, but also fragile. I can't imagine she is going to take this news—or the new otherworlder threat—well.

Bram tells us that Olette is with her sister right now.

"By now, Darius's guards should be subdued. They were only acting on his orders anyway, and now that Darius is dead . . . well, they'll be getting their orders from you," he says to Dryden.

A heaviness I'm not ready to deal with presses down on my chest.

Dryden is king now. Or will be shortly.

I can't think about what that means for me, for us, so instead I ask Bram how he found us. It can't just have been luck that he decided to check the tower.

Bram gestures toward the destroyed door, and I peek down to see two soldiers detaining Willow, a scowl on her doll-like face.

I take an aggressive step toward her, but Dryden grabs my hand to stop me. When I glance back at him, he says, "I promise you, she will be punished for her crimes."

Grief for Shayla rises in my chest, almost choking me.

Punished isn't good enough for Willow. I want her to *suffer*.

Dryden gives me a little tug and I drift back over to him.

"I know. I understand," he says, reading my face. "Shayla's death will be avenged, but we may need Willow, if for no other reason than to keep her father in check."

I take a deep breath in through my nose, trying to tap down my murderous thoughts. It takes more than a few seconds for me to rein myself in, but eventually I'm able to force a nod. "Fine, but only if you keep her in the dungeon."

Dryden's lips twitch with the hint of a smile. "Agreed. But first I have to go see if I can do anything about restoring the barrier," he says, gesturing toward the stairs.

"There's something that can be done?" I ask.

Dryden shakes his head and runs a weary hand through his hair. A gesture that reminds me so much of Neo. "I'm not sure. I wasn't there when Darius disabled it, but if there's a way to put it back up, I need to try."

"But what if what your brother said is true? What if the barrier is what caused fae to lose their magic?"

"I don't think we can believe anything my brother said. Even if he wasn't lying, we can't withstand an otherworlder invasion. The fae simply aren't prepared or strong enough. We need that barrier back up, at least until we have a plan."

I nod in agreement, making a mental note to tell him everything the book revealed to me when this is all over.

Dryden squeezes my hand. "Will you be all right for a little while?"

"Yes, of course."

Dryden asks Bram to come with him to take a look at the ember crystal, and they disappear into the room above, leaving me with the dozen or so soldiers and a room full of magical objects. I feel the pull, but for once I'm too exhausted to be dragged into their thrall.

As I wait for them to return, I go over to the window. I don't know what possesses me to do it. I've witnessed more than enough death today. And yet, I lean out, eyes scanning the ground below for Prince Varek's broken body.

At first, I think I must just be looking in the wrong spot. Maybe my tired eyes are playing tricks on me. But when I rub them and look again, the truth is unmistakable. There's no body.

No body means a very dangerous werewolf is still alive.

I spin, intending to bolt up the stairs to tell Dryden, but a sudden commotion from the landing below stops me. I glance through the trapdoor opening in time to see a soldier collapse and Willow bury a dagger in the other one before taking off.

I don't think, I just move, storming down to the landing and then the tower staircase after her. I catch sight of her below me. She's fast, already with a decent lead.

She can't get away. I won't let her.

Fire pumps through my veins as I tear down the stairs. Soldiers who were in the room with me follow, but they're too slow. They'll never catch her. It's up to me.

By the time I hit the ground level, I only catch a glimpse of Willow as she rounds a corner at the end of the hall. Pumping my arms and screaming at my legs to keep moving, I sprint after her.

Every step is a battle; my abused body fights me, but I force it into submission. Shayla's face flashes in my mind, and I push harder.

I turn the corner just in time to see Willow at the end of the hall. She glances back, and for a heartbeat, our eyes connect. She smirks, confident she's far enough ahead to escape.

No. No! I can't let that happen.

A door swings open in front of her, but Willow doesn't see it because she's still looking back at me. A pink-haired fae steps into the hallway, her eyes going wide just before Willow crashes into her. They tumble to the floor in a tangle of skirts and petticoats, giving me the chance to catch up.

When Princess Primrose sees me, she lets out a bloodcurdling scream. I'm not sure if it's just because it's me, or because I'm covered in blood. She scrambles back to get away, but Willow grabs her by the hair and yanks her to her feet.

"What are you doing?" Primrose shrieks, swatting at Willow, who shifts just enough to punch her in the face before putting her in a chokehold.

"My nose," Princess Primrose wails. "You broke my nose!"

"Shut up," Willow says, giving her a shake.

Footsteps sound behind me, but I don't take my eyes off Willow. She has an unhinged look in her gaze that says she'll do anything to escape. And anything includes hurting Princess Primrose.

True, there's no love lost between me and the pink-haired princess, but I bear her no ill will. Well . . . not too much of it. I won't pretend her crooked nose or the blood pouring out of it isn't giving me a small flicker of satisfaction, but I don't want her dead.

"Let her go, Willow," I say, taking careful steps forward with my hands up, trying to get closer without spooking her to do something drastic.

Willow might be tough, but I can take her. I'm street scrappy and fueled by revenge.

Something flashes in Willow's hand as she pulls a dagger from some hidden sheath. "Take another step and I'll slice her face up so bad her own father won't recognize her," she says, pressing the blade to Princess Primrose's cheek.

Primrose whimpers, and her panicked eyes dart to me, begging for help.

I freeze, knowing that Willow would do it.

"It's over, Willow. There are too many of us. You'll never get away. The smart thing to do is just drop the blade."

Willow lets out a laugh that sounds like her childish giggle. I don't think I've ever heard anything creepier.

"You're delusional if you think I'm going to turn myself over."

A soldier steps up beside me, and Willow's gaze tracks over to him. I catch a glint of something out of the corner of my eye and glance over to see the small dagger tucked in his belt.

Willow starts talking, saying that she wants full immunity and safe passage to her kingdom or she'll slit Princess Primrose's throat.

In the middle of her rant, I snatch the dagger and hurl it.

The blade makes a *thunk* when it sinks into Willow's forehead, snapping her head back.

Princess Primrose screams, shredding my eardrums as Willow's body crumples to the floor.

I stare at her lifeless form, expecting to feel satisfaction, but all I feel is sadness. Not sadness for Willow, but sadness that I didn't discover her sooner so I could save my friend's life.

At least now, justice has been served.

Chapter 41

I HARDLY SEE DRYDEN AT ALL OVER THE NEXT several days. Still bloody and only hastily patched up, he was officially named king in a private ceremony at sunset on the same day I killed his brother and Princess Willow. A larger, more formal ceremony will happen eventually, but Dryden needed to be crowned quickly to deal with the mess Darius made.

Overnight, Dryden suddenly had not only a kingdom to run, but a potential war to thwart as well. Dryden had soldiers scour the palace and city for Prince Varek, but the werewolf was never found. Deep claw marks were discovered carved into parts of the marble spire he jumped out of, leading to the belief that he somehow stopped his descent and climbed down the tower before fleeing. Dryden hoped he'd gone back to his land on the continent but feared he had gone instead to the River Kingdom, where parts of his army were being sheltered by Willow's father.

Dryden took the news that I'd killed Princess Willow in stride, pulling me into his arms and telling me he was just glad I was safe. I'm not sure how much harder my actions made things for him, but I don't regret it. Perhaps I should, but I can't help but be relieved that she's not alive to hurt anyone else.

Dryden and Bram managed to partially restore the barrier, but it continues to flicker in and out, and no one knows how long it will hold. Even now, otherworlders could be slipping into fae lands, a threat to our way of life and our very survival.

The only hope to stand against otherworlder invaders is to unite the fae kingdoms against our common enemy. A responsibility that has fallen to Dryden. But the task won't be easy. The Ember Kingdom's spies have reported that the River Kingdom is already carrying out Darius's plans and forming alliances of their own.

With so much uncertainty, the remaining tributes are all either preparing to go home or have already left. I was given back my old room in the palace. My belongings, minus the stolen items from the castle and tributes, have been returned to me as well.

News spread quickly about my real identity and the reason behind the deception. Most of the tributes who still remain at Whitespire whisper about me behind their hands. Even Tori acted a little different when I saw her. She was polite and kind, but things didn't feel as they did before. I can't help but wonder if Shayla had lived, if she would have cared or not.

The only tribute brave enough to outright confront me is Princess Primrose. Rather than thanking me for saving her life, she tells me she suspected all along I wasn't truly a princess and then blames me for her broken nose. However, right before she turns to go, she says that if I ever find my way to the palace of the Bloom Kingdom, she won't turn me away. She'll be happy to find a place for me to stay in their stables for the night. Considering it's Primrose, I take that to be as much of a "thanks" as I'll ever receive.

From the day I plunged the dagger into King Darius's head to now, I've been living in a strange state of limbo. I'm free to leave, but where do I want to go? Or do I even want to leave anymore?

I'm not angry at Dryden for not making time for me. He's the king now, on the brink of war, but it doesn't mean I'm not disappointed and confused. A small part of me mourns not only the loss of my friend but also the loss of the life I hoped I'd be able to have with Dryden.

Olette visits me frequently, though, and I always find her presence comforting. Since she's known the truth from the beginning, she's one of the only fae, besides Dryden and Bram, who don't look at me differently now. Even Eilowyn is cordial, but our interactions are strained. My mind keeps wandering to the what-ifs, making me poor company.

I'm only half listening when Olette tells me that Dryden has ordered Lord Sylvan to be sent to the Glacier Kingdom as an emissary. He is to reside there indefinitely with the mission of making amends with the Glacier Kingdom for my impersonation of one of their princesses. He's even been betrothed to one of their nobles from a lower station than his own. It's a fitting punishment, as I know he is going to detest living in such a cold and barren land, but I can't seem to summon the necessary joy at knowing the vile fae is getting what he deserves.

I'm glancing out the window, lost in my thoughts, when I hear Olette set her teacup down and sigh.

"I'm sorry," I say, refocusing on her and forcing brightness into my words and a smile onto my face. "My thoughts were just elsewhere."

Olette nods, her gaze more probing than usual.

"How's the queen?" I ask, more to take the pressure off me than anything else.

Although I do care. Queen Teresa seems to be taking Darius's betrayal just as hard as one would imagine. She's hardly left her rooms since everything happened. In fairness, neither have I.

Olette gives me a small smile, but there's sadness in her eyes.

"My sister is . . . coping the best she can. She'll make it through this, but she's going to need time."

"Yes, of course. She should do what she needs to in order to take care of herself."

I believe that, but I also hurt for Dryden. He's handling all of this on his own, and I can't help but wish his mother would offer more help. She may only be a dowager queen, but she's familiar with what it takes to rule. I'm sure he could use the counsel and support, but she's too fragile to offer it.

"Our lives, as royals, are not really our own, you know that, right?" Olette asks, shaking me from my thoughts.

When I refocus on her, the look on her face makes my stomach knot. Intuition says she's building to something that I'm not going to want to hear.

"I know there are obligations and demands on Dryden, if that's what you are getting at," I say, trying to preempt any warnings she may be about to give me.

Olette nods. "The kingdom is in a precarious position right now. We're on the brink of war, and alliances will have to be made if Dryden wants to prevail."

"Yes, of course," I say.

"As hard as it is to imagine, some kingdoms are going to side with the River Kingdom. If for no other reason than they fear their alliance with the werewolves and don't want to become their target."

My anger spikes. "Then they are cowards."

Olette nods. "They are, but nonetheless, it's going to happen. Dryden is going to need to collect allies, powerful ones, and there is one iron-clad way of uniting kingdoms." She pauses, and the feeling of unease in my gut amplifies tenfold. "Through marriage."

With those last two words, my body goes numb.

"You love him, don't you?" she asks softly, a touch of pity in her gaze.

Clearing my throat, I turn away from Olette, pretending to busy myself with pouring a cup of tea.

"I don't know why you would think that." My voice comes out high-pitched, and I pause to take a steadying breath. "Yes, we built a good rapport, but I'm no one of consequence. He's the prince—well, rather, the king now. To think that there would be anything that could come of us is just . . . silly." I force out a strangled laugh, completely failing to sound calm and composed.

Reaching across the small table between us, Olette lays a hand on my arm. When I glance over at her, I'm sure the truth is written all over my face.

"For what it's worth," she says, "I believe he loves you, too."

Hearing that makes it a thousand times worse. I can't stop the tears from flooding my eyes. Olette stands, her skirts swishing as she moves to fold me into her arms, letting me fall apart without saying anything. She strokes my back in soothing circles, offering me exactly what I need in the moment: comfort.

It isn't until the tears start to dry up that Olette pulls back. Taking my face between her hands, she gazes deep into my eyes. There's a shine in hers that says she gets no pleasure in saying this to me, but believes it has to be done.

"The courting season was a farce and is over, but there will come a time, probably sooner rather than later, when Dryden will have to pick a bride. A royal bride for not only the good of our kingdom, but for all of Vaeloria. And no matter how much it breaks your heart, you're going to need to let him."

A punch straight in the face wouldn't hurt more than those words. "I don't know how to stand by and watch that happen," I tell her honestly.

Olette nods, looking like she understands. "You don't have to be here to watch."

"What do you mean?"

"You're free, Rowan. You don't have to stay in Everlight, or even the Ember Kingdom, any longer. You can go and start the life you've always dreamed about."

I get a sinking sensation in my stomach. "You think I should abandon the kingdom? Abandon Dryden?"

A life away from Everlight is all I ever wanted. A fresh start. But that dream has changed, and now, any future without Dryden feels hollow.

A sad smile settles on Olette's face, and a single tear slips down her cheek. "I hope you know how much you've come to mean to me. I never had a daughter of my own, but if I had, I'd want her to be just like you. Brave and beautiful. Strong in mind and spirit. Compassionate. You're so many amazing things, and I want you to have a chance at happiness, but I don't think you're going to get that if you stay here and watch Dryden marry someone else."

The thought of Dryden marrying someone else is like a phantom dagger to my chest, stealing my breath.

"And if I'm being truthful," Olette goes on, "I don't think Dryden will marry as long as you remain at Whitespire."

The breath catches in my throat. "Why do you think that? Has he told you as much?"

Olette shakes her head. "He hasn't, but I have eyes, and so do the people around Dryden. When the two of you are together, it's like no one else exists. The idea of securing an alliance through marriage has already been brought up to Dryden by several of his advisers, and it's my understanding that he won't even consider it. There's an obvious reason why he'd react that way. I think he cares enough about you that he would trade the kingdom for you." A spark of hope ignites in my chest that's smothered the next moment when she says, "And if he did, that would be all of our undoing."

A weight bears down on me. One I don't want to shoulder, but one I must just the same. Part of me thinks it's unfair for Olette to lay this at my feet, but the other half sees the truth in her words.

"It's your choice," she says, a grim expression on her face. "I know you are probably split in two, and I'm so very sorry to put this burden on you, but you must know the consequences to be able to weigh them properly. Please know that whatever you decide, I'll support you. I just think you need to know the implications before you make a decision."

After taking a deep breath, she leans forward and kisses my forehead. She asks if I want her to stay, but I shake my head, telling her I need time to think. She nods, understanding, and quietly leaves.

I stay seated exactly where she left me for a long while, looking out the window, knowing the whole time what I have to do, but wondering if I'll have the courage to do it.

+

I DON'T GET the opportunity to see Dryden until the next day, and by then my mind is made up. I'm going to tell him that I'm leaving, like we always planned I would. As I walk through the hallways to the king's office, my resolve is strong, even if my heart feels weak.

Two guards are stationed at his door, but they don't try to stop me from knocking. Dryden calls for me to come in, and butterflies take flight in my stomach. Before entering, I inhale a deep breath through my nose, filling my lungs and hopefully clearing my mind.

After wiping the moisture on my hands dry on the fabric of my lavender overskirt, I turn the handle and enter the room.

My heart stutters when I lay eyes on Dryden. He doesn't look up when I enter, but rather he's standing behind his desk, reading some piece of parchment in front of him. His black hair curls over his forehead, and there's a crease between his brows. His injuries have faded, his magic having helped speed along the healing process, but he looks like he has the weight of the world resting on his shoulders. Something inside me cries out, wanting to take some of that burden from him, but I can't.

I pad across the red silk rug toward him, passing beneath a gold chandelier. As I watch him, an ache in my chest intensifies, a pull to go to him so strong that I force my gaze to drift from him to the map of Vaeloria on the wall behind him to stop myself from doing so.

I've never been in this room before, the king's office. I take a quick glance around, barely noting the deep mahogany bookshelves overflowing with thick tomes or the floor-to-ceiling windows framed with green velvet curtains.

"Rowan," Dryden says, drawing my attention. "This is a nice surprise." A smile brightens his face, and my gut clenches at how happy he is to see me. "Perfect timing, in fact. I want to show you something." Grabbing the parchment in front of him, he hands it to me.

"What's this?" I ask.

He nods to it. "Look for yourself."

Glancing down, I scan the contents of what appears to be some sort of official documentation. My breath catches when I finally realize what it is I'm holding. My head whips up, my eyes wide as I stare at Dryden with disbelief. "A proclamation outlawing the ownership of indentured servants?"

Dryden grins, and it makes him look devilishly handsome. "It should have been done ages ago." He gestures toward the parchment I'm still holding. "The proclamation doesn't just outlaw present and future ownership, it also holds owners responsible for paying back wages to the indentured for the years they were forced into service."

I think back to one of our first conversations in Olette's house when I didn't know who he truly was. He said he never agreed with forced servitude and that it was something he wanted to change one day. And I'd scoffed at him and said that unless he was the king himself, I didn't see much chance of that happening.

Yet now he's king, and he is actually doing it.

Stunned, I place the document back on the stack of papers on his desk and he rounds it to meet me. As he nears, I can tell he's about to pull me into his arms, so I sidestep him, keeping out of reach even though it's physically painful for me to do so. Dryden freezes, his eyebrows bunching.

"I'd hoped you'd be pleased by this news," he says, confused.

"I am. Of course I am. This means a great deal to me as well as so many others in your kingdom. It's just that I came here for a purpose and I don't want to waste too much of your time." I gesture toward the stacks of papers and parchments littered across his desk. "You're obviously busy."

He regards me with a tilt of his head, and I can see him trying to work out what's going on, why I'm acting this way. "You're never a waste of my time. I thought you'd know that by now."

Just get it out, I order myself. "I came to tell you that I'm leaving."

I had hoped I'd feel relieved after I got the words out, but I don't.

The shock is clear on Dryden's face. He shakes his head and

forces a smile. "No, Rowan. You don't have to leave anymore. You don't have to flee to another part of this kingdom or another. I'll provide you with whatever you could ever want or need. You can stay right here in Whitespire Palace."

He doesn't say, ". . . with me," but his eyes do.

Something inside me twists painfully. I don't know that I fully understood how much I wanted to be with Dryden until this moment.

But Olette is right. Even if it's what we both want, it can never be.

The fae in our kingdom would never accept me. I'd be blamed for the kingdom's downfall. Resented, at best. My life in constant danger from those who want me away from the throne.

So where does that leave us? Having a secret relationship, our feelings only expressed in hidden and stolen moments? Me eventually watching him wed another?

I swallow the ball of emotion threatening to clog my throat.

I knew this would be hard, but not this hard.

I shake my head.

The smile slips off his face. "What happened? Why are you saying you want to leave?"

"I'm not *saying* I want to leave, I *am* leaving. And nothing happened. This was the plan from the very start. Nothing has changed since then."

His eyebrows shoot up. "Nothing has changed? Is that what you think?"

I nod, looking anywhere but in his eyes. "Yes, I still want the same things I did the day we met. I want to leave the Ember Kingdom and start a new life."

The room grows silent. Dryden stares at me until he finally says, "But I don't want you to go." There's vulnerability in his words that pulls at my heartstrings.

I swallow, trying to gather my courage, but it feels like it's deserted me. "Yes, well. It's not about what you—"

"I love you."

I can't breathe. I literally can't breathe for a handful of heartbeats.

I lick my lips and his gaze drops, making my stomach flip.

"And you love me," he says, taking a slow step toward me.

I shake my head because I'm incapable of speaking.

He moves in closer, and I take a step back, trying desperately to keep space between us even though all I want to do is melt into his arms. When he takes another step forward and I try to take one back, I bump up against his desk. A smirk dances across his lips when he sees I can't retreat any farther.

"You do," he says confidently, shifting closer, all but eliminating the space between us.

Every part of me feels overly sensitized, from the tips of my fingers down to my toes. He's saying things to me I never even allowed myself to dream about. I know what needs to be done, but I don't know how much longer I can withstand this kind of sweet torture.

"I'm not sure of a lot right now," he confesses. "I never wanted to be king, let alone one under these circumstances. I'm not sure if the ember crystal's barrier will hold, or if Vaeloria will be overrun by otherworlders before a fortnight is out. I'm not sure which fae kingdoms are my allies or enemies. But one thing I know for sure is that I love you."

He moves in even closer, tipping his chin down so he doesn't have to do more than whisper for me to hear him. "You love me too, and I can prove it."

Taking my face in his hands, he kisses me deeply. My resolve shreds like tissue almost the moment his lips touch mine.

This is everything I remember from the last time we kissed, and at the same time so much more.

All of Dryden's longing and desperation and desire comes through in the way he holds me, the way his mouth moves against mine. The way he coaxes my lips to part and then sweeps his tongue inside, causing shivers to dance down my spine.

The ache in my chest intensifies, and everything that Dryden gives me, I give back, knowing this one stolen moment is the last we'll ever get.

His kiss is a confession. And mine is a goodbye.

I don't have the power to break away, so he ends up pulling back first. The look on his face isn't one I've ever seen from him before. There's a touch of wonder in his gaze. Happiness. And love.

"You love me, I know you do."

Yes. But I can't confess the truth.

"No. I don't," I say woodenly, dying a little inside with every word that I force to come out of my mouth. A mouth still swollen from his kisses.

His smile starts to fade. "I don't believe you."

I can't do this. I can't do this.

I have to do this.

"No, you just don't *want* to believe me." The coldness in my voice freezes the very air between us and turns my words into shards of ice sharper than any blade.

And they hit their mark. I see his heart breaking through his eyes, right before they harden with resolve. "Fine, I'll accept that for now, but I know you care for me. I have love enough for the both of us."

I pull away from him, at war with my body as I sidestep out of his arms, putting space between us. Space I want to snatch back the moment I create it.

I take extra care that my face doesn't betray the depth of my feelings for him. If he knows how I really feel, he'll never let me go, the kingdom be damned. I can't allow that.

"Yes, of course I care. We've shared some very intense times together, and that will bond anyone. But you're king now, Dryden," I say, doing my best to sound patronizing, like I'm an adult talking to a petulant child. "Someday you'll end up with someone of your station for the good of your kingdom. You can't let your subjects and perhaps all of Vaeloria come to ruin for a girl who simply *cares* about you."

There, I said it. And I hate myself for it.

Anger flushes his cheeks. "'Shared some very intense times together'?" His gaze narrows, and I swear he's looking straight into my soul. "You're lying," he says. "I won't let you go."

"You'll break your word to me? You'll deny me the freedom I've desired my whole life? You say you love me, but who's the liar now?"

I've trapped him with my words as surely as a fox caught in a snare, and my heart hates me for it. I know I've won before he even utters a word. He can't claim to love me yet force me to stay. The only way to prove his love is to let me go.

I see his slow acceptance of this truth in his eyes, and it kills me.

"You would truly walk away from me. From us?" he asks softly.

"I've never wanted anything more than my freedom."

Lies. *Lies.* All lies. I want him more than my freedom. I want to stay by his side and be his rock and have him be mine, but not at the expense of every fae in the kingdom.

If Dryden doesn't marry and form an alliance, like Olette said, the Ember Kingdom may not survive. I couldn't live with myself if I let that happen. I saw for myself the havoc otherworlders wrought on the fae in the past. Dryden might be the key to preventing history from repeating itself. And I can't be the weakness that unravels it all.

My heart and his are a small sacrifice when weighed against so many lives.

"I can't truly be free here. You need to let me go. And you need to do your duty to your kingdom."

He stares at me in silence for a few moments. Different emotions flash in his eyes too fast for me to read.

"You'd push me into the arms of someone else?" He no longer sounds angry. His voice is filled with sadness and laced with resignation.

No. Don't let me leave, I want to shout, but I have to shove those words down.

He looks away from me, which is the only reason I'm able to force myself to say, "We're not meant for each other."

I'm sure Dryden would easily read the heartache on my face if he were still looking at me, but he's staring out the window at the oranges and pinks the sunset has painted over the sky.

Dryden shuts down right in front of me, shifting from heartsick to stoic in the span of a few tense breaths.

The fae who turns back to me a moment later isn't the one I've fallen in love with—he's King Dryden of the Ember Kingdom. A male I no longer know.

"I'll have Bram deliver the money you were promised. He can also arrange your transportation to wherever you want to go."

A knot tightens in my gut, telling me I've made a giant mistake. Regret starts to rise in my throat, choking me, and I reach for him. "Dryden—"

He's the one who pulls away this time. "Thank you for your service and efforts in helping us unearth the truth behind Princess

Willow's and my brother's deception. The kingdom will forever be in your debt. Should you ever need anything, you should call on us."

I take a shaky breath. "Thank you, Dryden," I say, glancing down. I can't bring myself to look at his face.

"Considering the circumstances, I think moving forward, you should address me as King Dryden or Your Majesty."

"Of course, Your Majesty." The words taste like ash in my mouth.

"Goodbye, Rowan. I hope you find every one of your heart's desires."

My only desire is for you, my heart whispers silently.

"My hopes are the same for you," I reply, and I make the mistake of looking up and into his green eyes.

His mask slips a bit, and I see the depth of his feelings for me shining through. I wonder what he sees in mine.

"My only desire moving forward is to see my kingdom flourish and my enemies defeated."

He's trying to hide it, but I can tell that I've broken a part of him. Even though it would kill me to see him find love in the arms of someone else, I hope he does, because even though the words will never leave my mouth, I do love him. And if you love someone, you want the best for them, even if it means that's not you.

Chapter 42

I DECIDE TO LEAVE THAT NIGHT. I TELL MYSELF lots of pretty lies about why it's best to do so, but really, I'm fleeing because I know if I see Dryden even one more time, the truth will come spilling out.

I don't exactly know where I'm going to go, just that I have to go. Dryden, true to his word, delivered a small fortune to me. Shortly after I left his office, Bram showed up at my door with more gold than a person could spend in a lifetime.

And a parting gift from Dryden: the magic-infused dagger I tried to steal from him the first night we met.

I refused most of the money, wanting to take only what I needed to get started. Over the years, I've learned to live on close to nothing, so I don't need much. If I'm going to do this, start a new life for myself, I want to do it the right way. And the right way feels like forging my own path in the world rather than using Dryden's money to do so.

The dagger, however, I wanted to refuse, but couldn't.

And it wasn't because the magic called to me, though it still did. The moment Bram pulled the dagger out, I felt the familiar allure, but an interesting thing happened after I discovered my mystfinding magic. For the first time in my life, I finally feel like I have control over my impulses. So, although I found the dagger tempting, I could have left it behind.

No, I couldn't refuse Dryden's gift because even though I was leaving him forever, holding on to his dagger felt a little like holding on to a part of him.

My goodbyes were quick. There weren't very many of them. Besides Dryden, it was just Olette and Bram. Bram tried to talk me out of going when he delivered the coins, but I told him the same story I'd fed to Dryden about wanting to start over. Olette, of course, understood, but tears still filled her eyes when I told her I'd decided to leave.

It takes me hardly any time to prepare. I pack light, bringing only my small purse of coins, the clothes on my back, and Dryden's silver-hilted dagger. At the last minute, I grab the black leather book. I swore I'd never read it again, but now, knowing the otherworlders are a true threat to Vaeloria, the book feels too important to let sit forgotten on a shelf, its secrets gathering dust while danger gathers beyond our borders.

In the dead of the night, I creep through the dimly lit hallways and out of the palace, slipping out the front gate. It's easier sneaking out of the palace than it should be, making me worry for Dryden's safety. But I remind myself that he's not alone. He has Bram and Olette to look out for him, as well as a palace full of guards and a city filled with soldiers.

My plan is to buy a horse and then go from there. There's a stable on the edge of the city where I can get one, so I head in that direction. I hardly pass anyone, choosing the most deserted path through Everlight's dark alleyways and streets in the middle of the night with only the moonlight illuminating my way. As the streets become more familiar, I can't help my mind from wandering, which is why I don't notice the shadows creeping up on me until it's too late, and a bag gets thrown over my head, blinding me.

By instinct, I kick out, connecting solidly with flesh and bone. My attacker curses, and hands fall away from me, but before I can rip the bag from my head, multiple hands grab me, lifting me in the air despite my wild bucking.

Someone ties my hands and feet and then I'm thrown over a shoulder. I don't give up—the fighter in me won't let me—but I'm in a bad spot.

No one knows where I am. No one is coming to save me.

With my limited motion, I try to throw myself off my attacker's shoulder, but they clamp their hand over my legs, holding me in place. I'm frantically trying to figure out what to do when we stop, and the next thing I know, I'm being flipped off my attacker's shoulder and shoved forward. I trip and my shoulder hits a hard surface. The crack of a whip splits the night air, and the floor beneath me shakes with movement.

Where am I? A wagon? A carriage?

With my hands tied behind my back, I can't pull the hood off, but I can scooch to a seated position. My back comes into contact with something soft.

A covered bench, perhaps?

A hand grabs the material of the hood over my head and then yanks it off me. Disoriented, I glance up at the wolfish grin of a male sitting on a cushioned seat across from me. His eyes flash yellow.

"I told you. This isn't over."

Photo by Davide Esposito Fine Art

Julie Hall is a *USA Today* bestselling and award-winning author who traded her career in movie marketing for worlds filled with magic, danger, and slow-burn romance. She writes the kind of fast-paced, heart-wrenching fantasy stories that leave readers with epic book hangovers and a desperate need for more.

Her love of all things fantasy and supernatural started early—thanks to *Buffy the Vampire Slayer* marathons and a dog-eared collection of L.J. Smith paperbacks—and she's been chasing that same blend of heart, humor, and high stakes ever since.

Her stories have captured readers around the world and are known for fierce heroines, morally gray love interests, and twists that make you gasp out loud. She lives in Colorado with her husband, daughter, and two furry chaos-makers, forever chasing stories where love burns bright in the darkest moments.

VISIT JULIE HALL ONLINE

JulieHallAuthor.com
Julie.Hall.Author
JulieHallAuthor